Guinevere

Bright Shadow

Liminal Books

Between the Lines Publishing
1769 Lexington Ave N., Ste 286
Roseville, MN 55113
btwnthelines.com

Published: December 2022

Original ISBN (Paperback) 978-1-958901-19-9
Original ISBN (eBook) 978-1-958901-20-5

Guinevere

Bright Shadow

Sarah Provost

This is for
Edwina Trentham and Anne Logan
Believers

Prologue

There comes a time in late winter when the hills lie bare as bone and days follow each other like a steady drip of cold water. All manner of religious folk hold rites then, to coax back the sun or heal the old king or kill him to make way for the new. Though I am a priestess, there is nothing for me in that season but despair. It seems the skies will be slate forever, and the clouds hang heavy as millstones. Yet year by year the new life springs, and I am always astonished when ferns uncurl, and primrose and cowslip and purple thrift emerge from the sodden hills.

I used to think that if I watched carefully enough, I could glimpse them as they arched their way through dirt. There must be a moment when they appear, pale and tentative in the weak sunlight. I wanted to see that moment, but I never did.

What happened to us—the jumble of joy and evil, beauty and pain—happened like that. I thought if I watched closely, took account all the while, I'd know when it began, when it was ended, which of us to comfort, which to blame. I am old now. The story is over, all but the last cold fact, and I still don't know.

There must be a way to cast the sum, to go back and say 'This is how it happened. This is why. This is the result.' There must be a way to tell the story whole and put it to peace.

Part One

Chapter 1

The day could not have seemed more ordinary. I stood at a casement, holding the leathern curtain back, watching sleet streak the February sky, a sky as gray as the stone walls of our common room. Though it was just past midday, the brazier had been lit; it did little to lift the gloom. By its fitful flicker, a boy picked a listless tune on his harp. My younger ladies peered at their needlework in the dim light and talked in murmurs, while the elders swayed in a doze. Dame Arel suddenly let out a snort and woke herself, which set the others giggling.

I was not hearing. As I stood gazing out, my ears were filled with a rush of wings, a lark singing out its panic, falcon in pursuit. Nor did I see the frozen streams or the lash of ice on the distant hillside. In my yearning mind, the hills were heathered once again and the sun hot as I rode, hair streaming in a black tangle. Weyve was my first bird, and I loved nothing more than watching her rise up after her quarry. It made me feel I too could soar. But these days, I was as caged as my poor falcon.

The previous summer, our neighbor Ryance had come creeping. He was discovered barely in time to prevent us being taken at one drop. Both sides lost heavily, ours to the worst. My father was forced to retreat. Ryance ringed us round, and there he stayed.

I have since been in much greater danger, and have spent many a month in cruel waiting, but I remember that siege as the most painful. I was young. Time passed in days and weeks of crushing boredom, with little to do but lay out tedious embroideries, gossip, and dream. Then for a day or two, a furor, a skirmish! We'd take a few of their men, they'd take a few of ours, and we would settle down to wait once again.

We had been sitting there, doves in a cote, for eight long months. Our provisions were low, our numbers dwindling, and it was clear that the end, whatever it might be, must come soon.

In the common room, there was no movement save the flicker of needles in the cold light and the restless pacing of an old hound. The voices pattering around the brazier were so familiar, the songs of the harp so many times heard, the faces so often seen that they had become as alien as the nameless gods in the tapestries. I felt quite alone in the peopled room.

"Guinevere!" When I heard my name, it was with the startle of having heard and not attended.

"Guinevere! Dreamer! Let back the curtain—you're freezing me!" Catlin stood behind me, stout and scowling, feigning a shiver.

"With the quilting you have on your bones, you could sleep in a snowdrift and not get cold to the middle." I dearly loved to annoy Catlin. She was so solid, sensible, a sleeping dog to a puppy: I could never resist nipping her ears.

But this winter had brought changes. Restless, over-sensitive, we were both too quick to take a hurt. When I turned to join the laughter, Catlin's face was clamped with anger, and I saw I had struck too near. My body had not yet begun to round from boyishness into a woman's form, but Catlin's had, and she had also grown quite a bit stouter.

"Na, I'm sorry," I said. "I shouldn't tease. But there's no freshness in here all winter. When it isn't cold to cracking, I like to breathe a bit of free air. I'll close it in a minute."

"As you say, Lady," she replied, seating herself again and bending stiffly to the needlework in her ample lap.

"Oh, don't 'lady' me," I said laughing, for that had long been one of Catlin's favorite slynesses. She knew I hated to hear it from her.

She grunted and mumbled; I was forgiven. I picked up my work and meant to return to it, truly I did. But the pheasant I was embroidering made me think again of Weyve, and long for the day when I could ride out with her on my fist. I fell to gazing out the casement once more, watching plumes of smoke rise against the hard sky.

As I watched, the smoke grew dense and darkened. I stared a moment, puzzled, then hissed the room to silence. As the muted conversations and fragile music of the harp fell still, the ring of metal and thud of horses' hooves came clear. I turned to Catlin; my breath caught in my throat. "Where's my father?"

"In council," Catlin replied. "Isn't he?" I threw down my work and leaned out for a wider view. A small band of men burst from the forest, riding hard, their war cloaks torn and fouled. The black and gold bannerets were ours, but my father's standard was missing. At last, his griffin appeared, lagging, with only two or three accompanying him.

A second band of horsemen bolted from the trees, under a too-familiar red banner. "Ryance," I whispered. Catlin crowded into the narrow casement beside me as the rest of the ladies glanced at each other in alarm. Ryance's men pursued the griffin banner and closed with the riders. In the confusion of horses and swords, the griffin swayed and fell.

Our defenders galloped off toward safety, all but one, who stayed behind to hold off the attackers. I recognized the war cloak I had woven for my father. Finally, he too was forced to turn and flee. An enemy warrior thundered close behind him as he raced for the keep. Sleet lashed my face as I leaned farther out, my hands gone white on the stone.

For a moment both horsemen were lost in a hollow, and when they came over the crest of the nearer hill, the pursuer had caught up and they were skirmishing. One swift, chopping stroke, and the sword flew from Father's hand. His right arm hanging limp, he wheeled his stallion with his good hand and spurred headlong toward safety, Ryance's man hot behind him.

All this I watched, and watched, and could not move, a painted girl in a painted tower. At last I broke. Our riders had already reached the keep, where they milled in the courtyard with muffled curses, the clanking of harness, their horses wall-eyed and foaming. Leaning so far out that Catlin gasped and caught me from behind, I shouted out to them: "Go back! Help him! Go back!"

They lifted their streaked faces in dumb weariness. Slowly, too slowly, they gathered strength to swing their horses round and look where I pointed. At once my rally cry was echoed man to man. With a clatter of hoofbeats, they raced back over the bridge. When the red-clad pursuer saw them streaming toward him, he wheeled and fled. They reached the king in time to catch him as he swayed from his saddle.

I turned from the casement, colliding with Catlin who still gripped my waist. "You with me," I bid her, and called to the others, "Bandages! To the hall!" Lifting my skirts, I pounded down the stone stairs, Catlin after, and arrived in the hall just as the horsemen burst through from the courtyard. The horses whinnied and reared as I darted among them to where Davek steadied his lathered stallion, my father cradled in his arms. I caught the reins from the faithful, grizzled knight. Young Behr was beside me in an instant.

"Behr, help him down. How many others wounded? How many lost?"

"I don't know, lady. Many."

"They're coming with bandages," I said, swallowing the sharp bit of bone that rose in my throat. "Bed the wounded at that end of the hall. Careful, hold his arm across his chest."

The two men struggled to slide his weight gently from the horse. I handed the reins to Catlin, who had just arrived, red-faced from her rush, and slipped my arm under my father's shoulder. His head lolled back, and I staggered under the weight. His face beneath the steel was masked with blood, his eyes closed. The sounds around me became intolerably loud for an instant, then muted almost past hearing. A warm softness melted my bones, and my knees began to refuse me.

At that moment, Catlin caught sight of the king's face and let a resounding scream. I was startled into clarity and fought to retain it, taking deep, steadying breaths. Catlin dropped the reins and stood with her hands over her face, muttering prayers. "Catlin!" I said sharply, "Give me something to wipe his face." She dropped her hands, looked blank for a moment, then stooped to tear a strip from her underskirt.

I unlaced his coif, let fall the heavy mail and began to search his wounds as delicately as I could. Someone had dealt him a blow with the flat of a sword. There was a patch of crushed flesh just past the leather padding, where the rings of mail had cut into his forehead. Fortunately, the bone seemed sound. His nose was brast, but that's more blood than danger. I slumped a moment and let out the breath I hadn't known I was holding. "Nothing fatal. The main worry is whether his wits will hold after such a blow. Let's see to his arm before we move him further."

4

The two knights laid him gently on the rushes and began to strip his harness. He stirred and groaned but didn't regain his senses. They bared his shoulder, and Davek began to curse softly, working his way through all the gods he could remember.

The attacker's sword had hacked a thick collop from his upper arm, just below the hauberk, and bone glimmered in the raw flesh, nearly down to the elbow. This time there was no fogging: I saw clear and hard what I needed to do. "Stand close," I said to Behr. "If he stirs before this is done, you and Davek will have to hold him."

I'd need to draw the flesh together. The wound oozed blood rather than jetting, but it wouldn't heal whole with just a bandage. If it weren't joined, and joined thoroughly, he would never carry a sword again. With our surgeon killed a fortnight past, I had no choice but to risk him to my own meager skill. "Catlin," I ordered, "a needle and some silk thread."

What I did then, I did through a merciful darkness; my father did not stir. When I finished, I sat back on my heels and looked, for the first time, it seemed, at the two exhausted, mud-stained men before me. "Davek, are you whole? Behr?" They nodded wearily. "Then will you bear him to his chamber? Be certain he will know of your good service."

Not until they had raised him between them and borne him away did I allow myself to turn and meet Catlin's grave gray eyes. We took a long moment of silence, then fell together. Burying our smeared faces on each other's shoulders, we began to tremble and weep. I was just turned twelve that week, and she but two years older.

Torchlight flickered from the walls before my father stirred and groaned. I'd been sitting vigil to find if his wits were sound. When his eyes pried open to see me there, my hair tossed, my robe torn and bloody, he reacted as a father would. I should have prevented the shock. He struggled to rise, fell back.

Quickly I moved to assure him. "It's all right. I've been tending the wounded, that's all." I held a cup of broth to his lips and bid him drink, then settled him back against the skins and returned to my chair. I unclenched my hands and folded them in my lap, assuming a calm I did not feel.

After a glance at my grim face, Father closed his eyes, feigning sleep. "Don't bother," I said tartly. "Why didn't you tell me you were sallying today? And with thirty men against so many?"

"Guinevere," he replied wearily, his eyes still closed, "if you had known, you'd have raised a howl they'd have heard to the shores of Eire."

"That's why you left me ignorant," I said. "But why go out at all?"

He opened his eyes and raised himself a bit, wincing. "I needed to draw their men. I've sent messengers seeking help from the High King and wanted to keep Ryance busy till they were safely out the tunnel."

"And will he come?" I asked, a bit haughtily, perhaps. Father and I shared the failing of a most high pride. If the new king came to our aid, we would have no choice but swear to him, a very young man, and largely untried.

"If he's as noble as they say, he'll be no friend to Ryance. And he has enemies enough to need all the fealty he's offered." He tried to sit up straighter, groaned and fell back. "It must be soon. I can't lift a spoon, nor yet a sword."

"Here," I said, breaking pieces of oat bread into the broth, "eat this, and then you must rest."

"'Eat this.' 'You must do that.' You give orders as if you were the High Queen. Be careful I don't send you back to the nursery."

My face began to raise a flush, but if he saw me bristle there would be no cease to his teasing. So I smiled, and replied in kind. "Oh, aye. And who will stitch your wounds?"

"Did you?" he asked, startled. He stared a moment, taking my measure. Then he said briskly, "Well, daughter, I wish to eat some bread and broth, and then I wish to rest. You must go to your chamber and make yourself into a lady again. You look like a surgeon's knave."

I smiled, kissed his hand, and rose to go. At the door I turned. "I'll send your boy to lift the spoon for you," I said, with false cheer. "And if it comes so, I can lift a sword." Before he could reply, I dropped him a courtesy and was gone.

In the hall, men lay moaning on pallets as the women tended them and cleared the bloodied rushes from the floor. I looked around for Catlin and found her bustling from pallet to pallet with a cup of water and a kind—though brisk—word of encouragement. *Dear Catlin. The world could fall down around her ears, and she would sweep up the pieces and start seeing to dinner.*

Catlin came to me when I was two. My mother had been taken by fever, and when my father lost her, he almost lost himself as well. What was he to do with a toddling babe?

Catlin's mother Lia was a house slave in a nearby duchy. Father bought Lia to tend me, and her girl too. As a companion to me, he said, but really because Lia begged not to leave her own daughter behind. They might have been barbarians, but Father didn't hold with slavery, and he soon freed them both.

Lia died four years later, trying to bring forth a bairn. With the land in chaos, my father wanted a male heir to carry the black and gold. Of course there were unmarried ladies at the court, knight's daughters and such. But he told me once he could never love another as he had his Queen. Like most royal marriages, theirs had been a political arrangement. But the love between them came swift and strong. Though my mother had been gone now for ten years, he swore he would not marry again, an attitude that angered and frustrated his advisors.

They would have been satisfied with a bastard son. Bastards had no trouble laying their claims, and a kind and comely woman such as Lia would be no disgrace as a prince's mother, nor offer any demand to be the king's wife. But she was past thirty, too old for childbearing. Mother and infant struggled mightily, but both were lost. Catlin stayed, and I could not remember a night that wasn't made safe for me by her bugling snore and the bulky shape under the coverlet beside me.

Catlin caught sight of me and bustled over, trying to mask the worry in her eyes with an officious manner. "How does the king?"

"He woke, and his wits are sound. Did you hear—?"

"I did. Do you think he'll come?"

There was no need to sound the name, since it was being murmured in every corner of the great hall, and from there would spread throughout the kingdom. *Arthur. Arthur has been sent for. Will he come?*

Chapter 2

Sleet, snow, ice. Ryance's men kept to their fires while Father fretted in his bed, awaiting the return of his messengers. His wounds flamed and festered, then began to heal clean, aided by poultices I prepared. Of course he was uneasy, believing, as parents do, that his own child was yet an infant and couldn't know much.

"Have you forgotten I am priestess trained?" I asked him one afternoon as I salved the scabs on his forehead. "I've been studying the healing arts since I was a child." He tried to hide a sardonic smile at that. Annoyed, I wiped my hands and began replacing the dressing. "Doubt my skills if you wish, but they do seem to be working. How does your shoulder feel?"

"Itches like a thousand demons."

"Good. That means it's healing. But there are simples for the itch, too. I'll gather you some tomorrow. Hold still!" He had twisted abruptly to look at me. "You're making the bandage slip," I said, thinking his scowl was for the discourtesy in my tone.

"What do you mean, gather simples?" he demanded, his eyes sharp and hard.

"Why, herbs, sir. They grow everywhere hereabouts, even in winter, if you know where to look."

"Do you say, girl, you've been leaving the castle to gather herbs? With Ryance snapping at your hems? By the Bull!" He threw back the furs and struggled to his feet. I hastened to throw a robe over his shoulders. "Where is Catlin? Does she know of this?"

8

"Calm yourself, Father, and sit down," I said as firmly as I could. Even as I spoke, he turned pale and allowed himself to be led to a chair. "It's perfectly safe. I dress in rags and go out the postern tunnel. It doesn't take long to find what I need, and I always come straight back. Though I've been closed in so long," I continued unwisely, "I'd near gamble my life to go falconing."

"Falconing!" he roared. "Falconing? What folly is this?"

"Oh, hush, Father!" My own anger began to overcome my prudence. "I didn't say I was going, only that I wish I could. I've been inside these stone walls for months. It's hard to breathe."

"Guinevere," he said flatly, "you are not to leave the castle. Not for any reason, at any time, no matter how seldom or for how short a while. Do you hear?"

"But the poultices! We need —"

"I will do without the poultices."

"Aye, you will do," I flared. "But there are others still in need. We lost Aryn this morning, simply didn't have the skill to save him. Rolf and his brother are in danger yet, and there are many lesser wounds that still need tending. What king is this?" I asked angrily. "You risk your life on the battlefield to save them, only to let them die for lack of treating?"

"I am a warrior and a king." He was dangerously cold and quiet. "It is my sworn duty to protect my men. But you —"

"I am a king's daughter, sir, and no warrior, but I must do what I can."

"Silence!" he bellowed. "Will you deny me? By all the gods, will you say me nay? A king's daughter obeys her lord. As for being no warrior," his voice softened into gruffness, "I'm harder pressed to battle you than Ryance. Your tongue is sharper than his sword." We both fell silent for a moment. Then he continued quietly. "So you think I am no king? Tell me, Guinevere, will my kingdom fall for loss of a knight?"

"No, but loss of many —"

"Have kingdoms fallen for loss of an heir? You are my only living blood. If something happened to you, I..." he paused to adjust a fold of his robe. "The country would be torn. You must keep safe. Soon you will marry — don't scowl at me! You will, and you must wed someone strong enough to rule this kingdom well. Even if I throw down Ryance, how long before another takes his

9

place? You can do more for Cameliard by staying safe and marrying well than picking simples for sick knights. And who knows?" he asked, forcing a pleasant tone, "The High King himself may be on the way, and he's not taken a wife yet, eh?"

His smile faded as he looked at my face. "At any rate," the coldness returned to his voice, "you will not leave the castle again. Do as I command."

"As you say, sir." Slipping my hands into the wide sleeves of my robe, I gave him a stiff obeisance and walked out, my back straight as a sword.

Attracting no notice from the occasional churl going about his duties, I hunched across the frozen field, head bowed in a dingy shawl against the fat flakes of a late March snow. Pulling the cloak to further shadow my face, I scuttled with my basket like any crone down the path to the edge of the forest. At the border of ancient yew and elm, I stopped and peered about. No one was near, so I hurried into the dense tangle, heading for the marshes where certain mosses and worts wintered. I gathered, bent to the ground, making my crabbed way.

My basket was almost full when I caught the tang of woodsmoke in my nose and eyes. I froze, bent double, and peered through the slanting tree trunks, the gauze of falling snow. A tent, several tents, stood sentinel in the depths of the forest, huge ghostly mushrooms sprung up overnight.

I ducked behind a patriarch trunk. *Ryance runs here, does he? Such a fox deserves a fen to lie in.* Without noticing, I had been creeping from tree to tree, closer to the tents, until I could have touched the ropes stretched before me. These weren't war pavilions, flaunting commanders' banners and strung with shields. These tents were lurking, perhaps skulking closer to the castle by night steps. *Maybe we can raid tonight, catch him with his nose tucked under his beard. Ah, but look!* As the sweep of snow lessened a moment, I could see more tents stretched out beyond this circle. How many, there was no way to tell.

Rank upon rank, they marched threateningly out of the forest, marched inexorably toward my father's castle with its collection of torn and frightened men. A fierce anger began to build in me. I clutched the trunk of my screening tree, the rough bark biting my palms. Even a surprise attack upon this many foes stood no chance of success.

I hunched my back again and shuffled forward into the circle of tents, muttering under my tongue about simples and herbs. As I did, I glanced about with the quick hawklike twists of the neck I had seen so often in crones and peasant girls. Now I knew the gesture: it was spying.

There was little to spy. Though the embers were still glowing enough to make snowflakes sizzle, the camp seemed deserted. I stood near the center of the cluster, holding my basketful of simples. Should I trust my disguise enough to wait for their return? *But what is there to learn? We know their plans: kill off our men, tighten the siege and starve us out. Unless they choose to burn us out like rats.* I entirely forgot my disguise and began to stride around the fire like a swaggering boy. *They're probably out now challenging at our gate, damn them. Were I a man, I'd meet Ryance on the field and fly his beard from my standard. But I must stand by, watch him whittle my father to bone? No, by the gods, I shall do!*

I whirled to the embers and pulled out a glowing brand, then stepped to the nearest tent and held the torch to the fabric. It was damp with snow and burned feebly, but soon a wavering line of flame began to creep across the door flap. I went on to the next. That one too balked, then burned.

As I moved around the circle, I snatched another brand from the fire and began to strike with both hands, faster and faster, until I was running from tent to tent, always discovering more just beyond the veil of thick-falling snow.

So lost was I in my burning, I didn't hear the men until the first of them stepped into the opening.

He stopped and looked round, puzzled, at the smoldering tents. Then his eyes met mine, where I stood, torch in hand. For a moment we gazed across the clearing, hart and hunter met both unprepared. *Ryance*. He was young, not the greybeard I had expected, but his red badge and the bronze coronet on his helmet left no doubt he was the warlord.

Realization and anger dawned in his eyes, and he turned to the men jostling up behind him and pointed, shouting, "Spy! A spy!" Warriors poured from the woods and began to run toward me, reaching for their swords as they came. "Don't kill her," he shouted. "Bring her here."

I hurled my torches at them and ran, darting among the slanting tree trunks. The thunder of men in pursuit, the hiss of swords being drawn, then I was aware of nothing but my heartbeat slamming in my ears, my breath wrenching. Then even that passed, and I was a great bird, skimming the earth in silence, watching my dim snow-shadow run before me. I leapt from rock to rock across a narrow stream, leaving each the instant before it tipped.

The men behind me were skilled in pursuit, trained to run down their quarry. Despite the weight of their armor, they were closing fast. The fire raging in my side was beginning to pierce through my panic. I rucked my skirts up around my hips, stretched my legs as long as they would go and ran till my breath near burst. Far into the oldest part of the forest I came to a gully, too wide to leap. Across it lay a rotten log. Without pausing to consider the folly, I scampered across like a squirrel, my weight leaving as it was about to give way.

Dazzle spots danced in my vision. I began to falter and stumble but ran on as if carried in the hand of the Goddess, conscious of nothing but the thump of my own feet and the voice in my head insisting *run run run!* Only later, in memory, did I hear the sick sound of rotten wood giving way, the shouts, the clank of tumbling armor, the curses of the others as they milled on the far edge, watching their game disappear into the darkening snow.

It was full dark by the time I circled back to the castle. I hid in the underbrush and peered at the postern gate, wondering what I would do if Ryance's men were inside. Then it opened and Catlin's anxious face peered out. I dashed for the gate and slammed through, nearly sending Catlin asprawl. I leaned my back against the door, unable to do more than pant and stare.

"What happened?" Catlin whispered. "Are you hurt?" She put her arms around me and half carried me through the back hall and up the stairs to my chamber. "I thought you were lost! Your father's been looking for you." She nudged open the door with her hip.

"He's all right?" I asked, clutching her arm to stop her river of words. "Not attacked?"

"Better than all right! Arthur is come!" she said, jubilant, sitting me on my bed and kneeling to draw off my ruined hose. "He brought only his advance troops, but there are two thousand more, he says, on their way."

"Two thousand! Arthur has no two thousand men, has he?" I'd heard he was but newly crowned, not yet acclaimed in any surety.

"He has two other kings with him, Ban and Bors. They're brothers, come from Brittany. They've been aiding in his wars and he's to go to Brittany with them after he tidies up here. His words, not mine!" she said in response to my

12

glare. "Rather a swaggerer, he is. But an army of two thousand lends anyone a deal of strut."

"He's going to need them. Ryance is camped not a mile from here. I saw him, Catlin."

"You what?!" I could only nod. "Well, he's got a fine surprise coming to him. The king wanted you to meet Arthur, I think, before we're sent away. You have twigs in your hair!"

"Sent away? Where? What did—" My questions were cut off as Catlin bustled out to fetch water.

"It's a good thing he was distracted," she said, returning with ewer, bowl, and linens. "Here, you wash yourself. I'll get some fresh clothes."

"Catlin, stand still! What did you tell Father?"

"Nothing." She folded her arms over the linens, smug. "You'll have to make up your own story. He came sweeping in with Arthur and his ruffians in tow, frightening all the girls, and says, 'Where's the Princess Guinevere?' as grand as I've ever seen him. 'She's not here just now, sir,' I says, thinking to gain time, and out he stomps without another word. Too much on his mind, I suppose, to wait for you to turn up. Come now, hurry, I expect you'll be presented at dinner. What shall we do about your hair? Oh, I was sure you'd been taken." She threw her arms around me where I sat, limp and lifeless as a child's poppet.

My hands grew cold and trembled as Catlin hustled me down the corridor to the main hall, the fur tippets of my green wool gown trailing on the stones. My body ached so I could hardly bear it, but Catlin had insisted I wear my best. "It makes your eyes show greener," she said. "Arthur—"

"Catlin, please," I interrupted. "Father can do quite enough matchmaking without your help."

She looked about to argue, but subsided. She had foisted several bronze chains on me and managed to do my hair in a jeweled coif. I always hated that, but it was impossible to get it clean in time. Now she tried to grab one of my wrists to slide a copper bracelet on. "Will you stop?!" I snapped.

"You can't be presented to the High King looking like a hoyden. And mind your courtesy. He's here to help us, so bite your tongue and let him brag." We reached the entrance to the great hall, and Catlin gave me a quick hug and a mighty shove.

My entrance was less than graceful; I had to stop abruptly and regain my balance. I looked around, and as I had feared, every eye in the hall was on me. The long tables had been brought out from the walls and the benches were filled with knights and members of the household. But there was no feast, no pomp, only our own men weary and disheveled in their everyday leather jerkins, and a cold supper of bread and fowl. No High King. The clank of pottery and tinplate stilled for a moment and voices fell away as I entered, clad in all my royalty, feeling hot and foolish. A furtive snicker ran around the room, and my blood roared in my ears.

My father had been rapt in conversation with Davek, but now he looked around. One glance at my face and he clamped down the laugh I could tell was bubbling in his throat. I faltered for a moment under all those eyes, then dropped a quick courtesy to my father and slid into my place, casually bidding good evening, and asking after his wound.

The noise in the hall resumed, but my face flushed still warmer with Father's amused smile. "So this is where you've been all afternoon," he said. "No wonder Catlin was in such a hurly. How discourteous of us to burst in on you before you'd a chance to finish your trimmings."

"It was Catlin dressed me like a poppet," I muttered. "None of my doing."

"And a good result indeed! But alas, Arthur's gone back to await the rest of his men. You'll have to waste your glory on our own accustomed company, poor as it may be. He'll feast with us after the victory. You can trail your wing for him then, my dear."

"My only interest in the High King is whether he can back up his bragging." He chuckled and I gripped the table with both hands to keep myself from screaming in frustration. It was as well, I told myself, that he read my absence thus. At least I wouldn't have to stammer through a lie. But my anger at being thought such a fool as to cast myself at Arthur made me reckless when the topic of real importance came up.

Father signaled the boy and moved his trencher for me to share. "Well, we'll find out soon enough. I'd hoped to get you on the road this afternoon, but now you'll have to ride for Caerwent at first light."

"I'm to ride to Caerwent?" My father was about to speak, but I slammed my wooden cup on the table with a resounding bang. Several faces swiveled toward us, so I lowered my voice. "You think I'll be carted off to safety while these men face their greatest danger? My place is here!"

"We will not discuss it. Tomorrow Arthur expects the rest of his troops, and the next dawn we attack. If Arthur's men are as many and as mettled as he says, you'll be back as lady of the castle within the week. But if the battle is lost—Mithras prevent it—you must not be here."

I started to interrupt but was stopped by something in his face as he continued. "I wish there were some way I could send all the ladies to safety," he said. "It pains me to leave them here when we ride. Have you ever considered, in your girlish haze of honor, what happens to them if the enemy takes the castle?"

He stared down at the table and his voice fell further into grief. "There are two dreams," he said, "that torment me on the eve of every battle. One is the sight of all my good men broken and bleeding on the field. The other is a sound, the stomp of boots in the corridors, the swinish hoots and jeers of the enemy as they swarm the castle. Do you understand, Guinevere? First they take the wine, and then the ladies."

"Now," he said, straightening, glancing sidelong at my dismay, "let us enjoy this dinner and speak pleasantly. We may not see each other for a while."

He forced a worried smile, lifted his cup to me and drank. The darkness of his expression, the unaccustomed lines carving themselves into his face, made me hold my tongue. I bowed my head to his courtesy. As his eyes went down the long table, touching on his companions one by one, mine followed. The sight of so many empty places, so many maimed and bandaged men, filled me with a heavy sorrow. Suddenly the king stood and cried, "Where is the harpist? Let there be music, let there be rejoicing! Tomorrow begins the victory!"

The boy came running and broke into a merry tune, the men pounded the long table, and cups were lifted as the shout went up: "Lodegrance! Cameliard!" Father lifted his cup to them in return as I sat smiling, my heart cold and tight, my throat an ache of swallowed weeping.

15

Chapter 3

The next morning, before cocklight, Davek and Behr arrived to escort me to safe lodging. Catlin met them at the door, rolling her eyes, no doubt, to show my unsoundness of wit. "She won't go."

"Won't go?" echoed Behr. "She has to go. The King has ordered it."

"Where is she?" Davek demanded.

"Here I am," I said, coming out from my chamber, still in my dressing gown, "and here I shall stay."

Davek, drawing his bushy gray eyebrows down, stepped in front of Behr and confronted me. "The King has ordered that we escort you to safety. Are you refusing the King's orders?"

"I am. If the King won't recognize my duty, then let him deal with me after the battle."

"Are you asking that we too disobey the King's orders? Shall we let him deal with us as well?"

I have never liked to lean upon my privilege. In fact, my royal birth has more often barred me from my desires than smoothed my way. I could, however, be imperious as ice when it was useful.

"I am not *asking* anything." I drew myself up—as much as I could—trying to look regal, despite the dressing gown. All three stared, my tone was so unusual. "May I remind you, Sir Davek, who it was made you knight?"

"Your grandfather," he replied gruffly.

"And to whose service did he command you, most particularly?"

"To the service of your mother. But—"

16

"Were you not in my mother's service before ever you stepped foot into Cameliard or clapped eyes on King Lodegrance?"

"Yes, but Lady…" He faltered, and I took a step forward, pressing my advantage.

"Did my mother not swear you to my service, and in plain fact demand your unswerving loyalty to me as she lay in her final illness? Did she not charge you to protect me and my honor from everyone, including the King if need be?"

"I'm trying to protect you!" he burst out. "You're not safe here."

"My honor will not be safe if I go."

"Nonsense! A woman's honor lies in her bed, not in a battle."

"Nonetheless, I will stay." I turned away as if that decided all. "As you are my knight, you owe loyalty and obedience to me beyond what you owe the King. He will have no cause with you."

"Lady," said young Behr, bending his knee to me, "I too am your sworn knight. But Davek is right. You don't belong here, with battle swirling around you. Think of your safety!"

"Does my father think of his safety when he rides out with his sword in his left hand and a shield lashed to his useless right arm? Do you think you could stop him? Would you even try?"

The answer was foregone, so Behr switched his approach. "But with ladies…. You really must—"

I could see reason would go nowhere. I wrapped my dressing gown closer around me, the better to hide my trembling hands, and stood as tall as I could. "I will go to Caerwent if I am bound and flung over a saddle in my shift. Now, are you for it?"

Behr dropped his eyes immediately, and Catlin, smirking in the shadows, knew I had already won. But Davek, who had sat for hours with me on his knee, teaching me to say *fire* and *horse* and *table* when I was still in leading strings, exploded with all the wrath his love engendered. "Just what do you plan to do?" he thundered. "Carry a sword into battle? Do you want to tie that around your father's neck? How can he think about his men and his strategy when he has you to worry about?"

The skirmish was all but over. I reached out and put a hand on the elder knight's arm as he stood indignant. "My father will not be troubled. I'll keep to my rooms until battle's been joined, then come out to do what I can here. There are provisions to be sent to the field, harness to be mended and most importantly, wounds to be treated. I can do those things and oversee the ladies. Na, Davek," I said with a more cheerful visage, "I'll not wield a sword unless I must. And if you don't want my father worried on the eve of battle... don't tell him." I smiled sweetly and heard Catlin stifle a snort of laughter. Davek's scowl grew so deep it seemed his brow would break. Then he spun on his heel and marched stiffly away. Behr, working hard to keep a smile from his face, dipped his head to me and followed.

"Well," said Catlin as she closed the door behind them, "you've had your way once again. I pray you don't get us both killed, or worse."

It was a long day waiting, and a longer night. I don't believe my eyes closed at all, though Catlin made me a posset and grumbled about my tossing. Just before dawn I heard the horses and men preparing for the attack, the restless clank and shuffle, the quiet commands. In the first iron light, I peered out the window of my tower room, taking care to keep well out of sight. I sent a silent prayer after my father. So high and straight he sat in his saddle that no one would have guessed his right arm was bandaged to his chest, the reins and shield fixed to his hand with leather thongs. On the crest of the farther hill, I could barely see a mass of men, Arthur's troops, looking at that distance like one huge bristly beast.

The men fell into formation. In the eerie quiet, they began to move out of the courtyard. Father's stallion paced the bridge, with Davek beside him to be his right arm. Davek kept his eyes straight ahead, but as Behr passed in a later rank, he lifted one hand in the slightest gesture of farewell. I lifted my hand in return, but Behr dared not look up. As soon as the last foot soldier had left and the gates swung closed, I was out of my chamber and heading down to the main hall. "The youngest make bandages," I called. "Lyn and Marte to the stable to mend armor. And send Enola to the safe room to ready the herbs."

All preparations made, we waited anxiously. Soon a boy ran in with a shield come loose from its grip and was hurried on to the stable where the armorers waited. Another long wait. Catlin and I kept busy, making sure everything was in readiness, and offering words of comfort and encouragement to the women and girls who remained. They were soldier's

18

women—mothers, wives and daughters—since the few ladies in court had removed to Caerwent.

It was easy enough to tell when the battle was joined in earnest. They came flooding through the gates: boys, the lame, the old, bearing soldiers on litters, leading foaming, limping horses, carrying armfuls of smashed armor and broken reins to be mended.

I bandaged the head of an archer who had lost an eye. He picked up his helmet and tried to put it on, but it wouldn't fit over the bulky dressing. He called for another, jammed it onto his head, and grimly went out again.

I rushed to a young knight being carried in on a litter and unlaced his mail. When I wiped away the blood from his chest, there was no wound. Puzzled, I glanced at him. He stared back at me, in agony, then closed his eyes, and the life left his body. As he was lifted and carried away, I saw the back of his helmet was crushed. Before I had time to react, another man was laid before me, his arm gone to the elbow. I forced my attention to him.

In the lulls, we restocked the bandages, brought fresh rushes to cover the mud and blood on the floor, and tended to the less seriously injured. I sat for a moment, my robe bloodied and my hair hanging unbound, a piece of bannock bread in my hand. I took a bite, but was too exhausted to chew it, and sat like a dumb beast.

The pause was brief, and chaos erupted again. The next knight brought in was Davek. He was already dead, his eyes open and staring. I sobbed once, then steeled myself. I knew him to be a follower of both Mithras and the Great Mother, so I dipped a finger in the blood of his wound, drew the triple moon on his forehead, and sent him to the otherworld with the Goddess's blessing. I closed his eyes, laid my cheek against his grizzled hair for a moment, then turned to the screaming soldier on the next litter.

By late afternoon, we were running out of bandages. In another lull, I went up to my chamber and began ripping one of my gowns to strips, first cutting off the embroidery and setting it aside to be used again. *If I'm still a princess at the end of this day, and not a slave girl in the red livery of Ryance.* There had been wave upon wave of wounded, dead and dying. How many were left in the field? And how many did Ryance have? The memory of those rows of tents stretching into the forest kept coming back to me as I cut and tore, cut and tore…

Next I knew, it was full dark. *Was I awake, or was I dreaming?* Just as my father had told, there were heavy footsteps in the hall and unfamiliar voices yelling in triumph. My eyes flew open, but I stayed still as stone while I listened. Two soldiers laughed outside my door. "A right fine fortress. No wonder they held off the siege for so long."

"I hope he billets us here. Even the scullery maids are pretty."

Hopeless tears welled in my eyes. What had they done with my father? I blame my sleep-fogged brain for my actions then. I felt around in the dark for my scissors, the nearest thing to a blade in the chamber, and held them behind my back as I crept to the door and peered through a crack.

I saw the retreating backs of the troops who had passed, swaggering on down the corridor. Their red insignia confirmed my fears, and a sick knot formed in my stomach.

My father's chamber was on the same corridor, so as soon as the two swaggerers were out of sight, I bolted out the door to find him. Three men—three strangers—stepped from his doorway as I approached, and I ran right into them. One grabbed my arms. "Hold, girl!"

I stabbed at him, holding the shears like a dagger, but succeeded only in wounding his hand as he grunted in surprise and wrenched my paltry weapon away. The other two grabbed me. I flailed and kicked, but they managed, with many curses, to pin my arms behind me. "Let's have a look at you," one of them said. He grabbed a handful of my disheveled hair and yanked my head up. I spat at him, full in the face. He raised an arm to strike me but didn't deliver the blow. "Why, this is the little bitch who tried to burn us out!"

The soldier who held my pinned wrists craned to peer into my face. I would have spit at him too, but my mouth was suddenly dust-dry. "It is, the very one! He'll want to see her." I bucked and tried to kick him in the groin with my heel, but only hurt my foot on his chausses. "Be still, girl!" he snapped. "After today's rout, you have a new master."

They dragged me into my father's chamber, kicking and cursing. My father was not there. Instead, the young warlord I had faced across the clearing was easing himself out of his battle gear. I quivered as my last wild hope left me, but willed my heart to harden. I would not let them see my pain. I would not.

He knew me at once. "The urchin with the torches!" he said, half smiling. "Are you of this household?" Abruptly he scowled and thrust his face close to mine. "What are you doing here?" he demanded. "Have you come to burn us out again?"

"A serving girl turned against her master, no doubt," said the burly soldier whom I'd stabbed, surveying my draggled robes and tangled hair.

"Well? Speak, girl. How do you come here?"

"I come to this castle by right of birth," I said, my eyes hot with anger and scorn and tears I would not shed. "By what right come you?"

The warlord looked both puzzled and amused. "By right of birth, is it?"

I stopped struggling then. I would no longer reduce myself to fighting when clearly I could do nothing. *Let them do with me what they will. I will bear it with the knowledge of who I am, and the memory of my father's courage.* I stood as straight as my captors would allow and looked this monstrous interloper full in the face. "I am the princess Guinevere, daughter of King Lodegrance," I said, and a great dark calm flowed over me. I closed my eyes in the momentary silence that greeted my announcement, waiting in peace to accept whatever fate these blackguards would deal me. I hoped it would be death.

I didn't expect laughter. The sound lashed across me, and I opened my eyes to see the soldiers with their heads thrown back, roaring with amusement, while their leader smiled grimly. They loosened their grip, but I was too stunned to attempt escape.

"Lodegrance's daughter," said the leader sardonically. "Then why did I first meet you with a torch in your hand?"

"Because, sir," I answered, rigid with hate, "I had no sword."

The weight of contempt and fury in my voice slowly crushed the laughter. As the others stood with puzzled grins on their faces, the leader gazed at me, solemn. "Princess of Cameliard, are you?" he asked musingly. "And who am I?"

The guards looked at him, bewildered. My rage drained away, and a great sorrow came stealing in to take its place. "Why, you are…Ryance, my father's murderer," I said slowly, with a terrifying empty space opening in my breast. All my blood stilled and sank, and a hush fell in the room.

Slowly, the soldiers released my arms and backed away, staring from me to their leader. My words had taken my last strength, and I swayed despite my efforts. The warlord reached a hand to steady me, then to my amazement, bowed low. "Forgive me, my lady, for this appalling treatment. I am Arthur Pendragon, High King of Britain. Your father is in the hall with his men, fresh from his victory."

As he straightened from his bow, his face struggled to remain grave, perhaps show some sympathy. But when his eye fell on the scissors which one of his men still held, he burst forth in a gale of laughter. The sound bounded after me between the stone walls as I fled down the corridor to my chamber.

Chapter 4

I would have wished never to set eyes on Arthur Pendragon again, but there was nothing for it but to brazen through. I bid Catlin lay out once again my best gown. She tried to clasp a necklace of copper and emerald around my neck, but I refused. I love the feel of soft woolens and furs, and often, especially in spring, deck myself in the brightest and most unsuitable colors, but I have always detested jewels of any sort. They make me feel bound, somehow, as if the clasps and chains were connected to something more than themselves.

Catlin gave way on the chain but was adamant about the coronet. "You *will* wear it! It's a state occasion."

"Oh, bugger the state occasion!"

"Lovely. The future Queen of Cameliard speaks. Up with you now." She plopped the gold coronet on my head and adjusted it while I scowled, I confess, like a sullen child.

Perhaps it was because the worst had already been done, but for whatever reason, I was quite steady as I went down the corridor on my way to the main hall. I stopped at the head of the stairs and looked over the throng below. Our modest hall could never contain all of Arthur's nobles and officers in addition to our own, and the overflow filled the entire floor and out the doors. I had seen from my tower window the fires spread across the land until they were no more than dots of light, where the cottagers and soldiers and townsfolk were also feasting. Father was always generous with his people, and Arthur had added to the gaiety from his own provisions.

The crowd below me swirled with the colors of rich robes and the flash of jewels. All the various types of Britain were gathered there, since Arthur's army gleaned men from every kingdom, and the heads as I looked down on them showed the range. There were the russet hues of the northern Celts, ranging from deepest auburn through fox to flame. Saxon blood brought us the fair-haired ones, some rich and golden, some almost white. Roman blood showed in the ones with darker hair. Then there were the Black Celts, a tribe from the turbulent hills of Cymru, rugged and dark, like my father. My mother had been tall and fair, with hair the color of apricots, the very picture of a Celtic queen. Alas, I favored my father. My hair was black and unmanageable, to Catlin's despair. In contrast, my skin was pale and my eyes mostly green, but changeable. Where I got my stature from I have no idea, since my father was tall enough; like our tough little ponies, I was small, though spirited withal.

Catlin gave me a nudge, and I drew one deep breath and went down to the hall. This time, when I entered, I saw the full glory of our court. Every place at the long trestle tables was taken, and servants ran back and forth with fowl, fruits, and fish, sallets and sweets, a whole roasted boar and other meats, and of course skin after skin of wine and never-ending pitchers of ale, mead and small beer. This time everyone was too caught up in the festive clatter to stop and stare at me. Only the High King's eyes were on me, as he stood drinking by the fire with a group of officers, his and ours. He fixed me across the hall with a gaze as intent as that which had held me across the camp clearing.

All I had noted at that time was that he was not a man of years, as I'd expected. He was, in fact, not much more than a boy, his face smooth and shining among the scarred, grizzled visages of older soldiers. He started across the hall toward me.

Had he been solemn and on his dignity, and ignored me once the official greetings were done, I could have turned to my meal and excused myself as early as courtesy would allow. Had he teased me as a child, I could have marked him down for a boor and felt safe in my scorn. But the look in his eyes as he offered his greeting startled me somewhat: it seemed he looked with admiration. He made no open reference to the incident, only said, with an innocent smile, that he was pleased to see me again. Those around us snickered and chuckled. I bent my knee with as much dignity as I could. "Your Highness."

To my surprise, as I extended my hand for him to raise me from my reverence, he would not let it go. Instead, he tucked it under his arm and turned me to face his lieutenant, a tall man with a soft brown beard and mild blue eyes, and a most appealing slow, gentle smile. "This is my foster brother Bedwyr," Arthur said. "He defines the word 'loyalty.' And this—" he stopped a man careening past, somewhat the worse for wine, "—is my kinsman, Prince Gawain of Orkney." Gawain was a brawny young man wearing a northern plaid, with red hair flowing past his shoulders, his high color made even more ruddy by imbibing. Bandages and plasters in plenty showed he had been active in yesterday's battle, and a thick scar blazing a trail through his beard showed it hadn't been his first. He gave me a giddy smile and clumsy bow before charging on. "With these two at his side, that hound over there could win a kingdom," said Arthur.

"Only if the Merlin said it was to be," said Bedwyr.

Despite my resolve to be distant and coldly polite, I couldn't help asking, "The Arch Druid? He's here? The Merlin is here?"

"Wherever I am, he is. He's been controlling my destiny since before I was born," Arthur replied, with a trace of ruefulness. "Would you like to meet him?" I nodded, not trusting my voice.

The King maintained his grip on my hand as we approached the high table. In the place next to his was a gray-haired man in a plain white robe. "Emrys?" Arthur said smiling and laid a friendly hand on his shoulder.

I was thoroughly awed to meet the famous Arch Druid, the Merlin of Britain. Slowly he turned to face us. But when his black eyes met mine, there came into them a look of the most astonishing terror and hatred! All the noise in the hall fell away, and though I swear he did not make a sound, I heard a voice say, *Bright Shadow!* I stood as if glamoured, unable to move or speak. Bright Shadow is simply the meaning of my Celtic name, but for some reason hearing it caused a wave of guilt or shame or some such emotion to wash over me. I had no idea why. Then the clamor returned, and the Merlin smiled, all malevolence gone from his face. No one noticed anything amiss, but something heavy had passed between us.

He rose and greeted me with careful courtesy as I stood dazed and breathless. "I am Emrys, Lord Merlin," he said, "and you must be the warrior princess I've been hearing about. I am at your service, my lady." With a sweeping gesture, he offered me his seat.

"But my place is there," I protested, doubly confused and yes, frightened by the attentions of the High King and the quickly quenched look of hostility from this dark-eyed Druid. But it wasn't hostility, exactly. Not, for example, the pique of a fawner bumped from his right-hand place. This man looked at me with terror as well as rancor, as if there were a malignancy at my core that only he could see. But what most bewildered me was my own reaction, the helpless shame called up in answer, as if something in me admitted his unspoken accusation, claimed some awful evil as my own.

He smiled at me again as Arthur said, rather loudly, "What good for a man to be High King if he can't move a pretty maiden from her father's side to his own?" Several of those within hearing glanced around, raising amused eyebrows at this clumsy attempt at courtly gallantry. Arthur's ears reddened. "At least for the space of a victory feast," he added quickly as murmurs began to rise in the hall.

It was this quick amending, as if he feared I might be overeager for his attentions, that made my temper well up and cleared the haze of confusion from me. "I beg your pardon, sir," I said, "but I must ask you to excuse me. I am sure you and your men have much to discuss, matters beyond my ken." I took my hand from his possession and went to my place on Father's left.

The hall grew quieter. Some attempted to keep up their conversations without missing anything of what was happening, while others stared openly. Arthur stood awkwardly where I had left him as I seated myself. In the moment of quiet that followed, the implications of what I had done came clear. I had known it would be insulting, and I had known he was King of all Britain. But I hadn't put those facts together in my mind until I sensed the tension in the hall and saw the strain in my father's face as he slowly turned to me.

Arthur walked over and leaned against the table in front of me, so close I needed to crane my neck to look up at him. "Do you mean, Lady," he asked in a constricted voice, "that my company at this feast would be tiresome for you?"

There was no amending what I had done, and I don't know for certain whether I would have if I could, so I answered him as frankly as possible. "No indeed, sir. Quite the contrary. You see, the events of these past few days have left me not fully in possession of my tranquility, and to be honest, your attentions leave me ill at ease. Ours is a simple, rustic court, and often hard beset. I'm afraid I haven't been schooled in behavior appropriate to a High King."

Perhaps if he had been older, his dignity more settled, the offense would have seemed intolerable. But his face softened, and the flush of anger receded. He dropped to a chair beside me, and spoke quietly, not in the loud and regal voice he had used before. "My lady," he said, "I beg your pardon. I find I too am lacking somewhat in—what did you call it?—tranquility. Recent events have been.... I find myself in a position I never dreamed of. I became High King before I was even a knight! Nor was I trained to courtesy, only how to wield a sword. Will you forgive my bad manners? And would you come sit beside me? To be honest in my turn," he said, lowering his voice even further, "all this talk of military matters bores me too sometimes. And I fear we've made a ripple in the evening that should be calmed."

I needed to say something graceful to ease the awkwardness. But every lady in my court, with the possible exception of Catlin, had a tongue smoother than mine, which was cobbled and stubborn and often, as now, refused even the most blundering words. So I simply got up and took the arm he offered. As we walked to his place, the babble in the room rose again and people turned with relief to their food and drink.

As I took my new seat, I found myself the focus of several pairs of eyes: Arthur's, blue-gray and clear now as a child's; my father's, a bit dazed by it all; Merlin's, dark and opaque as the black jewel he wore on his breast; and yet another pair, which I had not noticed before, belonging to a blond young giant whose name, I later learned, was Cei. Those particular eyes watched us with unabashed merriment, and when I was safely seated to share a trencher with the King, he threw back his head and laughed and shouted, "Well done, Arthur! Well done, Lady!" and pounded the table till the cups bounced.

A server filled our goblets, and I tipped a few drops out before I took a long swallow to settle myself. Arthur cleared his throat. "A libation for the Goddess?" I nodded. "You should follow Mithras, the soldiers' god. He lets us keep all our wine for ourselves."

"You are not Christian, then, my lord?"

"No, though lately more and more of my men are. But soldiers are a superstitious lot, and I think most of them pray to any and all gods, whoever they think might help. And to speak true, I think they're all one in the end."

"Then you won't be establishing the White Christ in Logres?"

"I don't intend to establish any religion. Let each one seek his own truth and worship where he will."

"I'm glad to hear it. The Romans, and now many of the Christians, believe theirs should be the only worship. Even here, there were sacred oak groves burned and desecrated." Arthur shook his head in disapproval, but we were being plied with meats and dainties of all sorts, and the talk soon turned to lighter topics.

No victory feast is complete without bards retelling the glory. Once the major part of the feast was served, they took their places in the center of the hall. First our Dristan recounted the battle against Ryance in stirring terms, not failing to give honor to Arthur, while still emphasizing my father's courage and that of our brave warriors. Then it was the turn of Taliesin, Arthur's bard.

Arthur stifled a sigh beside me. Though he attended with all courtesy, I could sense he disliked sitting through a long recital of the Twelve Battles and the tale of his pulling the sword of state from the stone, proving himself the true King of Britain. As the tale reached its climax, everyone in the hall stamped and cheered and beat their cups and knives on the table. Arthur stood to acknowledge them, then slumped back into his seat and took a long draught of his wine.

Despite my earlier resentment, I was beginning to like this lanky youth next to me, and I was full of questions. "Where is the sword, Your Grace?" I asked. "Do you return it to the stone until it is needed? How did Merlin set it there?"

"Guinevere," he said, smiling gently, "this tale is the bard's fancy, changing fact into the stuff of legend. It didn't happen as he tells, and as all the world now hears it."

"But you do possess the sword of state?"

"Of course. It was my father's. When I went to my first battle, beside Uther Pendragon, he and Merlin were the only ones who were aware I was his son. I'm sure you've heard tales about my conception and birth…"

Fortunately, he paused to take a sip of his wine, so my blush went unseen. I had indeed heard many tales, ranging from sordid to magical, about how Uther Pendragon fell in love with the wife of Duke Gorlois, who swept her from court and protected—or imprisoned—her in Tintagel, an impenetrable fortress on the coast of Cornwall. Whether through Merlin's magic or the lady's connivance, Uther gained access to Ygraine and Arthur was conceived. As it happened, Gorlois was killed in battle the same night. Some say it was because of Uther's guilt, and some say it was the price Merlin demanded for his aid, but for whatever reason, the child Arthur was spirited away, shortly after his second birthday, to be raised in obscurity.

"Merlin had just taken me to meet my father," Arthur continued. "Uther was old by then, and very ill. He would have proclaimed me his heir…eventually. But a throng of barbarians launched a surprise attack before that could happen. We were fighting side by side, but he was weak, and struggling. In the heat of combat, my own sword was broken. He threw his to me. I caught it and led the charge against the Saxons while he turned back, all unarmed, to get behind the line. It wasn't until I tried to return his sword after the battle that I learned he had been cut down." His eyes clouded momentarily.

"And that's when it was fixed in the stone?"

"No stone." He smiled. "Well, Uther was the stone. He was reluctant, nay, totally refused to name an heir or contemplate the end of his rule, even though it left the kingdom in uncertainty. Men joked that one might as well try to pull the sword from a rock as from Uther's hands. When he threw it to me, he recognized me as his heir, his son, and the next ruler of Britain. But that wasn't poetic enough for the bards, so they transformed the jest into something to awe the world and glorify my reign." He smiled again. "You look surprised, Lady. Are there not tales told about you that have no basis?"

"I am not the subject of bards, my lord, since I have no exploits such as yours."

Arthur sighed. "I wish my own true deeds were enough, rather than hearing how I slew nine hundred men in one day's span or conquered a dragon…or pulled a sword from a stone." He took another draught of his wine, looking vaguely discontent. Then he turned to me with some enthusiasm.

"There is another sword meant for me, though. At least I hope it isn't another of the bards' inventions. Have you heard of the sword of Magnus

Maximus?" I had not. "You Cymri call him Macsen. He lived during Roman times, and tried to lead his men to take over Rome and liberate the provinces. Maximus was killed before he ever got to Rome, and his men brought his sword and other regalia back to Britain. They have not been seen since. The tales say they are in the possession of the Lady of the Lake, who will one day present them to the true High King. They don't say when, though." He chuckled, but I could sense a yearning in him under his casual manner. "My father's sword is the sword of state, and gave me the right to rule. But Macsen's sword is part of the Holy Regalia of the Druids, and carries a very different kind of power, beyond the scope of mere men."

My mouth always refused to wait for my brain. "Are you so sure, then, you are the true…" I trailed off, realizing that once again I had offered an insult to the man who held all our fates in his hand.

I needn't have worried. Arthur turned to me and caught my eyes in his. "Yes," he said.

After the bards there was dancing, at which Arthur proved totally inept. He danced with me, and with the foremost ladies of the court, enough to satisfy courtesy, and then sank back into his chair. Since there were only our few ladies and so many of Arthur's troops, we were all kept busy. Gawain was much like his kinsman and danced like a bear at a fairing. Bedwyr, though, was skilled, and especially good at showing his partner to her best advantage. But it was Cei who was the surprise of the night. For all his size, he capered nimbly, pavanned gracefully, and most importantly, made each lady he danced with seem as if she were exactly the partner he wanted. Every lady in the hall danced with him at least once, and Catlin, I noticed, several times.

I love to dance, but the events of the last few days suddenly conspired to drain me of all energy. The festivities looked to go on deep into the night, so I stood to take my leave. Catlin broke off a spirited dance with Cei and appeared at my elbow. I felt as though I might need her to carry me to my chamber. But then my spirits rose, if not my vigor.

"I hear you are an excellent horsewoman," Arthur said as he bid me good night. "I leave soon for Brittany, but tomorrow is a rest day for the men. Might we ride in the morning?"

"Certainly," I said with a sincere smile. With all that had happened, it hadn't even entered my mind that I was now free to leave the confines of the hated siege. I felt easier now with this young warrior who was our new High King, less constrained in his company... and he had no idea how much I wanted to ride Gala again and feel the wind in my hair.

Chapter 5

My hair streamed behind me, wild and tangled. His stallion's nose was at Gala's croup as we pounded around the final bend. I lay forward over her neck and urged her to her utmost. Clods flew and the thunder of our horses' hooves echoed off the bare hills. The stallion drew even with Gala's withers, but we were almost to the goal. I pulled her to a stop that nearly sat her down, then leapt from my saddle and raced to the ancient oak we had set as the finish. I slammed into the trunk just a hairbreadth before him, and we both rebounded and fell to the ground, laughing and gasping for breath.

"Only because you know the land, girl! If you hadn't edged me into that bog..."

"How discourteous of me," I crowed. "Look, your soft boots are all muddy."

We stretched ourselves out and relaxed. It was a mild day, fresh with the promise of spring. On the horizon, soft white clouds roamed like lambs in a blue meadow, and weak sunlight filtered through the branches of the great oak.

"This is a venerable old man, isn't it?" said Arthur, peering up through the branches.

"Venerable, yes, but sacred to the Goddess, so I'll thank you to speak of it as 'she.' I'll be made a priestess at midsummer, so..."

Arthur rolled to face me. "Tell me," he said, "do priestesses of your goddess see sin everywhere, as the Christ's priests do?"

"No. We keep the Beltane fires, and are free to—"

"Oh, I know about Beltane! That's where everybody goes out into the woods and makes the land fertile by, ah, showing the way? Lots of rustling in the bushes?"

"It's a very powerful rite!" I said, smiling in spite of myself. "Though they do seem to enjoy it."

Arthur moved closer, took my hand and began toying with it. "Seem? You haven't taken part yourself?"

This was clearly becoming a conversation between a youth and a maiden, rather than a king and a princess, and not one I wanted to take part in. He was handsome enough, certainly, and we were young. But I was well aware of my destiny.

I sat up and smoothed my hair, disengaging my hand from his. "When I go to Beltane, it will be with my chosen consort. I need to keep Cameliard foremost in mind, not romance."

"Oh, come! You'll marry and go to your lord's land. A bastard of yours would be no problem there."

"I'm not leaving here! Cameliard is my demesne and I intend to rule it after my father."

"But you'll have to marry. Would you like me to find you someone suitable to your rank?"

I suppose he meant no harm, since that was the way royal marriages were usually contracted. But I was stung and scrambled to my feet to remount Gala. "When I marry...*if* I choose to marry, I can find my own mate, thank you, like any Celtic Queen. I've already had suitors. A lot of suitors!"

I wheeled Gala, leaving the King unceremoniously leaning on his elbow. Before I spurred off, I heard him mutter, "May the gods help the one who gets you!"

Once again, I had transgressed in my treatment of the High King. But Arthur had nicked the two themes I held central in my life: my moira as the future Queen of Cameliard, and my dedication to the Goddess.

I was already being tutored by my father and his counselors in statecraft and diplomacy—though clearly not enough! My mother's death had been an unmitigated sorrow, but it also made my path clear. She was with child when the sickness felled her. Had her child been a boy, no matter how foolish, inept or even downright wicked he might have grown, he would have been the king. My only role in the world would have been to give myself entire to some stranger for political gain.

My religious training was a much more central part of my childhood. I had been trained to serve the Goddess from the time I could understand right and wrong. For such as I, there were four circles of training, with each spiraling upon the last.

From about the age of three to seven, all Druid children were gathered at regular intervals to learn about our worship. Dame Erma, a plump, jolly sort with the kindest of hearts, taught us about the Wheel of the Year and the basics of good behavior which truly, everyone should follow, pagan or no: honesty, compassion, reverence for the earth. The sons and daughters of plowmen, cooks, and woodcutters came together with the children of noble families, and we were all treated equally.

Our world was populated with many gods. Those who followed the old Brythonic ways worshipped Rhiannon, Brigid, Llyr, Cernunnos. They were tied to the land and celebrated the Great Marriage. My father's warriors were followers of Mithras: a secretive group, meeting and feasting in underground dens. I thought that odd, since they were dedicated to Sol Invictus.

We Druids met in open groves and among the standing stones. We revered the earth, and the sacred cycle of the seasons. We celebrated light in all its forms: moon, sun, stars, fire. Even the lowly glowworm and tiny flying creatures of midsummer contributed their little light to the world. Everything in the natural world partook of the sacred: oaks were particularly venerated, but people also held reverence for local spirits of springs, caves, hills.

I had never heard of the new religion spreading throughout the land until one day when I was four. Catlin and I were romping in the forest, accompanied by Dame Erma, who was foraging for the barks and roots, herbs and mosses she used to make her poultices. We scampered ahead of her, and discovered a cave in a hillside. We dared each other to go in, pushing and giggling. But when a man stuck his head out and glared at us, we shrieked and ran for the protection of Dame Erma's apron.

He looked to us half man, half beast. Despite the autumn chill, he wore nothing but a loincloth. His hair was wild and tangled, and his bare feet caked with mud. "Hush, children," said Dame Edna. "There's nothing to fear." She walked toward the cave, with Catlin and I clinging to her skirts.

"Good day to you, hermit," she said pleasantly. He stared at her a moment, then gave her a grudging nod. "Do you hunger?" she asked, reaching into her basket for some bannock she had brought along in case we girls got peevish. He stepped forward and peered into her basket of simples, then shook his head with a ferocious scowl.

"Witch," he said. His voice was a croak.

Dame Erma stiffened and dropped the bread back into her basket but maintained a civil tone. "Indeed, I am not. I am a healer."

"Damned," the hermit muttered. He leaned heavily on his staff and made a gesture that took in Catlin and me, cowering behind her skirts. "Damned," he said again, louder, and retreated into his cave.

Catlin and I stared wide-eyed at each other. Dame Erma gave a small cluck of disgust, then took our hands and started back along the path. We were full of questions, but it wasn't until we were home and munching on sweetmeats that she sat down with us to explain.

"That man you saw was a follower of a new religion. Some of them go to live alone, so they may dedicate their lives to worship without the distraction of worldly matters."

"But why did he call you a witch? Why did he say we were damned?"

"His religion believes there is only one god, and only those who worship that god are good people. They think the rest of us are cursed."

"Who would say that? Which god do they say we have to worship?" Our questions tumbled over each other.

"Their god's name is Christ, and his followers are called Christians. They came from somewhere far in the east, and they are growing in numbers."

"Are we...damned, then?" Catlin asked, with a tremor in her voice.

Dame Erma gathered us both close to her. "Of course not," she crooned. "You are good girls, and the Mother smiles on you. People believe different things, but if you listen to your teachings and are kind to one another and revere the world around you, you are blessed, truly. Now run and see whether Doran needs help in the kitchens."

Catlin was my constant companion in those early years. But then a new girl joined us. Her name was Nimue, and she had been sent to my father's court because her parents, minor nobility from Demetia, had died of a fever within a fortnight of each other. Her quiet manner hid a cutting wit and an appetite for adventure; soon we became friends.

Nimue was not a pretty girl. Her hair, in two thin braids, was the exact color of a carrot. She was stout, with small green eyes and a piggish upturned nose. Every inch of exposed flesh was densely dotted with freckles. The beauty among us, recognized even at that age, was Rhona. Tall and willowy, with golden hair tumbling down her back in waves, she moved among us like the very incarnation of the Corn Maiden, serene and smiling.

Under that loveliness, however, Rhona was malicious, and wily with it, so she seldom got caught in her little cruelties. She especially liked to bedevil the younger children. One day, she picked relentlessly on a little boy, pinching and poking him until he cried. Dame Erma didn't know why he was upset, so she simply tucked him under her comforting arm and continued with the lesson. After she left us, however, little Connor's older brother and two of his friends confronted Rhona.

"He's three years old! Why don't you try your tricks on us instead of the little ones?"

"I don't know what you mean," Rhona said, her voice dripping with disdain, and made as if to leave. But one of the boys pushed her back, and they began to crowd her, menacingly. I was wondering whether to intervene, but Nimue instantly stepped between them. She said something to the boys I didn't hear, and slowly, grudgingly, they gave way, casting poisonous looks at Rhona as they left. I expected Rhona to be grateful, but instead, she conceived a lasting hatred for Nimue.

At eight, I became an acolyte. There were fewer of us then. The boys mostly began their training in arms. Girls not of noble birth began their domestic training, except for any who felt the call to dedicate themselves to the Goddess. Catlin was an exception. She certainly held no desire to be a priestess, but I insisted she stay with me for two more years.

Those of us who continued with religious instruction were passed into the hands of Mother Arden, an unsmiling wisewoman, tall and thin. She spent much of this time teaching us herb lore and other forms of healing. A priestess must be able to heal her people from both physical and spiritual maladies, to resolve conflicts and foster peace.

There was no peace between Nimue and Rhona. Nimue was devout, exceptionally so, and intended to consecrate herself to the Great Mother. I was never sure quite why Rhona chose to continue with instruction, unless it was in the hopes of gaining some power. She grew ever more beautiful, and increasingly haughty. She continued to torment others, especially Nimue. It made me angry, but Nimue simply ignored her. And that, in turn, infuriated Rhona.

One sweltering August day, Rhona stepped boldly in front of us as we were walking beside the moat, while her faction waited giggling nearby. "Is it true?" she asked Nimue. "You're going to study at Avalon?"

"It is," Nimue replied.

"I don't see why," Rhona said. "My father is a duke, and yours is—oh sorry, *was*—a baronet. I could certainly learn about spells and powers more easily than some orphan from the forests of…"

"Avalon is not about spells and powers, Rhona. If you think it is, that's probably why you'll never be invited."

Lacking a ready reply, she gave Nimue a tight little smile and said sweetly, "You know, you really should be addressing me as Lady Rhona."

"That's enough," I said. "Why don't you leave us alone?"

"Pay no attention," Nimue said. "It's just talk. She shouldn't talk so much. Someday her tongue will turn on her."

I took Nimue's hand and turned us away to continue our walk, sending a glare to remind Rhona that if she wanted to talk rank, I was ready. Reluctantly, she rejoined her companions.

The next morning, we all went to the woods for another lesson in herbs and berries. Mother Arden sent us out in groups to see what we could find. "Remember, girls, keep your hands away from your eyes and mouth until you've brought your finds to me," she said, and sent us on our way.

Nimue, Catlin and I went together, and as we passed Rhona and her friends, Rhona whispered something that made them cackle like a gaggle of hens. Nimue turned and gave her a level gaze, and we walked on.

37

We were among the first to return with full baskets and were sitting on a log waiting for the others when Rhona and her friends burst into the clearing, sobbing wildly and pointing their fingers at Nimue. Rhona's tongue was black, and so swollen it protruded from her mouth. They ran to Mother Arden and began babbling through their tears about Nimue and curses.

Nimue calmly got up and went over to them. Purple drool ran from the corners of Rhona's mouth, and her overskirt was stained with purple as well. "She's been eating berries," Nimue said. "Doubtless she ate some she shouldn't have." Turning to Rhona, she said, "Lave your mouth in salt water. Don't swallow it. Let it sit a bit and then spew it. Keep doing it until the swelling eases." She put her hand on Rhona's shoulder and smiled benevolently. "You'll be all right."

Mother Arden gaped at her, then nodded decisively and grabbed Rhona by the arm, dragging her off to begin the treatment. Rhona decided not to return to instruction after that, and her friends gave Nimue a wide berth.

Only four of us became initiates at Mabon of my tenth year: me, Nimue, and two sisters who were so shy they never spoke except to each other. Like Nimue, they were intended for Avalon. Not to be priestesses, since that is a very public role, but to attend the priestesses. "I wouldn't be surprised if they were among those who take a vow of silence," Nimue said. "They're almost there already."

For the first time, Catlin and I spent much of our day apart. She could no longer attend the religious training and was to be prepared for some middling position at court. I wouldn't have it. Though her lineage was rude, I insisted she train to be my chief lady-in-waiting. There was some noisy opposition from those with more suitable daughters, but I went to my father. I made him understand that Catlin was not to be consigned to some lesser servant status. I simply couldn't do without her.

It pricked Catlin somewhat that Nimue and I spent so much time together. We had only the two silent sisters training with us, so we became ever closer. When our duties were done, Catlin and I would come together. But more and more often, Nimue joined us. She did her best not to intrude, but it was inevitable our talk sometimes turned to the day's teachings.

One evening as we were getting ready for sleep, I noticed Catlin seemed in an ill temper. When I asked a question, she replied shortly, "Ask Nimue. She would know." Then I grasped what the problem was.

"I'm sorry you don't like it when Nimue is with us," I said, "but it is really nice for me to have a friend."

She looked at me with a clouded expression. "You don't regard me as a friend?"

"What? No! You're not a friend, Catlin." Her eyes grew wide. "You are a part of me. Friends come and go, but you…" She threw her arms around me, and I hugged the comforting bulk of her tightly. I'd like to say she never minded Nimue after that, but that would be untrue.

As an initiate, I began to learn how to midwife souls into life and death, and some of the more arcane arts, such as scrying in water or fire. Seeing images in water came easily enough to me, though they were never of any import. But for some reason, I struggled futilely to see them in flames. Mother Arden said it was because I held a fear of fire. I was disquieted by this lack, worried that it would lessen me as a priestess, but Mother Arden assured me it would come with time.

I was not initiated into the deeper Mysteries. I could not, for instance, summon the Sight at will and act as an oracle, though there were times when glimpses came on me unbidden. The Sight is different from scrying, much more powerful. When the Sight descended upon a skilled priestess, she could see destiny, if she could read it. Even the most adept Seer, however, might be mistaken in interpretation, so only the very wisest were trained to cultivate the gift of prophecy. This and other advanced skills Nimue would learn at Avalon, under the tutelage of Morgan le Fey, the Lady of the Lake.

"I wish you were coming too," Nimue said to me one August day as we were paddling our feet in a pond, shaded by a massive elm tree.

"My father would never allow it."

"Why not? Being a priestess is an honorable life."

"Yes, of course," I said, watching the bumbling progress of a bee in a patch of campion. "But the Lady concerns him. There are rumors of sorcery…"

"Nonsense!" Nimue interrupted, a flush rising in her cheeks. "Sorcery is no part of earth magic. Nor for the worship of the Goddess."

"That's not the main reason anyway," I said quickly, fearing I had insulted my friend. "That's not my moira. I've been studying statecraft already, but once my religious training is complete, I'll concentrate on preparing to rule."

"Ah. Yes." We sat quietly for a moment, wriggling our toes among the tadpoles. "Is that what you want?" she asked, glancing sideways at me.

I paused to consider. Such a question was typical of Nimue, and she would not be content with a facile answer. "I do," I said slowly. "It's my fate, but it's also... my calling. Just as you never doubt your calling to the Goddess, I believe my life is to be dedicated to the welfare of my people. I'm devoted to the Mother too, of course, but I can do more to protect her and foster her worship from a throne than from Avalon."

Nimue nodded and sighed. "She does need protecting these days."

"What about you?" I asked. "Are you certain you want to turn your life over to her worship? Won't you regret not having a family?" I leaned back onto my elbows, gazing dreamily up through the canopy of leaves. "I intend to have a whole brood of children!"

"It's a sacrifice." Nimue looked down at me, her face knotted in determination. "But I'd sacrifice anything to serve the Mother, and do anything needful to protect her." She flopped down beside me. "Anything."

We dawdled there for much of that hot afternoon, dreaming and planning our destinies.

Chapter 6

We were preparing for Samhain, the end of the harvest and the beginning of the dark time of the year. This is the time when the veil between worlds is at its thinnest, when spirits walk among us and we pause in our daily lives to honor our dead and welcome their visiting souls with offerings. Most importantly, though, it is a time to acknowledge that the Wheel of the Year is turning, and dark times are coming when the world needs to rest. It is even more crucial to remind ourselves that the light would come again.

Our primary Samhain ritual was the lighting of the needfire, a towering bonfire on top of a hill. All fires in the village were extinguished, and later, new fires were lit from brands carried back down the hill. It was a solemn and reassuring ritual. Near our village was a particularly hallowed site. The hilltop where the needfire would be kindled was a nemeton, a natural opening surrounded by a copse of sacred oaks, many so tall and majestic it seemed they had been there since the advent of time itself.

It was a bright, sunny day, and we didn't see the flames at first. But then there was smoke in the sky, and alarmed murmurs ran among the people. Surely it was too early to light the needfire? It seemed everyone realized what was happening at the same time: the oak trees were burning. Shrieks and moans filled the air, and we all began to run up the hill toward the sacred grove. When we reached the top, we were struck into a horrified silence.

The youngest of the trees had already been consumed and stood like black sentinels. All the rest—all!—were ablaze. Some men ran off in a futile attempt to carry water up the hill, while the rest of us simply stood and stared. Catlin,

Nimue and I huddled together, too shocked even to weep. How could this have happened? And how could it be that the fire ate at not one or two trees in the huge circle, but all of them?

Then a breeze lifted, and the flames and smoke cleared a bit. The crowd began to cry out again, and this time there was anger as well as sorrow and despair. I closed my eyes, unable to bear the sight, unwilling to acknowledge what it meant. In the center of the clearing where the bonfire was held, there stood a cross. It was no hasty lashing of sticks, but stout, well-made. Whoever set it there wanted to make sure it didn't burn before we saw it.

There was nothing to be done. All we could do was stay with the majestic trees while they burned. All day and all night we watched, as at the deathbed of one's beloved. Sparks flew into the sky and woodland creatures fled to safety. We prayed. We lamented. The smoke hung over the countryside like a pall, catching in the back of our throats for days.

Our folk were filled with dread. The needfire promised protection through the dark time. What would happen without it? Would the winter be rife with illness? Would the game disappear from the woods, and the stores we had set aside molder? Would we starve? Despite the assurances of the priests and priestesses, the next months were burdened with gloom and fret.

I simply could not comprehend such an attack. How was it possible for a human being, one who could think and feel, to carry so much hate? And why? I understood rage against one who has harmed you. But what harm had been done to this despicable wretch by our worship? Even if we had offended in some way, why destroy these noble and sacred monuments to the glory of the earth?

Often, I climbed the hill to walk among the charred bones. Ashes underfoot instead of fallen leaves. And in winter, the fragile blackness stark against the snow.

Eventually, as winter melted into spring and spring blossomed into summer, the pain of it lessened. But the trees stood like a black crown on the summit of the hill to keep us reminded. Nimue, for one, needed no such reminder. She would never forget, nor forgive.

At midsummer of my thirteenth year, I received the tattoo of the Triple Goddess. I lay still as Mother Arden etched the design into my forehead with a thorn and rubbed the outline blue with woad. For the rest of my life, I would proudly bear the image of a full moon, with waxing and waning crescents on each side. This was emblematic of the Goddess in all her phases: Maiden, Mother and Crone.

Soon, it was time for Nimue to depart for Avalon. She was now a full head taller than I (though granted, most people were), and had slimmed into a pleasing form. We embraced, with tears on both sides. Then she held me away from her and looked deeply into my eyes. "We will meet again," she said, and turned to go. She looked as confident and regal as any full-fledged Ban Drui, despite the mingy carrot-colored braid hanging down her back.

The next years passed in a pleasant haze of household duties, falconing, seasonal festivals, planting and putting by. There were suitors, as I had assured Arthur, but none aroused even a glimmer of interest in me. Most were baldly dynastic offers, from men old enough to be my grandsire or little boys who still wielded wooden swords.

One who was near my age, my cousin Maelgwyn, was deemed by the bishops to be too close kin. It is the only time I ever had any reason to be grateful to the Christians. Although his kingdom of Gwynedd ran next to ours, Maelgwyn feigned it was not Cameliard, but myself, that he wanted. His fawning made my skin crawl. Fortunately, my father was still hale and had no particular interest in pledging me away. In fact, I gained from him a promise that he would never wed me against my will.

For Arthur, those were years of solidifying his reign. Once he returned from aiding King Ban in Brittany, he traveled the length and breadth of the realm, holding councils and leading skirmishes, until the various clan leaders were unified as client kings under the Dragon banner. The country was no longer Rheged and Lothian, Cameliard and Cornwall and Logres, but one entity: Britain. The Saxons had been mostly put to rest, and the land was peaceful and prosperous. As travelers and bards told us of his exploits and accomplishments, our concerns were set at ease, and we were proud to be aligned with him.

With the land at peace, the talk turned to his marriage. He seemed in no hurry to wed and produce an heir. According to reports, he was duly introduced to lady after lady, and heard the praises sung of those he had not met, but merely smiled and went his way.

It was early April of my fifteenth year, a morning full of lambs, with the land greening and streams rushing with snowmelt from the hills. Catlin and I, however, were huddled away in the darkest corner of the barn, candling the first bounty of fresh eggs. A boy dashed in, looking for my father: Sir Bedwyr and a contingent of horsemen had been spotted on their way to our holdings. By the time they paced into our courtyard, both Father and I were standing there, wildly curious and hastily tidied from our everyday duties. I was still blinking and trying to adjust to the bright sunlight—and hoping I didn't have straw in my hair—when Bedwyr dismounted and strode over to my father, giving only a slight smile and nod to me. When he spoke, it was with the high courtly speech which was seldom heard in our doings.

"King Lodegrance, I am come from Arthur Pendragon, High King of Britain, to bear his proposal of marriage to your daughter, the princess Guinevere. Will you give your blessing for her to be his queen?"

I was stunned to silence. Catlin came to stand beside me, clutching my hand. Neither man looked at me as my father conquered his surprise and replied, also using the high style. "With all my heart, Sir Bedwyr. And I swear by all gods, my daughter will devote her life to being worthy of this high honor."

They relaxed, smiled, and clasped each other's shoulders. Father turned to escort Bedwyr into the bailey while I was still trying to find words. Neither man looked at me as Father spoke again, in the ordinary tongue. "Well, we have many a toast to drink, eh? Did the king say—"

Finally, I came alive. I wrenched my hand from Catlin's, and it was certainly not the high language I spoke then. "Am I a breeding bitch or a pied mare to be passed from hand to hand?" I shouted to their retreating backs. They turned to look at me in astonishment. "Do you begrudge my keep, Father? If so, I'll eat less to come, or forage for myself in the meadow!"

"Guinevere! What—"

I rushed at them, and both men stepped back a pace. "I will not be passed off and robbed of my rule! I will be a Queen, as I am meant to be!"

Father recovered from his shock. "What is your plaint, girl?! This is honor!"

"Oh, high honor indeed! To sit and simper on someone else's throne? And who will rule here in my stead?"

"I will!" he thundered. His face was dangerously red, and Bedwyr was looking on in consternation.

I tried to rule my voice before I spoke again. "And when you're gone?"

"Bedwyr, give us a moment." Bedwyr nodded to Father, cast a bewildered look at me, and withdrew to look after his men. I braced myself to meet Father's towering rage, but when he turned back to me, he spoke calmly, sadly. "Resent your keep, Guinevere? Don't you think if I could I'd close you in the tower and keep you safe beside me?"

"Then why—?"

"I can't keep you safe! You were the child of my old age. I count myself thankful to see you grown."

"Nonsense. You're as hearty as—"

"Aye, I might live to eighty if the gods have use for me. Or I might be taken in my sleep tonight. And if—when—that happens, I have to be certain you're protected."

"You think our people wouldn't protect their queen?"

"With their lives. And it would cost their lives. How long do you think it would take Ryance or any other to set for your crown?"

"Set for and get are two things! There have always been warrior queens among the Celts. I could—"

"Warrior queens. What prattle! Without Arthur, they could take us tomorrow."

"You swore you wouldn't marry me against my will. You swore!"

"A true Celtic queen holds to her duty where she sees it, whatever the cost. Bind us under Arthur's dragon, Guinevere, or Boadicea herself couldn't hold back the tide that will come against you when..."

He faltered, and the sincerity and suffering in his eyes quashed the fiery retorts I longed to hurl. I took a deep breath and steeled myself. "Call Sir Bedwyr," I said sullenly.

Father relaxed and smiled and grasped my arm thankfully. "Put on a better gown, my dear, and we'll meet in the audience chamber. This should be done with all dignity."

For once, Catlin had little to say as she hustled me into my second-best gown and tried valiantly to arrange my hair. It wasn't until she asked, "Will you consent to a silver chain, Lady?" that the depth of her disapproval became clear. This was about more than my dislike of ornament. Her back was to me as she puttered in my jewel chest. I took her arms and turned her to face me.

"No. No chains." She had kept her eyes downcast the while she was attending me, but now she raised them and looked into my own. After a moment, the shadow of a smile appeared on her lips. She took a step back and looked me up and down.

"Well, the king requested dignity, but I guess this will have to do."

Chapter 7

There was little of dignity in the open-mouthed expressions of both Father and Bedwyr when we met shortly thereafter. Father was caught speechless, frozen in the act of reaching for some celebratory wine. "You'll... you'll..." Bedwyr stuttered in amazement.

"I'll parley. And if we come to terms... What?! You don't expect me to run to his heel just because he whistled, do you?" From their expressions, it seemed clear they did.

"Uh... when you say 'parley'..." Bedwyr said cautiously, "you mean...?"

"I'll discuss it. And if—"

"There is nothing to discuss!" my father thundered.

"Only my life! For as long as I can remember, you have schooled me to serve our people." Father tried to interrupt, but I wouldn't allow it. "I know, I know. As High Queen, I could serve all the people of Britain. And if that is what I am called to, all to the good. But I will not be chattel! Shall I spend my life granting knights my token and tossing sweetmeats to the crowd at tournaments? I'll be a real Queen, or he can find himself some prattling featherbrain to be his bride!"

A long silence followed. I waited, maintaining a difficult composure. I was somewhat concerned for my father, who appeared as stunned as a bull under the hammer. He was still groping for words when Sir Bedwyr stirred and prepared to rise. He smiled bemusedly at me. "With your permission, Lady, I will perhaps couch your message in somewhat gentler terms. But I will deliver it and bring you the king's response." At that my father half-rose from his seat, but Bedwyr forestalled his objections. "Rest easy, Your Highness," he said. "I know my brother well. He may be somewhat startled by this request, as were we, by the Light!" Father and I were both astonished when he chuckled. "But he will not take offense. Nor would he wish—" here he cast a significant glance at my father—"for a maiden to be his bride if she were in any way unwilling. We're only a day's ride away. I will return with his reply shortly."

Since the king had been making a progress among nearby clans, not holding court at Winchester, arrangements were made swiftly. We set out on a glorious spring morning, alive with birdsong after days of rain. Father and I paced down a forest path, Catlin and our retainers coming behind us. The canopy of leaves was not yet filled in, so wildflowers and flowering trees were at their peak. The waves of daffodils that flood our hills in early March were past, but bright yellow poppies took their place, as well as squill and speedwell, violets, valerian and the sweet-scented woodruff. Much as I tried to pay the attention due to such beauty, my fretful mind buzzed louder than the bees in the blossoms.

What in the name of the Mother had I been thinking, to put myself in this position? Father had held his tongue in the presence of Sir Bedwyr, but as soon as Arthur's envoy had taken his leave, I was made well aware of everything I had failed to consider. What if the High King and I could not agree? Then I would have two choices: to accept his proposal and condemn myself to the useless, frivolous life I despised, or to gravely insult the ruler of all Britain.

Though I tried to assure my father I would never put him in opposition to Arthur, he had misgivings. "What if your temper gets the better of you?" he asked. "For all that's holy, think before you speak!"

We entered a clearing where a regal pavilion stood, surrounded by Arthur's people. The dragon banner fluttered in a warm breeze. Sir Bedwyr stepped forward to help me from my mount, smiling warmly at me as he swung me down. "Welcome, Lady. The King awaits you, and food and wine are there for your refreshment. We'll take care of your people while you talk." He gestured to a table set with an array of breads, cheeses, and fruits, wine and ale, then offered me his arm to escort me to the pavilion.

I heard Catlin mutter, "He could at least come out of his tent to greet her." Everyone hearing, including me, gave her an incredulous look.

Because he'd been on a diplomatic progress instead of a military excursion, there were ladies in his retinue. Surely, they had taken a hand in appointing the pavilion, with its brocaded hangings and comfortable chairs and bright cushions, plus a table spread with a small feast of dainties. A regal-looking wolfhound sat alertly by Arthur's chair, and in one corner, a scribe perched on a stool. I smiled at that; it seemed Arthur was taking this discussion seriously. Indeed, he stood there looking as stiff and solemn as if he were about to negotiate rule of his entire kingdom…which he was.

In some ways he was changed greatly from when I saw him last. He had gained a bit in stature, though was still not much more than average height. He had grown a short beard and cropped his hair in the Roman fashion, and he seemed to possess more poise and gravity than he'd displayed as a stripling king. His eyes were as I remembered, though, shining with intelligence and enthusiasm. He gave me a strained smile as we exchanged greetings, and I could tell from his expression that I too had changed, and he was not displeased by what he saw.

Catlin and I had pitched a spectacular battle about how I would present myself. She was adamant that I should appear with all the power of my lineage: crowned, wearing the most magnificent of robes, and with a full complement of jewels. I wanted to take the opposite tack, and of course I had my way. I stood before the High King as a priestess, in a robe of rich, heavy white linen, simply cut and bare of any adornment, save the triskelion brooch I wore.

A Christian bishop stood on one side of the king, and Lord Merlin on the other. Merlin wore a simple Druid robe, while the bishop was clad in the opulently embroidered and gem-encrusted vestments of his office. He looked me over in a way so frankly appraising it approached insult. After thorough scrutiny of my attire and my bearing, the bishop's eye flickered once again to the Goddess tattoo on my forehead and my priestess brooch. He frowned, then took his leave of Arthur without addressing me. Meanwhile, Merlin stepped forward and bowed over my hand. "Well met, my lady," he said, "and may the Goddess smile on this, uh, conclave." Then he, too, left us to it.

Our discussion took the better part of the day, and there was some shouting before it was over.

"I cannot be purely decorative," I began. I hoped to appear calm, but inwardly, I was quaking at my temerity. He said nothing, so I took a deep breath and continued. "I've been raised to rule in my own realm after my father, and always assumed the man I married would be my consort, not me his. Being of service to my people has been bred into my bones, and I cannot consign myself to less."

"Of course. I, however, was raised humbly," Arthur replied, "all unknowing of my destiny. So I have not had your advantage."

Oh no, I've insulted him already! He bent to pour some wine and offered it to me. It was all I could do to keep my hand from shaking as I took the goblet.

"Therefore, I would welcome your experience and listen to your counsel," he continued, "as I do that of Merlin and the bishops. I cannot commit to following your advice in all matters, but I do pledge to discuss all major issues with you and treat your opinions with due respect."

I closed my eyes a moment and felt my clenched body relax. He poured some wine for himself, and we settled into our discussion.

It went well. He even proposed forming a special Queen's Council. Once I had settled into my new role and was able to make informed judgments about those around me, I would appoint counsellors and take up responsibilities that suited my interests. This appealed to me mightily, promising I could be heard on topics that particularly concerned me. Of greatest importance, of course, was the preservation of the home religion.

"I am a priestess of the Goddess as well as a worldly princess, Your Grace, and I am gravely troubled by the depredations of the Christians."

"Tell me what disquiets you," he said, and settled in to listen attentively.

"For time beyond time, my people have been under the protection of the Great Mother. When the Romans came, they spread vicious tales of crimes— even human sacrifice!—committed in the name of our worship and suppressed our religions with great force. They even massacred the entire population of Druids on the sacred isle of Mona."

"Oh, I know about this!" Arthur exclaimed. "Merlin made me read it in Tacitus when I was a boy. Gave me evil dreams! Suetonius and his legions on one side of the strait, and all the Druids of Mona ranged along the shore. But it was the wild-haired women shrieking curses who terrified the Roman troops— they thought the women were demons! The generals had to flog their men into action." He chuckled at that, and I fear I snapped at him.

"That may be, but once they attacked, they slaughtered every man, woman and child on the island." He paused with a bit of honey cake halfway to his mouth, taken aback by my tone. I held my breath, but he nodded gravely, bidding me continue.

"We outlasted the Romans. But now the Christians claim, against all wisdom, that their prophet is the only source of truth, their god the only god. And like the Romans, where they cannot convert, they kill."

"Oh come, aren't you exaggerating? No one is killing off pagans these days."

I took a moment to master my tongue, then took a deep breath. "Did Merlin never teach you about the bishop Patricius?"

He sensed my anger and said nothing, merely inclining his head for me to continue.

"Patricius is famed among the Christians for driving the snakes out of Eire. What nonsense! There have never been snakes in Eire. What he drove out—and by that I mean murdered—was every last one of the Druid priests, who bore serpent tattoos on their arms."

I saw that strike home.

"Still the White Christ gains worshippers," I continued. "And as they become more powerful, they become more dangerous to those of us who abide by the old ways. It isn't worldly power that's important to me, Sir. But I must ask for protection for my people and our way of life. Not just Druids, but all who follow their own gods."

"This new religion is certainly arrogant," he replied. "I am dedicated to Mithras, as are most who go to war. We celebrate his birth at the winter solstice, when Sol Invictus conquers death. But of late, the Christians claim we are usurping their celebration of their god's birth. How could a religion thousands of years old be imitating one only a few hundred years old?"

"At least they haven't destroyed your temples. They burned our nemeton, the sacred grove where we hold our rites. I had celebrated sabbats all my life in that grove. And I have heard of other groves burned or cut down."

"Temples of Mithras are underground," Arthur said with a wry smile. "And most Mithraites are warriors. That may account for their restraint."

We had been talking intently much of the day. The king rose to pour us more wine. I was satisfied with his recognition of my role in governance, but I needed assurance from him on this most important topic. I accepted the goblet and waited for him to seat himself again before returning to my plea.

"I am not asking you to suppress Christianity, my lord, only to let people worship as they...." Much to my surprise, he let out a hearty guffaw.

"Suppress them! Girl, you have no idea—" He stopped short when he saw my face, which must have looked like a storm about to break.

"With due respect, Your Highness," I said coldly, "I am a princess royal, and not used to being addressed as 'girl.' Nor being laughed at."

I didn't even have time to reflect that I had just destroyed my chances of succeeding at this parley. Instantly, he reached across the space between us and enfolded my hand in his. "Forgive me, my lady. I meant no disrespect. I feel so comfortable talking with you I just..." He shrugged and struggled for words, looking so distressed—the High King!—I had to smile. He gave me a relieved smile in return, and we both took a sip from our goblets, looking away from each other. When we set them down, he resumed.

"It's just that suppression isn't possible, you see, even if I wanted to. They become stronger every day. The bishops are now too powerful for me to omit them from my councils. Or from ceremonies of state, for that matter. If...if we were to marry, we would have to hold a Christian rite. Are you willing to do that?"

"If you are willing to have a handfasting as well."

"I am. And I swear to you my solemn oath I will never establish one religion above all others or oppress your people in any way."

That was what I needed to hear. I relaxed, visibly. The corner of his mouth quirked, and I saw a glint of humor in his eyes. "Should we marry," he said, "I doubt it would be a quiet union."

I answered with a half-smile of my own. "No. But it would be stimulating."

After discussing a few needful details, at last we came to an agreement and left the pavilion. Catlin took a step, then by sheer force of will, stopped herself from rushing up to embrace me. Arthur passed his gaze over my father, and Bedwyr, and lingeringly, Merlin. Then he smiled broadly. "We shall be wed at midsummer." Our people erupted into cheers. Even the Merlin smiled, though it was not overfull of joy.

Despite my occasional complaints about the duties and restrictions of being royal, I was certainly grateful for the help available to me as a princess and soon to be High Queen. With so little time to prepare, every hand was kept busy. I was grateful for the hurly. Though the king and I had come to a rational agreement and parted cordially, I had still not completely come to terms with the fact that I was to marry, and the High King at that. There was little point in fretting about it, though. The betrothal had been sealed, and I forced my mind to the practical issues at hand.

I needed a magnificent gown for the public Christian ceremony. I owned three court robes: the green wool, the white linen I had worn to parley with Arthur, and a scarlet velvet with embroidered sleeves. These were refurbished to meet the standards of a High King's court. "You'll need new robes for daily wear at Winchester," Catlin said.

"I suppose so," I agreed, "but these have still good wear in them. Let's distribute them among the ladies. And take first choice for yourself, Catlin."

She sniffed and turned a thunderous look on me. "Do you mock me, Lady? Only children and those with as sparse and niggling a figure as yours can make use of your unneeded garments. Those of us with a more womanly body—"

"All right! All right," I said, laughing. "We'll have some new daily wear made for you as well."

Arthur's court had been established at Winchester long enough for the planting of gardens and maintenance of a kitchen staff, but I took our excellent baker and such foodstuffs as we were known for. Our apples were rivaled only by those of Avalon itself, so I brought many barrels of cider. I took casks of honey and the mead we made from it, wagonloads of barley, and some of the strong "water of life" Father brought in from the Orkneys.

My father waived the bride price, and much to the displeasure of his advisors, Arthur declined a dowry. For his honor, however, my father sent him fifty of our tough little ponies with their tack, plus several dozen ladies in waiting, pages and warriors. His primary gift, however, was a splendid table he himself had received as a wedding gift from Uther Pendragon. It was formed in an open circle, so those serving could more easily tend to everyone. To be honest, it was too big for our hall, so we had never used it. Still, it was a handsome gift, made even more so by its connection to Arthur's father.

Arthur paid me the compliment of sending his two foremost knights, Bedwyr and Gawain, to escort us to Winchester. Though both equal in the king's esteem, there were never two so unlike.

Bedwyr was tall, cleanshaven now except for a luxurious mustache, and always elegantly groomed. With his gentle courtesy and graceful manner, he was to accompany me and my ladies and such nobles as were going with us. Rough, shaggy, irascible Gawain, who retained a northern burr in his speech, had little use for elegance, but displayed a rascally charm in abundance. (Catlin said our maidens were about equally divided in their admiration, and that which one was favored said a lot about the maiden. I asked her preference, but she demurred. "What, the wild Gael who looks and acts—and sometimes smells—like a poorly trained bear? Or the nimble courtier who would probably make a good lap dog?" Catlin was never one to mince words.) Gawain was in charge of the train of wagons, the herd of ponies, and the tradesmen, yeomen, peasants and warriors who accompanied them. The entourage was huge, ungainly, a barely controlled chaos, but Gawain was more than competent, and we made good progress.

It was drizzling when we set out, but I refused to ride closed in a litter. At home, I had been accustomed since I was a child to ride in a tunic and breeches. As I grew into maidenhood, there were mutterings from some of the ladies, which I studiously ignored. I did recognize that as future High Queen, such attire would be unseemly, so I had a riding gown made with a split skirt and wore my breeches under that. Catlin complained about riding in the litter with only "ninnies and fools for company," but when I told her she was welcome to requisition a mare and ride with me, she subsided. Catlin had no love of horses.

Sir Bedwyr rode ever beside me, and he was pleasant company, full of stories about growing up fostered in Sir Ector's household with Arthur and Cei. "Cei was Sir Ector's true son, and a couple of years older, so he lorded it over the two of us fosterlings when we were small." Cei was the blonde giant I had seen at the victory feast, where he certainly seemed well disposed toward Arthur.

"By the time Arthur was eight," Bedwyr continued, "he could hold his own in our mock battles, and in another year, he could easily best both of us, even though we were older and bigger. I've never seen anyone so quick with a sword! It's a good thing ours were wooden at first, and then blunted, or I doubt

Cei and I would have survived childhood." He chuckled, and I smiled warmly, charmed by the image of the boy Arthur.

"None of us knew who he was, of course, though looking back, we should have guessed he was someone exceptional. And it wasn't just his physical skills that set him apart. Cei and I held little interest in learning about history, military strategy, and such, but Arthur was keen for such topics. It wasn't until later that we learned his tutor had been Lord Merlin. Merlin looked very different then—and in fact, he still has something of the shapeshifter about him. I swear, when he's angry, he's a foot taller and twenty years younger.

"Anyway, when the truth of Arthur's royal birth was discovered, I wondered for a moment how Cei would react. I shouldn't have been concerned—he bent his knee to his 'little brother' without a moment's hesitation."

"I remember him from the victory feast at Cameliard. You and he were the favorites of all our ladies," I said. "She would never admit it, but I think Catlin was quite taken with him. He was so lively and gay." Bedwyr's face grew grave.

"He fought valiantly in all twelve of Arthur's major battles, but last year he suffered a grievous wound in what was really just a minor skirmish. The wound healed, but he will never ride with us again. It's changed him, I fear. There's little joy for him now."

His face cleared; such talk was perhaps too sad for a wedding journey. "While he was recovering, he made himself useful in setting up Arthur's court at Winchester. So useful, in fact, that Arthur recognized a true talent, and named Cei his seneschal. It's amazing what he can do. I mean, all three of us were raised in a very humble homestead, yet somehow he has learned to preside over a court with grace and refinement. I expect he's well occupied now with arranging the wedding festivities."

We'd been following a Roman road. It was not the best maintained, but Arthur was trying to restore as many as possible. The Romans had kept the land cleared on either side to an arrow's flight away, so ambush would be difficult, and they could march at "Caesar speed." There was a stretch between Fosse Way and Portway, however, where the road wound through forested land, and there it narrowed until it was little more than a path.

Though he was far back, behind the throng of people we were bringing with us, we could hear Gawain shouting and cursing as he tried to keep the wagons on the narrow path. Bedwyr chuckled and shook his head at the inventiveness of his profanities. "You can see why we don't ask him to escort the ladies," he said. Since the Saxons had been driven out, our only fear was robbers and brigands, so most of our fighting men were escorting the wagons laden with our household goods and the wedding treasures.

We came to a place where the path widened into a pleasant clearing, filled with ferns, meadow clary, and honeysuckle. I was about to suggest we stop here for our midday meal, but something caught my attention. It wasn't a noise. It was the silence.

As we entered the clearing, it struck me that I could no longer hear birdsong or the rustle of little creatures. I turned toward Bedwyr to mention the eerie stillness just as an arrow whined out of the surrounding forest and pierced his forearm. In an instant, men were rushing into the clearing from three sides, armed with short swords. Filthy and brutish they were, and shouted in a language I didn't know. The few knights riding with us tried to come to the fore, but the women and unarmed men were scrambling away from the attackers, and they hindered each other where the path was narrow. I heard Catlin screaming my name.

Bedwyr was laying about him with sword and whip, despite the broken-off arrow in his arm. One of the brigands fought his way close to me and tried to lay hands on my reins, but I kicked him in the face with all my strength and he staggered back. Bedwyr dispatched him and turned to the next. I had only the small dagger I wore at my waist, but I used it vigorously on the next one to come within my reach.

Above the tumult, I heard a crashing as if a giant were stomping through the woodland. How he managed to force his way through the thick forest I'll never know, but there was Gawain, lying flat against his courser's neck as they charged into the fray. Screams resounded as the huge beast trampled over the attackers. Other knights followed in the path Gawain cut through the forest, and the clearing was aswarm with our men.

With Bedwyr on my left, and now Gawain guarding my right, I was safe enough. Indeed, no one could have stood against the Gael, who was slashing and chopping with a fury almost inhuman. It didn't take long for the surviving outlaws to turn and run, leaving a score of their dead sprawled among the bloodied wildflowers. Our knights tried to pursue, but the thick woods hampered them. Gawain leapt down and went from man to fallen man, searching until he found one still alive. He tried to discover who sent them, and for what purpose, but the man died staring at him in silent defiance.

"Are you unharmed, Lady?" Bedwyr asked, and I was, only shaken and breathless. Gawain and his men continued to search among the bodies, trying to find a badge to identify whose men they were, but to no avail. I was tending to Bedwyr's wound and trying to soothe an overwrought Catlin when Gawain came up to us, his face flushed as red as his hair.

"Nae to tell who they were. My guess is common ruffians who set these ambushes whenever they spot trave1` lers and didn't know who they were tangling with. But if it was plunder they were wanting, it would have been smarter to wait for the wagons and attack them. Did ye ken they were trying to capture the princess?" he asked Bedwyr.

"No. I don't think they had any clear aim. But when you came charging out of the forest, they looked like they were seeing the Lord of Darkness himself come to drag them to the underworld. A good many of them went there, too."

"You'll mend?" Gawain asked.

"The only harm from this is that it hampered me. If you hadn't come when you did, I might not have been able to rout them." He paused, then cleared his throat and continued. "You know, Gawain, now that we're going to have a Queen, we'll need a Queen's Champion. When we reach Winchester, I am going to recommend that Arthur name you for the honor."

"As will I," I said. Gawain flushed with pleasure and dipped his head to me.

We went on our way with caution, Bedwyr and Gawain flanking me, and it wasn't long before the road widened, and the margins were cut clear again. When we put up our pavilions for the night, I checked the wounds of Bedwyr and the others who had been injured. Fortunately, all seemed to be clean and likely to heal well. It was harder to restore Catlin's serenity than it was to tend to physical injuries. She had no appetite for her supper, which was certainly unprecedented, and could not stop talking about trying to get to me. "I swear to the Mother, if we ever have to make such a journey again, I'll learn to ride so I can stay close to you," she said. I simply murmured at that, knowing her opinion of horses. I finally dosed her with some strong Orkney whiskey so we could both get some rest.

Chapter 8

When Gawain journeyed beside us, the conversation was always boisterous, and usually centered around his exploits, whether in war or in romance. I was a bit relieved, then, when the Orcadian finally cantered back to check on the wagons, since I was hoping to glean more knowledge about Arthur from his foster brother.

Truly, I knew little to nothing of the king, save for the bard's songs, and as I had learned, they were not to be trusted. I'd heard the stories about his birth, but there were many conflicting versions. In some, Merlin had cast a spell and glamoured Uther Pendragon into the likeness of Duke Gorlois, so Ygraine was all unknowing that the man who came to her was not her husband.

Bedwyr held a different opinion. "A lot of people say Ygraine and Uther truly fell in love on sight, and she was complicit in smuggling him into Tintagel. It would be hard to blame her, as Gorlois was reputed to be a man of evil temper and unwholesome habits. Whatever the truth of it, Gorlois was killed in a skirmish with Uther's men the night Arthur was conceived. The guilt of that made Uther willing to let Merlin take the child for fostering in secret, until he should become of age."

"What of his mother? She was willing to give up her child?"

"Eventually, she gave up all of them," Bedwyr told me. "She had two daughters by Gorlois, and as you might imagine, they were none too fond of Uther Pendragon. But Ygraine was besotted with him, which is why I believe Arthur's birth was the result of passion, not deceit and rape. As soon as Arthur was two, and deemed likely to survive, he was given to Merlin, and Ygraine raised no opposition. The younger girl had been entirely enamored with her baby brother, and when he was taken, came to open warfare with her stepfather. It wasn't long until both girls were sent away."

"What happened to them?" I asked.

"Morgause, the elder, is married to King Lot of Lothian. They live far north, in the wild Orkney Islands. Gawain is her eldest son, and there are several younger ones, three or four I think, all of them eager to join Arthur's court when they're grown. So apparently she harbors no grudge against him. The younger daughter, Morgan le Fey, is now the Lady of the Lake."

"That's Arthur's sister?" I exclaimed. "The High Priestess?"

"Half-sister. Arthur has no clear memory of either Morgause or Morgan; he hasn't seen either of them since he was a babe. But he recognizes Gawain as his nephew and gives him honor of place. Of course, Gawain could claim his position at Arthur's right hand by his combat skills alone. He's a great one for drinking and wenching and all kinds of pleasures during peacetime, but you've seen what he's like in a fray."

"I've never seen anyone so ferocious," I said with a shudder.

"Nor I, and I've seen many remarkable warriors. I wouldn't want to get on the wrong side of that redhead's temper! But he's as stalwart a friend as he is splendid a knight. When you're his friend, you're his friend for life."

Our conversation was cut short as Gawain whooped and hollered his way back to the front of the procession. I had to smile. As rough as he might be, and more than a bit of a braggart, something about Gawain gave him an irresistible charm, and laughter followed wherever he went.

Finally, Winchester was less than a day's ride away. The morning was gray, with constant drizzle and a thick mist shrouding everything. My musings, too, were vague and formless. For the last six days, whenever I was lacking the welcome distraction of conversation with Bedwyr and Gawain on the trail or the chatter of Catlin when we camped, I fell to wondering what, exactly, I was getting myself into.

What manner of king was Arthur, really? What manner of husband would he be? For that matter, what manner of husband did I want him to be? And what were his expectations of me as wife? Would I be able to meet them? Would I want to?

Arthur and I had discussed the larger political points at the parley, and he seemed respectful enough. I also felt sure there was no cruelty in him. Still, the fact remained I had but a few days' acquaintance with the man to whom I was about to pledge my life. I reminded myself that many, if not most, royal marriages were founded on less. But my thoughts prickled, and I was not overly eager for the journey to end.

After much discussion, Catlin agreed I should ride as usual until after the midday meal. A pavilion would be hastily thrown up, and there I would change into a more respectable gown and have my hair dried and dressed. I would have liked to resist riding the rest of the way in a litter, but Catlin convinced me I couldn't meet the king looking damp and disheveled.

As it fell, our plans went for naught. Well before midday, we heard the jangle of harness and men's voices, muffled in the mist. We could see nothing, but Bedwyr drew his sword and sent a rider back to fetch Gawain.

Our alarm was unfounded. It was Arthur who appeared out of the mist, looking as if he were floating serenely several feet above the ground. He was mounted on a magnificent white stallion, which only gradually was revealed. Behind him, his squire led a gray mare, richly caparisoned.

I gasped in surprise, and then stifled a laugh. So much for my grand entrance into Winchester! Despite my oiled cape, my cloak was sodden, my hair streaming down into my face, my leggings splashed with mud. Solemn and queenly as I tried to appear, I couldn't keep the corners of my mouth from twitching as I rode forward to meet him. He fought to keep an answering grin from his own face as he greeted me.

"Well met, my lady," he said. "I apologize if I've taken you unprepared…" Here he cocked an eye at my drenched appearance, though his own was no better: his golden hair lay dank under his hood, and water dripped from the ends of his beard. "You'll find patience is not one of my strongest virtues, and I was too restless to sit in my hall and wait for your arrival."

"I'm sure I shall look better at times, my lord," I replied, "but I'm also likely to look a lot worse."

Arthur laughed and gestured to the squire, who paced forward leading the gray palfrey. She was a beautiful creature, with a white star on her intelligent face, a graceful carriage and nobly arched neck.

"A princess who rides like the goddess Epona deserves a horse that matches her in spirit and beauty," Arthur said. "This is Etain. I hope she will be worthy of you." I adored my faithful Gala, but she was getting old, and no doubt would welcome a respite now and then from my demands. Arthur himself dismounted to help me down from Gala and up onto Etain. I immediately sensed a bond with her, as if the horse and I were destined to be together. I smiled down at Arthur, my breath catching in my throat.

"She's magnificent, Your Highness. Thank you."

"Please, just Arthur between us. Come. When I heard your party was approaching, I bid them set up a pavilion. Come get dry and rest yourself and have something to eat. My impatience has been satisfied," he said with a smile, "so there's no need to rush on to Winchester."

By the time we were approaching the town, my worried mind was somewhat set at ease. Arthur treated me with the utmost courtesy and respect, but what most impressed me was that he treated everyone so, down to the lowliest servant. He knew their names, listened carefully when they spoke, and answered their questions politely. When he talked with Bedwyr and Gawain, he included me in the conversation; everything they discussed concerned the good of his kingdom and his people. He even managed to charm Catlin, without being the least bit condescending or seeming to try too hard. *Surely, this is a good man. And a good man is bound to make a good king and a good husband.*

We entered into Winchester just as we were. Arthur managed to convince even Catlin there was no point in me decking myself in my finest only to be half drowned, for the rain was now a steady downpour. "Besides," he said, "I brought no regal garb. I know my Queen is going to outshine me, but let it not be on their first sight of us!" Those who came out to greet us, he continued, would be just as bedraggled as we, and might well be cheered to see their rulers, too, were subject to the weather. "Tomorrow, when I present you to the court and then to the people, we will give them their fill of pomp and majesty."

And indeed, when we came into sight of the castle, the way was lined on both sides with people cheering and throwing flowers in our path. They seemed, if anything, amused to see us arrive looking like drenched cats, and cheered all the more lustily. "Who needs the sun," Arthur said to me as we rode through the happy throng, "when we have your smile to light us?"

Once we entered the keep, it was much quieter. Arthur had again shown forethought and requested no formal greeting, knowing I would be at least tired, if not wet and cold. Only a few of his closest companions were there, including Sir Cei, who immediately bustled up to me with a dry wrap and a cup of hot broth, all the while clicking his tongue and looking askance at Arthur. "He may know all there is to know about warfare," he said, "but he has no idea how to treat a lady. Come, Princess, and I'll show you to your rooms." With a final glare at Arthur, he led us off. *So,* I thought, *he has a Catlin of his own.*

The next day was indeed filled with enough splendor to satisfy the crowds, and even Catlin. At the high table there were a phalanx of bishops, Bedwyr and Gawain and others of the Companions, and of course, Merlin, who greeted me courteously, and then turned his back. Arthur raised an eyebrow at his friend, then smiled at me with a little shake of his head. "He is plagued with visions sometimes," he whispered to me. "As if there weren't enough vexation in the real world. Pay him no mind."

Arthur had requested that I wear my plain white linen gown, and before the festivities began, he came to my rooms with a casket of fine jewels. "These are yours, my dear. Choose whatever you'd like to wear today." I caught a warning look from Catlin, so said nothing about my dislike of ornament. Instead, I began sorting through the treasures, looking for the most delicate, least oppressive items. Catlin, of course, was immediately by my side. I held up a slender chain studded with amethysts, but she shook her head decisively. "You want something bold with that gown," she said, and reached for a heavy golden torque. I was about to protest but something in Arthur's face made me hold my tongue.

"It was my mother's," he said. "Uther gave it her when he made her his Queen, and I'm told she treasured it above all. Will you wear it today? It would please me." I nodded and allowed Catlin to slip it around my neck, and she was right: it looked superb against the stark white linen. It hung heavy, like a slave collar, but later, when there was a quiet moment, I looked into the polished bronze on the wall and had a few stern words with myself.

This is not the mark of a slave. This is the emblem of a Queen. All your life you have looked toward being Queen of Cameliard, never guessing a higher throne awaited you. The responsibility is heavy. Wear it with pride and grace. And so I entered the great hall on the King's arm, feeling almost tall and dignified, almost like a Queen.

Again, Arthur showed the greatest consideration for his people. "Would you mind," he asked, "if we went to greet those gathered outside before the feast, rather than after? I expect they'd like to get to their own celebrations. The nobles who await you here are well fed and comfortably sheltered. It's easier for them to wait than for the folk."

Of course, I agreed. As hap would have it, the last of yesterday's lingering clouds parted just as we stepped out onto the ramparts, and the sun gilded us all. The people gave a mighty roar. I was unknown to them, but they greeted me as if I were sent by the Mother herself. Deeply moved by this welcoming accolade, I could only hope I lived up to their expectations.

Cei set forth an extraordinary feast: there were huge barons of beef and tiny roasted songbirds, an enormous salmon jellied with shrimps and crayfish, and tender young lamb in a pie. There were pasties filled with mushrooms and leeks, and sweet tarts of almonds and fruit. "If all this is just to welcome us," I marveled to Arthur, "what will the wedding feast be like?"

I barely had time to taste these delicacies in the continual round of introductions and compliments, gifts given and received. The guests were a varied group. Primary among them were Arthur's Companions, the mounted warriors who had secured his greatest victories. There were client kings who had sworn their loyalty to Arthur from all the territories and fiefdoms of Britain: rough men with huge mustaches from the north, suave clean-shaven courtiers with Roman haircuts from the south. There were those who conversed in Brythonic and others in Gaelic; many still spoke Latin, though not all with equal skill.

My growing regard for Arthur was only fed by observing how devoted his people were to him—Companions, nobles, client kings, and the common folk of town and field. When I went to my bed that night, I was exhausted, but fell asleep with a smile on my face. We would be wedded in a week, and I was well content.

I assumed I would be greatly occupied with the plans for the wedding, but Cei had done almost everything needful. He came to me several times a day for decisions, but I suspected he had held them back just to allow me to feel involved. We got on well. At first, his responses were, "An excellent choice, my lady." But now, three days before the wedding, he was calling me "lass" and treating me as if he were my own father, though he was only a few years older than I. I wished with all my heart my own father could have been there, but a message came that murrain had been discovered in the sheep, and he must remain in Cameliard until the crisis passed. I missed my mother, too, but that was an old ache.

Cei certainly was grumpy and cantankerous with everyone else. Well, except for Catlin. When we first arrived at Winchester, he studiously avoided her. Clearly, he didn't know Catlin if he expected her to let that pass. One night she cornered him after the evening meal and talked at him for some time before he could be seen to respond. They were still talking when I went to our chamber, and it was after moonset when she tiptoed in. From that point on, he was the soul of courtesy to her, though hardened knights were being felled left and right by his sharp tongue.

The next evening, Arthur and I sat playing chess in the great hall. High King or no, his court was much like ours at home. Everyone was in there, children asleep in corners, knights drinking and dicing, women doing handiwork and gossiping, hounds worrying bones on the hearth. Cabal, Arthur's wolfhound, lay stretched beside him, savoring the occasional absent-minded scratch of her ears. Merlin and Catlin sat nearby. Catlin took no interest in chess, or in games of any sort, but Merlin was attentive. As Arthur was about to make a move, he shook his head. "I'm glad you're better on the battlefield than on the chessboard. Strategy, Arthur! Think!"

"I'm just letting her win until we're married. Then she'll see."

While Arthur was reconsidering his play, a young man approached and bent his knee. He was still in disheveled, travel-stained clothes. "Sire?"

I glanced up, then glanced again. Though tired and sullied, and not particularly fine of feature, he was remarkably pleasing in appearance. He was slim, and carried himself with grace; clean-shaven, with long chestnut hair swept back. His eyes were particularly striking, set in a spiritual, ascetic face. Arthur smiled at the strapping squire. "Yes?"

"The Lady of the Lake has arrived, Your Highness." I drew in my breath. The Lady herself had come to do our handfasting! "She asks to seclude herself until she is needed for the rite," he continued, with a charming Breton accent.

"Is this usual?" Arthur asked. And in an aside to me, "The Lady Morgan is my half-sister, but we've never really met."

"Well, she's very... she seems to need a lot of solitude."

"So be it. And who are you?"

"Her ward, sir. Lancelot du Lac."

Suddenly Merlin rose in a towering rage. "Lancelot of the Lake? Morgan's son? Send them away!"

"What? Merlin, why?" Arthur's eyes were wide as he turned to his advisor.

"Flames on the lake! Morgan's son will destroy you! Arthur, I tell you I saw it."

"What now?" exclaimed Arthur. "First it was—" He broke off, with a glance in my direction.

Everyone around us had fallen silent. Catlin, as ever in any disturbance, moved to my side. The squire recovered from his surprise and bowed gracefully to Merlin, who stared at him with horror. "Your pardon, my lord, but the Lady Morgan has no son. I am the son of King Ban of Benoic. My mother, Queen Ygrette, passed over when I was young. I was fostered by Vivien, who was Lady of the Lake in our country. I served Lady Vivien until her death and have only recently arrived at Avalon to serve the British Lady."

"You see, Emrys? You told me yourself you don't always understand the visions you see," Arthur said. "Ban is a faithful ally. He and his brother came from Brittany to help set me on my throne. And if any malice lies behind the eyes of this goodly squire, I'm no judge of men."

The night before the wedding, we women were banished from the hall while the men roistered and drank. The roars of laughter and clattering of cups wafted across the courtyard to where Catlin and I sat with the ladies of the court. I turned my head toward the sound, and must have let a look of longing shadow my face. Catlin gave me a hard glance, and I returned my attention to Elaine, the pretty young maiden prattling at me.

"I heard the King's new order of knighthood is going to use the table you brought in your dowry. Since it's round, nobody has pride of place."

"Clever," I replied. "What are the principles of this new order?"

"Oh, I don't know. I wasn't really listening."

"Too busy trailing her wing for the new squire," another maiden put in. "She nearly stopped her breath and turned blue when he rode in. 'Oooh, Lancelot, I'm fainting!'" The maidens hooted and laughed. I smiled patiently. I was very tired, and very bored.

A rumbling noise from the hall could be faintly heard under the genteel murmur. Dame Helena, an elderly, bone-thin lady who wore a large crucifix, was reproving Elaine, and I could tell from the other ladies' expressions this was something she did often.

"What impression are you making on our Queen-to-be? Believe me, my lady, this kind of foolishness and frippery is not the norm. Ours is a good Christian court." I had been nodding over my needlework, but this pierced the fog that was overtaking me.

Before I could respond, Elaine said petulantly, "Speak for yourself. I am no Christian. In fact," looking around pointedly, "you are the only Christian I see here."

"There will be more," Helena responded serenely. "And until such time as we are all under the rule of the Christ, we should maintain a virtuous court. I trust, my lady, that you agree?"

Despite the importance of the conversation, I was tired to my very bones. As I struggled toward full wakefulness, blinking and trying to figure out what exactly I had been asked, Elaine smiled and said, "Oh, do let it rest, Dame Helena. I fear our new Queen is on her way to the Glass Isle, and in no wise ready to debate religion with you."

Catlin turned from her conversation. She came to me and took the work from my hands. "Come, lamb. You'll be stitching that to your skirts in a minute." The ladies murmured in sympathy. I smiled groggily and allowed Catlin to lead me out as they rose and curtseyed. I was not too sleepy to notice that Helena looked at Elaine with clear distaste.

As we crossed the courtyard, Lancelot stepped out from behind a column, startling us. "Who's that?" Catlin demanded.

"Sorry, no harm. I'm lost, I think. Can you tell me—" When he saw me, he stopped abruptly and dropped to one knee. "My lady!"

I was tired and cross, and he was blocking my way to my rest. "Oh, please get up. This isn't—" The squire rudely interrupted me.

"Forgive my discourtesy when I entered court, lady. I was overwhelmed and all I could do was deliver my message." Apparently, he didn't realize his attentions were entirely unwelcome, and true courtesy would let me pass!

"Squire, I've already had enough courtliness to last me, and I'm just beginning. Ask someone else to guide you. At the moment, I can barely find my own feet." I started to walk around him, where he still knelt on the rough stones. He grabbed my hand and bowed his head over it.

"My honor, my strength, and my skill are yours to command, Lady."

"Yes, well… thank you, squire. Good night." We walked on. I caught Catlin's eye and we both struggled to suppress our mirth.

I had been well asleep, but suddenly I sat up with a gasp. "What is it?" Catlin murmured sleepily.

"Snakes. A sword." I shook my head slightly, unable to recall exactly what had plucked me from my rest.

"Just a dream. Go back to sleep, pet. You'll need all your strength for tomorrow… and tomorrow night." Catlin chuckled and patted me as I lay back down.

Chapter 9

The day of the wedding dawned sweet and clear, with a fresh breeze to moderate the midsummer sun. I slept late: Catlin had stationed herself outside the chamber door to fiercely shush anyone who might make noise. As soon as I stretched and yawned, Catlin entered the chamber with cider, delicate wheaten bread, the best cheese to be found in the dairy and some luscious purple plums. "Where did you get all this?" I asked.

"I took their oatcakes and beer back to Sir Cei the Surly and asked him, very sweetly, whether he considered the repast fit for a Queen on such a day. He was as gracious to me as he seems able to be these days, but he had some words for the kitchen lad who prepared it." When she had set the tray down and made sure I was comfortable, she slid companionably into the bed. We shared the feast as we talked, though my appetite, usually quite sound, was lessened. "What's the matter, pet?" she asked. "Fretting about the wedding... or the wedding night?"

"A bit. Catlin, I know you've... I mean... What's it like? I don't know what I'm supposed to..."

"Never worry. You haven't been overly sheltered. You've seen the beasts in the field and couples in the dark corners of the hall. Besides, you're not supposed to know *too* much. Arthur is a man grown. Just follow his lead."

"Will...will I like it?"

"If you can relax, and if Arthur has any skill. And I wager you'll like it more as time goes by." Somewhat reassured, I snorted with laughter and fell to the bread and cheese.

69

Arthur's morning was apparently less pleasant. He looked pasty and forlorn. "I'm afraid I overindulged last night," he said ruefully. "I've never understood why men do that. I see how they suffer the next day. Now I'm the one suffering, and today of all days!"

I was half sympathetic, and half amused. He certainly didn't look very regal at the moment. "Is there anything I can do?"

"No. Cei woke me with a flagon of cold water and some willow bark to chew. Now it's just a matter of time. Good thing it isn't a morning wedding!"

When the guests gathered in the great hall early that evening, the spectacle was all they could have wanted. Hundreds of tapers burned, making the colorful garb of the assembly glow. Rich banners festooned the hall, and three bishops in scarlet regalia stood before a high altar erected at one end. Arthur was recovered from his shaky, whey-faced morning and stood resplendent in cloth of gold and a magnificent crown; his cape quartered by a scarlet Christian cross. He offered his arm, smiled joyously, and began leading me to the altar.

I was the one who was trembling, so much I feared my teeth might start clattering. The handfasting would be completely familiar to me, but I knew little of what to expect from this ceremony—nor for that matter, what my life would be from this point on. I wore a gown of silver tissue, the finest I'd ever owned, and carried herbs and wheat, for fertility. My hair was elaborately dressed, with pearls woven in, and covered with the most delicate of veils. In deference to the bishops, I had masked the triple goddess tattoo with a tinted cream. My legs were shaky as we approached the altar, but Arthur supported me as I knelt on the rich cushions. Then he knelt beside me and smiled at me again, and his face was so open, so full of happiness, that any lingering misgivings fell away. A choir of boys began to sing, their glorious voices soaring to the ceiling like birds in flight.

The ceremony was in two parts: the marriage, and my coronation as Queen. We exchanged vows, and I was touched to learn Arthur had insisted on using the traditional vows, with no modification to emphasize his superiority as King. We exchanged rings, his a heavy, solid gold, like a more elegant version of a battle ring. Onto my thumb he slipped a filigreed band of silver, set with amethysts and rubies.

The bishop who presided over these rites stepped back, and a second came forward to bless our union and offer a homily on the sacredness of marriage, with special emphasis on the duties of a wife. There was a murmur among those gathered when the second bishop stood back, and they grasped that no Mass would take place, no communion would be offered. The bishops stood for a moment with their eyes cast down. Arthur gave them a look, making it clear that was all the expression of displeasure he was prepared to tolerate.

As the third bishop approached, Arthur stood; I remained kneeling as he took a narrow silver crown from an attending priest and placed it on my brow. The bishop dipped his fingers in holy water and drew the sign of the cross on my forehead, smearing the cream I used to conceal my tattoo. He frowned, adjusted the crown to cover it, then raised me and presented me to Arthur. I bowed my head to him, and then we kissed. When we turned to the assembly to receive our acclaim, the roar was deafening. Even among all those people—knights, nobles, royalty—I had no trouble finding Catlin. Her smiling face was shining with tears.

The feast Cei had prepared was as extravagant as anticipated. Cei himself stood by to be our carver, assisted by the very best of his pages and kitchen boys. Feasts tended to be heavy on meat, and there was plenty of that in every form. But I was most delighted by lighter dishes that can only be prepared in the summer. Of the seven pottages, for example, I most enjoyed a chilled one of fresh green peas seethed with mint. Puddings abounded, made with the fresh milk that also went into cheeses, from delicate to hearty. Eggs were abundant now, so they were made into delectable dishes by boiling and stuffing, or transformed into smooth, rich custards.

With so many dignitaries who must be seated at the high table, I was not able to have Catlin beside me. Arthur and I shared a trencher, as did Gawain and Bedwyr on his right. Lord Merlin sat on my right, then the officiating bishops. Those worthies, ignoring all courtesy, conversed only among themselves, turning their backs on the Arch Druid. The bishop closest to him did not even share his trencher, preferring to take his meal from his brothers next to him.

As I lifted my goblet to drink, I spilled a few drops for the Goddess. Merlin took notice. He spoke to me in a low tone, so as not to be overheard by those seated next to him. "We were glad you consented to a Christian wedding. The bishops—"

"Are very powerful. I don't mind, as long as we have the old rites, too. But you're the Arch Druid. Don't you mind giving precedence to the White Christ?"

"Of course I do! But it won't be long before all Britain follows the Nazarene…thanks to you." Merlin spoke the last phrase almost absently, his eyes far away.

"Me? Why me? Lord Merlin, have you seen something? Tell me."

"A command from the new Queen?" His tone was less than courteous.

"No. In matters of the spirit, I bow to you… and to the Lady."

"Ah, Morgan. I'd asked her to make an appearance at the ceremony, or at least the feast, but she always does as she will."

"And did you also ask the bishops to come to the grove at moonrise?" Merlin made a slight noise of impatience and turned away. But I was irritated too. "Tell me, my lord, do you hold all women in contempt, or just me and the Lady?"

Merlin turned back to me and spoke harshly but keeping his voice down. No one had noticed the exchange. "I hate anyone, man or woman, who would bring harm to Arthur."

"I would never hurt Arthur! And Morgan's his own sister."

"You know not what you might do. And she bears no love for him now, however she may have doted as a girl."

"Nor for you, I should think." Despite my respect for his office, this man was annoying me greatly. I continued coolly. "It was you who helped Uther supplant her father, was it not?"

Before he could answer, a voice rang out in the hall. "A wedding boon, Your Highness!" Merlin and I smoothed our ruffled feathers and turned to see. Lancelot stood before the table, splendidly dressed. He was even more striking now that the weariness of travel and newness of the court had receded. His eyes were alight. "I ask to be admitted to your Fellowship."

Arthur smiled kindly at the youth. "There will be a tournament tomorrow, and if you're as likely as you look, I doubt not you will be knighted."

"I ask a boon of the Queen as well." He turned to me. "My lady, I present myself to be your Champion in all just causes. Will you accept me?" Gawain looked up and glared, indignant at his presumption. I didn't much like this pompous young man, either, and was at a momentary loss for words.

Arthur glanced at me, saw my hesitation, and noticed Gawain bristling. "You aren't even a knight yet, squire, let alone a Companion. Sir Gawain is the Queen's Champion. It is an honor that goes to the best knight of the company."

"I assure you, Your Grace, I am worthy." He stated it as a plain fact, not as a boast. There were some outraged murmurs from those nearby, mixed with a fair amount of snickering.

Arthur was amused by his confidence. Gawain clearly was not. "Well," the king said, "tomorrow's tournament will decide that." As Lancelot bowed and backed away, Arthur and I shared a smile. Impulsively, he leaned over and kissed me deeply. I was startled for a moment, but then a wave of warmth swept over me. I threw my arms around his neck and responded with equal ardor. No doubt there were frowning countenances among the Christian ladies, but the rest of the guests hooted and cheered, banging their knives on the table. As we broke the kiss, I felt myself radiant, glowing, as was Arthur.

Suddenly a murmur ran through the hall: "The Lady of the Lake! Morgan le Fey!" A woman robed in white, her face veiled, glided through the crowd, which parted to admit her. She wore an ivy crown on her dark unbound hair, and cradled a magnificent sword in her arms, a sword that seemed to gleam and shimmer with a power all its own.

I could barely take a breath. It was as if the Goddess herself had come to bless our union, and the entire company fell silent in awe. She stopped before the high table and addressed Arthur. "Brother, I bring you Macsen's sword, the Druid sword of power. It has been in my keeping, awaiting the true King."

Arthur squeezed my hand under the table, then rose and went down to her, his face solemn and glad. "With this sword," she continued, "you will unite all Britain and create a fellowship the like of which the world has never seen." As he came to stand humbly before her, she intoned, "My brother, I give you Excalibur."

Arthur reached for it. As she lifted it higher, the sleeves of her white robe fell back to reveal blue serpent tattoos, more elaborate than those usually worn by a Druid priestess. Arthur hesitated, halted mid-gesture, and gaped up into her face, as if in shock or even, against all reason, horror. Through the thin white veil, she smiled back at him and put the sword into his hands. "And, praise be to the Goddess, soon you shall have a son." Despite the joy of this auspicious blessing, all color and expression drained from Arthur's face. What was happening? Why was he not rejoicing?

Arthur stood frozen with Excalibur in his hands. The guests waited for him to say something, but he was silent. After a moment—without, I noticed, dipping a courtesy to the High King—the Lady turned and made her way back through the crowd. The court erupted into wild cheers as Arthur stalked woodenly back to the high table. I smiled hesitantly up at him, but he didn't look at me, nor did he sit. Instead, he stared at Merlin with a desperate, haunted look and walked out, carrying Macsen's sword stiffly in front of him as if it were tainted. Merlin rose and followed.

There was an anxious buzz among those assembled. Bedwyr and Gawain glanced at each other, puzzled, and then looked to me. I was all confusion: despite my elation at the blessing of a promised son, Arthur's reaction struck me cold at the heart. In my first act of queenship, I smiled reassuringly and spoke to the lieutenants clearly enough to be heard by those nearby, who would spread my words through the hall. "It appears my lord is overcome with gratitude for this great gift, and by the responsibility it carries. No doubt he seeks spiritual advice from Lord Merlin." They smiled, somewhat warily, and nodded, and soon the hall was alive with festivity again.

Arthur never returned to the feast. I didn't see him again until moonrise, when we took our places before a fire in the center of a glade. Lady Morgan was on the other side of the flames. The surrounding woods were full of people come to witness. Catlin edged close to me, and we shared a joyful smile. Merlin stood near Arthur. Both of them looked extremely solemn, even grim, though this wedding would be much more of a celebration than the earlier, more formal rite. I tried to catch his eye. Where was the man who had kissed me so passionately at the wedding feast?

In contrast to our earlier glory, we were naked now, except for ivy crowns on our unbound hair and a girdle of red berries about our hips. The palms of our hands and soles of our feet were painted blue with woad. I was exalted with joy. This, after all, was the rite that truly bound us. I glanced at Arthur, but he was staring straight ahead. It seemed he was taking pains not to look at Morgan. Nor, for that matter, did he turn to me. We knelt on the soft moss laid for us, facing Morgan, who was also sky-clad. A small girl brought a goblet to the Lady. She spilled to the Goddess, drank, then handed me the cup. I spilled and drank.

Morgan dipped a finger in a cup of sow's blood held by another small girl. She traced the tattoo on my forehead, then raised me. I smiled, feeling serene and complete, and turned to Arthur, who was still kneeling, his eyes focused on nothing. I handed him the wine. He tipped the drops for the Goddess, his hand shaking, then drank. I drew the red moon symbol on his forehead and raised him. We stood side by side as an ivy chain was draped over our shoulders, yoking us together. "Go now," said Morgan, "and consecrate your marriage, that the land may be fruitful and thrive."

Accompanied by drums and flutes, we were led in procession to a simple shelter made of tree limbs and deerskin, painted with symbols of blessing and fruitfulness. The two girls held the door flaps for us to enter. Once the flaps were closed behind us, the drums ceased, and the crowd stood in silence.

We stood side by side for a moment. I could not control my breath, now coming fast like a panting dog, now in far-apart gasps. Lightning flashed in my head. I was apprehensive, but also thrilled to take my place as a woman, a wife, and a queen.

I turned with a smile to my new husband. But his face was rigid and fierce, and my smile faltered. "Arthur?" Without a word, he took me by the shoulders and lay me on the furs. He parted my knees, then took a deep breath and closed his eyes.

I knew there would be some pain, and I suppose he didn't mean to be harsh, but I was completely unready. I cried out, and at that, the drums and music started again, and the people outside began to sing and shout. They rejoiced for much of the night.

Midsummer morning. The words gloss across your tongue like cream. The sun revels in its greatest glory, meadows bedeck themselves in crimson and blue and yellow, and the air is sweet as honey. It seems the earth itself is celebrating.

I woke that morning as if floating in a warm bath. Buoyant with joy, I luxuriated in the knowledge that my path glimmered bright before me. Arthur had opened himself to me whole-heartedly, and I was eager to take my place beside him. I was well satisfied that the man I would marry was a man of honor.

At our wedding feast, Arthur was jubilant. His ardent attentions filled me with bliss, and our future looked to be luminous.

Then the Lady of the Lake arrived, gliding through the crowd as if she were a swan. What great honor that she would come to bless our marriage! And when I saw that she carried the Sword of Power, I knew that Arthur's deepest wish had also come true. I did not believe I could ever feel more joy, until she affirmed that soon we would have a son. My heart was overflowing.

But when the Lady swept out, my husband did not return to me. Not then, not for a very long while, though his body knelt beside me at the handfasting.

It was as though I was walking in a sun-washed meadow, and a winged, ravening thing fell on me from the sky and closed me in darkness. That sudden.

By the time the midsummer moon had set, I was sere at my heart's root, and all my shining illusions lay in shards.

Part Two

Chapter 10

I spent the morning closeted with Catlin, who assured me the court would simply attribute it, with a smile, to bridal shyness. The steel will of a Celtic queen helped me maintain a serene facade as the party returned from the greenwood, but as soon as the door closed behind us, I turned to Catlin in anguish. "Is it supposed to be like that?"

"No, lamb." Catlin, my heart's sister, didn't have to ask what I meant.

"And after, he turned away and pretended to sleep, though I'm sure neither of us closed our eyes all night. It's as if he suddenly hated me, Catlin. What could I have done to make him hate me?"

"It might not be you at all. He seemed fine at the wedding feast. Could it be because you wanted a handfasting as well as a Christian rite?"

I shook my head. "He's not Christian, and I was clear from the start that the Mother must be honored. If he didn't like it, he would have said something earlier. He was fine until he was given Excalibur and left the feast with Merlin."

"Ah. Your answer might lie there. From what I see, it's not just your husband you have to be concerned with. I don't trust that sorcerer."

"You mustn't call him so. He's the Arch Druid. But he certainly doesn't seem well disposed toward me. You might think he'd be happy to see Arthur wedded to one of his own."

"I know only thing for sure about men, pet: there's no understanding them. Rest yourself now, and later we'll find ways to make it better." But my mind ached with relentless questions that denied all possibility of rest. What had I done? Did I say something amiss? How could I have offended him? And how would it ever be made better?

The wedding tournament far outreached in splendor any I had ever seen. Everywhere I looked there were pennants fluttering, richly decked horses, clamor and movement. And of course, the knights in their array. Each shield identified the knight when his visor was down. Gawain's shield carried a gold double-headed eagle on green, clutching a thistle in each claw. Bedwyr's was quartered black and azure. Lancelot entered with a vergescu, a shield covered by a plain white canvas, since he was not yet a knight. There were murmurs and muted squeals from my ladies, jostling each other down front.

Arthur was already seated on the royal platform. Merlin and then Cei sat beside him. I was glad I had insisted on having Catlin sit by me, against all custom. It took some doing. As senior lady-in-waiting, Dame Helena held rights to the seat. "Was this woman even born into a noble family?" she sniffed.

I stifled my distaste for the lady and replied, "Actually, Catlin was born a slave." Helena gasped in horror. "But I've never met anyone more noble in character." Dame Helena dropped me a courtesy and left, but I later learned that she took it to Sir Cei, the final authority in questions of courtly protocol. Cei agreed it was most unusual, unprecedented, and unmannerly, but my wishes were respected. That was the only advantage I had yet found to being High Queen.

Arthur was murmuring about something with Merlin as I took my seat on the platform. He tensed at my approach and gave me a smile that was clearly a mask. "Welcome, Milady," he said courteously.

"Milord." I dipped my head, my own smile as false as his. "Lord Merlin." Merlin nodded a greeting but did not try for a friendly face.

Arthur cast about for something to say. "We have a perfect day for our tournament."

"Yes." I groped for words of my own. I needn't have bothered. After this most perfunctory of greetings, Arthur turned back toward Merlin. I glanced at Catlin; her mouth was tightened into a line, and she gave the tiniest shake of her head. I straightened my back and turned my attention to the field.

As the knights cantered past the rail, Elaine gestured to Lancelot. She held out a length of ribbon and dimpled prettily. "Will you wear my favor, squire?"

"I'm sorry, uh…"

"Elaine."

"Forgive me, Elaine, but I am dedicated to the Queen today." He looked up at me and bowed, then trotted off, leaving Elaine with a smile pasted on her face and her ribbon drooping in her hand. Some of the girls snickered, but I silenced them with a look.

The first event was tilting. It was my favorite, a test of skill rather than brute strength. Competitors, riding at full speed, tried to catch a hanging ring on their lances. The first riders were boys and inexperienced squires. For them, the iron ring was a handsbreadth wide, but even so, many missed it entirely and endured good-natured hoots and jeers.

"Your lance will do you no good, lad, unless you know where to put it!"

"Pretend it's your fat little sweeting!"

At first, I sympathized with the youngsters subjected to this mockery, but they took it in good part, laughing and sometimes returning jests of their own.

For knights and experienced squires, the ring was gold, and not much larger than the point of a lance. Quite a few riders, including Bedwyr, missed entirely, and were subjected to the same raucous comments as the boys. Gawain nicked it but was unable to catch it securely. More failed attempts, then Lancelot caught it cleanly. He rode to where I was sitting and presented it to me on the point of his lance. I smiled and accepted it, bowing to his courtesy.

"The young Breton is off to a good start," Arthur said to Merlin.

"Indeed he is," I agreed. Both men glanced at me, then returned to their conversation. Heat rose to my face, and I resolved to be silent rather than court his attention.

Next was the quintain, always a crowd-pleaser. A post bore a crosspiece on a swivel. One end held a large poppet of a knight, stuffed with a heavy sandbag. A target was attached to the other end. One by one, each squire galloped at the target. If he failed to strike true, the crosspiece whirled about, and he was walloped from behind by his sandbag foe. One youngster, who charged at the quintain like thunder, missed and received an equally forceful blow that knocked him from his pony. He lay still for a moment, and I clutched at the arms on both sides of me. Catlin lay her hand over mine and watched, equally breathless, while the stewards ran out to attend the lad. Arthur's arm,

81

in contrast, lay under my hand like a piece of iron. The boy stirred and rose. Arthur was quick to brush my hand off when he stood to cheer.

An archery contest followed, so soldiers who weren't knights could take part in the tourney. It was won by a mountainous young man with flaming red hair and beard, from one of the clans of the north. As he approached the dais, his face turned an even more blazing shade of scarlet, and when he knelt to receive his prize from my hand, the poor fellow was so overcome that he stepped on the end of his tartan and could hardly rise again.

For jousting, the lances were blunted, but this was still a dangerous sport. A fall from a horse while wearing heavy armor is a hard fall, and there were often broken arms, legs, and ribs. Worse, if by ill chance the lance should shatter, the jagged edge could catch a knight with fatal results. Boys were not allowed to compete. Those squires with maturity and experience were tested beforehand, and Lancelot was one of those who entered the lists.

He was spectacular. In short order, Lancelot unseated every knight who rode against him, including Bedwyr, without taking even a single mark on his white shield. The crowd was wild with delight. Arthur and I both leapt up to applaud a particularly skillful atteint, but when turned to him in my excitement, his smile became strained and he looked away. I was hard pressed to retain a pleasant expression as I retook my seat.

Finally it came down to Lancelot and Gawain. They thundered down the lists at each other twice with no winner, but on the third pass Lancelot struck him solidly and unseated him. Gawain sat in the dust for a moment, taking his loss with ill grace, then rose and bowed to the royal dais and limped back to his pavilion without looking to either side.

Lancelot accepted his prize, a silver ring set with an ebony stone. He closed his fist around it, held it to his heart, then bowed and presented it back to me. I wasn't sure whether I should accept it and glanced around nervously. Arthur still was turned away from me, and Catlin was as startled as I. Dame Helena looked disapproving, as always. Fortunately, just as Lancelot's prolonged bow was about to become truly awkward, the motherly-looking lady seated next to Helena gave me a tiny nod, and I leaned forward to accept the tribute.

While the knights rested, the crowd was entertained with a mock battle. To say there was nothing subtle about it would be an understatement, but I laughed as heartily as anyone. Buffoons wearing hobbyhorses bashed each other with inflated bladders, roaring insults and taking pratfalls. Several were costumed as the leading knights of the court, and appropriate jests were aimed at them. "Sir Gawain," for instance, wearing an eye-blinding plaid, was constantly distracted by a jester dressed up as a red-lipped, eye-batting maiden with spectacularly padded curves. There must have been some last-minute changes in the romp as well, for as the mock battle wound down, a mummer bearing a white shield trotted in, and all the others scattered in panic while the crowd roared with laughter.

The chaos of the clown battle was nothing to the pandemonium of the final event. Afoot, armed with staves, all the knights and squires poured into the arena for a free-for-all. It was just thwacking, and I couldn't prevent an occasional cringe.

Soon there were only twenty left, then ten, then four. They were all tired, swinging wildly. Bedwyr connected heavily with Sir Agramore, who threw down his staff and left the ring. Gawain took advantage of Bedwyr's momentary lack of attention and dealt him a blow that laid him out. He sat up, shaking his head to clear it, and quickly scrambled out of the way as Lancelot and Gawain faced each other.

They could barely move, but neither would give in. It was almost comical, watching them swing and retreat at half normal speed, but clearly they found no humor in it. The watching crowd cheered wildly. Most of them were Gawain's supporters, but some were throwing their lot with this unknown competitor. At last Lancelot feinted and swept his staff around, catching Gawain behind his knees. Gawain went down hard. Lancelot offered him a hand to help him up, but Gawain shook it off. He hauled himself to a sitting position, tried to get up, but simply didn't have enough vigor left. He took off his helmet and glared at Lancelot, looked away, then turned back with a grudging smile that gradually widened. He extended his hand for help. They walked off with arms on each other's shoulders as the crowd cheered madly.

Arthur and I cheered too. But after the prizes had been awarded, he simply gave me a nod and walked off with Merlin. I gathered myself, smiled at the crowd, and took my leave.

The court assembled once again in the great hall that evening. The bruised and battered knights were in high spirits, though many winced as they lifted their cups. Lancelot entered, splendidly dressed, and bearing a shield that displayed three blue fleurs-de-lis on silver. He knelt before Arthur and laid his sword at the king's feet. Humbly, he swore his fealty and took the oath of chivalry.

Arthur stood and drew Excalibur, tapping him on the shoulder. "Arise, Sir Lancelot. I declare you to be a knight and a Companion of the King. And inasmuch as you have proven yourself to be both valiant and supremely skilled, I hereby declare you the Queen's Champion." There were murmurs among those watching, and many tried to sneak glances at Gawain. His ruddy visage flushed to a deeper shade, but he maintained a pleasant expression. As for me, I would much rather have been linked to the rough-and-tumble Orcadian than to this arrogant young newcomer. It was not, however, my choice to make.

As Lancelot stood, I left my place at the high table. I took a silver chain from my neck and placed it on his, then led him to sit beside me on the dais and served him with the Champion's portion. Elaine, at a lower table, pouted. There was a momentary silence, then Gawain began to pound on the table with his dagger, roaring "Aye! Aye!" and casting glances and nods to his fellows. The other knights joined in the salute as Lancelot looked around him, seeming both proud and humbled.

Later, Arthur and I walked among our guests, as was custom. I smiled and nodded at Dame Helena, but as I passed by, she clamped a bony hand on my wrist. "This was not well done, Your Highness."

"I beg your pardon?" I looked pointedly at the hand holding me, but she didn't seem to notice.

"Before the squire was invested, he should have consecrated himself with the vigil of arms, praying throughout the night, with his shield and sword on the chapel altar. He didn't even attend a Mass!"

"That is the Christian tradition. But Sir Cei is in charge of ceremonies, and I assume he conferred with Sir Lancelot beforehand regarding his religious preferences."

"It should not be a matter of preference. Any man deemed worthy of being a knight should be a Christian."

"And what of a woman worthy to be Queen?" I asked coldly. "In this court, Madam, knights—and Queens—are free to worship as they see fit. As are you." I disengaged her hand, smiled tightly and walked on. Helena turned to her friends and began a scandalized whispering.

When the festivities were concluded, Arthur and I walked side by side down the corridor leading to the sleeping chambers. The day had exhausted and relaxed Arthur somewhat, but he still had little or nothing to say. I was so nervous that I was no help in keeping up a conversation. My hands kept curling into fists, no matter how often I tried to relax them. We walked in silence, trailed by Donal, his page, and Catlin. As we reached Arthur's chamber, he stopped and turned to me. His eyes, however, skittered away from my face, and I saw something in them that almost made me gasp. If I read aright, he was feeling the same emotions I had when I first met Merlin: shame and humiliation without any apparent cause. After a slight hesitation, he kissed me on the cheek. "Sleep well, Lady." He and Donal went into his chamber, leaving us in the hall.

To be honest, I was relieved, but Catlin was miffed. "Hmph!" she snorted as we continued toward my chamber. "What kind of husband is that? A woman needs—"

Her tirade was interrupted by Lancelot, who appeared from a side passage. He was dead weary and sore to the bone, but his face brightened when he saw us. He bowed over my hand and smiled up into my face. "Your Highness." His fatigue had thickened his Breton accent

"My Champion," I responded, with an answering smile. "Well done."

"*Non*, my victory owes nothing to any skill of mine. How could I lose? I was inspired both by the Queen's glory and the woman's beauty."

"Thank you, Sir Lancelot. Good night. Enjoy a well-earned rest."

He bowed again and walked on, and Catlin looked at me with a raised eyebrow. "Is this the same arrogant pup we met last night?" she asked.

"He learns fast! Put a 'Sir' in front of his name, and instantly he's a paragon of chivalry."

"Well, he may be newly knighted, but he knows how to treat a woman better than some who are King!" I smiled at her indignation and linked our arms as we went on to my chamber.

Chapter 11

Young as he was, Lancelot stepped into his duties with little difficulty. Of course, there were some who resented him, especially those of the northern clans who held loyalty to Gawain...and who gained prestige from any honors paid their kinsman. Gawain himself, however, seemed to bear no such grudge. He was Captain of the Horse and leader of the Companions and seemed to feel the title of Queen's Champion was no especial loss. In fact, he and Lancelot became quite close, bonding as the best knights of the realm.

Arthur, too, was becoming fond of him. In short time, he became one of the inner circle: Gawain, Bedwyr, Merlin, and now the Breton. Lancelot not only possessed Gawain's military skills, but also Bedwyr's deep well of loyalty and at least some of Merlin's sagacity when it came to tactics. More and more frequently, Arthur and Lancelot could be seen with their heads together, pondering some question of policy or simply strolling in friendly conversation.

Often, now, I accompanied them. Despite the disastrous start to our wedded life, Arthur and I had eventually reached a place of affectionate companionship and mutual respect. After the first few weeks of our marriage, he grew warmer toward me and began to seek out my company more and more. And as I spent time with him, I came once again to admire his sense of justice, his humility, and eventually, the man himself.

It helped that we almost always slept apart. Though he had learned to be more considerate, I found no pleasure in the act. The warmth that once washed through my body at his kiss was gone. Arthur was a good king and an honorable man, and I held him in great esteem. When I was summoned to his bed, I went willingly, but without delight.

As for Lancelot, my feelings toward him warmed somewhat as well. Once some traveling musicians came to court, and we gathered to dance. Arthur simply didn't enjoy it, and danced but once, to please me. Cei seemed to have eyes for no other partner than Catlin, and Bedwyr was being kept busy with all the ladies of the court. I tried to sit patiently, but my feet were pattering out the steps under the cover of my gown.

Lancelot sat with us, and I leaned to him. "Will you dance, Sir?"

"I'm sorry, Milady," he replied, "but it would be most unfair to saddle any gentlewoman with my complete and total lack of skill."

We were comfortable enough with each other now that I could tease him without offense. "Why, Sir Lancelot! I thought you were eminently skilled in just about everything!"

He ducked his head with a half-smile. Arthur, between us, was conversing earnestly with Sir Agramore. "Shall we take some air?" Lancelot asked. I nodded; he rose and offered me his arm, and we walked out of the sweltering hall and onto a cool portico, shaded by flowering vines. He turned to me with a look of great earnestness.

"I was just a lad," he said, "when word began to spread on the Continent about the great King Arthur. He was little more than a boy himself, yet he ruled all Britain, and was pushing back the Saxons and reining in the abuses of evil nobles, and... I was intent on becoming one of his Companions. Vivien, my foster mother, dearly wanted me to become a Druid priest, but nothing interested me save swordplay and horsemanship."

He paused. Why was he telling me this? After a moment, he continued. "I cannot avoid saying it—I was the best. I conquered all who presented against me, whether in sport or in earnest. When Vivien passed, I was sent to Britain to serve Lady Morgan. I made it known that as soon as I came of age, I would go to court. When my chance came, though, I was terrified!"

We came to a bench and sat. "I hadn't considered," Lancelot said, "that being the best in Brittany might mean nothing in comparison with Arthur's famed Companions. The only way I could force myself to attempt such a reach was to put all such doubts from my mind and assume I would be the greatest of all. I fear I was a... *fanfaron?* A bragger? An ass."

He looked so heartily disgusted with himself that I began to laugh. "Yes," I agreed. "But we can't have it said the great Sir Lancelot is unskilled in something so simple as a pavanne. We shall have to teach you." At the horrified look on his face I laughed again. "No, not now. I wouldn't want to humiliate my Champion in public."

Errol, the dancing master, was reluctant to take on such a student, and I suspected Lancelot would look like a dancing bear among the nimble and elegant young squires who were learning the courtly entertainments. I was surprised. He was unskilled, certainly. In fact, I've never seen anyone of noble blood who had so little social competence. But he was not ungraceful. I noticed for the first time that he was only of average height, or even a little less (which made his military skills even more impressive when compared with the Gaelic giant Gawain.) He was strongly but compactly built, and moved with an animal grace, like the huge spotted cat Palomides brought back from his travels.

Lancelot struggled earnestly to master the intricate steps, and swore it was harder work than wielding a broadsword, but he took his failings with good grace and flashes of humor. Lancelot's cheerful demeanor soon won Errol over. And I confess, I was coming to like him more than I ever expected. By harvesttime, we were often in each other's company, even when Arthur was not with us.

There was little time for leisurely strolls, however. The weeks from Lammas to Samhain were the busiest time of the year for us women—not that we sat idle at any season. Everyone pitched in to help with harvest home. It had been an excellent growing season and the crops were abundant, but even so, it was imperative that nothing go to waste.

Grain was winnowed and threshed, then stored in underground pits. Beans were dried and put by. The dairy maids transformed the last of the fresh summer milk into cheeses and crocks of butter and set them to cool in the springhouse. Wagon after wagon of grapes arrived, to be made into the vats of ordinary wine required through the year, and the bounty of other fruits was dried or made into jams and honeys.

The herds were culled, and those beasts not worth feeding over the winter were butchered and their meat salted or smoked, while the rest were let loose on the denuded fields to manure them for next spring's planting. With the exception of slaughtering the larger beasts, these were primarily women's jobs. The laborers, both men and women, brought in the harvest, while knights and warriors continued their military drills.

I was making candles with Catlin, Helena, Elaine and Britt. We stood over a vat of molten beeswax, dipping and redipping wicks to build up the tapers. Britt, a plump young maiden of ten, stood by to take the finished candles and hang them to harden.

"Child, were you sleeping through the wedding tourney?" asked Elaine. "I don't see how you could judge Gawain the better knight. No one could stand against Lancelot."

"I'm not denying his skills," Britt answered, "but Lancelot's so serious! Gawain is always merry and jesting and teasing us about—"

"Young maidens shouldn't be thinking about merriment with full-grown knights," said Helena. "Better to keep your mind on godly things and being of service." I stifled a sigh.

"Which do you prefer, Your Highness?" asked Elaine, blithely ignoring Helena.

"I hold them both in high regard," I answered carefully, "and both are highly skilled. But I would caution any of my ladies against giving their hearts to Sir Gawain, even if you were old enough."

"It's not their hearts he's after," Helena sniffed, and we all giggled.

Britt took a finished brace of candles from Elaine and hung them. Elaine sighed and mopped her face with her overskirt. "It's true. Sir Gawain plays lightly indeed when it comes to romance, but Sir Lancelot acts like he's taken a monk's vows. He's the soul of courtesy, but…"

"He's Milady's Champion," Britt said. "He has no eyes for any other."

"He champions the Queen because she is the King's wife," snapped Helena. "I wonder whether he remembers that," she continued, almost but not quite under her breath.

I wasn't surprised by the innuendo—gossip is a plague in any court. Besides, any woman would have to be carved of wood not to notice Lancelot's kind, guileless eyes, his melodious voice and charming accent, his fine, sensitive hands.... Yes, there was something more than Queen and Champion to our relationship, but it was friendship, pure and simple. I wasn't about to let Helena continue in that vein. "Enough chatter. It'll be dusk soon, and we have a lot more candles to make. I want to finish the beeswax today, so we can start on the tallow tomorrow."

Britt sighed. "Now I know why my mother was always scolding me about using candles unwisely. 'Use a rush light! Candles come dear.' She must have spent days and days making them, and our court was very small."

Britt was a sweet girl, and I gave her a smile, glad to have the subject turned. "When next you see her, tell her that. Mothers like to be appreciated."

"Speaking of motherhood—" Helena began, but just then Catlin flicked a candle carelessly and spattered the older woman's hand with hot wax. Helena yelped and went to cool her hand in a bucket. I cast a glance at Catlin; it was probably more grateful than the rebuke I should have sent. She went on dipping as she murmured cheerful, insincere apologies.

That night, Catlin held out a robe for me. "Two more nights, Merlin said."

"That man keeps better track of my courses than I ever did," I grumbled, as I shrugged on the robe. "They all do! It's only been three moons. Do they expect me to pop out a litter every few weeks like a field mouse? I see them counting on their fingers and staring at my waist."

I caught sight of Catlin's face and realized I had allowed my voice to become sharp, even bitter. I hated to give Catlin concern. I grabbed a cushion from a chair, stuffed it under my robe and began strutting around the room. "I should wear this," I said, "and keep them guessing!" Catlin snorted in amusement. I threw the cushion back where it belonged and plopped down in the chair. "I wish I *could* produce a litter of princes and be done with it!"

"You get no pleasure from it at all?" Catlin asked gently.

The question made me uneasy, and I considered trying to evade it, but Catlin would never let me get away with that. "I like the feeling of having done my duty," I answered after some thought, "and the possibility of pleasing Arthur with an heir—and myself with a babe in arms!"

"And that's all? Is he still...?"

"Oh, no. It's not like it was at first. He's learned to be gentle, and we've actually become quite fond of each other. I admire and respect Arthur. He's a good man and a good king. But as husband?" I hesitated. "Something seems to keep him from taking any joy in me, at least in our bedding. He's kind, but our coupling is… earnest. I think once we have an heir, he'd be as glad as I to be affectionate and sleep apart." There was a quiet moment while we both considered the possibility. Catlin seemed about to speak again, but I interrupted her. "So I guess I'd better try to make it happen!" Giving Catlin a gay smile that fooled her not one bit, I wrapped my robe tightly around myself and went out.

A few days later, Arthur and I passed by the open door of the chapel on our way to the great hall and glimpsed a knight kneeling in devotions. We walked quietly on, Arthur deep in thought. At last he spoke. "They seem to find such peace, these Christians."

"I suppose. But I'd rather find my peace in an oak grove or sitting by the song of a stream than closed in a stone chapel."

"They find their gods where they will."

"Their *one* god, unconnected to the earth and seasons, who speaks only to the bishops and the Pope: mortal men, whatever they may claim."

"Well, the world is turning a new way, my love."

"It may be," I said firmly, "but we don't have to turn with it."

Once Samhain passed and winter closed in, the court settled into a comfortable routine. There would be no threat of raids by the Sea Wolves until the thaw, but despite the lack of overt conflict, preparations continued. Forges rang with the production of armor and weapons and Arthur and his advisors contemplated military strategy. Gawain was often gone from court looking for adventure of one sort or another. Bedwyr took a wife, as sweet and gentle as he, and though he spent his days with Arthur and the Companions, the lengthening nights found him secluded with his Avila. Lancelot, whom I so disliked when first acquainted, had become our close friend and Arthur's chief advisor, at least when Merlin was not in attendance. The Arch Druid was often gone for days at a time. He took private counsel with Arthur when he returned, but otherwise let nothing be known of where he'd been. At least he seemed to be better disposed toward me lately.

As Yule approached, I asked Arthur if the Lady of the Lake would be joining us for the holiday. He said only that she would not and turned away. I wondered whether there was some bad blood between them, perhaps because of their fathers. Arthur never wanted to discuss it, so I let it be. But it did nag at my thoughts sometimes.

One night, when Catlin's snores were keeping me from sleep more than usual, I remembered the one time I had seen them together. She had been veiled, and only Arthur was close enough to see her face clearly. What did he find there that affected him so? They'd not been in each other's presence since he was taking his first unsteady steps. Did seeing her stir up memories, perhaps some best forgotten?

Or did it have something to do with Excalibur? Was he indeed overawed, as I suggested to ease the discomfort among the wedding guests? That didn't ring true. Even if he was feeling overwhelmed by the responsibility and trust the sword of the Druids represented, why would it have made him so hostile to me? He was hostile no longer, but there was still some deep discomfort, particularly when it came to our bedding.

Was it something to do with the blessing she gave us? A child, a son. Was he angry with me for not yet producing an heir? But he became more fond of me as time went by, not less. And he had reacted to the blessing as if it were a curse. Why? With Arthur completely shut off from discussing it, and the Lady apparently not welcome at Winchester, I supposed I'd never know.

Morgan's absence left me the reigning priestess. I led a contingent of Druids to search for mistletoe, and cut it with a bronze sickle to deck doorways for protection against the elements. It served to guard against quarrels during the festive season, too, as tradition ruled that any enemies meeting beneath the mistletoe must throw down their weapons and embrace.

It was a merry time of year, especially since all three of the most common religions celebrated birth: the Christians held that their Holy Child was born then, and the warriors celebrated the birth of their chief god Mithras. For Druids, it was the rebirth of the sun itself.

Each group celebrated in its own way. Warriors followed Mithras and held secret rites in underground temples. The Christians had petitioned Arthur to allow a Christ Mass at court. Unfortunately, they held it on the same evening as the Battle of the Holly King and Oak King, the Druid masque presented at summer and winter solstices, with alternating victors. As it fell, by forcing everyone to choose, they found themselves missing no small number of their less committed Christians, for the masque is always uproarious and wildly entertaining.

Lancelot and Gawain played the two kings, with younglings of the court and town serving as their armies. Lancelot threw himself into his role, overacting madly and taking spectacular tumbles when attacked by the Holly King's child warriors. "He certainly loves children," Elaine said wistfully, and it was true; he almost always had a contingent of boys following after him. "A man like that should father a whole tribe," she continued.

I wasn't sure whether my discomfort resulted from Elaine's longing for my friend, which he clearly did not return, or from my own concerns about providing an heir. At any rate, I steered us back to the masque. "Has the Holly King ever died quite so dramatically?"

I watched with pleasure, glad of the distraction. Earlier, Catlin had come upon me weeping quietly in my chamber. "Your courses?" she asked.

I nodded, sniffling. "How long do you think I have? Before they want another Queen?"

"Don't be silly, lamb. It's only been a few moons."

"Six! Six moons, and...I heard Helena and some of her friends talking..."

"And they want a Christian Queen."

"Yes!"

"And someone else wants a Northerner, or even a Saxon to bind them to us, and everyone wants their daughter or sister or niece. And if—when—you produce an heir, it won't change that. Just mark it down to envy. Besides, do you really think Arthur would agree to set you aside?"

I considered her question carefully. "No. Not yet."

"Not ever, I'll warrant. The man may not be the world's best in terms of bedding, but never doubt he loves you."

She was right. Arthur and I were growing ever closer as time passed, and I was beginning to love him dearly. He often asked my opinion on issues he was considering, and when I went to his bed now, it ended not with silence or diffident mumbled endearments, but with long, comfortable discussions into the drowsy night.

During the days, Lancelot was always by our side, as was Gawain when he wasn't out looking for excitement, licit or illicit. Merlin continued to leave court at intervals throughout the dark months and kept to himself much of the time he was at court. Though clearly something was distressing him, he no longer looked at me with the fear in his eyes that always made me feel some vague guilt or shame.

Arthur, too, seemed troubled, and as the Wheel of the Year turned past Imbolc toward Ostara, he and Merlin spent much time closeted together. After these sessions, Arthur often needed to be alone. Even when we were nestled under the furs, our talk in the last weeks had turned mostly to inconsequential things, and he frequently fell silent. In public, he was always pleasant, but in moments of inattention his eyes turned grave.

One March evening, Lancelot and I were chatting as we entered the hall for our evening meal. There was no one else about at the moment, so I put a hand on his arm and drew him aside. "Do you have any idea what's troubling my lord?" I asked. "Is there some threat of invasion or something else he's not telling me?"

"I know of nothing military that might be distempering him," Lancelot replied. "There's always a threat from the Saxons, but no more this year than any other. If anything, somewhat less, now that the land is more united. I suspect they will bide their time."

"Until something disrupts our peace." I tried to sustain a calm demeanor as I asked him the question that had been tormenting me. "Lancelot, tell me true. I know the talk going around court. Is he considering setting me aside?"

"Lady, *non!*" Lancelot was vehement. "Trust me, that will never happen. Yes, something is gnawing at him, but it's not that. Never that."

I gave him a wan smile as the room around us began to fill up. Arthur was not among the arrivals, nor was Merlin.

Chapter 12

Despite Lancelot's assurance, I could not rest easy. The next day, I sought out Arthur and asked to speak with him privily. He led me into a small antechamber and turned to me with a warm smile, though his eyes looked more troubled than ever. "What is it, my love?"

"I've heard Merlin goes occasionally to Avalon." To my surprise, Arthur startled and tensed. He didn't answer, so I continued. "I'd like to go with him next time. Perhaps the Lady of the Lake could tell me why we haven't—"

"You are not to go near Morgan le Fey," he interrupted, straining to keep his voice under control. "She is a sorceress, and any contact with her could only bring us harm."

"She's our High Priestess!" I protested. "Whatever your personal history—"

"It is far more than personal. Please, Guinevere, trust me on this. Morgan is evil. Prayers from your own sweet soul will do more than any help you could get from such as she."

"They haven't done much so far!" I retorted. But seeing the hurt look on his face, I softened. "Won't you tell me why you bear her such ill will?"

"I cannot. Believe me, it's better this way. Just please, stay far away from that woman. Will you promise me?" Reluctantly, I gave him my word.

Sleep denied me that night. As queen, and especially as a ranking priestess, I should have some doings with Morgan le Fey. Yet I had given my bond to Arthur that I would not. This troubled me, but then I noticed Catlin was not trumpeting in her sleep as she usually did. I turned to her, and saw she was staring at the ceiling. "Catlin? You're awake?" I asked. She took a ragged breath, on the edge of tears. "What?" I gasped. "What is it?" Catlin was the most fearless and stouthearted of women. What could have upset her so?

"I..." she began, then stopped and took a deep breath. When no words followed, my fear overcame me and I sat up and grabbed her shoulders.

"Catlin, tell me! Are you ill?"

"No! No, it's just that...Cei has asked me to marry him."

I shouted in delight and embraced her, but to my surprise, she clung to me and began to weep in earnest. "Catlin, what? Don't you love him?"

"I do," she sputtered, "but..."

"But what? He seems a good man, and honorable. What is it?"

"How can I leave you?"

I pulled back and stared at her a moment in amazement, then laughed and folded her in my embrace again. "Why would you leave me? Cei is invaluable to Arthur. He's surely not thinking of leaving court?"

"No, he'd never leave Arthur. But if I'm married... What if you need me?"

"Then I'll call for you, and you'll be there before I close my mouth. Why would that change?"

"My nights will belong elsewhere."

"Ah. That's true." Dear Catlin. At this most important point in her life, she was thinking only of me. "But sometimes my nights are elsewhere, and that hasn't changed anything. And if I truly needed you, don't you think Cei would let you come to me? If he won't," I said sternly, "then I forbid this marriage!"

Finally, she smiled and sat up, sniffling. "I'd like to see him stop me."

I poured us each a cup of wine. "I suppose now I'll have to address you as Dame Catlin, being the honored wife of a knight and all." Catlin snorted at that. "When will you have the handfasting? At Beltane?"

We talked long into the night, until neither of us could keep our eyes open. As we settled back to sleep, I said, "Well, at least I won't have to listen to you snore every night. Have you warned Cei?"

"I don't snore," she said drowsily. And then the trumpeting began.

Arthur's silences deepened and lengthened, until he could hide his gloom from the court no longer. I could feel the uneasiness eddying among our people as I sat to the evening meal. Catlin patted my leg comfortingly under the table and made a tiny gesture to bid me eat, though I had little appetite. Merlin's seat next to Arthur was empty; he had been absent for several days.

The meal had ended, and we were listening to a bard when Merlin entered. His gaze went straight to Arthur, as always, but this time, Arthur looked back for only a moment and then his eyes skidded away. Without a word of greeting for the Druid, he got up and left the room. Merlin followed. Neither reappeared in the hall that evening, and in the morning, it was discovered that Merlin had left court again. He took all his books with him, as if he didn't expect to return for a long, long while.

That night, Arthur summoned me, though it was not our usual time for bedding. It was almost like our first time all over again. He thrust into me relentlessly, his face above me looking carved in stone. Tears fringed my eyelashes, but I said nothing as he continued to pound away. "A son," he whispered harshly. "Give me a son." And I knew that unless the Goddess granted my prayers, my time as Queen was almost over.

Since Arthur, for whatever reason, was dead set against my meeting with the Lady, I decided to visit a consecrated spot nearby and renew my pleas to the Great Mother. Less than a day's ride away was a copse of oak surrounding a sacred spring. It had been held as sanctified since time before time, and I thought perhaps if I removed myself from the bustle and fuss of court, my prayers could be heard more clearly. I wanted to go alone, with just Catlin to attend me, but Arthur wouldn't hear of it. He knew better than to try to forbid me, but he insisted I take a band of his men as guard. Bedwyr and his fellows set up a pavilion and built a small fire, then stationed themselves outside the oak grove, but within hailing distance.

At moonrise, I slipped out of my robe and stood sky-clad at the edge of the pool. Catlin also worshiped the Goddess, of course, but I asked her not to participate with me, since the boon I asked was wholly personal. She stood back, but being Catlin, she never took her eyes off me.

I used the horn cup that was always left beside a holy spring, and dipped up some of the cold, clear water, then offered the drops of tribute before I sipped it myself. It was early April, and I was shivering, but as I drank, a warmth spread through me, and I became completely unaware of my surroundings. I dipped a finger in the pool and traced my forehead tattoo, then anointed my breasts, my navel and womb.

I sang hymns of praise to the Goddess until the new moon was at its highest point in the sky. Then I waded into the pool and raised my arms in supplication. "Goddess," I began, "Great Mother, hear your daughter's plea. I ask not only for myself, but for this land that loves you. Britain needs an heir, a son to carry on Arthur's good works. Grant it, I beg you, Queen of All."

The sky had been clear, but now a thin cloud slid across the moon. The priestess in me knew it to be a bad omen – but not entirely so. What could that mean? I'll give him a son but the child won't live? I'll give him only daughters? The client kings and nobles would never allow a woman on the High Throne, so a girlchild would be of no help to the succession. Maybe it means he'll have a son, but only if he puts me aside and chooses another queen. I shuddered at the idea but was well aware where my duty lay. "I would that the child be mine, Goddess, but if that's not my moira, please send him a wife who will cherish him and his son and help them to be the glorious Kings they are meant to be. Ellithu!"

I dropped my arms and bowed my head in submission, then waded back to where Catlin waited with a warm robe and a steaming goblet. I had prepared the herbs myself, calling on my knowledge of those that would bolster Sight. As a young maiden, I had tried scrying for true love and other foolish spells, but once I was old enough to understand the power of the Goddess, I had never before asked for Sight. I lay down on the skins in the pavilion as my head started to swirl and my human vision clouded. I closed my eyes.

At first, I saw nothing, only roiling shapes, as formless as mist. Catlin lay down beside me and held me close, and if I could, I would have smiled.

Then... oh, then. I saw Arthur and myself enthroned, with all our folk in attendance. Arthur, in particular, looked older, with lines of worry or sorrow creasing his dear face. I too had lost the bloom of youth. But I saw what I'd longed to see, and my heart nearly burst with rapture. A boy stood just below our thrones, facing the assembled throng. He carried little of me, save my dark hair, but with the merest glance at his face, anyone would have known him for Arthur's son.

I began to sob with joy, and Catlin held me tighter as the darkness closed over me.

The ride back to Winchester seemed to take forever, though we made good time. I couldn't wait to tell Arthur what I had seen. But when we arrived midafternoon, the mood at court was even more anxious than it had been lately, and small groups of people huddled in corners, whispering. Lancelot, Cei and Gawain stood talking together, looking grave. I went straight to them, ignoring the ladies who swooped down on me as I entered.

"What's happened?" I asked. The men looked at each other, then Cei spoke.

"There's been... Raiders attacked a village near Avalon and carried off nine infants."

"What?! Even Saxons wouldn't..."

"It wasna Saxons," said Gawain gruffly.

"Who, then?"

After a pause, Lancelot answered. "No one can say. The riders were masked and bore no badges. They stormed into cottages in the dead of night and took the babes from their cradles. They knew which cottages to go to, and there were enough of them to do it all at once, so no one had a chance to be warned by the screaming mothers, or the fathers they struck down, or the wails of the terrified infants." Lancelot's voice held a bitterness I'd never heard from him before, and his face was made unfamiliar by anguish.

I stood locked in horror, trying to make sense of something utterly senseless. "The bairns were all boys, and all of an age," Cei added.

Gawain had been seething, walking away from us for a moment. He burst back into our little group now. "Three months or younger!"

"The Christians blame the Druids," Cei said. "They think they wanted the children for sacrifice. There are rumors Morgan ordered it, or even Merlin."

I gasped in outrage. "That's ridiculous! Druids don't—"

"*Non*, of course not," Lancelot said soothingly. "The Druids are saying the Christians did it, since the children taken were from pagan families. Truly, no one knows anything, my lady."

I looked around me, numb. The people of the court had drawn themselves into two factions, one on each side of the great room. The Christians glared across the room at the pagans and whispered angrily. The pagans did the same.

"Where is Arthur?" I demanded.

"He has commanded no one disturb him."

Arthur kept himself apart as much as possible for weeks, even from me. I was eager to tell him of the vision I had been granted, but under the circumstances, I thought it best to bide my time. My news seemed insubstantial in the face of such real sorrow. When I finally found a chance to tell him of it, he only smiled sadly and said, "Let us hope your prophecy be true."

No one ever learned exactly what had taken place, and the land was in turmoil for some time. They must have been taken out to sea: the bodies of the babes washed ashore a few days later, which ruled out their being used for sacrifice. But the Christians were still convinced such an atrocity must be the work of pagans. They went so far as to deface sacred oaks and standing stones by carving crosses into them, and by the time the furor finally died down under the weight of other matters, the Christians had more adherents than ever before. Elaine became a Christian, as did several more of my ladies, but I refused to allow anyone, Christian or pagan, to create division among us.

The Wheel of the Year turned, and turned again, and still there was no child. Helena, who made sure I missed nothing that might upset me, faithfully delivered her husband's report each time the council demanded I be set aside. Most recently, the charge was brought by Sir Hugh, a prosperous knight. (And one who, Catlin noted, had a marriageable daughter.) It seems Lancelot, Bedwyr and Gawain were all ready to leap to my defense, but Arthur forestalled any conflict with his calm, certain response. "You know I would rule my heart if it went against the welfare of my people. But my Queen brings no harm to the state. And we are still young. Who's next?"

That night, as we lay together in the firelight, I brought it up. "I heard what happened in council today. They'll be back."

"And back and back. Let them."

"But if it puts the kingdom at risk... if you need to..."

"Don't ever think it. I married for statecraft and found love. That's blessing enough, child or no."

I smiled and caressed his face, but then the darker emotions intruded again. "It seems so unfair. As if I were being punished, but for what? I haven't done any wrong. I haven't, Arthur."

"I know, love." He pulled me close, but as he did, I saw a shadow cast upon his eyes.

I had long been asleep but woke when I sensed I was alone in the bed. Arthur sat hunched in a chair by the fire, and the coals' glimmering made his face a mask. Pulling a throw around me, I went to him. "What is it, Arthur? Are you ill?"

At first, he didn't answer, but then in a harsh whisper, "It's not you. Truly, it's not you."

"What are you talking about?"

"If the gods are punishing someone... You are blameless, Guinevere. I might have done something, something I didn't even know was wrong... And if that led to other things, truly evil...." There were tears on his face. I leaned over and embraced him tightly, urging him from the chair, back to the warm bed.

"What evil could you have done, my love? I know you to be the best of men. Surely there's nothing..."

"But if you are suffering for some sin of mine... Maybe I should put you aside..." he said, and my body tensed, though I managed to remain calm. "So you could find a husband more deserving of you than I."

I brushed the hair back from his face, kissed him and looked into his eyes. "Arthur. None of us know the ways of the gods. It may just be our moira to wait a long time. I truly believe in the vision the Goddess showed me. We will have a son. We will." He took a long, shuddering breath and fell silent, and eventually, he slept. I lay awake a long time, wondering what he could have done to feel such guilt. Surely there was nothing. I knew him to be a scrupulous man, and finally reasoned he was accusing himself unjustly.

There was gossip, of course, as there is in any court. As the Queen's Champion, and our closest friend, Lancelot bore the brunt of it. I loved him, in the same way Arthur did, but I had to be very careful. Arthur didn't much care for riding as sport, for instance, so Lancelot and I often went out together. Once we were caught in a sudden downpour and spurred toward a stand of trees for shelter. As I scrambled down from Etain, I slipped in the mud and fell. Lancelot reached down to help me and I—there's no way to explain this—I took his hand and yanked him down into the puddle too. Oh, the shock on his face! But then he retaliated by slinging a handful of mud, and then I did, and by the time we staggered to our feet, we were clinging together, weak with laughter. Lancelot held the moment just an instant too long. I broke away and turned to cinch Etain's saddle, laughing gaily and prattling about nothing. There were many glances askance as we rode back into court, rain streaking our filthy faces and clothes, but I held my head high, knowing that whatever evil they might think, I had not stepped a foot wrong.

We were watched and watched. Dancing a reel, women in one line, men on either side. I paced through the steps with Arthur on my right and Lancelot on my left, twirling from one to the other as the figure was called. Elaine watching. Helena watching. Everyone watching.

The Wheel turned. Elaine refused all other attentions; Lancelot treated her kindly but remained aloof. Catlin and Cei made an excellent marriage, and to the surprise of all, Cei began to soften and sweeten like an autumn pear—as long as no one disturbed the efficiency of his domestic rule. The Saxons remained fairly quiet, with only occasional sorties that needed to be put down. The crops were bountiful. Morgan was secluded at Avalon. If only I would ripen and swell, everything would be perfect.

One hot evening in late August, as we sat to our meal, a messenger approached the dais, bowing to me. I was seated between Arthur and Lancelot, since Catlin was feeling ill and had declined to sit at table. "Your Highness..." he began, but my heart leapt, and I interrupted. He was a youth from Cameliard!

"Why, it's Pryderi, isn't it?"

"Yes, Ma'am. But Your Highness..."

In the moment of his hesitation, I noticed he had obviously ridden hard. All my pleasure at seeing a face from my own country was suddenly doused by the knowledge of why he must be there. I grasped the edge of the table for support, as both Lancelot and Arthur leaned toward me. "My father... When?"

"Four days past, milady. He made a peaceful death, taken at his rest."

Lancelot touched my hand, and I grasped his gratefully. Arthur immediately began to deal with the statecraft. "Who rules Cameliard in the Queen's absence?"

"Her cousin Maelgwyn, Sir, King of Gwynedd to the north."

I was still dazed by the news and so unable to make much response when Arthur turned to me. "Is this Maelgwyn a good man?"

"I... I don't.... Pryderi, my father's ritual, was it...?"

"I left immediately to bring you the news, my lady, but Maelgwyn is a devotee. I'm sure he sent the King to the Goddess with full rites."

"Thank you. Excuse me, I..." I could no longer contain my grief. As I rose to leave, Lancelot stood. Arthur spoke to him.

"Send some men to visit Cameliard. We'd better make sure of this Maelgwyn."

"I will, sir," Lancelot replied. "And I'll see to this lad while you..." He inclined his head toward me. Belatedly, Arthur rose. As I left the hall, I heard him whisper to Lancelot.

"I feel so helpless when she weeps."

As I lay sobbing on my pallet, Arthur clumsily patted my back and made soothing sounds. He meant well, I know, but still I was relieved when Catlin burst in. He swiftly moved aside for her and slipped from the room as we clung together. Catlin was as distraught as I; she had known my father for almost all her life and had no other parent since she was small.

It was several days before I could rejoin the company. During that time we were reminded that as one life goes, another comes. Catlin was spending most of her nights with Cei, and recently she had been joining me later than usual in the morning. After the blow of my father's death, she started coming to me earlier again, and I soon understood the reason she had been delaying. When she brought in the tray of oatcakes and ale to break our fast, she was pale, and her brow was dotted with sweat. She ate nothing and made a dash for the garderobe before I took my first bite.

When she returned, pallid and shaky, I faced her down. "When will the babe come?" I asked. "And how long have you known?"

"I was going to tell you," she said miserably, sitting beside me and taking my hand. "But then your father..."

I nodded understandingly, but what I understood was that she had kept it from me as long as possible to spare my feelings. And it was true I had experienced a pang deep in my core when I realized she was with child.

"And when...?"

"In the spring. I wondered whether..."

"What?"

She took a moment before she answered. "Would you mind if I named it after your father, if it's a boy?"

"Of course not! I'd be honored, and so would my father, I know. Oh, Catlin—" All my hidden ache disappeared for the moment, and I embraced her fiercely. "You'll be such a wonderful mother!"

I wanted to visit Cameliard myself to see how my people were faring, especially since my only memories of Maelgwyn concerned his unwelcome attempts to marry me. But Arthur was about to host a conclave of client kings and could not accompany me. I knew I would be safe enough with a small escort, but Arthur was uneasy, and the conversation continued for days.

Helena, of course, made her opinion known. "Your father is gone, milady. What good can you do there now?"

"I want to see my people. I'm their Queen."

"As I understand, they have a regent. And though you may be Queen there, here your duty is to your husband."

"Thank you, Helena," I said icily. "When I need to be schooled in my duties, I'll be sure to ask your advice."

What finally decided it was Catlin. She was having a difficult time, with sickness every day that left her weak and exhausted. Between my concern for her and my reluctance to be in Maelgwyn's company, I agreed at last for Bedwyr to go and bring back reports.

It was clear Bedwyr liked Maelgwyn no better than I did. "There is just something repulsive about the man. I could find no fault with his governance, though," Bedwyr reported. "The people seem content with him, though of course they still miss their Queen." He smiled at me. "I wish I could convey all the greetings and good wishes they sent for you, milady, and condolences for your father."

"When last I heard from my father," I said, "he had both a Druid and a Bishop to advise him. Is the Druid still there?"

"He is, but the Bishop is gone. It's my feeling Maelgwyn intends to remove the Christians from positions of power, but slowly and carefully, to avoid protests." This troubled me, as my father had welcomed all religions, but I had to admit I was relieved that my people still followed the old gods.

"You saw no sign of persecution?" Arthur asked.

"No, sir. Maelgwyn is a Druid, and prefers to be surrounded by his own people, but I saw no evidence that he was mistreating Christians."

Arthur and I spoke at length later, and we decided to make another visit the next summer, both of us, to be sure all was well.

Chapter 13

Arthur wasn't fond of riding for pleasure—I suppose riding to war so many times killed the joy—but he did enjoy hawking. There was a September day when the heat was so stifling that Arthur, Lancelot and I decided to spend the afternoon in the forest. Much to my surprise, Elaine asked if she could go too. She didn't own a falcon and never showed an interest in any sport, but there was no reason to refuse her.

She showed up richly dressed and coiffed, daintily riding sidesaddle on a palfrey that had no business trying to keep up with our coursers. I studiously avoided looking at Arthur or Lancelot for fear I would burst out laughing. As for me, I was myself: wearing breeches and riding astride, hair hanging in a braid, with Weyve hooded on my wrist. My peregrine and Arthur's gyrfalcon were rousing their feathers in joyful anticipation of flight. Lancelot's fist was unencumbered. Falconry was not part of his upbringing at Avalon, so he was just learning. He'd been given an elderly kestrel to train with, but due to its age, he hesitated to bring it out in the intense heat.

It took us longer than usual to arrive at the clearing. Elaine's languid pace was especially irritating, since on such an oppressive day we'd normally have been tearing through the woods at a breakneck pace for the cooling wind. We stopped, finally, to remove the jesses and hoods from our birds. Elaine fanned herself ostentatiously. "Would someone help me down, please? I'd like to sit under a tree and catch my breath."

"But they're about to stoop," said Lancelot. "Don't you want to follow?"

"And watch them kill a poor lark?" Elaine made a pretty moue. "I really don't see the pleasure in this sport." I wanted to ask her why she'd come, but the answer was obvious. She smiled coyly at Lancelot. "Your hand?"

Concealing his reluctance, he dismounted and went to lift her from her palfrey. She simpered up at him as he set her down, but at that moment Arthur's gyrfalcon took flight, spiraling up and then speeding off toward the east like an arrow. "Yes, Toran! Fly!" Arthur shouted, and spurred off after him.

Lancelot watched the bird until it was out of sight. Elaine tried to lead him to the tree. "Will you sit, Sir?"

Weyve's hood was giving me trouble, but just then I got it off and loosed her. We all watched as she soared, riding the currents, then flew off to the northwest. With a wild whoop, I started after her. Apparently Lancelot left Elaine to sit under her tree by herself, for I could soon hear hoofbeats pounding behind me.

We rode like demons, splashing through brooks, cresting hills, and urging our horses to their utmost. Finally, after a long pursuit, we got tangled in a copse of willows and lost sight of Weyve. That happened all too often, but she would come back. She always had. We reined to a stop by an inviting pond, sweaty and exhilarated. Lancelot slid from his horse to kneel and drink at the brook that fed it, then dunked his head and shook it like a dog. "Whoo! That's a fine bird! What's her name again?"

"Weyve, the outlaw girl. I named her too well, it seems," I said as I too dismounted. I wanted to dip my hand into the water for a drink, preferring not to use Lancelot's method. But a buckle on my gauntlet wasn't cooperating. I worried at it until I was getting exasperated. Lancelot noticed and came to my aid. He smiled at me, his eyes sweet and affectionate, then bent his head and began to work the buckle free.

At last it let go. Lancelot drew the glove from my hand and let it fall. But he still kept my wrist, and held his face averted. I should have moved away, but something in his utter stillness held me as if I were glamoured. When he raised his head to look me full in the eyes, there was no smile. His face was taut and deathly pale. He pulled me toward him, and I did not resist.

His lips brushed my forehead, and I breathed him in, a long, deep breath. I shuddered and closed my eyes as his lips traveled along my cheek. When his mouth met mine, it was with such tenderness that I could do nothing except meld into it. What we were saying to each other with that kiss had little to do with lust. Only our lips touched, and our hands where he still held mine.

In that instant my life was changed forever. There was no sense of urgency. Instead, a wave of peace billowed over me. It felt like coming home after a lifetime spent wandering. Had it really always been this simple, this pristine? The miracle of his lips on mine could only have lasted a moment, but in that instant I understood all I had been missing in my life. And then, as I was about to vanish completely into the ecstasy of it, I understood what the future held as well. And it was dire, agonizing. It was utterly impossible.

I broke away. I turned from him and buried my face in my hands. He came to stand behind me. "Can you tell me you don't love me?"

"Don't say that! It is—"

"Treason. And an appalling sin, and a betrayal of the man I consider my brother. But how can we deny—"

I whirled to face him, wracked with fury. "Go back to Brittany!"

"No!" My sudden anger shocked him.

Despite the sweltering heat, my very skin seemed encased in ice. A deep breath failed to crack it. "Then you will leave the court. You have holdings in the north. Go."

"Is that truly what you want?"

"It's what must be. Go to Joyous Garde and…and take a wife, and… never return. I command it."

"You command me?" He went paler still, now with anger as much as consternation. As for me, my face was flushed, and wet with heat and tears. The shell of ice retreated to my heart, where it thickened, and would stay. A moment passed.

"I beg you."

He hesitated, then swiftly turned and leapt onto his horse. I heard him crash back into the forest as I sank to the ground, biting my hand to keep from howling.

By the time I had composed myself, Weyve had returned and was sitting on a branch waiting for me to gesture her back to my fist. I scooped up water from the pond and doused my face, but it was some time before I was presentable enough to go back to the meadow. Arthur was sitting under the tree trying to chat with Elaine, who looked thunderous. Toran had brought back a brace of fine hares, which Arthur had already dressed. Lancelot was nowhere to be seen.

Arthur leapt to his feet. "There you are! Lancelot told us Weyve played one of her escaping games. He was feeling ill, and headed back. Probably the heat. I'm about ready to go back too. Are you, ladies?"

Elaine heaved a great sigh. "More than ready," she said. I stood for a moment gazing at Arthur. My husband. I was flooded with love for him, this kind, noble man. My life was forever bound to his, and he deserved all my devotion and respect. There was no denying this.

But at the same time, I could not deny my grief at the prospect of seeing Lancelot no more. Our kiss had awakened me, in a way I had not known possible. When our lips touched, I felt a fluttering like thrushes in my blood, and lost all consciousness of a world outside. Only the two of us existed, and a radiance that bound us all around. My love for Arthur was deep and calm and steady, but when Lancelot's lips touched mine, our souls were merged forever. How was I going to live with that?

The next few weeks seemed to stretch forever, but the leaves on the trees were just turning when Arthur and I stood in the courtyard, watching Lancelot help his glowing bride onto her palfrey. Elaine threw her arms around his neck, almost knocking them both off balance. Lancelot gave her a strained smile and gently unwrapped her arms. Arthur and I wore equally forced smiles.

Lancelot mounted, then turned to salute us, though without meeting our eyes. As they rode out, I could feel my smile freeze into a grimace. I started to turn away, but Arthur folded me into an embrace. "We'll miss him," he said.

He asked me to his chamber that night, and made love to me sweetly and tenderly. But I don't think either of us closed our eyes until dawn.

Merlin returned to court shortly after Lancelot's departure. He had been gone for more than two years, and we'd heard no reports of his whereabouts. "He often takes himself off into solitude," Arthur told me, "but never for this long." He sent out scouts. Finally, one reported that the Merlin had been seen in Caledon, far north of Hadrian's Wall, on the bleak, untamed coast of the

Hibernian Sea. Arthur sent a message requesting his immediate return to Winchester, and Merlin complied. There was some stiffness between them for a while, but it passed.

"A priestess of Avalon to see you, Milady." I was heartily glad of the interruption. I wasn't obligated to do anything I didn't choose to do, but my father raised me to take my part in all the work of the court, not just the rituals and statecraft and feasting. And so I sat with the others, spinning, the most tedious chore I could imagine. I tried to disguise my eagerness as I abandoned my spindle and distaff and hurried after the boy.

She was alone in the room when I entered, her back turned to me as she examined a tapestry. She stood straight and tall in her white robe, and the lock of hair that escaped her veil flamed brighter even than Gawain's. When she turned, I was already hastening across the stone floor to embrace her.

"Nimue!" We laughed and wept as we clung together. Finally we stood apart, grasping hands and smiling as we examined each other. She had not altered much. Her body was slim and strong, but she had already lost much of her stoutness before she left for Avalon. Her freckles had faded somewhat from spending much time indoors, but they were still strewn densely across her face. Her hair was still lank and thin, her eyes still keen, her smile still broad and warm. And yet she was transformed completely.

She wore the power of Avalon like a crown. It shone from her face, wrapped her in an air of command. For just an instant, I felt small and slight, and even somewhat shy of her withal. But it passed quickly. There was no question the power was there, and could be called upon in an instant, but it was like a mist that hovered around her, hiding nothing of her essential self. Soon we were seated side by side in my solar, chattering like girls again.

"Why did you not let me know you were coming?" I asked. "I would have been better prepared to welcome you."

"Exactly why I asked Lord Merlin not to tell you," she responded.

"Merlin?"

"I am sent to study with him, through the winter at least. The Lady Morgan favors me, and is preparing me to succeed her."

I shouted with delight and embraced her. "My Nimue, to be the Lady of the Lake! I am thrilled, but not the least surprised. The rest of us taken together were not as devout as you."

"The excellent training I received in Cameliard helped immensely. You must thank your father for me."

When she saw the shadow fall over my face, she took my hand in hers, and the conversation turned to all that had happened since we had seen each other last. I did not mention Lancelot.

Catlin was still grievously ill and concerned about nurturing her babe. I spent much of my time with her, tempting her with the tidbits poor fretful Cei provided, laving her brow with cool water steeped in herbs, and trying to provide such comfort as I could.

I prepared potions for her, but they didn't seem to do much good. It was common for women to have such bouts when first with child. But this was different, and dangerous. I went to Nimue, to ask whether she might know some more effective remedy. She did, and earned Catlin's sincere gratitude. But Catlin was greatly weakened, and I forbid her to rise from her bed.

I was grateful for Nimue's company during this time. Talking with Arthur was fine, but I missed Catlin's chatter. Women, no matter how close they are with their menfolk, need other women to talk to. It was especially satisfying to talk with Nimue. Unlike most of the ladies at court, she was not interested in gossip or frivolity. That is not to say she had no humor; her wit was keen. But just as when she was a girl, she never hesitated to dive into deeper topics.

One evening, when the great hall was particularly raucous and unruly, we retreated to my solar for a quiet game of draughts. As she sat pondering her next move, she asked casually, "Remember when we were girls and talked about our different callings?"

"I do," I said, smiling. "You have certainly done well in yours."

"And you?" she asked.

The question startled me and left me somewhat discomfited. I tried to pass it off with a droll question of my own. "I am High Queen, am I not?"

"You are indeed. Certainly a higher destiny than you ever expected." She fell silent, again contemplating the board. *So like Nimue, to drop such a comment and leave me to ponder it.* I gazed at the board as well.

"As a girl, I looked no higher than to rule Cameliard when my father passed. But now, I know little of how my realm fares. Except it is under a regent I don't admire."

"Maelgwyn."

"You know him?"

"Only that he is a very devout follower of the Mother. You should be pleased about that, at least. But you were not able to choose your regent yourself?"

"He was already named by the time I learned of Father's death. With me so far away…"

"Of course. And you are fully immersed in your duties here, I imagine." Our game had been forgotten. I stood and paced the room restlessly.

"Yes," I replied. "Arthur often asks my opinion, and there's the Queen's Council…."

"Tell me about that." She poured us each some wine.

"I have some excellent people. Cei is my chief advisor, and Sir Bors and Sir Agramore—"

"Yes, but what do you do?"

I scoffed at that. Nimue's questions always went for the throat, but that was part of why I liked her. "At first, very little. When the Council was formed, all we were sent were questions of court decorum and an occasional quarrel within a family. I went to Arthur and convinced him we should be given more authority. We now handle more important domestic matters, and rule on questions of religion—"

"For Christians also?"

"Well, no, the bishops rule them. But Druids, Mithraites, all the pagans."

"As you should, being the ruling priestess here in Morgan's absence."

I leaned forward to lay my hand on her arm, but she reached for her wine. "Do you know what lies between Arthur and the Lady? He will tell me nothing, only that she is not welcome here. It doesn't seem right."

"It is not. And she is more than unwelcome. She's banished."

"I didn't know that. Arthur confides in me, of course, but on that subject he... I suspect it might have something to do with..."

"With what?"

"Well, since we're talking about fulfilling destinies, I haven't fulfilled the most important of mine: to give Britain an heir. Nimue, can you help me? You know potions beyond—"

"No. I'm sorry. We cannot command the gods to give us what we want. You know that. They give us what they will and leave it to us to puzzle out how to live with it. Anyway, that's not what's most important. You are not a breeder. You are a woman and a priestess and a Queen. What's most important is, are you happy? Have you fulfilled your moira?"

"Oh yes!" I said with a bright smile, though a prickling began behind my eyes. "If only I could bear a child. Everything else is—"

"What about your knight?"

"What?! How do you...?" At that moment, Arthur bounded in, oblivious as a puppy. I didn't know whether to be frustrated or relieved.

"Ah, there you are, ladies. Come, I sent the roisterers away, and Taliesin is going to give us a new song." Nimue smiled, gathered up her skirts and exited gracefully. I followed, with a distinct lack of composure. I evaded private talk with her for the next few days, and the subject was not broached again.

It soon seemed Nimue had always been a part of the court, sitting next to Merlin at table, joining the other maidens in their chores and merriment, and charming everyone she encountered. The aura of power she evidenced upon her first arrival was muffled as she became just another inhabitant of the household, but I could tell it was never gone.

Merlin was not immune to her charms. He hung upon her gay chatter at meals, sat aside with her of an evening talking earnestly, and spent a part of each day instructing her in the duties and burdens of being the High Ban Drui, once Morgan passed the power to her. Morgan was still young, of course, but preparation for such high office took as much as twenty years.

Nimue frequently traveled back to Avalon, but we never spoke of it. As for Arthur, he was wary at first, but soon accepted her into the company. I believe he actually became fond of her.

"She's about as different from Morgan as possible," he said.

"Except in their devotion to the Goddess," I replied. "I don't think even Lord Merlin has given his heart and soul as completely to Her worship."

Not that she held herself apart in any way. Like Merlin, Nimue was something of a shapeshifter. Most of the time, she was just another maiden at court, laughing and jesting with the rest. When the need arose, however.... Once a particularly callow squire made a lascivious joke about the Goddess. Nimue's eyes blazed, her face paled so that even her freckles disappeared, and her entire bearing changed. I swear she grew two hands taller. She didn't have to say a word. The squire quailed before her, stammering apologies. She stalked off, but when the two were together in a room again, you would not have known from her good humor that there had ever been anything amiss between them—except the boy treated her with utmost respect.

Many a knight tried to catch her favor. But because of her priestly status, or because they didn't want to run afoul of Merlin, or simply because she showed no interest whatsoever in any of them, they never pressed their suit too strongly.

Chapter 14

I was pleased to have an adept priestess by my side for the winter celebrations. Despite being of the highest rank, Merlin never showed much interest in rites and ceremonies, preferring to study relentlessly. But my people needed those rites, not only to mark the passage of the year, but also to keep us connected: the Christians convened every week, but we only came together eight times throughout the year.

Nimue was spending more and more time in Merlin's rooms. Officially, she was learning Druid lore. It soon became clear, though, that their relationship had changed from student and mentor to friends, and then to something else. As they grew closer, Merlin's attitude began to change. He was absent at Samhain, and a bystander, mostly, at Yule. By Ostara, he was taking part in every festivity. And it was widely known by then that Nimue was sharing his bed.

It was good to see the old man happy, but... he *was* an old man, and Nimue only my age. My ladies were in a particularly giddy mood one day as we were weaving reeds into Brigid's crosses in preparation for Imbolc. The chatter turned to Merlin and Nimue, and there were whispers and smirks in plenty. The silence that fell when Nimue entered the room made it obvious what they had been gossiping about.

I shooed them out and tried to cover the awkwardness with an inane comment about the coming holiday, but Nimue just cocked her head and gave me an appraising look. She took up a handful of reeds and began intertwining them skillfully. "They cannot imagine why I prefer Lord Merlin to the dashing

116

knights trailing at my skirts. I suppose you wonder the same thing." I glanced aside, not wanting to pry. But I also did not deny it.

"What I see and the world sees are sometimes different things," Nimue said.

"Does he…? I mean, some say he's a shapeshifter."

"Not in the way most understand it." She considered for a while, then put down her weaving and turned to me.

"Think of the chicory flower. That lovely hue, like the sky as dusk begins."

I saw them vividly in my mind. "I love that color. When I was small, I always wanted to pick huge bunches of them and bring them inside." I laughed a little.

"But you soon learned the folly of that. What happens to chicory flowers when you pick them? The beautiful blue?"

"It turns to ash, almost at once."

"Exactly. When I am with Merlin, it's the opposite of that." She turned back to her work with a small, secretive smile, and though I cannot say I totally understood her meaning, I understood that was all she was going to say.

Arthur and I discussed it, too. "Merlin told me once he was fated to love her, and she him. That he had been waiting a long time for her to appear."

"How very romantic," I said. "I would never have looked for such whimsy coming from Merlin."

"The way he said it was strange, though," Arthur responded. "There seemed little romance in it, and no whimsy. It was more like…a statement of fact. As if it were something to which he resigned himself."

"That is odd. But he does seem to take more joy in life when she's around."

"He does indeed."

Arthur and I both missed Lancelot, in our own ways. Messages came for Arthur a few times a year, telling of a skirmish on the northern border or how the local farmers were doing. Whenever a traveler passed through Joyous Garde on his way to Winchester, Elaine sent along more personal news.

After we returned from falconing that disastrous day, Elaine had attributed Lancelot's sullen countenance and my distance from him as my reprimand for being so discourteous to her. It seemed she could not comprehend any event that didn't have her at its center. So when Lancelot asked her to be his wife and accompany him to Joyous Garde, it confirmed her belief—and she considered me her benefactor. At every opportunity, she sent me long, effusive letters detailing her happiness, despite her husband's inexplicable moods. She shared her joy when she was with child. She also shared every detail of her pregnancy, labor and birth. I did not receive these letters in the spirit in which they were sent.

When news came that Elaine had borne him a son, I couldn't decide which was worse: the ladies who peeped at me to see how I might react, or those who diligently avoided looking at me.

There were many nights when I struggled against the memory of his lips on mine. Sometimes I even hoped for a major attack, such that Arthur would have to call him back. Then I chided myself for my utter selfishness. Besides, it was I who sent him away, to protect us both. And now he had a wife and a son. It was almost too much to bear, but I bore it. I had no choice.

As February grudgingly made way for March and the roads became more passable, a messenger arrived from Joyous Garde. He bore an official missive, which was read out in open court. The only reference to me was, "Greetings to my lady Queen." The rider also delivered a private message to Arthur, which talked of matters of state and strategies to avert the spring raids. And as always, there was a personal letter for me from Elaine.

This most recent one was replete with news about Galahad, their little son. How clever the lad was, how beautiful, how like to his father except for his golden curls. I hauled Catlin into my chamber with me after reading it. She sat quietly while I paced and ranted, until finally I dropped down beside her and buried my face in my hands. Catlin put an arm around me and pulled me so close I could feel the bairn moving in her womb. "You don't respond to these letters, do you?"

"Never! You might think she would understand they are not welcome."

"And you don't send messages to him?" I just stared at her, the idea was so ridiculous. "Good. Best you put him out of mind entire, pet."

I sighed. "The Goddess knows how I try. But Nimue seems to think he might be my moira."

Catlin went still beside me, and the arm around my waist grew heavy. "You told Nimue?"

"No. I didn't have to."

"If Nimue knows, then likely the Lady does too. And hap Accolon has your secret as well." Accolon was Morgan's lover. He was also a knight, and at court more often than not.

"What difference?" I said dully. "They have always whispered of it, and no matter how long he is gone, the whispers continue."

"Whispers are vexing," she said, "but the truth could be dangerous. You were right to send Lancelot away, no matter how heavy your loss. But what is this nonsense about moira? The first thing the Goddess asks of us is to harm no one. Even though he's not at court, Lancelot is still Arthur's greatest hero. If your fondness were known.... Your moira has always been to rule, to be Queen, to aid your people. Your moira is your throne. Not Lancelot, nor no other." She paused, then looked away. "Anyone who tells you else has not your weal in mind."

"Catlin," I said gently, "I know you and Nimue have never been best congenial, but surely she means me no harm."

"There is something about her that doesn't ring true," Catlin said. "I have no doubt of her devotion to the Mother, nor her affection for you. I sometimes wonder whether she has something to gain by her close association with Lord Merlin..."

"The Lady sent her here to learn from him."

"I know. There's nothing I could point to, but she gives me unease." She looked at my troubled face. "Mayhap I'm jealous," she said with a little laugh.

I smiled but said nothing.

The hard skies of winter at last gave way to the soft clouds and running rivulets of spring. The time for her child's birth grew closer and Catlin's illness eased. Other discomforts took its place, however. On a gently rainy afternoon in April, when the smell of the thawed earth was strong, several of us ladies were working on a large tapestry. Suddenly Catlin said "Oof!" and pressed a hand to the side of her bulging belly.

"Making his presence known again, is he?" I asked.

"I wish just once he would choose another spot."

"You should have seen me when I was carrying my twins," said Lynde. "I was big as an ox. One kicked here, the other there. Slept not a wink the last two months."

"Then there's getting up ten times a night to piddle in a cold pot," chimed in Elin.

"Ah, don't worry, Catlin. You'll catch up on your sleep after he's born. About seven years after!"

All the ladies laughed, and Helena looked up with a cool smile. "Aye, carrying them may be hard, and raising them harder. But worse not to have them, don't you think? I thank the Christ for blessing me with my four bairns, trouble though they be."

An uncomfortable silence fell. I got up and walked out of the room. Catlin hurried after me, with a poisonous look for Helena as she went.

Catlin brought forth a bonny boy in May. Little Lodegrance made up for all her sickness and discomfort by arriving swiftly and without difficulties. That was a great relief, for she was now in her mid-twenties, late for a first child. I was with her, of course, through the birth. And when the midwife had washed and swaddled him, and he had suckled and begun to drowse, Catlin handed him to me. He was so tiny and fragile it stopped my breath. Tears were running down my face, but I could not cease from smiling. I had never lost faith in the vision the Goddess granted me and continued to hope for a son of my own. But until then, this infant, like his mother, owned all my heart.

The Wheel turned. Lancelot had been gone from court for more than three years now, but it seemed the gossip and viciousness never stopped. One evening, when Arthur and I were away from court for a few days, Catlin was sitting quietly in a hearthside nook winding yarn, little Lodegrance playing with spools at her feet. She sat facing the fire, and behind her, Accolon, Nimue and Helena sat with a group of minor knights and ladies, mostly Christian. There was also Father Edalwurf, the priest who ensconced himself when the Christians pressured Arthur into creating a chapel for them within the castle. Apparently our absence made people feel they could speak more openly than usual. When I returned from our visit to a neighboring duchy, Catlin came to me, practically breathing fire, to tell me what she had heard.

"I hadn't been paying them any mind, but something about the tone of their voices caught me. I didn't know the first voice. He says, 'Oh, Arthur's still young and hale. But the Saxon shore is swarming. He'll have to go against them in the spring. What if he's killed, with no heir?'

"'All the more likely with our best knight sitting cozy by his fire.' That was Accolon.

"One young knight—I'd like to box his ears—said slyly, 'And who knows? If Lancelot were here, the Queen might bear a princeling after all.'"

She glanced at my stricken face. "I'm sorry, but best you know. Someone laughed aloud, and Helena had to have her say. 'It's nothing to jest about. Her barrenness shows there has been some terrible sin committed in this court, you can be sure.'

"Nimue noted the sin might be the King's, but the priest trod heavily on that. 'Remember, madam, the original sin was Eve's. And it's not the king who is cursed. He has a son, or so rumor goes.'" I gasped, but Catlin was too outraged with the telling of her tale to notice.

"'Aye, and so does Lancelot!' They all laughed this time. I couldn't help myself—I turned around to sneak a look and see who these wretches were. But I turned right back. Nimue was standing, and I tell you, she frighted me. She stood so tall! And her face was white and strange. Everyone got very quiet. And when she spoke, the voice rolling out of her mouth, well, it wasn't hers." Catlin took a deep breath to steady herself.

"'Have respect!' she says. It was like a command from...I don't know. 'The Lady Guinevere is your Queen, and a priestess beloved of the Goddess. You scoff, priest? Know you well, the Goddess still rules this land. Your Queen holds her people in her heart and does all in her power to keep them safe. She is no beast to be bred! Has she no child, another will come, and return Britain to its rightful worship.' And she swept off. They were silent for a moment, then there was some muttering, and soon they all went their ways. I waited until I was sure I would not be noticed before I scooped up Grance and left."

I sat astonied. Catlin cast a worried look. "I did right to tell you?" I nodded, unable to find my voice. "I thought you should know what is being bruited. And who your friends are. I do regret," she said shamefaced, "that ever I doubted Nimue's goodwill. But what is this about Britain's rightful worship?"

I had not yet begun to think of that. My entire being was caught on one passing comment. "Arthur has a son?" I said wonderingly.

"Of course not!"

"But maybe... before we were married..."

"If anyone, wench or lady, had borne a son to the High King, don't you think she would have trumpeted it to all the world by now? This is idle gossip, lamb. Put it from mind."

She was probably right. After all, half the court "knew full well" that Lancelot and I had been swyving like foxes until Arthur banished him. Certainly, the existence of such a child, if he existed, could not have been kept so totally covert. Nor would there be reason to. A royal bastard was an asset to an otherwise childless king, not a scandal. So I did not let myself brood on it, and every moon I grew more skilled at managing my sorrow.

I was thinking on nothing particular as I walked past the safe room and stopped to savor the aroma of sweet and medicinal herbs. As it happed, I overheard some conversation between Nimue and Merlin. I know I should have walked on, but there was a bit of an edge to her voice that caused me to linger, and greatly unlike myself, even to peek in unnoticed.

"Lord Merlin, I have known about tansy and orris and asafetida since I was a child. I was sent here to learn those things even the Lady cannot teach me. What about the dragon's blood you gave the King's father to make him invisible to Gorlois' guards?"

Merlin tsked and shook his head. "Rumors, my dear. I let them talk. It is often wise to let people think you have more power than you really do."

"Yes," she replied. "And to keep some powers hidden."

"Ah, you are a clever student," Merlin said. "I wish I had time to teach you everything I know."

"I have no need to return to Avalon soon. Nor do I desire to." She reached out to lay a gentle hand on his cheek, and I suddenly understood what she had meant when we talked at Imbolc. They kissed, and when they parted, Merlin's eyes were bright and clear of rheum, a fresh color bloomed in his face, and he held himself as straight as a much younger man. He smiled at her, but his smile seemed to me somewhat sad.

"Nor would I have you leave. But I fear our time together will end sooner than either of us would wish."

"Truly?" She seemed startled. "Why? Does the King have plans for you?"

"No," Merlin replied quietly. "But Morgan does." They both went still for a moment, then Merlin picked up another herb.

"Elodea," Nimue said with a sigh. "For marsh fever."

Chapter 15

Gaheris and Agravain, Gawain's brothers, were almost identical twins, both of them a good deal taller and broader than average. They had huge hands, and russet hair, and beards braided in the northern style. Like Gawain, they wore tartans and retained an Orkney brogue. But while Agravain's blue eyes were piercing, Gaheris's were dull and placid, and that difference was reflected in their personalities. Agravain was bold, Gaheris shy. Agravain talked loudly and unremittingly, while Gaheris was mostly silent. Agravain always had a leman, usually a servant girl; Gaheris tended to avoid the company of women.

It was the opinion of many in the court (though emphatically not Agravain) that Gaheris was something of a lackwit. For this reason, there had been some opposition to his being knighted. But Agravain held enough influence to bring his brother along with him.

Behavior at court, even for those who were not bound by the vows of chivalry, was expected to be kind and compassionate, or at the very least, polite. But as with any large group of people, there were some who did not hold themselves to this standard, especially those who had not yet gained full maturity. Whenever these found Gaheris unaccompanied by his brother, they seized the chance to ape his clumsy walk or engage him in conversation intended to confuse him.

Edda was a notable exception. She was not much more than a child when she came to court, accompanied by her brother, a new-made knight. She was not the comeliest of maidens. Both she and her brother were fair-haired and weedy, with slightly protruding teeth. Edda had the further disadvantage of eyes so pale they were almost colorless, and which also protruded. Although the two were of noble blood, their parents had no wealth. The family lived like the laborers who were, strictly speaking, in liege to them. I think this was part of what made Edda so sweet—she had not the arrogance I saw in maidens who benefitted from greater advantages. Edda took a liking to Gaheris, defending him against those who tormented him, though she herself was often plagued by unkind comments. Sometimes I would see them walking in the gardens at twilight, his head bent to her soft, modest voice.

I blame myself in part for what happened. I came across Edda alone in the dairy one day and took the moment to speak a word of praise for her kindness toward everyone at court, especially Gaheris. She blushed and ducked her head, but I could tell she was well pleased. It might have been that my approval led her to act unwisely, for that very night she ran into the ladies' quarters sobbing and holding together her bodice, which had been ripped to the waist. While Catlin tried to calm her, I shooed everyone out. Wide-eyed and whispering, they went, but it was obvious that the entire court would know about this in a matter of moments.

Catlin had given Edda a wrap to cover herself, and she was now sitting in a chair, trembling, while Catlin coaxed her to take sips of warmed wine. I sat on a stool in front of her and took both of her hands in mine. "Tell me," I said.

At first, she just shook her head, but I waited, and finally her whimpering lessened. "We were sitting by the fishpond," she began.

"You and Sir Gaheris?"

She nodded, her eyes welling with tears again. "This afternoon, Mar— someone said something cruel to me, and I was feeling sad. He told me I must not credit it. He said—" She choked back a sob. "He said I was bonny, and clever withal. He was so kind. So I—" She wrenched her hands from mine and covered her face. "Oh, it's my fault! It's all my fault!"

I urged her to another sip of wine while Catlin made soothing sounds. When she had regained some control, I asked quietly, "What happened then, Edda?"

"I put my hand on his cheek. I didn't mean anything. I just..." She took a shaky breath. "He took my hand and held it, and kissed my palm, and I...I allowed it. I even smiled. But when I tried to retrieve my hand, he held it tighter. And then... he leapt on me! He was kissing all over my face and my neck and then he tore my—" She shuddered and clutched her wrap more tightly around her. "I scratched him, and he fell back, and I ran. I'm so sorry, my lady. I never meant..."

I tilted her chin up and made her look at me. "This is not your fault, Edda. Go with Dame Catlin now and try to rest. We will deal with this on the morrow."

Edda heaved a deep sigh, wrung of tears for the moment. "All my life," she said quietly, "I've dreamed of coming to court. If you send me away...."

"No one is sending you away. It was Sir Gaheris who offended, and the King will deal with it. You are blameless. Trust me."

The whispering spread through the court so quickly that a band of men had already set out to seek Gaheris by the time I returned to the public rooms. Since he and Edda were often seen walking by the pond, the men went there first, but found no one. Agravain was not among the party.

Eventually they found both brothers in the chamber they shared. Agravain stood in the doorway, telling the men his brother had been there, ill, all evening. He was sleeping now, and Agravain would not let them in. "This is absurd. We will find the truth of the matter tomorrow."

At my request, Arthur held the hearing privately rather than in open court. Catlin and I were there with Edda, as was her brother, Devin. Sir Devin, I should say, but he was a most unlikely looking knight. Agravain accompanied Gaheris.

Arthur directed Edda to tell her story first, and she did so, her voice shaking. Agravain watched her closely throughout but did not interrupt. When the girl finished her narration, the king turned to Gaheris. Arthur and I had discussed the matter the night before, of course, and were both inclined to be lenient, providing the man be made to understand completely that such behavior must not occur again.

Gaheris stood as if in a stupor, with three blazing scratches on his cheek. Those scratches, combined with Edda's obvious distress, made the outcome foreseeable—except it wasn't. When Arthur turned to Gaheris, Agravain stepped in front of him and addressed the king.

"I am heartily sorry for this maiden's trouble, Your Highness, but she is mistaken if she thinks it was any of my brother's doing." Edda and Devin gasped aloud, and my mouth dropped open in shock and dismay. "Sir Gaheris was ailing last night and stayed in our room all evening. I was there, tending to him."

Arthur was furious, but only his eyes showed it. In a dispassionate voice, he asked, "And the scratches?"

Agravain shrugged. "He was fond of the girl, and after we heard she had been attacked, he ran out to find her, and was scratched while pushing through the trees by the pond." We all stared, but he stood his ground, gazing back at us with perfect calm.

"This is—" I started, but Arthur gestured me to silence. He left his throne and approached the brothers.

"Stand aside, Agravain." When he complied, Arthur stood in front of Gaheris and looked fully into his face. "Is this true, Gaheris?" No reply. "Were you with Agravain all evening? And the scratches are from tree branches?" I almost pitied the man. He blinked and fidgeted, his eyes flickering from Arthur to his brother. "Gaheris?"

"Yes, Your Highness. What my brother says is true."

The room was suffocating with outrage and disgust. Edda stood weeping quietly. Devin fumed, but a glance from the king kept him from any outburst. Agravain resumed his position in front of his brother. "So you see, Sir, if the girl was attacked, it was—"

"If? *If* she was attacked?" I could not keep the contempt from my voice.

He hesitated, as though reluctant to speak his mind. "Pardon me, but she is…not a maiden of great wealth or beauty. Sir Gaheris is a Prince of Orkney. She might have much to gain from this supposed dishonor."

Edda's brother leapt to confront Agravain. Standing close, he was a head shorter than Agravain and half as burly. White with fury, he took a deep breath, and backed off a step. When he had regained some control, he said, "You wish to protect your brother. I understand. But it must not be at the cost of my sister and her honor! As you are a sworn knight, sir, you must retract this slander."

Agravain closed the small distance between them. Staring into Devin's face, he said quietly, "Are you giving me the lie, sirrah?"

Devin stood straight as a sword and held his gaze, though he couldn't prevent his hands from trembling. "In your teeth."

A look of satisfaction spread over Agravain's face. "Then it shall be decided with trial by combat." The room went still. Agravain turned away and put a hand on his brother's shoulder.

"Wait!" I almost shouted. "It was I who brought this charge, not Lady Edda. You shall fight my champion, not hers."

Agravain turned to me and cocked an eyebrow. "Sir Lancelot is your wonted champion, my lady, and he is not here. Surely you do not expect Gawain to take arms against his brothers?"

"There are other—" I began.

"No. This is my battle," Devin said firmly, "I will be the one to champion my sister and defend her honor. It is my right, and mine alone."

"Devin, no. Please!" Edda said.

Devin went to her and took her hands in his. "We are good people, Edda, and the truth is on our side, is it not?" She nodded, her chin quivering. "This man is a liar and an oath-breaker. He is trying to protect his brother, but he does so by foreswearing himself and dishonoring a true maiden. And he made his brother party to his lies. What Sir Gaheris did was wrong, but this man is evil. God will not let evil triumph over good. That is the whole intention of trial by combat."

I went to them and looked searchingly at this young man. His eyes were clear with purpose. "Yes," I said, "but Sir Devin, mistakes can be made. Accidents can happen. This is not a perfect world."

"God is perfect, my lady, and I am perfect in my belief and my trust in Him. If you were Christian, you would understand."

Arthur shook his head resignedly. Agravain made the slightest of bows and swept out, trailed by his brother. Edda slumped to the floor.

There was much headshaking in court in the days to come. Gawain did his best to dissuade his brother, but Agravain held firm. As for Gaheris, he stayed out of sight as much as possible, and when he did appear, he had a haunted look. A few expressed some sympathy for him, but for the most part, he was roundly shunned.

The day set for combat arrived too soon. Arthur and I sat on the highest level of the arena, with Gaheris on his right and Edda on my left. Gaheris was no longer just a quiet man—now he was nearly mute. He bowed his head quickly to Arthur and me but could not bring himself to look at Edda. She was trembling violently. I gave her my hand and she clasped it tight.

Both men wore linen tunics with leather breastplates and were required to throw down their helmets and gauntlets. Each was armed with a short sword and a small round shield. The combatants swore an oath: as the sun began to sink lower in the sky, they would align themselves so the light glared in neither man's eyes.

The sun had no time to move from its position. With his advantage of height, weight, and experience, Agravain pressed his attack instantly. It was evident that he could have cut down Sir Devin at any moment, but he preferred to toy with him, like a cat with its prey. He would slash at Devin, pressing him into a retreat, then turn his back and walk away. By the time Devin collected himself to attack, Agravain was on him again.

Edda was muttering prayers and hiding her face against my shoulder, and in no time the crowd was shouting, "Yield! Yield!" The trial could end only when one combatant yielded or was slain, and no one wanted to see this young man die. As Agravain pressed harder and granted fewer respites, everyone was begging the boy to give over, including Arthur and me. Even Edda stopped hiding her face and shouted with the rest.

Finally, Gaheris jumped to his feet and joined his voice to the chorus pleading for surrender. Agravain glanced up at him, and then with a sneer he began to slash and thrust at Devin mercilessly. He was going for the kill. He swept Devin's feet from under him and reared back for the final blow.

The noise from the crowd was overwhelming, yet Edda's anguished voice cut through. "I lied!" she screamed. "Devin, yield! I lied!" It was difficult to say whether Devin heard or not, but Agravain did. He froze with his sword in the air, then lowered it to poke contemptuously at his fallen foe. Turning his back, he walked away with head high and a smile on his face. As we all turned to stare at the sobbing girl, Gaheris let out a roar and leapt from the stands to disappear into the crowd.

Edda ran down to her brother where he lay bleeding. For a moment, everyone held back, trying to take in what had just happened. Then several knights went to her aid. They lifted the young man up and carried him off.

In the morning, Edda and Devin had fled. Gaheris was gone as well.

As soon as I could find some time alone with Arthur, I told him, rather heatedly, that such a mockery of justice must never, ever happen again. He raised troubled eyes to me and said, "What could I do? I tried to convince the lad to approve another champion. And when she admitted to lying—"

"Edda said that to save her brother's life. And now they've lost everything and will henceforth live in shame."

"I know, love. It's an imperfect system, to be sure," he said mildly.

"It is one more way the world rewards the strong and punishes the weak, no matter what they merit," I replied hotly.

"The bishops say it is God who decides."

"I doubt Edalwurf would hold to that teaching were he put in the arena with Agravain. There must be a better way to decide right and wrong besides finding who is the bigger brute!" My dudgeon was overtaking me, and Arthur started pacing, as he always did when troubled.

"It's the way of the world. I became High King by defeating those who opposed me. From the rule of realms to ownership of a strayed lamb, the strong always win against the weak."

As he passed me in his next circuit of the room, I took his hand and drew him down to sit on the bench beside me. "Arthur..." I waited until I had his full attention. "Change it." He looked startled, and I hurried on. "You've already changed the world in many ways. You are revered as the king who united Britain against the barbarians, who created the Companions and established the code of chivalry. Wouldn't you also like to be known as the ruler who brought wisdom to the realm? The king who conquered injustice?"

I could tell he was moved by the idea, despite the gentle smile on his face. "And just how would I do that, love?"

"I have no idea."

Chapter 16

So began the work of finding a new system of justice. It became a focal point of Arthur's life for several years, and the legacy that resulted, his greatest source of pride.

The bishops, of course, were outraged: "You take justice out of the hands of God and put it into the hands of man!" Arthur demanded at first that trial by ordeal also be banned, an idea I heartily supported. The ordeal, by fire or by water, was primarily used in cases of sorcery and witchcraft, and those accused were predominantly women.

The Church was even more infuriated by this demand, as it concerned offenses in spiritual rather than worldly matters. The idea was abandoned—as Arthur expected it to be.

"You were using it as a bargaining pawn! What about the innocent women who are drowned or maimed?"

"I had to give the bishops something. There are far more deaths from combat than ordeal. Statecraft rests on compromise." I suppose he was right, but I stomped away nonetheless.

With combat no longer an option, how were judgements to be made? Obviously, Arthur could not hear even a tiny part of all the disputes that arose throughout the realm. "The Companions go out to right wrongs," I said. "What if you sent them out to judge these things?"

"The Companions are military. They right injustice by force of arms when there is no question who is guilty. But where there are conflicting stories, well,

131

the Companions are skilled fighters, but I couldn't swear that all of them are wise." I had to agree with that.

Nimue shared Merlin's trencher these days. One night as Merlin turned to speak to Arthur, I saw Nimue pour him more wine. But then she stared at it with a strange, almost grieving expression. Merlin turned back and saw her face, then picked up the cup and drained it dry. He put a hand over Nimue's, and smiled.

"I've grown weary, my dear. It's time for me to take my rest." He kissed her forehead and left the table.

Merlin began to sicken, but slowly, slowly. He was immensely old, a greybeard already when Arthur was born. But somehow, we had thought he would live forever. Nimue devoted herself to nursing him, but soon Arthur and I stood by his bed, where he lay unmoving, his eyes open. Nimue wiped his lips with a wet cloth. "He can't speak or move, but he could live a long time. Like a bug in amber, poor man." She broke down weeping, and I put an arm around her while Arthur, with tears standing in his own eyes, gently pressed Merlin's hand.

Edalwurf assumed Merlin's place at councils. He even attempted to claim the seat next to Arthur at table. However, Gawain and Bedwyr took him aside and spoke to him quietly but firmly. The seat remained empty, with Merlin's cup turned upside down at his place.

The search for a new means of justice continued. We tried having local lords decide matters in their own lands, but the lords consistently sided with whichever plaintiff was richer and more influential. And if the lord himself were a brigand, his people held little hope of justice.

"I miss Merlin," Arthur sighed one evening, rubbing his brow. "He always gave me the wisest advice."

"Such as 'Don't marry Guinevere?'" I asked laughingly.

He told me once how Merlin had fallen into a spell when Arthur suggested marrying me. It gave me pause, since obviously it had been a Seeing, but Arthur found it comical. "'A boy,' he said, something about a boy and water. I told him my tastes didn't run that way! Never could decipher what it had to do with you."

It had become something of a jest between us when we bickered, he saying Merlin had been right, and I telling him to go find his boy. I was trying to tease him out of his mood. Judging from the look he gave me, it didn't work. "Go sit with Merlin a while," I suggested. "That often eases your mind."

And in fact, it did. Ulfin was there, tending Merlin. Ulfin had been a young man, a Saxon slave, when Merlin bought him and freed him. Even now, when Merlin was gone in all but body, the ancient Ulfin remained devoted. When he saw the king, he excused himself and started to leave, but Arthur stopped him.

"I asked him to bide with me a while. We talked about the early years, when I was a youngling under Merlin's tutelage. Then I asked him how the Saxons settled conflicts among themselves. He said they use compurgation."

"Ah. And what might that be?" I smiled indulgently. Arthur was stirred up about something and was wearing out the floor with his pacing.

"Well, Saxons are great oath-takers. Each man in a dispute is required to find people who will provide supporting oaths and they're sworn to speak truthfully. A case such as Edda's would be decided not by the sword, but by how many believed her, and how many believed Agravain's version of events."

His enthusiasm was contagious. "The maiden would have been upheld!" I said, elated.

The system was far from perfect, but it worked. Assizes were held regularly throughout the land, and those who were poor or weak held, for the first time, a chance of seeing justice done—at least in the civil court.

I was on my way to confer with Cei about a coming feast when I heard the sound of weeping from a small side room. I stopped and looked in. Little Wynyth, one of my younger ladies, was the source. Standing over her and whispering harshly was Helena. "What is going on here?" I asked.

"Nothing that need concern you, madam," Helena replied, while Wynyth put her head in her hands and began sobbing with great heaves.

"As Queen, everything that happens in Britain concerns me, Dame Helena, and most especially things happening in my own household. You may leave us." She gave me a look of such scorn that I put a hand on her arm as she passed me. "Mend your arrogance, and mend it soon, or you will leave this court. I have had quite enough of your insolence."

Her startled look told me I had let her unsuitable behavior go on far too long. She stiffened, and seemed about to speak back to me, but then dipped her head in submission and murmured, "Yes, Your Highness."

I turned my attention to Wynyth and waited until the girl calmed herself enough to talk. "What is it, Wynyth? What troubles you so?"

"I'm so sorry, Your Highness," she said, with a fresh burst of sobbing.

"And what are you sorry for? Whatever it is, it can't be that bad."

"Oh, it is, milady, it is! But Dame Helena says I mustn't tell anyone, that everyone would hate me, and maybe... maybe kill me for my sin."

"I am your Queen, not Dame Helena. And I say you can talk to me. In fact, you must. What is this horrible sin you have committed?"

There was a long pause, and then she burst out, "I have... oh God forgive me! I have corrupted a priest."

"What?!" I took her hand and with the other, tilted her chin and made her look at me. "Tell me exactly what happened."

"I...I had impure thoughts, and my confessor made me describe them. He was very angry, milady, and said he would show me what comes of such evil imaginings."

"I see," I said, trying to keep my voice expressionless. "When was this?"

"Just after Ostara—I mean Easter. And now... my courses... Dame Helena says I must be sent away before anyone sees what I have done."

I closed my eyes a moment, struggling to keep my rage under control and trying to find the words to comfort this poor creature, hardly more than a child. "Listen to me, Wynyth. For the time being, you will be my handmaiden and stay with me in my rooms. Later, we'll think of what to do. For now, you will have to be strong. Nothing that happened is your fault."

Her face was pure misery. "Why are women so full of sin? I didn't want to be evil."

"Whatever the priests might say, women do not carry sin. Women carry the spark of life, and life is blessed. Your confessor is Father Thomas, is it not?"

She nodded, looking terrified. "Please don't punish him for my sin."

I could see I was not going to convince her otherwise, at least not now. "Go find Dame Catlin and tell her you will be serving me closely for a while. Now dry your eyes and be about your duties."

I set out in search of this rogue priest. Before I found him, however, I ran into Arthur, walking with Bedwyr. When he saw the fury in my face, he excused himself from Bedwyr and asked what was distressing me. I was so angry I could barely tell him what had passed. "I will bring him in front of my Council!" My voice shook. "He cannot abuse a maiden so and not face his crime!"

"Are you certain that is the best course?" Arthur asked. "Might it not be better to deal with it privily?"

"Better for whom?" His calm regarding the matter enraged me more.

"For the maiden. Why make her shame public?"

"It is not her shame! People should know what a viper he is!"

"Yes, but..."

Eventually Arthur drew from me a promise not to confront Father Thomas until I had calmed myself. I feared that in my present state, I might not be able to control myself as a Celtic queen must, so I agreed. And while I pondered, I considered Wynyth's father, a baron in a nearby holding. I had met the man, and could guess how he would deal with this dishonor. To be honest, if I thought it was the priest he would kill, I might have let the situation be known. But I feared for the girl.

Still, I wanted to confront the caitiff directly, and argued fiercely when Arthur discouraged me. "Let Bishop Edalwurf deal with it. The maiden is a Christian. For a pagan, a priestess, to interfere..."

"It is not interference when he abused one of my own household!"

After long dispute, Arthur convinced me it would be best to leave him to his superiors. Tension between the factions was strong, and the Christians might claim that condemnation from a priestess was due to my prejudice, not to his crime. "If his superior condemns him, there can be no doubt of his guilt."

That evening I saw Arthur conferring with Edalwurf. The bishop left before I reached them, and would not meet my eyes.

"You spoke to him about Father Thomas? There will be a trial?"

"No need for a trial, my love. He confessed it, and will do heavy penance."

"And?"

"And so he has been shriven." At my astonished look, he amended, "Forgiven."

"I know what it means! And what of the little maiden who is no longer a maiden? What of her child?"

"The Church will take her in, and the child will be raised by nuns."

"She has no choice in this matter?" His silence was assent. "So she will be mewed up in a cloister for the rest of her life while he roams free."

"He will do penance..."

"It seems no matter what you do, if you say a few prayers—and give a healthy gift to the Church, no doubt—the evil you've done is wiped clean. No wonder so many follow the White Christ!" I stormed off and could barely be civil to Arthur for some time.

I kept Wynyth with me until she began to swell. Then she was taken to the convent to bear her babe. She never returned, choosing to stay where she could be near her child. At least I was able, after facing down Edalwurf, to get Father Thomas sent from court. I feared, though, that the same thing might happen wherever he went.

Shortly after Lammas, Nimue came to my solar to bid me a reluctant farewell. It had been suggested to her several times that she return to Avalon; though Lord Merlin would never recover, she was loathe to go. She spent several hours of every day at his bedside, holding his insensate hand. Then, too, our girlhood friendship had deepened into a true and lasting bond. But now the Lady of the Lake had stopped suggesting and given her a command.

"Will you visit me?" she asked. "I miss your companionship already."

"It might be hard for me to get away." I smiled uneasily. "I hope you can return to us often."

Nimue sighed and took my hand. "Keep close watch on the King, my dear. I fear he is set against not only Morgan, but the Goddess as well, and I would have you both safe."

Startled, I asked, "Are we in some danger?"

"We all are. We entrusted the safety of our people to him when the Lady invested him with Excalibur. It rests upon him to protect the home religions, but he does not seem very active in our defense."

"He tries to remain open to all beliefs." The justification sounded weak to my own ears.

"But some beliefs threaten others."

I could not respond. Truth be told, I had grown increasingly troubled about the extent to which Arthur had begun supporting the Christian view in almost any conflict. Nimue let me sit with my thought for a moment, then rose and drew me into an embrace.

"Take good care," she said. "You are my sister in love, and my sister in worship. I have never known another."

We clung together for a long moment. I would miss her dearly.

It was a cold, windy day in October when I stormed out of the kitchen and headed for the stables, looking for my husband. He had told me he would be meeting with Bedwyr, Gawain and Palomides to discuss a new type of saddle. At the time, I'd been intrigued by this idea Palomides had brought from the east; I was always desirous to improve my riding skills. But such plans were swept from my mind entire when I heard Cei's news.

Arthur saw me approaching and smiled in welcome. But once he registered the look on my face, his smile disappeared. The three knights saw it as well and took their leave as quickly as hares.

"What's amiss, love? You shouldn't be out here. Look, you're trembling." It was true I had rushed from the kitchen without a wrap, and the horses were stamping and blowing clouds of white breath in the cold air. But my blood was afire, and I was shaking more from rage than from the chill.

"I had to hear it from Cei, Arthur? Tell me this is not true!"

He knew exactly what I was talking about. He put on an ingratiating face and tried to wrap an arm around me, but I shook him off. "Nothing has been decided yet," he said. "I was going to talk with you about it."

"Were you? Or were you just going to tell me about it once it was done? And what is to discuss? The Samhain feast will take place on Samhain, as it always has."

"Well…" Arthur started to pace, as was his wont when presented with a difficulty. "You can have all the usual rites then, certainly, but the next day is All Hallows, and the Christians—"

"Intend to turn yet another Druid sabbat to their own purposes!"

It was insidious. Every great religion celebrates the turning of the year from light to dark and then to light again. Yet the Christians claim that only the birth of their god should be celebrated in late December, and only his rebirth in the spring. When they found people were reluctant to give up worship of the Goddess, they elevated their miraculous "virgin mother" as an object of devotion—though that is about the only instance when they showed any good will toward women. All cultures also set aside a day to honor their dead; the Christians used to do it in May. But one of their Popes decided to move All Saints' Day to November 1, in direct conflict with our Samhain rites on October 31.

"Why must they always encroach?" I demanded, while Arthur paced to the end of the stable and back. "All Hallows is a holy day of little import to them, but for us, Samhain and Beltane are the two poles of the year."

"No one is denying you the rituals," Arthur said. "They just want to have one feast rather than two. Both holidays honor the dead, so why not—"

"It's not the same!" I shouted. Arthur stopped pacing and glared at me. I lowered my voice and tried to speak reasonably. "Yes, we honor our dead. But there is much more to it than that. The needfire—"

"You can have your needfire."

"But the celebration, Arthur, you cannot just proclaim it moved to the morrow. Once the fires are relit, we rejoice."

"You can rejoice as well the next day." His face was closing to me. "And it isn't only about the needfire. Guisers in masks, setting out treats to appease evil spirits... such rustic superstition seems ill suited to a civilized court."

I gasped. "Civilized? Worship of the Great Goddess is not civilized? Arthur, you swore to me before we married—"

"Much has changed since then."

"Indeed it has. You have broken your vow not to favor one religion over another. As Christians gain worldly power, you bend to them. You've built a chapel, established Edalwurf as advisor, given free rein to their priests.... You've even banished the Lady of the Lake!"

"That has nothing to do with religion," Arthur said stiffly. "She is evil."

"Do not set yourself against the Goddess, Arthur. The people—"

"The people can do as they please! I won't keep anyone from their beliefs, Guinevere, and that is what I promised. But for me and my court, there will be no more official sanction for pagan rituals."

"And for me?" I was breathless with rage and disbelief.

"Do as you will, my lady. I won't stand in your way. But never bring Morgan le Fey into my sight. We will not speak of this again." He strode off, kicking aside a piece of tack that had been carelessly dropped in the straw.

I went to Etain, leaned my head against her withers and closed my eyes. A few tears leaked onto her glossy coat. I angrily brushed them away, then mounted her bareback and took off for a wild ride through the water meadows, earning myself Catlin's indignation and a fortnight of coughing and rheum.

The Samhain rites were solemn that year. I stood atop the hill where the needfire waited and looked back at the castle, glimmering brightly with candles, rushlights, torches and hearthfires. Then I gazed at the countryside around. One by one, the fires went out in cottages and crofts, and lines of tiny sparks, like the glittering insects of deep summer, began to stream out of the villages and up toward the crest of the hill. My people, carrying candles in carved-out turnips to light their way, began to gather.

I spoke to them of the Great Mother's promise that the light would come again. We mourned our dead, and dropped bits of food for their spirits, though we knew full well we fed only the woodland animals. I sacrificed a calf, in hopes that all the other beasts driven in from the fields for the winter might survive. Its blood was collected in shallow bowls, and four little maidens carried them into the fields in the four directions, scattering drops of blood on the fallow land as a blessing for next year's crops. Finally, the people lit brands from the great needfire and wended down the hill to their homes, where they would relight the fires that would warm them all winter.

A joyous feast at the castle should have followed, but instead, each family would have to hold its own humble celebration with whatever meager stores they had. When I returned to the great hall, an uncommon number of people were still gathered. I think many were pagans who wanted to see their priestess but did not attend the rites for fear of seeming backward. The rest, of course, were Christians. Helena stared at me coldly, her eyes traveling from the hem of my gown, draggled with ashes, to the crescent tattoo traced in blood. She shuddered and turned away. As she left the hall, a great many followed. Those who stayed looked as defeated as I felt.

Chapter 17

Gradually the Samhain controversy died down, and Arthur was prudent enough not to interfere with Yule celebrations. The Christians held their Christ Mass in the chapel, Mithraites celebrated the birth of their sun god secretly, underground, and the rest of us cheered at the Battle of the Oak King and the Holly King. Lancelot was still sorely missed, though Gawain played his part with enthusiasm. His opponent that year was Lancelot's cousin Bors, a very able knight, but far too shy and gentle to fully enjoy his boisterous role.

Yule was also when knights errant returned to court and squires hoping to become knights came to try their capabilities. By sheer good fortune, Catlin and I were witness to one of the most astonishing moments of the season.

Gawain and Bedwyr were sparring in the snow. No matter the weather, Gawain skirmished with someone every day to keep his skills sharp. He even made use of a heavily weighted weapon, so his broadsword would feel light when taken up in battle. He and Bedwyr were not equally matched, but with the extra weight, they were close enough to make the exercise worthwhile. As Catlin and I were passing on our way to visit a new mother in the village, a stripling squire, armed and with a blank shield, rode up and stopped some distance away to watch the match. He lowered his vizard to hide his well-favored face before he approached more nearly.

"Sir Bedwyr!" he called, leaning casually on his pommel. "Don't you need a more worthy opponent than that clumsy red-headed lout?"

The two knights stopped and gaped at him, as did Catlin and I. Gawain flushed with anger, but it was Bedwyr who spoke first.

"If you've come to Arthur's court to be a knight, squire, you'd best work on your courtesy."

"Aye, youngling," said Gawain. "Run back home to your mother and take more lessons at her knee."

"You come too," the squire rejoined. "Maybe she could teach you to handle a sword."

Gawain started toward him, and the squire lightly dropped off his horse and drew. Bedwyr backed away as they began to spar. Gawain was powerful, but the squire was incredibly quick and graceful, and gained an advantage right from the start. We were all astonished to see Gawain trying in vain to keep up with him, looking like a bear beset by a terrier.

In moments, Gawain was winded. The squire ducked behind him and bashed him in the back of the head with the flat of his sword. Gawain was wearing only a light helmet of boiled leather, and the blow knocked him sprawling into the snow and mud. His sword flew out of his grip. Instantly, the squire put a foot on Gawain's neck. Alarmed, Bedwyr started toward them.

"Lost your sword, Sir Oaf? My brother taught me to hold my sword at all costs. Here, take the one he made me. Practice with it as much as I did, and maybe you'll learn to fight."

He reached under his cloak and pulled out a wooden sword, which he threw down in front of Gawain. Gawain stared a moment, then with a roar, caught the squire's ankle and brought him down. The two rolled about in the dirty snow.

"You arrogant pup!" Gawain shouted. "About time you got here! Been snoozing by the fire with that fleabag of yours?"

When they sat up, to our amazement, Gawain was laughing. The squire, lifting his vizard, was laughing too. "Poor old hound's been dead for years," he said. "Probably still smells better than you did when we shared a pallet."

Gawain beckoned to his confused friend. "Bedwyr! This is Gareth, the runt I've told you about. We'll have to teach him some manners. Mother was always too easy on him. The baby, you know."

With his skills and his courtesy (despite his first impression, he was the soul of chivalry), Gareth soon became a favorite of all the court. Well, almost all.

The Orkney clan comprised four boys, all true-born sons of Arthur's half-sister Morgause and King Lot of Lothian. One might expect those boys to have grown to be enemies of Arthur—their mother, like her sister Morgan, had been banished by Uther Pendragon, and Lot was one of the challengers most ferociously opposed to Arthur's claim of High King. But Morgause was a plump, pleasure-loving woman who was perfectly content as Queen of a wild northern land and mother of a pack of wild boys. And Lot, after several pitched battles with Arthur, recognized his legitimacy and became one of his strongest allies.

Gawain was eldest of the clan. He was devoted to Arthur, and proud that Arthur claimed him as kin. The twins, Agravain and Gaheris, had come to court as soon as they were of age.

Gaheris had returned from his self-imposed exile, announcing that he had been washed of his sins when he was baptized. During his flight from court, he had taken refuge at a monastery, intending to shelter there only for the duration of a storm. But he converted almost immediately and remained sequestered for months. He even considered becoming a monk himself, but finally decided he could better serve by being in the world. The stammering young man Gaheris had been replaced by an outspoken advocate for Christianity.

Gawain, like most knights, was a Mithraite, though not especially devout (except on the eve of battle). As for Agravain, he claimed no religion whatever, but continued to defend Gaheris against any ill word.

Agravain's affection for his twin did not extend to his other brothers. He and Gawain mostly avoided each other. But Agravain had little use for Gareth, calling him ugly names and sneering at anything Gareth did or said. Gareth paid no heed. I suppose he was used to such treatment from a young age and had learned to ignore his malevolent brother.

Gareth idolized Gawain but believed Lancelot a god who walked the earth. From the time he was in leading strings, his primary playthings were a wooden figure of the great knight and the toy sword Gawain made for him. He was aware, of course, that Lancelot was no longer at court, but held hope he would return. Even Gawain, close as their bond was, took second place to Gareth's childhood hero.

Gareth was very well-liked by the ladies, and he clearly enjoyed their company. But he and I formed a special friendship. He was wittier and more exuberant than most of the men at court. I looked forward to chatting with him, and to dancing with him at various feasts and celebrations—he was so very graceful and self-assured, yet without the least hint of vanity. Catlin adored him, and he became like an elder brother to little Grance, no longer a baby but now a lively, noisy boy.

I did wish, though, that Gareth might talk less of Lancelot, who had not visited Winchester since he left with Elaine. That was all to the good, of course. But often I ached to see his face or hear his voice, melodious as any bard's. He and Gawain still shared a close friendship and exchanged messages regularly. Whenever official missives arrived, they always contained greetings to his Queen. But these were read out in open court, and therefore completely impersonal. Mercifully, the effusive missives from Elaine had slowed, then stopped.

As the winter softened, Arthur and I were at peace with one another. The Yule celebrations successfully avoided conflict, as did Imbolc, which the Christians do not recognize. He continued to resist the occasional demands to put me aside, and I had become practiced at dealing with my monthly grief. We enjoyed each other's company, Arthur and I, laughing often, discussing affairs of state and spending more and more nights together. We seldom spoke about religion, though, and there were still times when he seemed beset by some private anguish he would not share with me.

Often, during those times, he could not sleep. One night in early March, I was drowsing at his side while he lay wakeful. "Guinevere? Are you awake?" I drew myself up against him and murmured a sleepy assent. "I... I will not be celebrating Nouroz this year."

"Why is that, Arthur? Most of your Companions still follow Mithras. As their leader—"

"I intend to take communion at the Easter mass."

I pushed away from him and sat up. "What?!"

"I have decided to become Christian."

I tried to take a breath, but it was denied me. "You cannot. You promised..."

143

"I am breaking no vows. This is not a betrayal of our agreement, Guinevere. I promised I would never interfere with the old worship, nor establish a state religion, and I am not. This decision is for myself, not for the realm."

My mind cast about frantically as I again gasped for breath. "What would Merlin say? Would he advise—"

As I watched, his face transformed from resoluteness to the deepest sorrow. "Merlin would understand full well what I am doing."

"But Arthur, the Christians say there can be only one god—theirs. They want all power in their own hands. If you join them, they'll be tenfold stronger! What do they offer in return?"

"Forgiveness."

He spoke with such profound sadness that despite my own shock and turmoil, I embraced him in sympathy. "What do you need forgiveness for? You're a good man, a good king. What have the priests said to you? They see sin everywhere!"

"I see it, love. I look into my soul and I see such black sin that the old gods would cast me down forever." I was about to protest, but he cut off any further argument. "The Christ died so my sins could be forgiven. I will celebrate His resurrection."

The High Mass held at Easter took place in the great hall, as there were far too many celebrants to fit into the chapel. Word of Arthur's intention spread, and people came long distances to bear witness. The hall was replete with jeweled communion cups, gold censers and bishops in rich vestments. Arthur was first to approach the altar and kneel for communion. I can only imagine the rapture that must have flooded the people watching.

I was not there. I sat by Merlin's bed, holding his warm but unresponsive hand. *You foretold this, Lord Merlin. But how is it my fault? We never sinned. I sent him away, and still this disaster happened. Why? What could I have done?* The Merlin lay unblinking, mute.

The home religion celebrates three spring sabbats, one in early February, one in late March, and one on the first of May. Though Imbolc celebrates the first stirrings of the seeds underground, aboveground is still locked in deep winter. By Ostara, the longer days and milder weather cheers us, but the festival isn't widely observed among pagans, especially since the Christians renamed it Easter and made it perhaps their most important holiday.

Beltane, though! By May Day, spring is in full bloom. Trees flaunt a lacework of new green leaves, wildflowers abound in the woodland, lambs gambol and chicks peep stridently. The world is awash in fertility and the joy of new life. Humankind responds with its own erotic joy and begs blessings on the fertility of women, beasts and crops. In daylight, youths and maidens weave their dance about the Maypole, and at night, as the Beltane fires roar, many a lad and lass come together in the fields and woods, and the Goddess smiles on them.

Beltane and Samhain, the two primary sabbats, evoke the most disapproval and dismay among Christians. Arthur had other matters on his mind—the Sea Wolves were gathering again—so while he continued to go to Mass, he made no other public pronouncements. Nor did we speak of it in private. Now that the King was one of them, however, Christians in the court felt free to condemn and complain.

My women and I were brushing down the winter's furs and woolens and airing them in the courtyard on a sunny, breezy April day, before strewing them with herbs and storing them in chests until they were needed again. It was easy enough work, but lately I had been feeling achy and lethargic. I wanted nothing more than to go someplace quiet and rest, so I was somewhat irritable. The maidens were chattering and giggling about the holiday, though it was still weeks away. Helena had been holding her tongue recently, but she considered herself in charge of the maidens' morals, and so Beltane was a topic on which she held strong opinions.

"Free to worship is one thing, but Beltane is just an excuse for lechery and licentiousness. And each year a new crop of bastards!"

"A Beltane child is not a bastard," I snapped. "Such infants carry the blessing of the Goddess. We're meant to procreate, and to take joy in it. It's only your religion that makes barrenness a virtue."

"Then you must be virtuous indeed," Helena muttered, just loud enough for me to hear.

Everything in me stopped: heartbeat, breath, everything. I grew still as a standing stone. My women looked at me anxiously, thinking Helena had gone too far at last. I searched out Catlin with my eyes and she came to me, took my arm and led me to a quiet corner. "The moon!" I whispered, barely more than a gasp. "The moon was a crone last night. My courses come with the maiden."

I could feel myself turn inward as my hands slowly came to rest on my belly. Catlin embraced me fiercely as the ladies began to crowd around. "Oh, bless you, lamb. At last!"

I am suddenly shy, my eyes cast down. The very pebbles look like pearls in the dawning of this delicate possibility. This babe is no more than a whisper in the womb, but already I feel replete. The spring breeze sings a love song, and the song of my body rings out, a triumphant hymn.

Implausible, impossible: the ultimate hope achieved, pristine as a flowering pear. I feel roots delving deep in the dirt. New leaves throw trembling sunspots on the ground, and I tremble with them. Oh, glorious! I am the sun, oblivious to all but my own shining.

There is no past, only the holy and radiant Now. Such splendid heartache, not from sorrow, but overmuch of joy.

Part Three

Chapter 18

The celebration was beyond all imagining. The people of the court threw down whatever was in their hands to dance and shout for joy, and even the workers in the field stopped their toil and gathered around the castle, singing and cheering. It was all so sudden and tumultuous that I could barely get a purchase on my own emotions. And when Arthur took my arm and led me out for the people to see me, I was nearly overwhelmed by the force of their elation and good wishes. Again, I had reason to thank the Goddess for Catlin, who stepped in and whisked me away to my chamber. "Rest," she said. "Let the others rejoice for you while you get about the business at hand."

I didn't think I could rest with all the excitement, but next I knew it was dark. I was for the moment unattended, so I slipped out to find Arthur. I assumed he would be in the great hall celebrating with the others, but on my way there, I passed the chapel. He was at the altar, on his knees, giving thanks and weeping. I did not disturb him in his devotions.

The weeks that followed were the happiest of my life. In public, I was smiled upon everywhere I went, and in private, Arthur and I were blissful. Never before was he so completely at ease in the world. Despite occasionally fussing about my health and that of the child, my husband wore an air of utter satisfaction.

Folk say a breeding woman is prone to haphazard feelings, leaping from joy to rage to sorrow with no reason. That wasn't the case with me, at least not in those early weeks. For the most part, I felt serene as the moon. But one night a dream woke me in terror, and it took days before I could put it to the back of my mind.

Arthur and I were riding through a fog, with Lord Merlin and Morgan le Fey close behind. Swirling shapes in the mist resolved into huge white wolves, half the size of our horses. Arthur reached for his sword, but in the twisted way of dream, he held only my small dagger, and I was carrying Excalibur in a massive scabbard hung from my pommel. I tried to throw it to him, but it was too heavy, surely the weight of twenty broadswords. I looked back at Merlin and Morgan, beseeching them to help, but they both shook their heads and held out their hands, palms toward me, as if warning me not to give it to him.

I pulled the sword from its sheath. Without the scabbard, which was worked with Druid charms and symbols, it was much lighter, and I tossed it to Arthur. He caught it and held it up. But then, so slowly I could see each crack and fissure forming, Excalibur shattered in his hand. Until that moment, there had been no sound. But now Merlin and Morgan wailed like a ravening wind, and the howling wolves were upon us. It was only Arthur they attacked. Morgan grabbed my reins and led me away. I tried to look back but was unable to turn my head. The ferocious noises told me clearly enough what was happening. I tried to scream but couldn't.

Except apparently, I did, loud enough to wake the entire bastion. When I battled my way to consciousness, Arthur was holding me firmly with one arm and smoothing my hair back with the other hand. "Shh, shh, it was just a dream," he said, kissing my forehead and murmuring soothing sounds. Sobbing, I choked out what I had seen, and he gave me a gentle smile. "It's the Saxons, love, the Sea Wolves. You're just worried about the coming battle. Don't be. We're in great strength, and we'll send them back to their own lands in no time." He poured me a cup of wine, and I began to settle. He pulled me close as we lay back down. "Nevertheless," he chuckled, "I'll be sure to have Excalibur out of the scabbard and in my hand before we close with them."

The day came too soon when Arthur had to lead his troops to the Saxon shore. He even considered sending Gawain to lead them in his place, which astonished me. But there were still months before the birth, and after such a long peace, this battle was crucial. He must be present.

He and his men were in the courtyard, armed and mounted. Bedwyr stood holding his reins. Arthur leaned from his saddle to kiss me. "I'll clear this nest of Saxons and be back before your belly blossoms. Bedwyr will be with you, and Gareth, and a contingent of knights and well-proven squires. And I've sent word to Lancelot to be ready to ride if he's needed. God bless you, love."

"May all the gods ride with you," I replied. Only the discipline of a Celtic queen kept the tears from my eyes as he rode off.

Then Beltane was upon us. We pagans prepared to go Maying. We were all dressed in green, decked in ribbons and flowers, ready to ride to the greenwood before the dew was off the grasses.

"All we have left here are boys and old men," Lynette complained, fixing a yellow ribbon in her hair. "They'll never get it up! We should send for Lancelot!"

Tart-tongued Dilys replied. "He's Christian and he's married. He won't do you any good. But that Gareth looks like he could raise a maypole all by himself!" While the maidens gleefully chattered and bustled, the Christian ladies sat with their embroidery, mouths pursed tight.

There was a little skirmish in the courtyard, as Bedwyr tried to talk me out of riding Etain. "Please, ride in the litter."

"I'm not an invalid. Your wife rode till the horse couldn't carry her."

"My children bear my happiness, lady, but yours bear the kingdom."

Catlin, of course, had to join in. "You'd never forgive yourself if…"

With a sigh, I dismounted, and let Catlin hand me into the litter.

It was a perfect morning. Bedwyr rode ahead, and Gareth claimed it as an honor to be one of my litter bearers. The rest of the party, mostly maidens and young squires, was on foot, singing and weaving wildflower garlands as they walked.

Suddenly, silently, a band of men dressed in black stepped out of the forest and confronted us. There was a moment of utter stillness. Then one threw a dagger with deadly swiftness and Bedwyr fell from his saddle.

Chaos followed: ladies screaming, the men and boys trying to hold off the attackers, Catlin trying to position herself in front of me. Gareth, especially, fought like a madman, but we were completely outnumbered.

Their leader appeared, mounted. As his men dragged me kicking and flailing from the litter, he reached down and hauled me up over his saddle, face down, nearly tearing my arm from my shoulder. Catlin clung to me, screaming, but he kicked her in the side of the head, and she fell. As he galloped off with me, I could see Gareth fighting his way to Bedwyr's horse. Then the brigand pressed my face to the horse's lathered withers, and I could see no more.

I thrashed about with all the strength of panic, trying to fling myself from the horse, no matter what injuries I might sustain. It was hopeless. My captor threw his leg over mine, pinning them at my knees, and all my efforts were effectively curtailed. After a short distance, he slowed and entered a clearing where his henchmen awaited. One of them approached and yanked me down from the horse, headfirst. I hit the ground hard and lay there stunned for a moment, and he took advantage of that to wrench my arms behind me and bind them tightly. My feet were bound as well, and then I was hauled upright.

The leader dismounted and approached me now. He grabbed a fistful of hair and forced my head back. "You might as well make it easy on yourself. We have a long way to—" I twisted my head to the side, ripping out hair as I did so, and bit his forearm as hard as I could. I tasted blood. He shouted and drew back his fist.

I woke slowly, and in pain, to find myself in the softest of feather beds. "Ah!" a stout little woman exclaimed as I turned my head to look about me. "You're awake. Slowly, my lady, don't sit up too quick-like. You took a nasty lump on your pate, and a bruise on your cheek." She tried to hold a cold cloth to my bruise, but I twisted away, staring at her. "It won't show much by firelight," she assured me with a smile.

Looking over her shoulder, I saw that the room where I had awakened was richly furnished, and a gown was laid out on a chair nearby. "Where am I? Who are you?"

"I'm Clare, my lady. Come, let's get you washed and dress your hair."

I was still dazed and could comprehend nothing. "I... I don't understand."

She held a cup to my lips. "Drink this. It'll help clear your head. Oh, my lady, I'm so glad you've come!" She dropped a courtesy to me as I sat up, bewildered.

"But...come where? I was attacked—"

"I'm sorry about that, Your Grace. You were not to be harmed in any way. Believe me, the brute was severely dealt with when the King heard."

"But the King is in—"

"He's in his throne room, waiting for you! Come now, hurry."

My head was beginning to clear somewhat, and I could see I was going to get nothing of sense from this woman. Wherever I was, and whatever I was about to face, I would do it better without this torn, stained gown, bloodied lip and rat's nest of hair. I had a feeling I was going to need every ounce of regal dignity I could summon.

I permitted her ablutions and cooperated as she dressed me in one of the richest gowns I had ever seen. The woman was humming merrily as she served me. She looked askance at my tangled hair, a look that reminded me so of Catlin that I almost burst into tears. Where was she? Was she all right? And Bedwyr, and Gareth, and the rest?

"Not much we can do now but cover that, my lady." She efficiently tucked the mess under a gold net. "We'll get it washed and dressed later. No time now. Here's your honor guard."

She opened the door to admit four ceremoniously dressed men. *More guard than honor*, I thought. I downed the last of the spirits, shook my head to clear it, then drew myself up as well as my aching body would allow and took my place to be escorted. Clare, whoever she might be, clasped her hands in delight and smiled on me with a radiant happiness. As we walked through stone corridors, I tried mightily to find something familiar, something to tell me where I was and what might be happening to me. A smell, a sound, something. There was nothing. I was led into a well-appointed throne room crowded with courtiers. There on the throne sat a man about my age, quite handsome and very regal. For a moment I didn't recognize him, but then he stood, turned to greet me and smiled, and my heart went to dust.

"Welcome to Gwynedd, cousin," Maelgwyn said. He had changed much, at least in a bodily sense, from the obsequious boy who once bid for my hand. He now had an impressive bearing, but that smile was as repellant as ever. I nodded coolly in response to his greeting, noting he addressed me not as High Queen, or even Queen of Cameliard, where he was my regent, but simply as his kinswoman.

There had been a great stir among his people as I entered. Now he stepped down from the dais, took my arm and turned me to present me to the crowd. They erupted in cheers, as if this were some sort of state visit instead of an abduction. I gazed out at them, trying to hide my puzzlement. Quietly, I said, "Why am I here, Maelgwyn?"

He replied as quietly, while smiling and gesturing to the crowd. "To save my country. And yours. And our Celtic heritage."

"Save them from what?"

"Arthur." And with that, he swept me away into a private chamber behind the throne.

"The High King is on the Saxon Shore, fighting for Gwynedd and all the client states," I said hotly. "Why aren't you with him?"

"Your High King," he sneered, "went into battle with the dragon on the front of his shield and the Christian goddess Mary on the back. How long do you think it'll be before the Pendragon is gone forever?"

"True, Arthur has become Christian. But he doesn't force it on anyone. What is your complaint?"

Maelgwyn's entire bearing changed, and with a feral snarl, he leaned over me. I hadn't been truly afraid until that moment. "He held Excalibur, the Druid sword of power, as a cross to bless his troops!"

"Excalibur?! No!" I let my shock show, which was a mistake, and quickly tried to bring the conversation back to a rational tone. "That was wrong. But what has it to do with my being abducted and abused?"

His expression gentled, and he reached out as if to touch the dark swelling on my face. I shied away, and he pulled his hand back. He was irritated for a moment, but then regained his polite demeanor. "I'm sorry you were treated so poorly. I never meant to cause you any harm. In fact, I brought you here to invite you to put the Christian traitor aside and marry me."

"What?!"

"He betrayed our people. We entrusted him with the sword of power, but now that the bishops have him in their grasp, they won't rest until the sacred oak groves are burned, our nemetons utterly destroyed."

"No. He'd never do such a thing. He promised me. Arthur is—"

"Arthur is not a Celt. He descends from Ambrosius Aurelianus, and he'll give us back to Rome. He already owes his loyalty to the Pope, not to us. You see how the people welcome you, Guinevere. If we marry, Gwynedd and Cameliard would form a base from which the Celtic nation could rise once more and rule!"

"You're mad," I said flatly, all caution forgotten. "The Celts have no reason to rebel against Arthur."

"Reason enough, and Celts will always follow their Queen."

"A Celtic Queen does not betray her lord."

"Oh, come. You don't love Arthur. You married him so he'd protect your people. Now your people need protection from him. I know you, Guinevere. You'll do what's right."

I could see reason was not going to help me here, so I appealed to his kinship. "My dear cousin, please. Let me return to Winchester. I'll see that there is no retribution."

"No. You'll stay here."

"You would hold me against my will?"

"Whoever holds the Queen holds the land. It has always been so. I'd hoped you might put aside the Roman and come willingly. But one way or another..." He stepped to the door and opened it. The guards entered, closed ranks around me, and led me away.

Chapter 19

Clare was with me always, as was the guard outside my door. She was a chatty little woman, so as she carefully untangled my hair, I tried to learn whether the people of Gwynedd were indeed in favor of Maelgwyn's appalling plan. They were. Among the Cymri, the old religion still held almost uncontested sway with the people, and they were shocked and angered when Arthur joined the Christians. We had heard of some mutterings, even a few small, easily put down rebellions from the predominantly pagan realms, but hadn't grasped the depth of their resentment.

And why had I not heard about his inexcusable insult to Excalibur when they heard it here, so much further from the battlefield? Could Maelgwyn have made it up to rouse the people against their King? But then I remembered the dream I'd had: it had clearly been a Seeing. What could he have been thinking? Even if the greater part of his army were now Christians, using part of the Sacred Regalia in this way was deeply, deeply wrong. It's as if he had found the Christians' Grail, and then used it to hold wine at an orgy.

"No one blames you, Your Highness," Clare said. "Everybody knows you would never forsake the Goddess. Your people love you! I'll never forgive the way that brute treated you, and now you're here, believe me, no one will harm you again. I won't allow it." She sounded so much like Catlin in her indignation that my heart ached.

After that first presentation, Maelgwyn kept me apart from his people. He took his meals with me, and behaved in a gentlemanly fashion, for the most part. I think he was trying to convince me that life with him as a husband and consort would be pleasant enough. But each time I saw him, he asked whether I had made my decision. There was no decision to make, of course, but I pretended to be considering; if I could make him wait long enough, I might find a way to escape. I even sat to a game of chess with him on one occasion, ignoring his heavy-handed sallies about capturing the queen. The foods he provided were rich and plentiful, and I was supplied with a sumptuous wardrobe and any comforts I could want. But I was never allowed to leave that room, and the guards were always present outside the door.

It was late in the afternoon of the fifth day. Maelgwyn hadn't joined me for the midday meal, so I expected him at supper. He came early. I had set up the chessboard, hoping to while away more time, but as soon as he burst through the door, I knew this would be a different kind of visit. He had been drinking. His eyes were red as a maddened bull, and his clothes and hair were disheveled. He gestured for Clare to go, but the terrified woman shook her head and moved to stand between us. Maelgwyn took her by the arm and threw her bodily out of the room, then locked the door behind her.

I tried to present a calm and pleasant bearing, but before I could say anything, he kicked over the table that held the chessboard and advanced toward me, backing me toward a wall. "What is—?" I began. He smashed me with a backhand that sent a flash of red over my vision. Grabbing my shoulders, he pushed me so hard my head bounced off the stone wall.

"We are done talking, madam."

I tried to run past him, and he grabbed my arm. The sleeve came off in his hand, but he grabbed my hair and hauled me back. I groped for the little dagger I always wore, but of course they had taken it from me. He spun me around, and this time, rather than a slap, it was his fist that met my jaw. I fell to the floor. I tried to crawl away, but he grabbed my foot and wrenched it so hard that I screamed and was forced to turn over. Then he was on me.

"No! I'm with child!"

"A traitor's brat," he said as he clawed at my skirts. "It will yield to one of my own."

I cannot bear to remember what he did, except that he did it for a long time. Twice he left me on the floor and went to pour himself some wine, which he drank while staring down at me coldly. By the second time, I thought that if

I did not die of this, I would die of thirst. But I would not ask to drink. Then he returned, and soon after that, there is nothing there for me to remember, even if I would.

Chapter 20

Oblivion. And then I opened my eyes one night and discovered that I could see. Until then, it had not mattered whether there was hearthfire, candle or brazier, whether it was day or night, whether my eyes were open or closed. I lived in an eternal blackness. Now, by the dim gray light of early dawn, I saw I was in a small room with stone walls, and there was a figure slumped in a chair beside my pallet. As my sight slowly cleared, I began to think it was Lancelot. Surely, I thought, I am dreaming still.

In my daze, I spoke his name, and his eyes opened. When they met mine, he fell to his knees and embraced me, sobbing. "I'll never leave you again," he choked out. "Never. Never leave you."

Catlin—oh, it was Catlin!—came to stand behind him, laying a comforting hand on his shoulder. She was in tears as well, but smiling, smiling. I tried to keep my eyes open, to give them a word of solace. I could not. I succumbed again to darkness, with the sound of his voice in my ears.

It was several days before I could speak more than a word or two. Mostly, I wept. Little by little, as memory returned, the weight of my grievous loss bore down on me. It seemed I would never be able to rise from this well of despair. Nothing Lancelot nor Catlin said could hold any consolation. But even as I mourned the loss of the small life I had held within me, the life of my own body began to reassert itself.

When at last I was able to order my mind a bit, I tried to piece the past back together. "How did I get here?" I asked Lancelot. "Did you…?"

"Gareth spurred straight to Joyous Garde to fetch me. Had I been at Winchester, I might have… but I was too late."

"Maelgwyn?"

"Dead."

I would want to know, eventually, all that happened. But I had not the strength to think of it now. "How long have I been here?"

He shifted his eyes and looked out of the casement a moment. When he turned back to me, he said gently, "Litha was last week."

I was slow to comprehend. "It's… past midsummer? But it was May Day… Great Goddess!" I tried to rise. Catlin pressed me gently but firmly back down. "Where's Arthur?" I asked. "He should be home by now."

"Eosa brought the Horse Tribes in to aid the Saxons. They probably won't finish much before winter."

"Does he know? About…?"

"He knows," Lancelot replied, with a grim expression. "He sent two missives. One was a private message of thanks, and concern for you. The other was an official, public reprimand for killing Maelgwyn before he could be brought to trial."

"No!"

"The King is determined to hold the rule of law over combat. And in truth, I slew the man dishonorably. Never in my life have I violated the code of chivalry, but when I saw…" His countenance was haggard, no doubt from the long weeks of watching. Now, as his gaze turned inward into memory, his expression became a terrifying mix of rage and despair. He stood abruptly. "If you will excuse me, my lady." And he was gone.

Catlin came to sit on my bed. She smoothed back my hair, then cradled my face in her hands. "He has tended you day and night. All this time. The court, as you can imagine, has had much to say. I'll tell you more later, but now you should rest. Just know," she said earnestly, "that you could have no finer Champion." She kissed my forehead and left me to the sleep that was overtaking me.

The story came out slowly, over several days, and very little from Lancelot himself. "Well, he has earned himself a new name," Catlin told me. "They call him the Knight of the Cart. Maelgwyn's men had been set along his path, since they knew he'd come for you. They should have known they couldn't stop him, but in the skirmish, they killed his noble horse Martel. He slew them all, but their horses had run off. Rather than lose time pursuing them, he stopped a rude fellow taking his poultry to market and relieved him of his horse and cart. So the greatest knight in all the realm rode up to the castle gates to rescue you, knee deep in feathers and chicken shit!" She laughed heartily, and even I had to smile at the image.

He refused to say much of anything publicly about my abduction. When he brought me to Winchester, he had sent Gareth ahead to find Catlin. They managed to convey me through a back entrance, while his men made a great commotion at the front gate, so no one would see me in my ruined state. He and Catlin had taken it in turns to watch over me, allowing no one in, even to tend the chamber, except Cei. "We had to feed you like a babe," Catlin said. "It was quite a sight to see the great warrior spooning broth and oat bread into you like pap to a mewling infant."

I turned my head away. The picture she painted brought my own lost babe to mind, and also Lancelot's Galahad, now absent his father. Catlin's light laughter died in her throat. She said no more, only grasped my arm in sympathy, and left me to my mourning.

I knew nothing of the rescue itself, and it was clear he was unwilling to talk about it. He told the court only that Maelgwyn had treated me ill and was now dead. Of course rumors flew, but he would say nothing more. Nor would he allow anyone in to see me. Many murmured that he was stepping above himself, but who was going to confront him?

Only Catlin had heard the full report, in a whispered confession during one long night of waiting for me to awaken. "He used the peasant's cloak as a guise to get into Maelgwyn's castle," she told me. "In the courtyard, he saw a stout little woman carrying a tray of food, and somehow guessed she would lead him to you."

"Clare," I murmured.

"He followed her, and when she unlocked the door where you were being held, he was close behind her. The room looked empty, and he was about to handle her roughly to find where you were, but as soon as she saw him, she begged him to help you. You were... lying on the floor. He went to you, but you didn't know him." Catlin turned away and began toying with items on a tray nearby.

"Go on," I said. She hesitated, then turned back to me and took my hand.

"Maelgwyn came in. Lancelot didn't see him at first, all intent on you. The woman shouted to warn him, but Maelgwyn was on him before he was ready."

"He was hurt?" I gasped.

"No, no. But he said he fought badly, undone by his fury at the beast. Maelgwyn was besting him. And then... Lancelot parried wrongly, and his sword was shattered."

My heart was pounding. Catlin stopped her tale and offered me a cup of water, but I pushed it away. "What? What happened?"

"He said he heard a ferocious scream, and only later knew it for his own voice. When Maelgwyn gathered himself to deal the death blow, Lancelot leapt on him, all unarmed, except for the jagged bit of broken sword. Maelgwyn was pinned, unable to strike. The coward yielded. But Lancelot was so enraged he...he buried the blade in the caitiff's throat, up to the hilt." She was quiet a moment, then said with fire in her voice, "And well served, too! I would have done the same!"

Numbness overcame me at first. Then two warring emotions began to well in me. The first was a barbaric lust for Maelgwyn's blood; if I had been in my senses at the time, I swear I would have wallowed in it. But then. Lancelot held to his honor more fervently than any other. For such a man, such an act was almost beyond imagining. I looked up at Catlin. "It must have tortured him."

"Aye. Many a night we talked of it. If I'd let him have his head, he would have confessed it and given up his shield. But I finally made him see it would only cloud the issue, when everyone should be focused only on what an inhuman beast it was that he slew."

"Clare? Did no one question her?"

Catlin shook her head sadly. "When Maelgwyn went for Lancelot, she tried to stop him. Clouted him over the head with the tray she held."

"And?"

"He ran her through. I'm sorry. It seemed she wished you no harm."

I swallowed the constriction in my throat and hoped someone had sent her on her passage with the blessings of the Goddess.

Perilous as it was, Lancelot, Catlin and Cei held close the information that I was recovering for several days, giving me more time to regain some vitality before I had to face the court and their questions. Finally, however, it could be put off no longer. "Do you feel strong enough to meet with Edalwurf?" Lancelot asked. "I promised him that as soon as you were able…"

I drew a long breath and let it out with a sigh. "If I must. But only if you and Catlin are here."

Within the hour, the bishop bustled in, oozing sympathy and compassion. "We are all so grateful for your safe return, Your Highness. But I wonder, might it be possible for us to speak privately? This is such a delicate matter…"

"No. Sir Lancelot was there, and Dame Catlin can know anything I know."

"And we are indeed grateful to the Queen's Champion for delivering you to us and avenging the King's honor."

"The *King's* honor?"

"Well, the people mustn't know what happened there. It is most appalling, my lady, but if it became common knowledge that you were… dishonored, His Highness would have no choice but to put you aside. The law…"

It was a good thing for Edalwurf that I was too weak to move from my bed. "It was not my dishonor! I was abducted and brutally raped."

Edalwurf gave the slightest suggestion of a shrug. "Of course. But you must understand, we are in a difficult position. Maelgwyn is dead. We have no way of knowing for certain what happened there."

Catlin actually squawked in indignation. "We have what our Queen has told us!"

"Yes, of course. But we also have reports of her playing chess and smiling and speaking him fair." The man's glibness enraged me as much as what he was saying.

"To bide time until I could escape!"

Edalwurf had been taking pains to keep his tone solicitous, but when he spoke now, there was a sharpness in his voice. "It is said you returned wearing a very rich gown, not the one you rode out in."

"And soaked in blood!" Lancelot's hand went to his dagger, and he could barely restrain himself from approaching the bishop. "The blackheart nearly beat her to death!"

Edalwurf raised his eyebrows. "A lover's quarrel, perhaps?" All three of us were shocked into silence. The bishop continued before any of us could voice our furious objections. "At any rate, the law is clear. Congress with any man but the King is treason. There can be no question about the blood of an heir."

I threw back my coverlet and struggled to rise. "According to *your* law. Celtic Queens… A priestess…" I was so incensed I could not continue. Catlin eased me back to my pallet. It would be impolitic to let this man make me lose control of my emotions, so I drew a deep breath and tried to calm myself. "Anyway, thanks to Maelgwyn, there is no heir," I continued.

"A tragedy indeed. Especially since it took so long…"

"You offend me, priest."

"You should be grateful, madam. With the land at war, I've agreed to hold your secret…for now."

I could bear no more of this. "I need to rest. Leave me. Both of you." The men bowed and went out. Lancelot looked back as he went, pained sympathy in his eyes. Catlin glared them out the door.

I refused to see anyone but Catlin for the next few days. My strength was returning quickly now that I was able to eat the hearty, nourishing fare Cei prepared for me, and Catlin helped me first to sit in a chair, and then to move around the chamber. My visible wounds and bruises were healed by then, and one day she convinced me to walk out with her to my private garden, to enjoy the beautiful summer day for a few minutes.

Midsummer was peak time for the roses, so I didn't take much convincing. As we opened the door to the walled space where no one entered without my permission, the blooms spread before me in what seemed a thousand variations of red, pink, peach, yellow and white. The perfume was so overpowering that in my weakened state, I almost swooned from it. With Catlin supporting me, I quickly recovered. She led me to a secluded bower, then slipped away with a few murmured words. I thought it odd that she should leave me thus.

I had sat there brooding for only a few moments when Lancelot approached. I frowned: this had been planned. Lancelot looked grave and drawn as he sat down beside me.

165

"Best not sit too close. My stain might rub off on you," I said.

"The sin was his, not yours. And mine, for not getting there in time. By the gods, I wish Edalwurf carried a sword!"

"Careful. I hear you're a Christian now."

"Well... officially. My foster mothers would never forgive me. Vivien was certain I was meant to be Arch Druid."

"Then... why?"

The slight smile he wore disappeared, and his eyes filled with compassion. "It was Elaine's most ardent wish, especially after Galahad was born. There was so little I could do to make her happy..."

It was the first time her name had been mentioned, and we went silent for a moment. Best to face it straight on.

"When do you leave for Joyous Garde?"

"Never," he said firmly. "I'm not going back. My place is here with you."

"Lancelot. I owe you my life. But I can't—"

"You *are* my life. I swear I will never impose myself on you, will never so much as look at you in any but the most respectful manner. But I will never leave your side again."

Before I could respond, he took my hand and kissed it fervently, then strode off, leaving me bemused. Catlin said nothing when she returned, but it seemed her arm around my waist was as much a comforting embrace as a support for my faltering steps.

Gareth had been pleading to see me, and I allowed visits from him and from Bedwyr, who was recovering slowly from the thrown dagger that had pierced his side, barely missing his heart. And as I continued to heal, it was Gareth who gently urged me to rejoin my people. "With the King so long gone, they need to see you, my lady," he said. He was right. Still, I was loath to find out how many had been poisoned by Edalwurf's insinuations, and in no haste to present myself at court. Before I could say as much, Gareth added shyly, "Besides, it seems I am to be knighted soon, and I wanted to wait until you could be present." Well, what could I do?

As always, I had to fend off Catlin's choice of lavish gowns and jewelry. Some things never change. Dressed in a simple blue robe, with my hair down, I entered the hall with Lancelot and Gareth on my right, Catlin and Bedwyr on my left. My knees trembled so that I thought I might fall. "Stand close," I murmured to Catlin, but she was already there with a hand at my elbow.

"Breathe," she whispered.

As we entered, a silence fell over the hall. It lasted until I reached my place at the head of the table. Standing there, I could see all eyes on me. I dipped my head to my people, and gave them a wan smile, the best I could summon. My smile strengthened, though, as they began to rise, even the Christians. They stood for me, everyone, and they roared their welcome and their relief. By the time I sat, there were tears running down my face.

Their good will was sincere, but for many it was sorely tried when I took up my duties again as Regent in Arthur's absence. I suppose they would have held doubts about a woman in the role under any circumstances. But for the last months, while I was unable to serve, a group of mostly Christian men— including Edalwurf—had presumed to rule in my stead, supposedly with the advice of the Queen's Council. In practice, however, backed by the Church, they did as they pleased. When I returned to the throne, they were loath to give up their power and influence.

We battled almost instantly about the rule of Cameliard. Once it was known that Maelgwyn was dead, a new regent had to be chosen to rule in my name. Edalwurf and his cronies took it upon themselves to select one. They chose Niall, a wealthy duke who owned extensive lands within Cameliard. Of course, he was a Christian. When I learned of this, I could have confronted a dragon and breathed more fire!

I said nothing, however, until I met with my council; I would act first and defend my actions later. When I entered the council room, I found it more crowded than I had expected. While I was unavailable, Edalwurf had declared the two groups should be united; his faction was much larger. After the greetings and well wishes were over, I wasted no time.

"I have appointed Sir Selwyn, son of my father's chief advisor, to serve as regent in Cameliard."

Sounds of dismay ran around the table. "But...he is only a knight! Niall was chosen by the council," Edalwurf said. "While you were...indisposed."

"I have sent Duke Niall a message thanking him for his service."

"Why do you go against the council's wishes and advice?" asked one of Edalwurf's men.

"Why indeed!" sputtered Edalwurf. "She wants a pagan in power."

"My people are primarily pagan, Bishop, so my choice suits them well. And I know Sir Selwyn to be wise. I have no knowledge of the duke." Their grumbles and plaints continued. "Besides," I added, with an edge to my voice, "I heard no advice. I was simply informed that a decision had been made. While I was... indisposed," I added. If Edalwurf wanted to threaten me with disclosure of my rape, I was ready for him.

"You might at least have consulted the council," said one of my own partisans. I could see some feathers needed to be smoothed.

"I will most certainly depend on your wisdom, Sir Wallis, in all questions where it is appropriate," I said warmly. "I took great pains in choosing my council and have utmost faith in your good advice. However, I did not choose many who are here today, and feel no need to recognize their authority."

A babble of voices rushed over one another. I spoke more loudly to make myself heard. "Who is more suited to choose her regent than the reigning Queen of Cameliard herself? The matter rests."

"This is—" Edalwurf began. I did not let him finish.

"The Queen's council was complete, Bishop, but new faces have been added in my absence. In the interest of full representation of the people of Britain, I am willing to let a number of your allies remain, equal to the number of those I selected. You may choose which ones."

Edalwurf leapt to his feet. "You cannot—"

I remained seated and spoke with what I hoped appeared perfect calm. "I can. And if it is not acceptable to you, I thank you for your good offices, and dismiss all who were not of my original choosing."

I waited. Burning looks were exchanged among the Christian faction, while my chosen ones tried to hide their smirks. Finally, Edalwurf sat, his face aflame.

"Good," I said. "Let us adjourn until tomorrow, so the bishop can choose those he wishes to attend my council." I rose, and waited pointedly until all had risen in respect, and walked out, my head high.

There was even more pleasure in store for me that day, for in the evening, Gareth knelt before the court while Lancelot knighted him. The boy's eyes were brimming as he was raised and embraced by the man he had worshiped since childhood. Bedwyr, still gaunt from his wound, was the first to congratulate him. "Imagine when the Captain comes back to find his little brother already a knight! And made so at the hand of Gawain's own dearest friend." The joy on Gareth's face showed he was imagining just that.

There continued to be squabbles in the council, reflecting the hostile factions that had developed in the realm. This division was infecting the way our people treated each other, and I hated to see the spreading rancor.

The Christians believed pagans to be primitive, almost uncivilized, and even began to spread again the old rumor about human sacrifice. Pagans resented the fact that Christians were fast becoming the wealthiest faction in the realm. Our social traditions were being sorely affected as well.

For Druids, the Goddess reigned above all, and women were priestesses, healers, judges. In the Christian view, however, the only role for women was to serve. Women were prohibited from presiding or assisting at their rites and forbidden even to speak during worship.

This disdain of women was influencing our entire way of life. Though the Druid tradition granted women mastery over their own affairs, civil law prevented them from even owning property if any male could claim rights, no matter how vague. Ancient knowledge of herbs and healing was derided as rustic ignorance, even witchcraft, while male practitioners returned to the barbaric practice of bloodletting. Midwives lost their status and were now treated as servants.

Nevertheless, when I was sufficiently healed in body and spirit to bear an examination, it was a midwife I called in, an elderly woman known to be the wisest in the realm. She said nothing as she poked and prodded, nor even when it was over, and she was laving her hands in a basin. When I could not bear the suspense a moment longer, she turned to me, with an expression of deepest compassion. "I'm sorry, my lady. You won't bear again."

She dropped a courtesy and went out, leaving me silent and numb. Catlin closed the door behind her, then began combing my hair. After a moment I spoke, my voice flat and impassive.

"Catlin. Send for Morgan le Fey."

"But Arthur…"

"Arthur isn't here."

Chapter 21

Morgan came at once. Heeding Catlin's advice, I brought her in privily, though I had no intention of hiding my action from Arthur when we were together again. I had sent him a brief missive once I was well enough, but there was no response yet. I supposed he was caught up in military matters, or maybe the messenger never got through. In any case, it seemed best not to discuss such personal matters except face to face.

My only acquaintance with Morgan was when she did our handfasting, but she greeted me warmly, as a sister in the Old Religion. And as such, I could trust her with the truth of the situation. She had, of course, heard about the abduction through common talk, but the details were as unknown to her as to the rest. "I wish you had called out to me," she said when I finished. "I could have helped you use your powers. Maelgwyn could have been taught what happens to—"

"I have no skill to call you. I do not make use of those powers," I said, "since I act more in the worldly realm than as a priestess."

"But you are a priestess. These abilities are available to you, and you should know how to make use of them. Had you used the Sight, you might have known what Maelgwyn intended."

"I have no talent for it. Mother Arden despaired of me."

"Nonsense. You're merely afraid of what you might see. If you let yourself look freely, with your whole soul, you can see past, present, and future. You can see the entire world, and the forces that frame it."

171

That seemed a bit grand to me, and I held back a smile. "Mother Arden said I held a fear of fire."

"Yes, well. Try looking backward at first, instead of forward, if it frightens you to know the future."

There was a brazier hanging nearby, empty of fuel during these hottest days of summer. Morgan reached out a hand, and with a roar, flames surged from it. Catlin and I jumped back. Morgan took my hand and drew me near the brazier. "Let me show you." She went to stand behind me. She was much taller than I, and when she put her hands on my shoulders, I felt uneasy, even frightened, a bit. Catlin saw the flash of fear and started toward me. Morgan held up a hand. And Catlin—intrepid, unruly, unstoppable Catlin—stopped where she was, as if she had no power to move further. She sat down, folded her hands in her lap, and waited placidly.

"Close your eyes and draw a deep breath," Morgan said. I obeyed. She put one hand gently on my head. "Now breathe out the world around you, open your eyes and look into the very heart of the fire."

With her hand on my head, I began to feel such a deep calm that I was totally accepting when I saw *fire on a hearth, not a brazier, and a room beyond it. There a younger Morgan sat at her ease with Accolon, her gallant. A small boy was playing with carved animals on a low table. I could not stop looking at him. I thought him somehow familiar, but then he was not much more than a babe, with plump arms and a chubby face not yet grown into itself. I smiled as I watched him, so solemn at his play. When I glanced up into the room again, I saw the young Morgan gazing back at me, her eyes meeting mine through the curtain of flames. That did startle me, and the vision disappeared.*

Catlin blinked and stood, looking confused. I turned to the actual, tangible Morgan standing behind me. "That was a wonder!" I said, delighted. "How did you do that?"

"I did nothing. You did it yourself."

"Was that your son?" I asked.

She nodded and smiled. "Now, shall we sit and ease ourselves a bit before we proceed? Nimue sends her greetings."

We spoke for a while about Nimue, then our talk turned to the Druid realm. I assumed she would be strident about the depredations of the

Christians, but while she deplored their more outrageous offenses against the home religions, she seemed surprisingly unworried about our future.

"Maelgwyn might have held a good purpose in his heart, but that doesn't excuse his actions. I fear others might try to take matters into their own hands. That is foolish. We need to be patient and wait for our time. It will come." I wondered what Arthur held in his heart against this pleasant, intelligent woman.

Our talk turned to news of the kingdom, and when that was exhausted, I began prattling about the weather. I suppose I was putting off hearing what she might have to say. She smiled and led me to my pallet, brisk but solicitous.

Her examination was thorough. After, she accepted a cup of wine from Catlin and sat waiting until I had rearranged my robes and joined her. "I'm afraid the midwife was right," she said gently.

"But there must be some potion, some charm! Without an heir, the Christians will—"

"Be at peace, sister. The Goddess will be served. There is an heir."

I was struck motionless. "What do you say?"

"The time hasn't come to make it known. But Arthur has sired a son. A pagan son."

My heart bucked in my chest, and I fought for breath. "I...I see." My voice faltered. "Who is the mother?"

"I am."

My first shock was nothing to this. I heard Catlin gasp, as if from far away, though she stood right behind me. My vision narrowed to a pinpoint, and I swayed in my seat. Catlin put her hands on my shoulders, and after a moment, I could see again. Morgan sipped her wine, affecting a casual air, but over the rim of the cup her eyes drilled into mine. I struggled to find my voice. "But you're—"

"I'm the Lady of the Lake," she said smoothly. "The survival of our people, and of our Goddess herself, depends on me. So I took steps to assure it."

I could do nothing but stare. Finally I shook myself and croaked, "When?"

"Just before you were wed." She gestured again...

Flames. Not in a brazier, but in my vision, fluttering before me like a sheer curtain, through which I saw the great hall at Winchester. Arthur and his men were

173

drinking and roistering, and there were rope dancers, acrobats, jugglers, fire eaters. It must have been the night before our wedding, for there were no court women present.

Into a moment of relative quiet came the haunting melody of a bone flute, soon joined by an exotic drumbeat. A dancer moved into the space in the center of the room. Her arms, shoulders and breasts were covered with blue serpent tattoos, and she had a barbaric beauty that made even the most lively talk falter and die. She danced, slowly at first, and with great dignity. But as the drumbeat became more insistent, her whirling became more primitive and enthralling, until every man in the room was spellbound and flushed with lust. They began to pound on the tables with their daggers in time with the ever-increasing drum, and the dancer's erotic movements stoked their fire.

I closed my eyes and shook my head, hard, trying to clear the vision. When I opened them again, I saw that the woman sitting before me and the dancer were the same.

"Arthur didn't know who I was until I gave him Excalibur. And don't think I haven't heard what he has done with it! The time will come to deal with that."

It seemed my mind was working at half speed. By the time I grasped one bit of information, there were two more capering ahead of me. I struggled to sort out what was most important.

"He…didn't know you?"

"The last time I saw my brother, he was a tiny lad, barely weaned from his nurse. He was squalling and screaming as they wrested him from my arms." Her voice caught for a moment. "As was I. I never saw him in the flesh again until that night. But I had the Sight from a young age and followed him. At first he seemed quite ordinary, except for the fact that Merlin was keeping him close. By the time I understood what he was destined to be, I knew what I must do."

Her hand moved again, and before I could resist, *I was in a hallway, watching Arthur reel toward his chamber, supported by Gawain and Bedwyr. "Fine now, thanks. Just need to sleep. Here's Donal. Ho, Donal." His page lay unconscious on the floor. Arthur carefully tipped himself down to shake him. The boy didn't respond.*

"Aye, had his fill, too. You all right?" Gawain asked, with a somewhat bungled tongue.

"Mm. Just lie down. G'night." The other two walked on. Arthur reached to open his chamber door, but found it was not latched. Put on his guard, as much as his condition allowed, his hand went to his dagger. He slowly pushed the door open and peered around the room, lit only by a few glowing coals in the hearth.

There was movement among the skins on his bed, and the dancer—Morgan!—sat up, naked, and smiled at him. Her hair made a wild black cloud around her face, her kohl-rimmed eyes alluring. In the fireglow, the serpent tattoos seemed to slither across her skin. Arthur gaped a moment, then smiled back and moved toward the bed, peeling off clothing as he went.

She lay back invitingly. Arthur leaned to kiss her, but fell onto the bed, laughing. She rolled with him and knelt astride, her long unbound hair covering them. He fumbled with her breasts. Soon she was moving over him as he lay passively. His eyes were closed, and she watched his face intently, unsmiling. As if from a distance, I could hear someone whimper and moan. It was me.

The coals in the hearth suddenly flamed up brightly, casting wild shadows on the walls, as Arthur's eyes flew open and he strained upward in his spasm. Then he fell back with a sigh and slipped into a deep sleep. Morgan slid from his bed, took up a robe and glided out past the sleeping page. She stopped and turned to look back at Arthur before she closed the door. Her expression was an odd mixture of tenderness and triumph.

Morgan released me. Like a child's dancing-toy when its strings are cut, I slumped into a heap. When I forced myself to look at my tormentor, her eyes were shining, and she was smiling.

"Do you see? A child twice royal, son of the High King and the Lady of the Lake! No one could deny him. When he comes into his power, Britain will return to the true religion and the invaders will be cast out. He's just a boy now, but his time will come, and come soon."

"That boy? The one you showed me?"

"My son and Arthur's." There was unmistakable pride in her voice.

Her words nearly wrenched me apart. I knew that child, from the vision I had long treasured. The dark-haired boy who stood with us before the throne was Morgan's son, not mine. Never mine.

My thoughts skittered in all directions, like pebbles cast on a frozen pond. "Does Arthur know?"

"Oh yes," she said. "He sent my old friend Merlin to murder him. Quite a few infants died in the attempt."

"No!" I doubled over in pain. After a moment, I straightened. I must know all. "But you said there is an heir."

"The boy lives. Merlin has his wiles, but he was no match for me."

"I don't believe you. You may have deluded Arthur with your treachery, but Merlin would never knowingly—"

"Ask him. You have the Sight now, and it still lives in his mind, what he did. And did with Arthur's permission, I might add."

Understanding crept slowly at first, then rushed in like a mighty wind that crushes all in its path. "The guilt... He was always talking of sin! You're the one sent him to the priests!"

"That was unexpected. But it will all come right again when our son is recognized as High King. A pagan King."

The weight of what had been done settled on me. There would be no undoing. "You have destroyed Arthur," I said. "And the Christians will never accept your son. You have destroyed Britain as well."

Morgan leaned forward, even reached out as if to take my hand. I flinched away. Her eyes burned with an expression that seemed almost pleading. "Guinevere. I saw our destruction coming, our way of life trampled down. I did what was needful to save our land, and the Great Mother herself, from that god of nails."

I recovered myself enough to look her in the eye and speak without a quaver in my voice. "You have shamed us all. Arthur was right about you. You will leave, now, and you will never come back here again."

Morgan closed her eyes and inclined her head with a slight smile, then withdrew in icy dignity.

Chapter 22

My mind swirled and stormed like a great ocean, so many different facts and images and horrors churning together that I could not grasp any one of them. I turned to Catlin, who read my face and grabbed a basin. Everything inside me came spewing out, and I felt would henceforth be an empty vessel. As indeed I was.

With that thought, my mind settled on the one piece, out of all I had heard, that I could grasp completely. I sat back, and let it settle into fact. Looking up at Catlin, I spoke in a voice as hollow as I felt. "He has a son. Arthur has a son."

Catlin, bless her, for once knew when to speak and when to hold silence. She went to fetch me a cup of water and a wet cloth. Then she sat across from me, and we simply stared at each other for a while, until I burst out with a sound somewhere between a sob and laughter. Even to my own ears, it was a sound so appalling that I hope never to hear it again. "Eight years!" I cried. "He has known for eight years, while I…"

Catlin said nothing, only grasped my hand tightly as I worked through this disaster. "That's why…oh, Great Goddess, that first night…the shame of it kept him from… And his conversion. The Christians forgive sins. How he must have suffered! His own sister!" I loosed Catlin's hand and began pacing, marking the width and length of my chamber, over and over.

Catlin let me pace for a while, then said quietly, "He could not have known her. She carries the blame for that alone."

"Yes. But… eight years!" Another idea forced its way into my regard, and my voice rose shrilly. "And what of Merlin? What of that?" Again, she said

177

nothing, but her thoughts swam across her face. A scream built in me, winding tighter and tighter, but I would not let it out. I choked on it instead. *Those babes...*

I went for my door at a run. Catlin leapt up, but I commanded her to stay. It was fortunate I met no one as I bolted through the passageways to the room where Merlin still lay in his oblivion. Ulfin was sitting with him when I rushed in. "Get out!" I shouted. The faithful old man leapt to his feet. He bowed quickly to me and stumbled away.

I threw myself down in the chair and stared into the waxen face of this man who had taught and protected Arthur when he was a child, advised and supported and yes, protected him as man and king. My mind raced along impossible tracks. This man could not...and yet. His absences from court, many and short at first, then the long disappearance after... I had to know. Morgan said the Sight was within my power now, but was it? Did I want it to be?

Slowly I reached out and grasped his hand. I closed my eyes and sent my will out. At first nothing happened, and I was about to abandon the effort. But then, through the darkness behind my closed eyes, *I saw a cloaked figure riding, almost invisible in the murk of a midnight forest. Just a glimpse, and it was gone. I waited, and the next image was clearer: Merlin was in the room I had seen earlier. Morgan stood clutching an infant tightly and sobbing. But then her tears turned to laughter. I could not understand what was happening. She handed the baby to Merlin, casually, and turned away. Merlin stood confounded. After a moment, he lay the infant down and unwrapped its swaddling. It was a girl.*

I began to be aware that I was breathing in gasps and holding Merlin's hand so tightly I was in danger of crushing the fragile bones. I stood and reeled around the small room, trying to steady myself. I was utterly confused. What was I seeing? After a moment I understood: it was a cruel deception, a prank Morgan played on Merlin to amuse herself.

I turned to the wall and leaned against it, pressing my forehead into my arm, sick with dread, half-knowing what I would see if—when—I looked again. Trembling, I sat and reached once more for the wizened hand.

This image came like a thunderbolt. *Merlin stood at the top of a hill, looking down at a peaceful village, bathed in the faint light of a waning moon. A band of armed and mounted men waited behind him. At a nod, the riders poured down the hill toward the village.*

Merlin watched, rigid and impassive, as the riders barged into cottages and came out with infants in their arms, followed by screaming mothers and raging fathers. The action was quick and merciless. They thundered back up the hill with their tiny captives. Merlin wheeled his horse before the riders met him, and led them off, keeping his face averted.

A moment of blackness. I was being given this in bits and pieces, and I did not want to see what was next. It came anyway.

The band stood on a rocky shore where a coracle waited. The men dismounted, each carrying an infant. Their leader looked to Merlin, who nodded. One by one, they deposited the wailing infants into the fragile boat of willow and skins. Then the leader pushed it out into the sea. Merlin's jaw was set in steel, but his eyes grieved.

As the sky lightened in preparation for dawn, Merlin stood alone on the craggy beach looking out to where the coracle was barely a speck in the distance. But when the wind veered and shifted, the wailing of infants could be heard, mixed with the cries of gulls.

Shuddering, I threw the old man's hand from me and leapt up, pressing my back against a wall. Sickened to my very core, I never wanted to look on his face again. I started for the door.

But...I still didn't understand. Why had this happened? How was it that Morgan's son still lived? And there was yet another thing I needed to know: was Arthur complicit in this wickedness? My teeth were clenched so cruelly my jaw might break, but I sat back down and reached for his hand again.

Nothing. Only blackness. I waited and waited. At last, despairing, I allowed my eyes to open. Merlin lay as he always had, immobile, insensible. But as I watched in amazement, a tear seeped out from his closed eyelid and slowly trickled down his furrowed face.

I pressed his hand to my forehead, fervent. "Please, Lord Merlin. Emrys. For the love of the Mother, tell me. Did Arthur know?"

It came in bursts, in fragments.

Merlin was seated as Arthur paced angrily around his chamber. "It's not just you she means to ruin," Merlin said, "but everything you have built, everything you will build. You have barely begun your work here, Arthur. Long before your conception, I knew what you would be, what you were destined to do. We cannot let her demolish what you will create."

"But... can't you just find that child?"

"I have tried. But Morgan is as powerful in her ways as I am in mine. She has blocked my ability to know him."

Arthur knelt next to Merlin and looked up into his face. "Emrys, as you love me, how can you ask me to bear the burden of such a sin, when I am nearly broken already by the first?"

"It was not your sin," Merlin said firmly. "You didn't know her. The weight of that is entirely on her. And the weight of this? It will be on me."

"Sin is sin. It besmirches everyone. I will not escape whole from any of this."

"No. Probably not. But at least, Arthur, at least we can save Britain."

Well. I had wanted to know, and now I did, and my heart was shattered. I put my head down and sobbed. But I had not let go of Merlin's hand. Nor could I. Despite my profound desire to be anywhere else, I somehow understood that Merlin had more to tell me. Reluctantly, I closed my eyes.

In Arthur's chamber, Merlin sat slumped on a stool while the King paced furiously. Arthur strode over to him and grabbed him roughly by the shoulders. "How many? Tell me, old man, how many?"

"Nine," said Merlin, without looking up.

"Nine?" Arthur reeled back, groped behind him for a chair and sat heavily. His head dropped, and when he looked up again, his face was pure suffering. "Nine innocents? Nine untainted babes? I will carry them on my back forever, and all that I do henceforth will bear that stain." He pressed the heels of his hands against his eyes and heaved a great, anguished sigh. "I hope you are certain it was worth it."

There was no answer. Arthur dropped his hands and stared at the powerful Arch Druid who sat across from him, now looking like an old and broken man. "Merlin?" He had barely enough breath to speak the name.

Merlin would not meet his eyes. "I was watching the coracle go out to sea," he began. "And the Sight came on me."

"No," Arthur said. "Please no." I could feel my heart pounding, my throat aching, and I wanted nothing so much as to run far away. But I could not. Merlin continued.

"Suddenly I was not looking at the open water at all. Instead, I was inside a fisherman's hut. I could hear waves crashing against a cliff, the malevolent hiss as they receded. A woman sat at a rough table, folding and refolding a length of soft cloth. An empty cradle beside her."

His voice was choked, and he stopped for a moment. Arthur's face had turned to stone. "Go on," he said, and there was no mercy in his voice.

"*I heard steps approaching. The woman leapt to her feet. A man pushed aside the hide covering the entrance. He carried a bundle in his arms.*"

Arthur groaned but said nothing.

"*She turned back the wrappings. It was an infant, only a few days old, with a thatch of black hair. He opened his eyes and began to wail. With tears running down her face, the woman unfastened her bodice, the front of it already wet with milk. Taking the babe, she held him to her breast, and he began sucking greedily. She asked her husband, 'How long will we keep him?'*

'*I don't know. Until he's old enough for training, is all they told me.' And he tossed a heavy bag of coin on the table.*" *Merlin fell silent.*

Arthur sat as though carved of oak. "*So it was all for naught,*" *he said.* "*The child lives.*"

"*We can find him. He's by the sea somewhere. I saw the people —*"

"*NO! No more! You will take no further action in this matter. Is that clear?*" *Merlin turned his head aside, closed his eyes and nodded.* "*You had best leave court for a while,*" *the King said heavily. Merlin nodded again, then dragged himself out the door, moving and looking like a man a hundred years old.*

I released Merlin's hand and it fell to my lap. I could not say how long I sat there, but when I finally stood, it took me some time before I could walk to the door.

I still tired easily, so it wasn't remarked when I didn't join the court that night. I persuaded Catlin to spend the evening with Cei, and while she was gone, I wrestled viciously with my emotions. Should I send Arthur a missive? No. I would wait for him to come back, and only then tell him what I had learned.

Part of me fiercely wanted Merlin gone. Seal him in a cave somewhere or put *him* out to sea! Let Nimue take him to Avalon, let Morgan have him. But then, his evil actions had been in defense of Arthur. And he was already a prisoner in his own body. Grudgingly, I decided to let him stay, but I would never go near him again.

And what to do about the child? Surely it—he—should not be left to be raised by such as Morgan. And if I would not conceive again…

Mostly, though, I dwelled on the betrayal. How could Arthur have kept this from me, knowing how I was tormented by the lack, knowing my fear that he would have to put me aside? All he had to do was say there was an heir… but how could he, without revealing the mother? Despite myself, I ached for him, for his guilt and sorrow. It must have been intolerable.

I grieved and was furious by turns: I had given up my realm for him, I had given up Lancelot for him. It was because of his conversion that I had been raped, and yet I was to bear the blame, while he…. It was unendurable.

Catlin returned, bearing a tray of dainties Cei sent to pique my appetite, but I could not eat. We sat together, she and I, sometimes talking, sometimes weeping, sometimes in silence, until well after moonrise, when the people of the court were long retired. I was pacing once again, and saw that poor Catlin was nodding where she sat. I knelt beside her, putting a hand gently on her knee. When she opened her eyes I said, "Catlin. Go back to Cei." She started to protest, but I cut her off. "But before you do, find Lancelot and send him to me."

I was gazing into a cup of wine when the door to my chamber opened. Lancelot came to stand behind me and put his hands on my shoulders. I tipped my head back to look up at him, and he bent forward, placing a kiss on my forehead. I hadn't known for certain until that moment what I intended, but the tenderness of that gesture removed all doubt. I stood and turned to embrace him. I kissed him, tentatively. He hesitated, leaned back, and gazed at me, then returned my kiss, softly at first, then with growing passion. Without a word, he picked me up and carried me to my bed.

I suppose I expected it to be ecstasy, an exaltation that would transport me to some blissful realm the likes of which I had never known. I was wrong. It was better. When we finally came together as one, it felt like coming home.

Chapter 23

I couldn't call it joy, exactly. Not with the horrific discovery that finally brought us together, nor the guilt accompanying every moment. The fate of Britain hung on a balancing point. News from the Saxon shore was encouraging, and the realm was thriving. Arthur's rule of law brought the country a measure of freedom from the robber barons, highwaymen and other brigands who had spread terror over the land. The king was beloved by his people. Still, if my liaison with Lancelot became known, it could bring Arthur down and Britain with him.

And it wasn't just concern for the kingdom that gnawed at me. As angry as I was with him, I loved Arthur. The respect and awe I held for him in the early years had grown into a deep and abiding affection. I could no more deny my cherishing him than I could deny that Lancelot and I were destined to live out our desire, our devastating need for one another. With Arthur, I was a Queen, and with Lancelot I was a woman. I could surrender neither role, nor could I completely surrender to one.

Lancelot and I rode out often that August. There was talk, of course, but not much more than there always was, even when there had been no basis for it. One day we were lying together in a glade, our horses cropping contentedly nearby.

"You know you'll have to leave," I said.

"I know." And he kissed me.

"Arthur…"

"And Elaine..." He kissed me.

"Go back to Joyous Garde."

"I will." He kissed me, and we moved together in the dry grasses, feeling the heat of the earth and hearing the buzz and clatter of summer insects.

In public, Lancelot continued to seem serious and somber. But in private, I discovered that he also had a playful, mischievous side he kept well hidden. When we had the privacy to laugh aloud, we often tumbled like kittens in a basket. We sang together—his voice was as mellow as any bard. We regaled each other with stories of our past, or imitations of members of the court. (His Cei was perfection, and when I did Dame Helena, he rolled about in glee.)

Each night, late, he came to me, and we clung together like children stranded in a wilderness. But often sleep eluded us both, and there were times when we lay washed in misery.

"Go then," I said. "Your holy conscience..."

"I'm devoted to Arthur. And not just as King. I love him like a brother."

"I love him too. Never think I don't."

"I know. But I lead the Companions! Squires come from across the sea to be knighted by my hand. How can I keep that honor if I..."

"And what of my honor? Do you think my conscience is sound?"

"Then let me go. Before the whispers get any louder. Before we're both lost."

"It's too late."

I turned to him then, and despite our grief, despite the respect and love we held for Arthur, our passion for each other once again proved its power. We could no more leave each other than a nightingale could separate from its song.

And so the weeks passed, in pain and rapture, until the trees were fading to dun and the night wind began to bite. But it was one of those fine days that sometimes happen in autumn when I sat beside Bedwyr in the stands. The sun still gave some warmth, the air was crisp, and the sky was that breathtaking blue you see only when all other colors begin to leach from the land. Lancelot and Gareth were overseeing a junior tournament, with young squires and even pages in the lists.

"It was Lancelot's idea," Bedwyr said. "With so many still on the Saxon shore, the young ones coming up weren't getting the training. He and Gareth did all the work."

On the tourney field, two heavily padded little pups were having at each other with wooden swords. I laughed as they flailed away, with little skill but endless enthusiasm.

"It's a wonderful idea. The boys certainly love Lancelot, don't they."

"Aye. And Gareth follows him like a duckling. Imagine when Gawain returns to find his little brother not only a knight, but Lancelot's trusted lieutenant!"

One of the younglings took a hard blow to the stomach and was trying to pretend he wasn't crying. Lancelot went to him to be sure he was all right. On the wide calm river beyond the tourney field, a barge slowly floated into view, topped with a black pavilion and with black banners fluttering. I gestured to Bedwyr, who also looked at it with curiosity. An old man began to pole the barge toward shore.

"Gareth," I called out. "Greet that bargeman and enquire his business."

Gareth arrived at the bank of the river just as the barge gained the shore. He waded in and helped to secure it, then spoke to the bargeman. I don't believe the fellow answered, just gestured toward the pavilion.

Gareth lifted a curtain and looked inside. Then he backed out slowly, ran partway up the hill and called to Lancelot. Still jovial, Lancelot started down the hill, surrounded by a pack of jostling boys. When he saw Gareth's face, his smile faded, and he broke into a run.

He jumped up onto the barge and swept aside the draperies. There lay Elaine on a bier, a letter in her hand. Lancelot stood and stared as the boys piled up behind him. It took a while for him to wrench his eyes from Elaine's corpse and see that there was someone else in the pavilion, his white-blond hair and pale face stark in the dimness.

"Galahad!" He started toward the lad, but the boy's expression froze him where he stood. Galahad looked at his father, then at the other boys clustered around him, and then at his father again. His eyes condemned him.

I told Catlin she could go to Cei that night, but she stalled and busied herself with unneeded duties. Neither of us knew whether Lancelot would

185

come, and she didn't want me left alone. Finally, she bid me good night. Lancelot came soon after. He entered my chamber with Elaine's letter in his hand, looking twenty years older than the day before.

I started to go to him, but he held out the letter to me instead. His bleak eyes and harrowed face wrung my heart. I took the letter from him and moved away to read it while he stood where he was, frozen in misery.

My Lancelot, it began, *I fear I can no longer hold off Death. He comes for all, but I had thought to have more time. Galahad still needs me, and while I lived, I could keep faith that you would return to me. In truth, I should count darkness as my friend, for releasing me from such bootless hope. I have been shriven and am cleansed of my sins. I ask only that you do the same, if not now, when you are able, so that we may meet again. And as God forgives you, forgive yourself.*

I turned back to him, wanting with all my heart to embrace him, but his desolation was a wall. "I should..." His voice caught in his throat. He took a breath and started again. "I should repent."

"Yes," I said, and his eyes flickered toward me, startled. "If you are indeed a Christian in deep belief, you should put aside your sin, do penance, and be forgiven. Edalwurf will be happy to keep your secret. It will give him one more source of power over you, over me, and Arthur. If you truly believe what we have between us is a sin."

"But you? What do you...?"

"I count it a great disloyalty. I tried, we both did, but our love was stronger than our wills. I think perhaps my greatest offense was urging you to marry Elaine, just to help me resist you. She loved you, but I knew you could never return it. It was cruel of me to let her think you might. I'm deeply sorry for that. But as for sin..."

He was trembling. I poured a cup of wine and held it out to him, careful not to let our fingers touch.

"You were raised in the Old Religion. You know the Goddess doesn't judge, isn't vengeful. She is more saddened by cruelty and injustice than by love that falls where it should not."

"Elaine's last wish..."

"Was that you be shriven when you are ready. And to forgive yourself. Can you do that, Lancelot?"

I held him through the night while he sobbed.

Lancelot ensured that Elaine was buried with all propriety. Catlin heard rumors that Edalwurf resisted giving her the proper rites, claiming she was a suicide. I never asked how he was persuaded otherwise. I only know that Lancelot, Gareth, and Bedwyr went to him with Elaine's letter in hand, and afterwards, he made no more protestations.

The bier was carried with great ceremony to the burial grounds, where a rock-lined tomb awaited. Elaine's body, wrapped in white linen, was carefully lowered, and Edalwurf read the rites. Lancelot and Galahad stood on one side of the grave, Bedwyr, Gareth, Catlin and I on the other. Almost all the people of the court were gathered, but there was a margin of empty space around me, another around Lancelot. One by one, the mourners filed past, dropping what remained of the season's rusty flowers into the grave.

Lancelot and Galahad were last, except for me. As soon as Galahad had laid his tribute, Helena swooped down like a raptor and bore him off. By the time I filed past the grave, most of the people were walking back down the hill. Lancelot trailed behind Galahad, who was being shepherded by Helena and Edalwurf. My loyal friends waited to escort me back to the palace, with Catlin grumbling all the way about the disrespect the others had shown me.

With the exception of Agravain, who could never hold silence when there was trouble to be stirred up, no one was so bold as to make open accusations. People glanced askance when I was seen with Lancelot, but held their tongues, at least in our hearing. Galahad made it clear, young as he was, that he intended to fulfil his mother's hopes and be trained as a priest. He was not inclined to follow his father as a knight, nor indeed, to have much contact with him at all. This was a sorrow, of course, added to his other sorrows, but Lancelot respectfully submitted to the boy's resolve.

Nimue had long ago returned to Avalon, and while I greatly disliked her association with Morgan le Fey, she regained my trust when I called her to court and questioned her about her knowledge of Arthur's son.

"Yes, I knew it," she admitted, "but it was not my knowledge to share. Nor would I cast abroad anything I learned in confidence from you."

"Who else knows?"

"A few of the elder priestesses. And Accolon. Visitors sometimes peer closely at the boy, who bears his lineage rather too clearly. But no one has ever said anything."

I asked her to tell me about him. "His name is Mordred. He seems wise beyond his years, a solemn child, well grown and well mannered. He is steeped in Druid lore. I wish Morgan could be content training him to become the Arch Druid when he is old enough." There was a catch in her voice as she said that, and I could see she still mourned the Merlin she had loved. "But she is training the lad for a much more ambitious role. I should not gainsay the Lady of the Lake, but in truth, I lief he were raised away from her influence." I said nothing; her concern echoed my own.

It was in my mind to ask her if she knew about Merlin's actions, but I did not. Nor did I try to learn anything by other means. I'd had quite enough of the Sight and did not wish to know more. What I had seen could not be unseen, much as I might wish it, and the wickedness of the world that was visible to everyone was all I could deal with. Though there were times when I could have used a warning...

It was after Samhain when news came. The court was loosely assembled after the evening meal. Lancelot and I were playing knucklebones. Everyone else was sharpening tools and weapons, weaving, spinning, playing with the hounds or simply taking their ease. Gareth and Catlin sat by us, Gareth harassing Lancelot for steadily losing games to me.

Bedwyr rushed in and began to make his way to where we sat. But before he reached us, a herald stepped through the doorway and blew his clarion. "Hear ye!" he called. "Our troops are returning from the Saxon shore. Our victorious King Arthur is but two days away!"

There was a silence, as everyone looked or tried to resist looking at me and at Lancelot. I schooled my mien to show only calm welcome, but I was a welter of happiness, anger, and fear. As for Lancelot, he sat frozen with guilt. Finally, Catlin broke the moment by jumping up and bustling around.

"Gareth! Take out a party for game. The rest of you to the kitchens with me. We have a victory feast to prepare, and only two days to do it!" She herded everyone out, leaving me and Lancelot alone. We stared at each other, but found we had nothing to say.

Lancelot came to my chamber late that night, and we talked until the sky began to pale. Our earlier wordlessness was overwhelmed by our fears, by the knowledge that once Arthur arrived, we might never find a private word, let alone a touch, a kiss, a caress. There was no question that we should give over, bless the time we'd had together, and keep safe. But there was also no question that we would not.

Chapter 24

The next day was crammed with the busyness of preparations. The banners my ladies had been stitching for months were hung along the road leading to the castle. Cei was a whirlwind, flying from larder to fish well to buttery, a train of kitchen boys trying to keep up. The stables were made spotless, hearths swept, the round table polished until it gleamed like threshed wheat. Catlin and I were kept running from one task to another, which should have made the day go by like an arrow. And yet it seemed one of the longest days of my life.

At last, most of the household retired. Lancelot and I had said our farewell the night before, and I asked him not to come to me that last night. Cei was still frantically bustling around, so Catlin and I were bedfellows. Exhausted as I was, I could not rest until she made me a strong posset. Tears seeped from my eyes as she held me and murmured sweet old airs from our childhood. Finally, I slept.

It was midmorning when the messenger galloped in to say Arthur was approaching. The entire court turned out in their best to welcome the King and his army. After the usual scuffle with Catlin, I wore a simple gown of a color between blue and green, and the torque that had belonged to his mother Ygraine. My hair was down, covered with a white veil, and I wore my rose-gold coronet. As I approached the hall, I stopped for a moment to control my trembling and bolster my composure. At last, I stepped onto the dais, where I was flanked by Lancelot and Bedwyr. There was a deal of malicious whispering and giggling in the assembly.

The great doors opened, and Arthur rode in at the head of his company, clad in his well-worn armor, but with a fresh tabard bearing the red Pendragon. He carried his helmet and wore a simple but commanding crown. Gawain and Bors rode as his escort, and he looked very royal. But when he saw me, his dignity collapsed in a joyful grin. I reached deep inside myself and found a smile to answer him.

The whispers stilled for a moment. Arthur dismounted, and Lancelot led me down the steps and presented me to him. It took every bit of my resolve not to cast a backward glance before I curtseyed and stepped to Arthur's side. As we ascended the dais together, the buzzing started again, louder.

Somehow, we got through the endless feasting, the bard's songs, the distribution of spoils. Gawain was singled out for honors. Arthur told the company how the Prince of Orkney had saved his king's life on the battlefield, not once, but twice, and rewarded him richly with lands and treasure. Gawain tried his best to look humble, but the smile he flashed as he knelt before his uncle showed his rascal spirit was undimmed.

There were more festivities to come, but late in the day we were able to repair to our rooms for some private time. That time was not spent as Arthur had expected.

When he tried to take me in his arms, I turned away. He assumed it was because of the rape, and began to apologize. There was certainly much we needed to talk about—my abduction, the loss of our child, the insults from Edalwurf, the desecration of Excalibur—but foremost in my mind was the son he kept hidden from me for so long.

When I had finished telling him what I'd learned from Morgan, he sat slumped in misery on a stool, his head in his hands. I stood stiffly, with my back against a cold wall.

"Send for him," I said.

"And who shall I say he is?"

"From all reports," I said, "you'll have no choice but to tell the truth. And even if he didn't bear your stamp, the boy deserves to be recognized. None of this is his fault."

"The bishops..."

"Oh, the bishops will indeed exact a price. But we're in their power already. And the pagans will likely be pleased, no matter how it came about."

Still he sat slumped, with his head in his hands. I had lived with my anger for months now, and it was no longer so fresh a wound. Seeing him broken tugged at my heart. "You're the best King this land has ever had, Arthur. The people will forgive you anything."

At last he looked up, and his eyes burned into mine. "But will you?"

He was lean from the long campaign, and at the moment, all the pride of his royal victory counted for nothing. He looked haggard, and very much alone. As I started toward him, he stood with his head bowed, bracing himself for my condemnation. I wrapped my arms around him, and he wept.

Arthur met first with Edalwurf, his confessor, and then with the Church council. When he left me to go to that meeting, he was apprehensive, but firmly resolved. When he returned, he was broken. He slumped onto a stool and would not meet my eyes.

"Every moment. Every salacious detail. The same questions over and over again, just to be sure my humiliation was complete. They charged me with not only fornication, but incest, despite the fact that I was all unknowing."

"But you are absolved?" I asked.

"Oh yes. When my penance is complete." He spat the word *penance*.

I moved to embrace him, but he held up a hand to ward me off. He winced at the gesture, then lifted his fine linen tunic to show me a garment of burlap so coarse it had already abraded his skin to rawness and specks of blood. I gasped.

"I must wear this for a year. I am allowed only bread and water for the next three months. I will never again taste wine." He delivered these strictures flatly, with no emotion, and when I protested the harshness he shook his head and bowed his body into an even more humble posture. "It is no more than I deserve."

"Well," I said, "we'll deal with it. I suppose it could have been worse."

"It is," he replied, his voice hollow. He struggled for a moment but could not make himself say more.

"Arthur?" His silence was frightening me. His eyes seemed hardly human, so empty were they of anything but pain. Again, he tried to speak but could not.

I began to tremble. When I stepped away to find a chair, he spoke it to my back. "I am to declare Britain a Christian nation."

I froze, certain I had not heard those words. But when I turned back to him, the truth of it was evident. If I hadn't been about to sit, I swear I would have fallen senseless to the ground. As it was, I collapsed into the chair and stared at him wordlessly. I wanted to rage, to scream, to pummel him with my fists, but I had become a woman made of stone. He gathered breath to speak, but I gestured him to silence. At last I rose and, with unsteady steps, walked to the door.

"Guinevere," he said. I stopped but did not turn to him. I went out and closed the door. It was four days before I could bring myself to speak with him again.

The conversion was to be officially announced at the Christ Mass, but word spread in the weeks before. There would be no battle between Oak King and Holly King, at least not at court. The Yule log was allowed, and greenery, but the celebration of the return of the sun became a celebration of the Son. Images of their holy mother were everywhere, in an obvious attempt to replace the Great Mother. I could not understand this strange religion, which was so against the natural joy of coupling that they put forth the nonsense of a miraculous virgin birth. And even as they venerated the "undefiled" mother, they stripped power from women as completely as they could and held us responsible for all the sorrows and errors life comprised.

I wondered, too, at the way the pagans accepted this establishment of a state religion where there had been none before. I suppose the everyday life of the people was not much changed. The tide had slowly been turning, and now there were more Christians in most of Britain than pagans.

Then, too, there was to be a pagan prince, son of the Lady of the Lake, no less. Since Arthur had no other child of his body, Mordred would be considered his heir and successor. Morgan herself counselled peace and patience. That might have surprised me, but I knew her vision of the future. I vowed to do my utmost to purge this boy of Morgan's poison. Arthur had assured me I could

193

raise him in the Old Religion, and I was determined to instill in him all the best that religion entailed.

After much discussion, it had been decided that Arthur and I should receive the boy privately. As we waited, Arthur paced, tracing with his steps the old Roman mosaic of Janus on the floor. His face was drawn, and he looked as ill at ease as I'd ever seen him.

I stood high above the portcullis and watched their approach. Mordred was tall for eight years, slim and graceful, and held his seat well on a chestnut gelding. He was pale, but he bore his head high. Next to him paced Morgan, dramatic on a huge black stallion. Both were dressed in black, stark against the snow, and Morgan's face was veiled. I tried, for the lad's sake, and ultimately for my own, to breathe away my hatred for that woman. I was not entirely successful.

The gatekeeper stepped out to greet their impressive retinue. There was a brief, intense argument, then Morgan moved aside to let Mordred pass. The gate opened, and the boy entered, with several of his men. The rest accompanied Morgan as she turned back the way she came. I did not see her give the child any word of parting.

There came a rap on the door and Cei ushered the lad in, washed and tidied after his travels. His face was unreadable, and I wondered at the poise and discretion in one so young. He knelt before Arthur, who raised him kindly and turned to introduce him to me. I had seen him briefly in my vision—that memory never failed to stab at me—but seeing him in person was startling. Though his hair and eyes were dark as opposed to Arthur's fair coloring, the lines of their face, the strong jaw and high broad forehead with well-defined brow, were identical. More than that, it was the intangibles, the way he walked, how he held his shoulders, even the timbre of his voice that marked him as Arthur's son.

"I saw you ride in on that fine chestnut," I said. "You have excellent horsemanship for one so young."

He brightened somewhat, bowed slightly and replied, "Your Highness is known for your skills throughout the land." I thought this could be the basis for a bond between us, and determined to go riding with him as soon as it could be managed.

"Mordred," Arthur began. He stopped and cleared his throat, then tried again. "I apologize for my absence from your life. I know what it is to be brought up ignorant of your identity and your heritage—"

"But I was not ignorant, Your Highness. My lady mother told me of my lineage when I was quite small."

"I see," said Arthur, hiding his surprise at being interrupted. "And what did she tell you?"

"That I was to rule Britain one day. Unless, of course..." he stammered, turning to me and flushing, the only discomfiture he showed. I nodded at him, to show I had not been offended, and he turned back to Arthur.

"And I know you are my uncle as well as my father. But my lady mother told me there was no shame in that. Just as you had been born in unusual circumstances..." He stumbled over the words, and I was reminded with a start that the person discoursing so dispassionately was but a child. "So I too was born for a purpose, and it mattered not how it was brought about."

Apparently he had been rigorously schooled in this speech, and now that it was delivered, he seemed to deflate before our eyes. Gone was the self-possessed young man, replaced by an uncertain and anxious boy. He stood staring at the floor, his trembling hands clasped behind him. It was time to leave them to talk with each other alone, so I stood and turned my chair to face Arthur's. "Come, Mordred, sit here," I said, but he only stared at me. I took his arm and gently led him to the seat, and let my hand rest on his shoulder a moment as I took my leave, saying that I hoped we would ride together soon. His eyes followed me out the door.

There was less surprise than might have been expected when Arthur introduced his son in the hall that evening. The mood of the assembly was subdued, with people talking quietly among themselves and casting glances at the boy who sat on Arthur's right, wearing Pendragon scarlet.

Since I had begun to develop my powers, all my senses were heightened. The Sight sometimes came upon me unbidden, as once when I'd wondered yearningly where Lancelot was, and instantly found myself spying on him in the stables. I had hurriedly shut that door in my mind. Voices, too, sometimes

195

came clearly to me at times when I would never have heard them with common ears. Now I heard Helena as if she were speaking beside me.

"It's a grievous, grievous sin. But we must hate the sin and forgive the sinner."

A voice I didn't recognize replied. "I don't even count it a sin. Everyone knows Morgan is a witch. She enchanted him."

"At any rate, great good comes of it," said Helena. "He will earn his pardon by saving the souls of others and bringing them to the Christ."

"That won't please our Queen."

Helena sniffed. "She could use some forgiveness herself. Better his one sin, confessed and repented, than hers held to and repeated as often as she gets the chance."

Lancelot, fortunately, was seated on the other side of Mordred. He and Gawain, Captain of the Horse and Chief Braggart, were regaling the wide-eyed boy with tales of horsemanship and daring. I turned to Bedwyr and began a conversation about nothing, my face a burning brand.

Lancelot and I had supposed we could avoid each other in public when Arthur returned, but that proved impossible. Besides, it would only draw attention. The three of us had been boon companions before, so why should that change? Gawain and Gareth were often with us. Gawain doted on his youngest brother, in his gruff way, and both of them loved Lancelot as much as the king did.

There were times, too, when it was just the three of us, that it almost seemed Arthur was deliberately leaving us alone. We would be out riding, and he would turn back for one reason or another, telling us to go on without him. At other times he lagged behind, or pushed so far ahead that we had space for private conversation. It made me very uneasy. I even wondered whether he might be laying a snare, but Lancelot vehemently denied it: "It would be beneath him." When the two of them were alone together, Lancelot said, Arthur's manner toward him was unchanged. Gossip swirled, though as Lancelot pointed out, it always had, even when we were innocent. Through it all, Arthur and I treated each other with utmost tenderness and respect. And Lancelot continued to be as essential to me as my very bones.

Chapter 25

There was an entertainment the evening of Mordred's arrival. A traveling troupe of actors had arrived late in the afternoon, and it seemed a good distraction from all the turmoil in the court. After the evening meal, we gathered in a receiving room where benches had been hurriedly set up. Arthur, Gawain and Lancelot had excused themselves. Important duties, they claimed, but I suspect they simply had little interest in such things. I sat with Gareth on one side and Mordred on the other.

The presentation was a morality play, in which Pride ran roughshod for a while, but then was viciously checked and thrown down. To be honest, I found it rather boring myself, and it had none of the swordplay or rough humor that might have appealed to a young boy. And this particular boy had already had a challenging day. As the actors droned their platitudes, Mordred's head began to droop. He struggled to keep his eyes open, but it was a losing battle. I put my hand on his shoulder, about to tell him he could be excused if he wished, but to my surprise, he fell over sideways and landed with his head in my lap.

I was at a loss for a moment, and then I heard whispering among the other spectators. Gareth silenced them with a glare, and I too looked around forbiddingly. As they quieted and I returned my lackluster attention to the play, a wave of sadness for this child washed over me. His cap had fallen off, and I stroked his hair. An expression of great peace came over his sleeping features, and he burrowed more comfortably into my lap.

Mordred became an accepted part of the court surprisingly quickly. Of course, he was tested by the other boys, partly because he was joining the pages in training a year after everyone else, partly because the circumstances of his birth were familiar to all, and partly because, well, they were boys. He had some protection from Gareth, who had charge of the pages.

Not that Mordred needed much help. He was already quite an excellent horseman for his age, and the skills needed for hawking and hunting came to him easily. Mostly he ignored the gibes and insults tossed his way, but when a tormentor needed to be dealt with, he was dispatched easily and firmly, though without cruelty. At least, the physical scraps were straightforward. Gareth confided, though, that he had suspicions about whether such disagreements were actually put to rest. Even though Mordred won most of his battles, bad things happened to his opponents, sometimes long after the problem seemed to be solved.

"There's a lad named Marc, an orphan. He has the dirtiest mind of any little boy I've ever known, and growing up with Agravaine, I heard a lot! He said something to Mordred, something so foul no one would repeat it, not even the ones who love to carry tales. They scuffled, Mordred bloodied his nose, and they gave each other wide range from then on."

"That doesn't seem…"

"But then last week there was an accident. A practice sword broke, which almost never happens, and Marc got a deep wound on his arm."

"Mordred was wielding the sword?"

"No, another boy. But Mordred was there. And as I said, those two avoid each other, so it was odd that they were even in the same sparring group. What worries me most, though, is that the wound festered. Badly. Almost as if there had been some taint on the sword." Gareth paused, uncomfortable, knowing my fondness for the boy.

"But you don't know? Can't you examine the sword?" I asked.

"No one can find it. And…" again he hesitated, "it happened just after Mordred returned from visiting his mother at Avalon."

"How long ago had the boys quarreled?"

"A month or more."

"You really think an eight-year-old boy capable of such a thing?"

"No, most of them can't hold an idea in their head for more than a moment. But with a mother such as he has..."

"No one despises Morgan le Fey more than I, Gareth, but I try not to hold her son accountable for her evil."

I found it difficult to countenance Gareth's concerns, especially since there was never any proof he could offer. Between riding out together, which we did often, and teaching him about Druidry, Mordred and I spent a lot of time in each other's company. He never expressed any bitterness about his origins, and spoke respectfully of both Arthur and Morgan. In fact, he seemed sometimes too sincere, taking everything with utmost seriousness.

The only time he let his guard down was when we rode. As I'd suspected, he shared my love for horses. At my suggestion, Arthur had given him a fine courser rather than the common rouncey usually provided for younglings. Both of us loved to give our steeds their heads, and tear across the countryside as if chased by demons. At the end of such a wild ride, we were usually laughing like dafts. Mordred's face glowed, and he carried himself with less rigidity. I think it was the only time he relaxed enough to just be a boy.

I began to teach him falconry, too. Bors had found an eyas, an unfledged peregrine, and offered it to Mordred. I was hesitant. A boy his age was usually given a more manageable bird, one that was already trained. I feared Mordred was too young to have the patience for training, but he proved me wrong. He walked for hours with the falcon on his glove, feeding it tidbits.

"Remember this is a wild thing," I told him. "It will never obey just to please you, as a good dog might. And you can never train a bird by making her fear you. She must learn to trust you before all else." Eager as he was, he followed every step slowly and carefully, first letting Astra, as he called her, off his fist on a short creance until she learned to return, then training her to her prey with a lure, then letting her range further and further until the longest leash was discarded. Finally, we were ready for his first hunt.

"Do you think she'll bring something down?" he asked excitedly as we rode out.

"Very likely," I replied. "Just remember we have to do our part, too. She's not going to bring her prey back to you."

"I know," he replied. "I must give chase and be there when she comes to ground, or she'll eat the prey herself and get fed up."

"And if that happens, Astra will be ruined. You would have to let her go. So keep a close eye and ride hard. Are you ready?"

Mordred removed her hood and jesses, and we were off. Astra performed brilliantly, as did Mordred. I held back during the chase, letting him choose his path, and we reined to a stop just as the falcon was dropping to earth with her prey. Swiftly, Mordred slid from the saddle, took the dove from Astra, rewarded her with a tidbit, and had her hooded. He was breathless with excitement. "Well done!" I cheered, and much to my surprise, he ran to me and threw his unencumbered arm around me, burying his head in my waist.

I was startled, and tensed somewhat, and he flinched away from me. There was a flash of shame in his eyes, and if I am not mistaken, of anger as well. I had no wish to discomfit him further. I ruffled his hair and bid him remount. "We want to get Astra to the mews to rest." He nodded curtly and was quiet for much of the ride back.

Mordred grew apace. It seemed no time at all until he had lost the soft edges of a child and stretched into a gangly twelve-year-old. It had seemed natural, when he first came to court, that he would cling somewhat to me, since the boy had never had any real mothering. But by the time he was ready to be a squire, he still had no other attachments.

Usually, the lads who trained together as pages, and then as squires, formed strong bonds. This was encouraged: when they later became knights, it was imperative that they protect each other in battle, and live up to the other rules of chivalry that were instilled at an early age. But Mordred seemed to go his own way. The other boys tended to avoid him; when they couldn't, they treated him with the deference due the heir to the throne, but never with any exuberance or affection. For his part, Mordred seemed barely to notice them, preferring to spend his time with adults, or by himself.

As for his father, Arthur could never see the boy plain. He tried to develop a relationship with him, but they were ill at ease with each other. Mordred was always respectful. In fact, his attitude toward Arthur was so scrupulously correct I sometimes wondered whether it bordered on mockery. And Arthur tried his best to treat Mordred as his honored son, but there was no warmth in him for the boy. In our private moments, he admitted he could never entirely put aside the circumstances of Mordred's begetting, though it was no fault of the child's. There was also Merlin's prophecy, which often crept into Arthur's mind when he looked at the lad.

On a day when heavy rain kept all within doors, Arthur and I slipped away from the company for a few hours in the afternoon. I had told Catlin she too could remove herself, so when it came time to dress again, I had to rely on Arthur's tender but somewhat clumsy ministrations. He finished lacing one sleeve onto my bodice, his tongue poked out with concentration, and moved to the other. Before we had turned to our pleasures, he had spoken again of his concerns regarding Mordred. I returned to the subject, hoping to ease his worries. Despite my adamant opposition, the Christianization of Britain had occasioned no dire results.

"You've always done your utmost to assure both factions are treated fairly; once it became clear you would not allow pagans to be persecuted in any way, the land settled into a balance. There is no reason to think that will change when Mordred becomes king," I said. I turned to him and kissed him, which almost made him drop the sleeve. "Hopefully many years in the future."

"Merlin said it would tear the land apart. And I can't imagine Morgan had any such cheerful prospect in mind…" He again applied himself to the laces.

"Merlin had a lot to say, and none of it has come true," I said tartly.

"I can only hope you are right, love," he said, and stood back from his task. The sleeve was laced askew, but I pretended not to notice. Catlin could put it right later.

For some reason, Mordred seemed to actively dislike Lancelot. He never failed in courtesy, but it was clear there was none of the hero worship most younglings bestowed on our foremost knight. This was made abundantly clear one evening when Mordred was called into our private chambers. Arthur was looking quite pleased with himself, as, no doubt, was I. Mordred arrived, sleek and well-groomed as always—he never looked rumpled or grimy like other boys. "Well, Mordred," Arthur said, "It's time for you to enter service to a knight. I'm pleased to offer you the opportunity to serve as squire to Sir Lancelot." We waited for his reaction, but it was not what we expected.

"That would be a great honor, sir," Mordred said, but with none of the expected emotion. Then he dipped his head humbly. "If it please Your Highness, I would prefer to serve Sir Accolon."

Arthur and I both gaped at him. Lancelot usually had no regular squire, since we judged it might create rivalry among the boys. For Mordred to be named to the post was a signal honor, befitting a king's son. But Accolon? He was at best an ordinary knight, one of the least of the King's Companions. And he had been Morgan le Fey's leman for many years. Though he had never opposed Arthur in any way, that association alone made him suspect. Arthur's face clouded, but his tone was mild when he spoke again. "Why Accolon? He's hardly the most distinguished..."

"No sir," Mordred assented. "But I have known him since I was very small. Since I was brought back from my foster parents, in fact." He paused, and Arthur's eyes bored into Mordred's. The boy continued, smoothly. "And as you know, he spends a good part of his time at Avalon. I would like to accompany him there." He paused again, then said, "You did say you would not keep me from seeing my lady mother."

I glanced at Arthur, whose face was stony. But still he kept his voice light when he replied. "Very well, Mordred. It shall be as you wish."

In truth, we had never made any attempt to keep Mordred from his mother. Arthur was adamant that she never appear at court, but Mordred visited her regularly. He seldom spoke of her to me, and when he did, it was with that same careful correctness.

One afternoon, after a strenuous ride, we had cooled our horses and rubbed them down, and were currying them in the stables. Etain was still in her prime, but sometimes found it hard to keep up with Mordred's younger, larger steed. I was taking special care with her as I groomed her, feeding her treats now and then to thank her for the exhilarating ride.

Mordred and I always talked easily in these moments. He was telling me about Accolon's quirks. A squire spent almost all his time at the beck of his patron, even sleeping on a pallet at the foot of his bed. "He refuses to sleep in any room with only an arras covering the entrance, and always has me put my pallet tight up to the door. I asked him why, and he said it was just a foolish habit. 'If evil wants in,' he said, 'it'll find a way.'"

"Hm." I was thinking that Accolon's long liaison with Morgan had no doubt made him well acquainted with evil, but of course I said no such thing. I was regaling Mordred with stories Catlin had relayed to me of her boy Grance's knight and his ridiculous requests, when Lancelot rushed in.

"There you are." he said. "Come quickly! Palomides is back from the east, and you won't believe the marvels he brought!" He took my hand and began leading me off.

"I can't leave Etain," I said.

"Mordred, you'll finish for the Queen, won't you?" Mordred nodded and gave him a thin, tight smile. Lancelot, laughing, pulled me away again. "Wait until you see..."

Lancelot was telling me about the exotic treasures when I glanced back at Mordred. His face had grown pale, and his mouth wrenched grotesquely, as if he were in great pain. I stopped abruptly, taking my hand from Lancelot's. "Mordred, what is it? Are you all right?"

"Fine, my lady. Just a cramp," he replied, with the same tight smile, and rubbed the small of his back.

By the time the boys of the court were fourteen or fifteen, they discovered an urge that soon enough turned into an all-consuming quest: the search for a maiden who might serve as a mate, either temporarily, or as an eventual wife. Country boys, of course, fell under the same compulsion, and often at an even earlier age. But things were less complicated when it was simply the pairing of a healthy, pretty maid and a strong lad with good prospects.

At court, however, even childish liaisons were taken seriously, with due consideration to respective rank and lineage. A parent or guardian had the final say, and while some were content to let their charges have their head until marriage was spoken of, others kept close control from the start. Parental strictures caused much unhappiness, and the older ladies and I spent a lot of time comforting sobbing girls. Even when there was no opposition from their elders, romantic rivalries among the lads resulted in fistfights, and hairpulling was not unknown among the maidens.

None of this turmoil touched Mordred. He had become a handsome young man, but even if he'd been foul as a toad, his status as heir to the kingdom ensured that the maidens would do their best to enthrall him. They worked their charms: a delicate ankle flashed in a dance, soulful eyes fixed on him in the tourneys and jousts, enticing smiles and carefully planned chance encounters. But Mordred remained politely aloof.

I spoke of it once to Arthur, who looked discomfited and turned the question aside. There was, of course, much talk among the boys and young men about their quests and conquests, and it generally found its way to the ears of their elders. Gareth in particular was a confidant for many of the lads, but he too seemed loathe to chat with me about Mordred's romantic prospects.

When you want to know about the armaments inventory or the condition of the distant keeps, ask a man. If you want to know something closer to the heart, ask a woman. Catlin knew my concerns about Mordred's isolation, and so she found out. He was not at all bereft of female companionship. He had plenty, just not the right kind and not for the right reasons, at least to my reckoning. We learned that Mordred had a reputation for bedding servant girls: many, and never the same one twice. He didn't stoop to harlots, but he paid the girls he bedded to keep their mouths shut, and he never, ever, evinced any interest in a maiden who might be considered an appropriate match for him.

It all sounded cold and calculating to me and didn't seem to fit with the warmth and affection he showed me when we were together. But his regard for me was not echoed in his attitude toward other women. Catlin, for instance, often noted that although he observed all the rules of courtesy, he still treated her rather dismissively. At times we even quarreled about the lad.

"There's something about that boy makes my bones itch," Catlin said one hot, humid day after Mordred had paid a visit. There hadn't been a breath of air for far too long, and everyone was walking a knife edge. At least, that's what I told myself to excuse my snapping back.

"Oh, yes, and Grance is perfect. How would you like it if I talked that way about your son?"

I saw her bite back her answer, and I turned away, mopping my face. She didn't have to say it: Mordred was not my son. But he was the boy I saw in my vision years ago. At that time, I believed he was mine. The yearning had lessened with the years, and with the sure knowledge that it was not to be. Every now and then the bishops made another attempt to have Arthur put me aside and marry again, in hopes of producing a legitimate—and Christian—heir. On that he remained unmovable.

I can't say we became a family. Arthur was never able to accept the boy fully, but Mordred eased some deep ache within me. As did Lancelot.

The wheel had turned and turned. It seemed I had spent half my years torn by two devotions. I loved Arthur with every grain of tenderness and admiration I had within me. Our marriage had certainly had its difficulties, but often I reminded myself of the clear-eyed, kind-hearted young man I had met and grew to love before Morgan le Fey wedged her evil between us. Despite the guilt, rage, and deception she had engendered in him, that man was still there. He was the greatest king Britain had ever known, and Morgan notwithstanding, a fine husband. Our life together was affectionate and respectful. He was a good man, noble down to his bones.

Lancelot was also a good man, and true. But that had little to do with our passion for each other. Nor, despite the snickerings of the court, was it purely pleasure that brought us together repeatedly. Our bodies were merely a means to express our souls. Well, I shouldn't say "merely." It was as if we were two halves of the same being, and when we came together all the world was made right. When my eye fell on Arthur across a crowded room, I smiled with pride. But whenever I caught such a glimpse of Lancelot, my breath stopped for a moment and everything inside me grew taut with longing.

These days, the morning light wasn't kind to me. A web of fine lines had traced themselves around my eyes, and my body was not so supple, nor my waist so slim. Even a few wiry silver strands glinted in my black hair. As for Arthur, his war wounds deviled him when the weather changed, and though Lancelot still leapt to his saddle with the blithe grace of a cat, he had grown lean and sinewy. And still we loved, the three of us, entangled in a dance that seemed it would go on forever.

Chapter 26

The winter Mordred was knighted was a hard one. We hadn't expected it. The harvest had been good, so there was plenty of grain. But even before Yule, sickness swept the court and the countryside, and didn't loosen its grip until almost Ostara. As always, it was hardest on the very old and the very young. There were times when we buried someone almost every day.

One of the first to pass from us was Dame Helena. Though I had little affection for her, I helped nurse her as I did the others. She was a fretful patient, despite the assurances of her priest that she was about to reap the rewards of a "blameless" life. Perhaps she kept herself blameless by casting all blame on others. For years, since I had threatened her with banishment, she had kept her accusations aimed only at my ladies. But now, nearing death, she felt free to return to her favorite subject: my infinite sins. Weak as she was, she still left blue bruises on my wrist, where she would clamp on while alerting me that pagans burn in hell for all eternity. I can't say I grieved when she died.

The weather added to our distress. Although there was little snow that year, the cold pierced to our very bones, and it seemed our fires gave but feeble heat. My women and I spun with chilblains on our fingers. Warriors continued to prepare for the summer invasions and were warm enough as long as they were exerting themselves. Once they stopped, though, the wind bit into them, and many fell ill. Gawain and Lancelot petitioned Arthur to suspend training on days when the weather was particularly evil. Fortunately, those three remained in health. Gareth and Mordred both struggled through bouts of fever, but they were young and strong, and survived.

Game was scarce. But even if the forest had been chock-full, there were few men able to go on the hunt. Our stores of meat dwindled until we were hard pressed even to make broth for the sick. One foul day, Cei took out a party of kitchen boys. All of the boys were unskilled, and Cei hadn't hunted for years. He was also just recovered from the sickness. Had Catlin known about it, she would have persuaded—well, ordered—him not to set foot outside the keep.

It was already full dark when they straggled back, the boys dragging Cei on a makeshift sledge. Every year there are hunting accidents. Often, blame falls on a boar, vicious creatures that they are, or a sow bear protecting her young. Poor Cei was the victim of a badger. The animal had darted from the undergrowth directly into his horse's hooves. The horse reared, Cei fell, and a murderous rock was waiting for him.

Strong as she was, Catlin's grief ate at her, weakened her, until she fell ill in her turn. All the deaths in the realm didn't add up to one moment's thought compared to the terror I endured when she lay unconscious. I spent all my days and nights holding her hand, bathing her fevered brow. The only time I left her was to check on Grance, who was also ill, but conscious. I feared for him, mourning his father and worried about his mother, but he was strong. I don't think Catlin could have survived losing both of them.

At last, she opened her eyes and gazed at me. "Was it a dream?" she asked. I shook my head, and we wept in each other's arms. I have to confess my tears were not only—or even mostly—grief for Cei but blessed relief that I had not been reft of Catlin.

Finally, the winter broke and life returned to normal, though less populous. When Mordred was knighted, and named a Companion of the Round Table, the assembly was scant. Morgan, of course, was not present at the ceremony, so Mordred left court shortly after for an extended visit at Avalon.

It might have been the enduring sadness for all those we lost, or fears of the barbarians gathering once again on our borders. For whatever reason, there was a great deal of unrest in the court that spring. Minor slights were blown into brawl-worthy insults. The petty sniping, snarling and general bitchery among my ladies was so exhausting that I had to send a few away. The widespread belief among the Christians of the court, who were now in the majority, was that the winter's pestilence had been their God's punishment for having unbelievers in positions of power. Obviously, they meant me, and my paganism wasn't their only plaint. The priests never stopped thundering about how women should be subservient to men, should not speak in public, had no role in ruling, and so on.

I had known from the beginning that being consort to the High King would be very different from ruling in my own land, and I was vigilant in my efforts not to overstep. When I formed my Council, I took care not to include any who were especially needed by Arthur, such as Gawain, Bedwyr and Lancelot. I had named Cei to be chief of my advisors, and now that he was gone, called on Gareth to replace him. Arthur was well pleased when I told him my decision. "Not only is he a very able man, but he will represent the Orkney faction, a balance to Bors and Lionel, and others of Lancelot's kin."

There had lately grown a rivalry between the northmen and the Bretons. At first it seemed friendly enough, just the sort of laddish behavior one saw all the time among pages, squires and even knights. But recently, even though Gawain and Lancelot remained the closest of friends, their relatives and allies had begun to scorn and denounce one another; the Bretons were mostly Christian and the Gaels mostly pagan. It irritated me no end.

My liaison with Lancelot was also being constantly bruited, but then, when was it not? By now they should be bored with the same old gossip. And maybe they were, because that spring it seemed to take a particularly nasty turn, with some arcane theories. One version had it I was a witch and had ensorcelled the perfect Christian king and his perfect Christian knight in order to take over the kingdom for the pagans.

Another was that my apparent romance with Lancelot was just a cover: he and Arthur were the lovers. It was so unlikely you might think it a jest, but this rumor particularly horrified the Christians. The Druids pay little heed to such things, believing that if you hurt no one, you may do as you will. And the Mithraites condone and even encourage it, as part of the bonding that helps warriors protect each other in battle.

Some said I was a Saxon spy and blacked my hair with charcoal every morning. Others, citing my barrenness, held I wasn't human at all, but a demon sent to destroy Britain. It was all so very hurtful, and wearisome. Even though it had been going on for many years, it was worse this year, and the wagging tongues were wearing me down entirely.

Finally, I could live with it no longer. I summoned Lancelot, to tell him we must give over. I arranged to meet him in a secluded bower. The garden was walled, and opulent at midsummer, protecting me from any eyes that might peer from a casement. Catlin was posted at the only door. I had always refused to be attended at every moment, even before there was a need for such privacy, so my absence was unlikely to be noted. We were safe in the green calm, yet my heart thumped as if I were fleeing a catastrophe, and I labored for breath to speak.

"It's like a thousand little cuts every day," I said, trying not to give way to sorrow. "And then we're together, and you heal me. But the next day, it's a thousand and one."

"I see it in my men, too. Those arrayed against me give me scornful looks, but what pierces most deeply is when those who love me avoid my eyes."

For our honor, for Arthur, for Britain, it had to end. There were tears, and vows that our love would live forever. When he stood to leave me, Lancelot forced a ragged smile and said, "I'm supposed to be the invincible knight. I can face any foe. But to take one step away from you is the hardest task that has ever been set me." Our hand were clasped. I bent to kiss his, then slowly pulled mine free. He stood there for one more moment, then turned and strode swiftly away, taking an indispensable part of me with him.

That summer was as hot and stifling as the winter had been cold. In an attempt to escape the baking heat of the keep, a large party went out from court to spend a day in the countryside. It wasn't much better there. When we'd done this in times past, we'd never had to think about transporting tables and pots and food and serving ware and such. But without Cei, it was chaotic. Catlin, of course, couldn't stand the disarray. She marshalled some of my ladies. I should have helped too, but I simply couldn't bring forth the energy.

Lancelot and I had been trying to avoid each other, but it was difficult in the confines of the court. Of course he had to take his accustomed place at meals and other public gatherings, but it also seemed that whenever I turned a corner or mounted a staircase, he was there. For a while he tried to engage me when we came upon each other privily, but I held firm. Now we passed with eyes averted. Still, every time I saw him, the wound bled afresh.

He had been keeping himself apart on this outing, spending as much time with his horsemen as possible. I was sitting by myself under an oak, having shooed away my ladies. I suppose I was brooding. Arthur eased down next to me, and I stirred myself to be pleasant to him. None of this was his fault. Still, our conversation was halting. At one point, we were both looking around ourselves uncomfortably when I caught sight of Lancelot. He saw me at the same time, and began to turn away, but Arthur also glimpsed him just then. "Lancelot!" he cried. "Come join us in the shade."

No no no, find some excuse. But there was none, and so he came to join us. Worse, the only place he could reasonably sit was on my other side, trapping me between them. Catlin would have found some way to ease the situation, but she was occupied, and my mind is not so nimble. I sat and listened as they made awkward jests, trying my best to put in a merry word now and then, but the effort was simply beyond me. Everything green had turned brown, the leaves drooped in the heat, and the clatter of insects was deafening. My riding gown clung to me wetly and sweat streamed into my eyes, down my back and sides. Arthur and Lancelot were both looking at me, waiting for an answer to some inane question I hadn't heard. I clambered to my feet, declaring, "I can't bear it!"

They both looked up at me in surprise. I forced a smile. "I'm going down to the stream and put my feet in. It might still carry some coolness."

"Good idea," Arthur said. For a moment I feared he'd come too, but he settled himself more comfortably. "I'd accompany you, but I'm compelled by that fine meal to take a nap." Relieved, I patted his shoulder and turned to make my escape. "Lancelot, go with your lady, will you?" Arthur said lazily. I nearly screamed.

Breaking through the woods to the stream bank well ahead of Lancelot, I plopped myself on the bank and awkwardly began to tug off my boots. When he got there, he offered to help but I turned away, wrestled the second boot off and dangled my feet into the lukewarm water. He sat down beside me, and I buried my face in my arms.

"Go away. It's hard enough being around you when we're under the eyes of the court, but alone…"

"You don't want me here?"

I lifted my head, and my despair was overcome with a sudden rush of bitterness. "When I can't touch you? When my mind is so rapt on you that I can barely attend to Arthur? Better not to see you at all."

"I know. I thought I could just…be near you, see you and hear your voice, and that would be enough. You'd think after all these years… Well. I was wrong." He groped for a pebble and threw it into the stream.

My anger faded as quickly as it had come. I sighed and leaned back on my elbows, looking up through the dry leaves to the blazing sun. He too leaned back, our shoulders touching. I didn't move away.

"Do you want me to leave?" he asked, carefully not looking at me.

"No. I want you beside me like this for the rest of my life. But it might be wisest."

"I'm afraid I'm not much good at being wise."

"Nor am I." For a moment the racket of insects died down, and we could hear the gentle burble of the stream. I turned to him. "You'll have to stay away this time."

He smiled at me, that sweet, slow smile that always made my heart stumble. "Then you'll have to promise not to get abducted again."

"I'll do my best."

His smile went away. "You know, I would have come back in any event. Leaving Elaine and Galahad would have been harrowing, but being away from you was eating my soul. Soon I would have had to leave or die."

I turned away. I did not want to think about that time. Then, it had been pure longing for what I assumed I could never have. Would it be different now, having spent these years together? Would memories of our joy in each other sustain me? Might it be better? Worse? It didn't matter. It would be unbearable.

He stared at the stream, and we were quiet a while. Then he sighed and turned back to me, brushed a damp strand of hair from my cheek.

"Gawain and Gareth could lead the men, I suppose. Maybe it's time I take my leave, go tend my orchards at Joyous Garde."

"Remember the spring we went there together to plant them? Those silly-looking little sticks! Now they're blossoming, and bearing, and we…" My throat tightened, and I looked away so he couldn't see how fine the thread that held me. I turned back to him when I heard his wrenching sob. We clung together, weeping like children who had been beaten. We succumbed to one last, long kiss, a kiss that would have to suffice in all the years to come.

At last we pulled apart. Lancelot reached out and wiped the tears from my face. "We'll always love each other, won't we."

"I'm afraid so."

And then we heard someone approaching through the woods with deliberate noise. We flinched apart as Arthur came into the clearing.

"Ah, there you are," he said, wiping sweat and gnats from his eyes. "I just wanted to let you know, love, that Gawain and Gareth and I decided to stay out here and do a night hunt. So leave us a cook and some provender." His gaze was carefully trained past the stream and out over the misty hills.

Lancelot got to his feet. "A night under the stars sounds wonderful. I'd stay with you—" Arthur gave him a sharp look. He seemed somehow eager, almost hopeful. "But I was just telling your lady that I'm leaving tomorrow for Joyous Garde. I'll need to prepare tonight."

Arthur's brow wrinkled. "This is a sudden decision."

"No. Not really."

Arthur glanced at me, but I was staring at my toes, white and distorted under the water. He clasped Lancelot in the soldier's embrace. "Go safely, my dear friend, and take my blessing." He started back into the woods, then turned to Lancelot again. "And be careful tonight." We both looked at him, puzzled. He shrugged, but there was some sorrow in his eyes. "Just that… there are such rogues in court these days."

He crashed off through the woods, leaving me with Lancelot. Panic surged in me, and I had to fight to take a breath. "Arthur, wait!" I called. "I'm coming with you." I grabbed up my boots and ran after him, the bracken like daggers to my tender feet.

I sat in my chamber that night with a piece of damp embroidery in my hand. I couldn't have told you what the design might be. Instead, I was staring into the middle distance, not seeing the candle flame or the rich tapestries hanging on the walls. Catlin sat across from me, supposedly mending a kirtle. In truth, she was spending more time glancing over at me, but she did not interrupt my musing. A quiet tap at the door behind me, and I startled to attention.

Catlin opened to Lancelot, who embraced her warmly. Then she went out, with a last sympathetic look at me. Lancelot barred the door and came to sit beside me. I couldn't bring myself to look at him, but reached out my hand, and he grasped it, stroked it, then swooped to press his lips to it. I bent to kiss the back of his neck, and we sat together in silence a while. Finally he straightened and looked searchingly at me. The pain in his eyes echoed my own, and the lines on his face seemed drawn with a dagger. "Come with me," he said quietly.

"I can't do that to Arthur, and no more could you."

"No. But..."

"When?"

"First light, before the court is well stirring. Bors is putting a fresh edge on my sword—he's coming with me—and then all will be prepared."

I wanted nothing more than to scream and rage and make impossible demands, but I called on the Mother for strength to keep my voice calm. "Gawain and Gareth will sorrow that you didn't take your leave of them."

"I know. But I feared Gareth would want to come with me, and his place is here with Arthur. Saying my farewells to Arthur and..." his voice caught in his throat. "And to you... that's all the leave-taking I could manage."

"Galahad?"

"I tried to see him, but he was at prayers. I wish —"

BOOM! An armed fist struck the door and the sound reverberated throughout the chamber. Agravaine shouted through the wood. "Come out, traitor! We have you!" Other voices shouted, whooped and cursed.

We stared at each other as if our lives were draining from us. "No," I whispered. "No. Not now."

"Lancelot, show yourself." This from Mordred. "No heroics, there are eight of us. No one needs to be hurt."

Finally Lancelot moved, looking around in panic. "I don't even have a sword!"

I went to a chest and found the small ceremonial dagger I use in the rites and held it out to him. "This is all I have."

"Keep it. Defend yourself."

Agravaine, Accolon and others continued to pound and shout. "Surrender, traitor!" "Unbar, you coward!" Lancelot started toward the door, but I pulled him back.

"Take this and use it. They need more than eight to hold you. Get through and ride!"

"No," he said quietly. "It's over. I deserve..."

"You'll be quartered and I'll be burnt. We don't deserve that."

"Arthur would never harm you."

"Open, sir. Do you think we'll go away?" This was Mordred, trying to sound reasonable. Lancelot turned toward the door, but again I pulled him back and made him look at me.

"He'll have no choice. To him, the laws are sacred, you know that. If he were here... he'd tell you to ride."

The pounding and yelling were unbearable. Lancelot broke away from me and went to the door.

"All right! Stop that noise! I'll surrender to you, Accolon. Not to Mordred."

"So be it," Accolon replied.

I was stunned with shock and betrayal, unable to believe he would surrender his honor so cheaply. But I was mistaken. He kissed me, took the little knife, pulled the drapery from the bed, and wrapped it around his left arm as a shield. He went to crouch by the door and signaled for me to stand ready to open it. I positioned myself across from him, and our eyes met one more time. I strode across the distance between us, gave him a warrior's kiss, then took my place again.

He nodded to me as Accolon began to pound again. I unbolted and threw open the door, so quickly that Accolon was caught off balance. Lancelot hauled him into the chamber, flung him down and cut his throat in one swift move as I slammed and bolted the door. He tossed the dagger to me and started stripping Accolon's harness. I went to help him don the armor. Finally, we kissed once more, a kiss of fire and grief. "I'll come for you," he said, cupping my face in his palm.

Then he opened the door to let in the mob and began fighting his way through. As they poured in, I used my dagger to help clear him a path. Of the seven remaining men, he was able to dispatch three right away, and I

214

accounted for one. Another wrested the dagger from me and held me, kicking and screaming. Mordred and Agravain faced Lancelot, jockeying for position.

Suddenly, Mordred tried to bolt. Agravaine was startled, and Lancelot took that opportunity to hurtle through, crushing Agravaine against the heavy oaken door. The oaf holding me loosened his grip a bit, so I struggled harder until I had his attention again. I had no chance of escape, but I wanted to give Lancelot time to get away.

He caught Mordred and pinned him against the wall, eye to eye, just outside my chamber. Had it been me, I swear I would have killed him where he stood. But Lancelot hesitated. "You," he said with pure contempt, "a king's son. Arthur's son. A spying, sniveling, despicable..."

With deliberation, not taking his eyes from the terrified man, Lancelot drew his sword along Mordred's cheek. He would not kill him. But he would leave his mark on him. Mordred screamed.

Agravaine shook his head clear and charged at him. Lancelot threw Mordred into his path and leapt out a casement to a roof below, and then to the ground. The knight who held me dragged me with him. By the time we looked out, we could see nothing in the darkness, only hear hoofbeats pounding away.

I gasp for breath in the stifling heat, but my throat will not open. Sweat trickles my spine, and I press my back to the stone walls, but they hold no coolness. I can smell my own fear, rank as weeds. I wish for an abyss, but all that gapes and yawns is time.

Owls sob and screech from their trees, and despite the heat, I hear the honing winds of winter. Shadows unravel and creep from the walls, and in their depths, the feeble rushlight becomes a tower of flame.

Each heartbeat is a blow against ribs bruised from within. I am beaten, like a bear that sits whipped in its cage. I, too, am hunched like a brute, not yet dead, but lifeless. What keeps me in my body? I fear my very bones might be visible.

My thoughts, weak and random, cannot be mustered. I am a hollow hum of despair. I kneel, I stand, I wander wall to wall in a seizure of grief.

Insects chitter in the hot night wind. Minutes river through me, some rapid, some slow as silt. Had he left a heartbeat early or come a deep breath late... Were we not parting, he would not have come at all.

Rage does not serve.

The Great Wheel will turn, and season follow season. The wheel of humankind, though, no one can say. In the high window, only the plummeting stars and a pockmarked moon.

Part Four

Chapter 27

We could have been worse served. I was still Queen of Cameliard, at least for the time being, and under Arthur's rule of presumed innocence, I suppose I was still Britain's Queen, so we were treated with some circumspection. We were not put in the foul dungeon but held in a strongroom with guards at the door. It was clean enough, and there was a small window, so it wasn't entirely airless. We had water to drink.

I say "we" because Catlin had joined me in my confinement. It seems she had seen the armed men headed for my chamber and attempted to warn me, injuring a guard when he tried to pull her away. They weren't going to lock her up, having larger concerns on their mind, but she demanded it. I'm sure she would have injured someone more severely if they'd refused.

The strongroom was situated in the outer wall, high above the gate. A troop of horsemen had gone in pursuit of Lancelot, and when I heard hoofbeats approaching the keep, I feared they were returning already, with him in custody, or worse. But then someone called to the gateman; it was Arthur's voice. I sank to the floor, trembling. Catlin knelt beside me and held me, hard. I think that was all that kept me from flying into a thousand jagged fragments. I can never thank the Mother enough for giving me Catlin.

After a moment, she hauled me to my feet and shook me gently. "Come now," she said, "you can't meet your husband and King looking like this." While I stood numb, she pulled my night cloak around me and tied it, then roughly wiped the tears from my face and smoothed my wild hair. She began to plait it, but then we heard footsteps approaching. She abandoned the plait and stood beside me. We heard voices outside, and she gave me a sharp poke in the back to make me stand up straight. Holding her own back erect as a ship's mast, she turned her head and looked me full in the face. "The Mother will protect you," she said, "and keep Lancelot alive to be her instrument."

Arthur stood in the doorway. Catlin dropped him a quick courtesy and went out with the guard. As the door closed behind them, Arthur and I stood silent, both of us fighting back tears. I took a hesitant step toward him. "Arthur…"

"No," he said harshly. "Don't." He turned away for a moment, gathering himself. When he turned back and spoke to me, his voice was choked, but with sorrow and grief, not rage.

"I've never blamed you for loving him. But how could you let…" He stopped and drew a deep breath. "Do you know what this means? Not enough that I'll lose my Queen—and the bishops will make sure of that—but the Companions, all of it, everything we've built together will be broken…"

My fear and guilt drained away, replaced by a wave of certainty. "No," I said. "No. This is not the end. The realm will stand. Most of your Companions love Lancelot almost as much as they love you. His enemies will never allow his return, but neither will his friends allow harsh retribution. When he is gone to Brittany and I am no longer Queen, your Companions will stand beside you. What you have built for Britain will survive. It must, and it will."

I was certain of that. For me, for Arthur, for Lancelot, this was tragedy indeed. But whatever spite or political ambitions fueled this attack, it would be rooted out and destroyed, and the realm would remain whole. Arthur was staring at the floor, unable to see past this disaster.

"Ambitious knights and religious rivalries mean nothing in the face of the Sea Wolves," I said. "You have united us and defeated them. Your people will not abandon you."

He shook his head wearily. Still not looking at me, he asked, "You are treated well enough?"

"Yes. And Arthur, know that though you lose your Queen, your wife still and always loves you." He lifted his head, and our eyes met. He took a step toward me, then whirled to pound on the cell door.

219

The pursuers returned without Lancelot. I suspected they had not ridden very hard nor searched very thoroughly. Gawain and Gareth had been away from court with Arthur, but Bors and Lionel were part of the company and would have tried to ensure no harm came to their kinsman. Of course, the Christians still hoped for a Christian queen, but they bore Lancelot no particular ill will. Everyone assumed he had fled to Brittany, and except for Mordred, no one pushed Arthur to pursue him.

Mordred came to visit me once. How he dared, I do not know. He stood in abject humility, the slash on his face glowing scarlet and studded with crude black stitches. He'd brought a basket laden with rare treats, exotic fruits, and the most delicate pastries. He set it on a table, then bowed deeply to me.

"I beg you, Your Highness, to accept my apology. I never intended this for you; it was only Lancelot I sought. I thought sure he would be taken, and the king, for his great love of you, would forgive you. But here you are, caged and held, while that blackguard runs free. Had I to do it over—" I could hear no more. I grabbed him by his arm like a wayward child and dragged him to the door, where I began pounding for the guard.

"The king will pardon you, Lady," he babbled. "I'm sure of it. And you'll see, when events have run their course, that it was all for the good. The Old Religion must—"

The guard opened, and I thrust Mordred out into the corridor. Catlin came behind me with his basket of delicacies and threw it out after him. I paced a while, trying to conquer my rage. When I finally calmed myself, Catlin set down a serviette with two of the lovely pastries. I looked up at her, and she shrugged.

We were in custody for more than a fortnight, and Arthur never came again. But he moved us to more comfortable quarters and made sure we were provided decent food and appropriate clothing. He even appointed Catlin's son as one of our warders, knowing Grance would make certain his mother and I were treated with respect. He also knew Grance's honor would not allow him to do anything against the law.

Catlin harried me endlessly to use the Sight, but I would not. "I am no oracle," I told her. "What Seeings I had—and those were many years ago— were given me by the Arch Druid and the Lady of the Lake, people of great power. Even so, I saw only what had already come to pass. I cannot auger the future. Even if I could," I continued, "I'm not sure I want to see what's to come for me."

I confess I did not tell her the entire truth. There had, in fact, been several instances when the Sight came upon me without my willing it. It was true I never saw the future, always the past. Once, just once, I saw my mother singing to me when I was a bairn, and I treasure that, but I could never call it back. Sometimes, too, I could see or hear or smell things happening at the time. More often, I heard something I would rather not have heard, such as the hurtful gossip in the court.

But it was not under my control. And most often, it was nothing of import, simply a hint, an inkling of small matters, such as a visitor. I knew, for instance, that Gawain was trying to screw up his courage to visit us.

He finally arrived, looming in the doorway, awkward and mumbling. I drew him in and bade him sit and refused to listen to his apologies for not being at hand that dreadful night. I could see he was ripped asunder by grief, both for Lancelot, his friend and fellow warrior, and for his King. "Aye, he suffers, my lady," Gawain said. "Donal tells me he paces all night. He eats but little, and though he maun hold court, he scarce hears what is said to him."

Gawain never came again, but Gareth visited every day, and his company was most welcome. He never spoke of that night if he could prevent it. Instead, he diverted us with court gossip, recited stories and regaled us with song, as skilled as any bard. He was determined to lighten our days, and I loved him more than ever. Just once did he mention the disaster, and I rather wish he hadn't. Once again, I learned something I would prefer not to have known.

"My brother sends his greetings, my lady. I keep telling him he should come again to see you, but he can't bring himself to do so."

"Surely Gawain knows I bear him no ill will. None of this was of his making."

"He berates himself daily for agreeing to the plan. If he hadn't, he thinks, he might have saved you, and his dearest friend."

"Wait," I said. "What plan? He knew this was going to happen?" Something began to buckle inside me, and I could hardly get air enough to force my next question out. "Did Arthur?"

It simply never occurred to me that Arthur staying away that night was anything more than a terrible falling together of events, either fated or by chance. At most, I assumed the conspirators took advantage of an unforeseen opportunity. But if it had been planned? It took a moment for Gareth to realize I hadn't known. He turned ashen and began to back away. I reached out to grasp his arm, and the room wavered around me...

Knights were gathered at the Round Table. Arthur and Lancelot were not yet present. Accolon, Agravaine and Mordred stood together. They were making show of talking privately, but in fact they carefully pitched their voices to be overheard.

"If only the Picts were as easily conquered as Lancelot," Agravain said, "we could spend every summer at home."

"What are you saying?" Mordred asked. "No man has ever defeated Sir Lancelot."

"No," Accolon chimed in. "It took a woman. Arthur's too bewitched to see, and we who still have eyes say nothing."

The other knights could no longer pretend not to hear. Gareth and a few others shifted uneasily. Gawain colored with anger. "Mickle noisy for nothing, Accolon," he said. "Best shut your vizard."

"Why? Everyone knows Lancelot spends less time in the King's council than under the Queen's skirts."

"I know nae such thing."

"Then you're the only one who doesn't," Agravaine said. "If he used his sword as much as he uses his—"

"Enough!" Gareth shouted. "I won't have it."

"Why stuff your ears against the truth?" Mordred asked mildly. "I think we ought to hear what he has to say."

"That's no surprise," said Gawain. "Whenever there's some shit to be shoveled, you're right there with your little spade. Leave it alone, Mordred."

"We've left it alone for years." Agravaine said. "It's time we spoke up."

Gawain looked him up and down contemptuously. "I haven't heard you squeak so loud since Turquin held you in his dungeon. If Lancelot hadn't come for ye, you'd be cold at your heart's root today. Half the men in this room owe him their lives, including me. Now stint!"

Arthur entered, and there was a moment's silence. Then Agravaine broke it. "I will not."

Accolon stared at Gawain. "Are you with us?"

"Some quarrel here?" Arthur spoke pleasantly, but his eyes were stern. Gawain looked around and saw the set faces of the others. He walked out without another word.

"What's got that redheaded temper up this time?" Arthur asked, turning to Gareth, who began fumbling for an answer.

It was Accolon who spoke. "He's more loyal to a treasonous friend than to his king. My lord, Lancelot holds your Queen as his own and has for years."

There was a long silence as Arthur turned away and went to his seat at the Round Table. The others followed. When all were seated, he spoke,

"This is a heavy charge. The law has banned trial by combat, so Lancelot can't kill you for such slander any more. But the law also says you need proof."

Mordred had been keeping himself apart since Arthur arrived, but now he spoke earnestly. "The issue has been poisoning the Companionship for a long time, sir. It should be settled. Spend tomorrow night on the hunt, and we'll either give you proof or put the charge to rest.

"You'd have me set a trap for my friend and chief knight?"

"What harm," said Mordred, with a pleasant smile and shrug, "if he's innocent?"

By the time I gathered my senses again, Gareth had fled, and Catlin was pouring me a cup of wine. Though she was not privy to my Seeing, she was more than adept at reading my face. Her jaw was set, and her brows beetled: she would have something to say. I took a sip of the wine and set the cup down. "He had no choice," I said. "He knew about us, he always knew, but couldn't say so. Mordred caught him in a trap as neatly as he caught us."

"He could have warned you!"

"He tried. But we didn't understand him."

"Then he should have tried harder. How could he—"

"Catlin. He did all that honor would allow."

"Honor!" Catlin spat the word as if it were tainted. "Men trot out their precious honor when it is most convenient for them."

"Come now, Catlin. Women are bound by honor, too. And loss of it is a heavy burden." I looked around meaningfully. "As you can see."

"Yes, and where is Lancelot? He fled and left you. Your husband betrayed you. And these are the two most honorable men in Britain? I am up to my back teeth with men and their accursed honor."

There was little profit in arguing with her, and I had no spirit for it anyway.

Lughnasa passed, the light from our little window faded earlier each day, and still we waited. Did Arthur intend to keep me locked away forever? Lancelot was presumed safe in Brittany, but Mordred constantly demanded that he be brought back to stand trial for treason. I also heard he pleaded for leniency for me, which I found hard to understand.

Gareth was certain I would not be brought to trial, only held for a time, and then banished, or maybe even pardoned. "There aren't many left to testify," he said. "Only Mordred, Agravaine and Lovel. Not one of them of any good repute. And all they can truly bear witness to is that Lancelot was in your chamber. They can say nothing about what he was doing there."

"We were only saying goodbye," I said miserably.

"You see?" Gareth insisted. "They simply don't have evidence to convict you of any crime. That's why they aren't calling for a trial."

Chapter 28

And yet they did. It was almost Mabon when I found myself summoned to stand in open court before the king, who was flanked by Edalwurf and Mordred. I hadn't seen Arthur since midsummer, and I was shocked by his appearance. He had wizened like a dried apple. His face was carved with deep lines, and he even seemed smaller in stature. I wanted nothing so much as to be able to hold him and tell him how sorry I was.

I had asked that they send me one of my better gowns, a simple gray one devoid of any trim or embroidery. I must admit I was shocked when Catlin made no objection. Arthur himself sent along a modest crown and the golden torque that had belonged to his mother. I stood as tall as I could in that hall packed with what seemed like every member of the court and people from miles around, but I felt very, very small. Edalwurf glared at me. Mordred sat with the expression of a small anxious dog. And Arthur refused to meet my eyes.

I didn't have to be there. The night before, Gareth had entered my cell beaming. "You're free, my lady!" he exclaimed. "His Highness sent me to tell you he intends to grant you a full pardon tomorrow, the bishops be damned." Catlin gasped and leapt to her feet as he continued. "I think—" he could barely speak for his delight—"I think he may even intend to reinstate you as Queen. Oh, my lady, I am so glad!" Catlin moved to embrace me, but I held up a hand.

I couldn't bring myself to look at Gareth, so shining and eager. "Please tell my lord and king that I cannot and will not accept his offer." Catlin understood

225

immediately, and sank back into her chair, shaking her head in resignation and despair. Gareth looked as though I'd clouted him with the flat of a sword.

Of all the blessings Arthur brought to Britain, it was his system of justice that most made him swell with pride. It was Arthur who instituted the concept of judgement by a group of nobles and codified the laws that defined a crime and set forth the appropriate punishment. No one man, despite his rank, his wealth, or the size of his army, could set himself above the law. Not even the High King. If ever I doubted Arthur's love for me, the fact that he was willing to overthrow "the King's justice" set all such fears to rest.

He had united Britain and won us years of peace after the battle of Badon Hill. But the various barbarians still threatened to overrun us, and probably always would. His true legacy, what set him apart from every other high king, emperor, or ruler of any stripe, was the rule of law. A pardon by decree would lay it all to waste.

I tried to explain all this to Gareth, but he could not be made to understand. When finally I ended the debate and dismissed him, there were tears standing in his eyes. As for Catlin, she had kept silence through my explanation and Gareth's arguments. Now she stood, took our bedding from a chest, and began to make up our pallet on the floor. "Well?" I challenged. "You have nothing to say?"

"Would it make a difference if I did?" When I didn't reply, she continued. "I knew you wouldn't accept, and I suppose the king did too, but he had to try. Why do you think he sent dear sweet Gareth instead of coming himself?"

And so I stood in the great hall, with an assembly of knights and nobles seated behind Arthur, and the people of the court crowded in wherever they could fit. I had asked Catlin not to employ the formidable elbows which she usually used to secure the place closest to me in any public gathering. I needed her out of my line of vision. Surprisingly, she understood.

Since Arthur was personally involved, he could not serve as presiding judge, a role Edalwurf was all too eager to take over. He began his questioning by asking Arthur where he was that night, and whether Lancelot and I knew he would be away from court. Then Agravaine recounted his tale, embellishing it with the worst innuendo whenever he could. Several times Mordred tried to interrupt with a different interpretation, but Edalwurf refused to allow it.

When Mordred's turn came, his version was shaded to imply that Lancelot alone bore full responsibility for being there, and I had been unwillingly compromised. He called upon Bors, for example, to testify that I had sent no message summoning Lancelot, nor commanded him to attend me.

Then they turned to me. Edalwurf smiled unctuously and addressed me respectfully as he asked the question again.

No," I told them, "I had not sent for Sir Lancelot."

"Did you know he might come?"

"I try not to think overmuch about what someone else may do or not do. Since he was about to leave court, it was possible, yes, that he would come to bid his Queen farewell, as was meet for my champion to do."

"Why delay his farewells until late at night, when he would have to find you in your chamber?"

"He had just decided to leave that day. As leader of the Companions…" I cast a glance to those knights, most of whom looked sympathetic, then continued, "…and a prominent figure at my Lord's court, there were many duties he needed to attend to. And he planned to leave before the court was well astir."

"Why had this decision to leave been made so suddenly?"

"As I said, I try not to predict or interpret the thoughts of others." There was a ripple of amusement among the listeners; Edalwurf silenced it with a scowl.

"If you considered that he might come, that it was appropriate for your Champion to say his farewells, why were you in a state of undress?"

"It was late, and since I hadn't commanded him, I assumed he wasn't coming."

"Why were you alone with him? Why were you not attended?"

I was growing impatient with his questioning and paused for a moment to get my irritation under control. *Just tell the truth,* I told myself. "I knew there was nothing to fear from such a man of honor as Sir Lancelot. I didn't know there were others of less honor who might wish me harm, or I would have pulled every lady of the court from her bed to attend us. And had every lady of the court been present, they would have seen or heard nothing except our farewells. He kissed my hand, as he might in front of all the court, or all the world at large."

There was a stir of uncertainty. Gawain stood and called for the trial to be ended, that there was no proof of treason or adultery. Many of those in attendance murmured agreement. None of those who did so were Christian.

"We will carry this event to its conclusion, Sir Gawain, and then you may vote as you will." Edalwurf turned back to me. "Your Highness, was this the first and only time Sir Lancelot had been within your chamber?"

"No," I said, and both Edalwurf and Mordred leaned forward eagerly. I paused just long enough to let the tension build. "I am told that he and Dame Catlin attended me assiduously when I was ill."

Edalwurf's exasperation was growing. "Were you alone with him at any other time?"

"Yes. We often rode out…" His impotent rage caused him to interrupt my answer, and many in the hall shook their heads reprovingly.

"Did he ever touch you other than to kiss your hand?"

"Of course. Dismounting, escorting me into dinner…"

Again, there were murmurs, and even some amusement in the hall. I could not find it in me to enjoy this dreadful repartee. It was not in my nature to play at cat and mouse, and I had to hold myself back from blazing with defiance. The bishop's face raged so red I would have feared for him, if I did not so much fear for myself.

"Were you ever intimate with Sir Lancelot du Lac?!"

"He was—is—one of my dearest friends, and we often spoke intimately."

Edalwurf turned away. When he turned back, he had calmed himself, and smiled on me. That smile made my heart skip a beat with fear. "Your Highness, this must be most distressing and exhausting for you, and I do regret it. Take a moment to rest and refresh yourself."

Rest indeed. As if I could. It took a supreme effort to keep my hands relaxed at my side, not allowing them to tremble or clench. I tried to catch Arthur's eye, but Edalwurf put an arm around his shoulder and turned him away from me. They were having some intense discussion, and Arthur was shaking his head vehemently. I could feel the slight buzzing in my head that presaged the Sight. *No! Not now.* It could not be helped. Though Edalwurf's voice was pitched well below my hearing, I heard: "It's not my place, Your Highness. Such a question should rightly come from her husband. We could clear the hall…" I wrenched myself away and turned to look for Catlin.

She had used her elbows well and was standing behind me. Our eyes met, and I saw it in her face. Catlin had not the Sight, but truly, she didn't need it. She always understood. We kept our faces smooth as we gazed at each other, knowing what the bishop wanted. If he forced Arthur to ask me directly...

And indeed, that's what he did. Edalwurf ordered the guards to clear the hall. As they were herding everyone out, except for those knights and nobles who would sit in judgement, Catlin slipped under a guard's arm and scurried toward me. The guard grabbed her roughly, but Arthur leapt to his feet and roared, "Leave her!" She came to stand beside me while the hall emptied of onlookers. Arthur remained on his feet but turned away to collect himself. I scanned the faces of those who would judge me. Gawain and Gareth, Bedwyr and Bors, there were many who met my eyes with the greatest sympathy and compassion. But there were more, many more, whose faces were hard, lips set in a sneer.

Arthur turned to face me. His skin was as grey as his eyes and sagged as if he had aged twenty years in that short moment. Mordred quivered beside him, his scar blazing. On his left, Edalwurf tucked his hands into the sleeves of his scarlet robe and gazed at me serenely.

"My lady..." Arthur began, then broke off. He swallowed hard and began again. "My Queen. I must ask you here, in this court, did... did you and Sir Lancelot du Lac commit treason and adultery?"

Utter silence, all eyes on me. I could feel Catlin straining beside me, could see Gawain, Gareth, all the friendly faces, even Arthur, each of them begging me, *Lie. Lie!*

I drew a deep breath, tried to find the last morsel of strength inside me, but still my voice broke as I answered, "Not treason, my Lord." And then, sobbing, "Oh Arthur, never treason. We loved you." Arthur's face shattered. As the guards moved to escort me from the hall, I could see Edalwurf making a grimace of false pity and regret as he turned to the king.

It appeared the guards were intending to lay hands on me, so I swallowed my sobs, stiffened my back, and gave them a baleful glare that stopped them in their tracks. As they glanced at each other uneasily, I made a deep courtesy to Arthur, and this time it was I who was unable to meet his eyes. The four guards closed around me and escorted me out. They didn't touch me. Behind, Catlin marched, accompanied by two skittish guards.

It's hard to say how long we waited. We sat and paced and sat again. Bread and cheese were brought, but neither of us could eat. Nor did we talk, since there was nothing useful to say. At last we heard footsteps in the corridor. Thinking it was the guard come to take us back for sentencing, we stood and faced the door, our clasped hands hidden by our gowns. But when the door opened, it was Edalwurf who stood there. Catlin and I returned to our seats.

"What are you doing here?" I asked coldly.

"I have come to save you, Madam," the bishop replied. "As you know, the punishment for a woman who commits treason—and betraying the King is the very definition of treason—is death at the stake. But you have many friends, myself included, who do not wish to see you suffer. I have come to tell you that you can be spared." Catlin tensed, then slumped back. She knew what was coming, and so did I.

"You are to be my savior?" I asked.

"Not I, Madam, but the Savior of all. Accept His mercy, which he offers to even the most loathsome sinner. Repent, vow yourself to the Christ and you shall be saved both in heaven and here on earth."

"So if I submit myself to your authority, I can live out my life in a convent. If I do not, I am consigned to the flames?" He nodded. I walked to the door, pounded on it for the guard. "I'd rather burn."

I admit I was startled by the expression that met my declaration. It was not rage or frustration or even pity, which would have been surprising enough. It was satisfaction. This man had no interest whatever in saving my soul. He would be delighted to see me burn. "As you wish, Madam," he murmured, and went out.

Things moved quickly after that. Soon enough, I was standing again before the dais. If I'd harbored any doubt about my fate, it would have been removed as soon as I saw them. So I was well prepared when Arthur looked out over my head at the gathered court, and in a hollow, cadaverous voice pronounced sentence. "Testimony set before this court shows the Queen taken in treason and adultery. Sentence of law commands that she be burnt."

He started to rise, heavily, but Mordred put a restraining hand on his arm and whispered, "Him too."

Arthur gathered himself to speak again. "Sir Lancelot du Lac, taken with the Queen, is also sentenced to death. A troop will be sent..." He stopped speaking and sat for a moment, trying to go on. Then he rose and walked out, leaving the court buzzing.

Catlin could not sit down. She paced and paced in our small room until she made me dizzy. I knew what she was thinking, and didn't want to get into a discussion, so I held my silence. Finally she burst out. "Where is he?"

"I don't know. Nearby."

"People are saying he escaped to Brittany."

"He wouldn't."

"Oh?"

I had used up so much self-control during the trial and sentencing that I had little left. I snapped at her. "Do you really think a man as honorable as Lancelot would leave me here to bear our guilt alone?"

She did not reply, only lifted an eyebrow, and looked pointedly around our room. I flounced angrily into a chair and turned my face away, unwilling to acknowledge that indeed, except for her, I was alone. She began pacing again, then stopped and sat across from me. "Why hasn't he tried to get word to you?"

"Perhaps he has, but it didn't get through."

"You know Gareth would have risked anything to bring you a message."

"But how could he get to Gareth?"

"I don't know! But he has friends enough at court. Bors—"

"Bors was absent from the sentencing. Where do you think he might have gone?" My voice softened. "Do you really think Bors doesn't know where his kinsman is? You said it yourself, Catlin: the Mother will help us, and Lancelot is her instrument."

"Lancelot is a Christian," she said gloomily.

Gareth held no such doubts. "Don't think it for a moment, my lady! He will come. The king himself is sure of it. It is all that sustains him."

"Oh? You know that for certain?" Gareth was not a person of spiritual power, but the bond between us was now so close that I could easily access his thoughts. He simply held out his hand to me, and I took it...

Arthur sat brooding in his chamber. Gawain and Gareth entered. He turned his gaze on them but didn't speak. With his usual bluster, Gawain broke the silence. "We ask to be exempted from the Queen's guard."

"You lead the Companions now," Arthur replied. "You have to be there."

"I won't watch her burnt."

"Lancelot will come for her," Arthur said firmly.

"And if he doesn't?"

"He will."

"But I can't bear arms against Lancelot, either," Gareth protested. "It was he who made me knight! Ever since I was a child I— Please, sir."

"It's a duty no one wants. When rescue comes, there won't be much resistance."

"There are some who want it," Gawain said.

"Some Christians, I suppose," Arthur conceded.

"Some pagans too, sir. Even my own brothers. I don't know why, except for jealousy of a knight finer than they could ever hope to be. Thank Mithras I have one brother left who I can stand to look at," Gawain said, giving Gareth a jostle. If he was trying to lighten the mood, he didn't succeed. Arthur just gazed at him without expression.

"I suppose, as chief of the Companions, you could stand with me. But Gareth, you'll have to serve."

"Then I'll serve in the livery of a common soldier. I won't sully my knighthood and my arms in such low service. And if Lancelot comes—"

"He'll come."

"I won't strike a blow against him."

"The law requires—"

"Then bring me before your precious court!" Gareth himself seemed stunned at this outburst. Gawain and Arthur stared at him as he continued. "I won't do it. How can you? How can you burn your Queen, and raise arms against the noblest knight that—"

"Enough," Arthur said wearily. "Wear what you will, strike or don't strike, but the law must be served. I have no choice but to carry through with this spectacle. And if God hears my prayers, unworthy though they be, Lancelot will come."

Gareth was still indignant, and about to say more, but Gawain firmly led him out.

232

When I loosed his hand, Gareth looked discomfited. "I should not have spoken so to my liege lord. But I was—"

I gathered him into an embrace.

They came for me the next night. Catlin, Gareth, and I had spent most of the day in prayer, and in reminiscing. We all tried to maintain a calm confidence, but as Gareth knelt to me, his knees shook. "I swear to you, Your Highness, if—when!—when Lancelot comes, I won't lift a sword against him. And I will help you in any way I can."

"My dear Gareth," I said. "I know it. Just don't put yourself in any danger. Neither Lancelot nor I could bear it if you were hurt." He kissed my hand, rose, embraced Catlin in a rough hug and pounded on the door. He kept his face to the door until it opened.

I had been worried that Catlin might be accused of abetting treason, and indeed there were those who tried to levy such a charge. But Arthur was adamant. He sent a message with Gareth saying she was free to stay at Winchester with Grance, or if she preferred, he would help her find a place elsewhere.

"What do you think you will do?" I had asked her.

"I'll go wherever Sir Lancelot takes us."

"Oh? So now you think –"

"Of course he will come. He'll take you to safety, and after a proper interval, Arthur will pardon you both."

It was hard to think about what might happen after, especially since, no matter how earnestly I reassured myself, I wasn't certain there would be an after. And if there was not… there was this night to be endured. I have always believed that fire must be the worst death.

Grance entered and spoke with his mother quietly. Like Gareth, he assured her he would do nothing to prevent a rescue. Then he gave her some instructions, which I couldn't hear. After he left, she gave me a wry look and said, "It appears Lancelot will have to take you barefoot and clad only in your shift. I hope he has some decent attire waiting at Joyous Garde. But men never think of such things, do they." Then, still chattering bravely, she unlaced my sleeves, released my kirtle, and helped me out of my blue-and-grey gown. My hair, too, had to be unbound. For probably the last time, Catlin unplaited it and

233

combed it smooth. It struck me that I must look like a virgin on her wedding night. An aged virgin, but still...

There was a soft tap at the door, Grance's signal that they would be coming for me momentarily. Catlin and I clung to each other. We were beyond words, beyond tears. The door opened and my guard assembled. Catlin tried to take her place beside me, but it was not allowed. I must walk out alone.

The stone corridor seemed miles long, yet it also seemed I reached the end of it in the space of a breath. I could see dancing flames as we entered the courtyard, and quailed inwardly, but it was just torchlight. The entire court was gathered, with the exception of Arthur, Gawain and Mordred. The crowd was quiet, uneasy, murmuring among themselves. Edalwurf stood waiting for me.

In a booming voice, he proclaimed, "Madam, I beg of you, do not go into the flames an unconsecrated heathen. Will you take the sacrament?"

"My life and my death belong to the Goddess. Where is my husband?"

"The King waits above to give the signal."

I looked up at the crenellations surrounding the courtyard but could see nothing. "Will you tell him, please, that I die loving him?"

"If you love him, take absolution and join him in heaven."

"You forgive everything, don't you. For a price."

He gave me a look of utter disgust. Then he hooded his eyes, bowed his head in mock resignation, and stepped back. My heart was pounding so hard I was sure everyone watching could see it pulse beneath my shift. For a long moment it seemed certain I must waver and break, but I drew the deepest breath I could, shook my hair back, raised my head and looked into the eyes of the soldier who led those coming for me.

It was Gareth, clad in the armor of a common soldier, his shield covered with white canvas. His face was partially hidden by his mail coif, but there was no mistaking those kind eyes. I blinked in surprise but showed no other sign. If this was part of some plan, I didn't want to give it away. He and another soldier I did not know clasped my arms and led me to the pyre.

Chapter 29

Fire. It was a part of many pagan observances. At Beltane, Imbolc, Samhain, fire is a blessing and a protection. In older times, each year the Queen chose a new King, who knew that at the end of his reign, he would be expected to climb just such a pyre and be sacrificed for the land. I had tried, during the sleepless night, to convince myself I too was making a sacrifice for Britain, that my death would allow Arthur to bring the kingdom together again and satisfy those who wanted to bring down his realm for hatred of me and of Lancelot. But as I faced the stack of wood, as high as a man's shoulder, that concept could not sustain me.

A great pole had been driven into the earth and wood stacked around it to half its height. A small platform had been built there, with a ladder leading up to it from the side. And there I must stand, to be displayed to all in my agony. It was Gareth who helped me up the steps and bound my wrists and ankles. As he stood, he whispered, "Never fear!"

Once Gareth came down, the executioner mounted the platform and kneeled for my forgiveness, which I granted. I could see his eyes under the black hood, and they were full of pity. Still, he checked my bonds and tightened them, since Gareth had left them far too loose. Had I known it would be Gareth who bound me, I would have begged him not to do that. I could not trust myself not to try to wrest free once the flames were lit and did not want to make a spectacle of my contortions. So I was grateful for the tightened knots.

As he stood behind me cinching my wrists, the executioner whispered to me. "I have put nerium among the wood, my lady." Again, I was grateful.

Nerium creates a poisonous smoke, and with luck, I might be overcome before the flames fully reached me.

He moved to bind my eyes, but I said, "No." I searched again for a glimpse of Arthur but could not find him. "Let me go to my death with my eyes open. Let me see the moon, and the Mother waiting to welcome me." He nodded and gave over. I tried for a smile of thanks but failed. He dipped his head to me before he went back down the ladder.

The blacksmith's boy trotted up with his torch and stood beside the executioner. All eyes turned to where Arthur must emerge and give the order. Mordred appeared in a casement, looking down on the crowd, his face twisted in misery. Then he turned to say something, presumably to Arthur, who must have been standing back, unseen. Mordred was gesticulating and shouting, but his words could not be heard. The torch trembled in the boy's hand, the crowd began to murmur, Edalwurf scowled, and still Arthur did not appear. It became increasingly obvious that he was waiting for Lancelot.

I could not breathe and didn't know what I wished for more: to be saved, or just to end the wrenching suspense that was ripping me asunder. Edalwurf paced back and forth at the foot of the pyre, muttering, and casting baleful glances at the window. Gawain appeared, looked down briefly, and backed away. The crowd's murmurs grew louder, and a few shouted out. "Burn her!" "Pardon! Pardon!" "Harlot!"

Catlin managed to force her way to the front of the crowd, and I saw Grance sidle to stand in front of her, as one of the line of soldiers holding the spectators at bay. Her eyes were huge in her ashen face, but she held my gaze unwaveringly.

Finally, Arthur took his place at the window, Mordred beside him, still pleading passionately, Gawain standing well back. My eyes met the King's across the distance, and for the briefest instant, I forgot my own fear and was lost in sorrow for his dear, anguished face. He turned away for a moment to gather himself.

And then we heard hoofbeats. Edalwurf screamed in frustration, grabbed the torch from the blacksmith's boy and thrust it into the kindling. It began to burn, sullenly at first; then small flames started licking up toward my feet. I could not hold back a whimper.

Bors, who had hidden himself among the crowd, was working feverishly to throw open the gate before the soldiers near him could prevent it. He managed to crack it before they shoved him aside, but it was enough for Lancelot to burst through, surrounded by a party of horsemen.

They formed a wedge and thundered through the foot soldiers, then spread out to fight, leaving Lancelot free to make his way to the pyre. I had never seen his face so grim. People in the crowd ran about in howling chaos, some trying to get out of the way of the charging horsemen, some closing ranks against them. Lancelot's men brandished their swords, clearly trying not to use them lethally, only to open a path for our escape. And it seemed most of the King's soldiers, too, forbore to land a killing blow.

The heat was growing at my feet, and I bit my tongue until it bled to prevent a scream. I gasped and cast about me, muddle-headed from the nerium fumes wafting up, not knowing where to look. High on the wall, Arthur and Mordred leaned forward, grasping the stone opening of the window. Catlin, rejoicing, began to wallop the soldiers nearest her, until Grance grabbed her and bundled her off bodily out of the melee.

Edalwurf raced around the pyre in a frenzy, striking with his torch. Gareth barreled toward me. He dealt Edalwurf a blow with the flat of his sword, knocking him into the fire. The bishop screamed and scrambled and slapped at his robes, and Gareth turned to me. The bottom rungs of the ladder were aflame, but Gareth leapt to where he could get a purchase. His face was alight with joy as he clambered up and ducked behind the post to cut my bonds. And Lancelot bore down on us, ramming his way through the panicked crowd.

Then he was there. My ankles were freed, and I drew my feet up away from the flames. When Gareth's sword cut through the bonds at my wrists, I braced my feet against the post and launched myself toward Lancelot. He caught me and thrust me across his saddle, then wheeled to make our escape.

Gareth leapt down from the pyre's platform and landed right in front of us. Lancelot's war horse reared and struck out with his hooves. Gareth scuttled away behind his white-covered shield to evade the flailing hooves, then popped up beside us, shouting and brandishing his sword in triumph. I had managed to pull myself upright in front of Lancelot and could see his ecstatic face, but Lancelot could not. Struggling to regain control of his horse, trying to hold onto me, he saw only a soldier with a sword. He struck. And his sword twisted in his hand.

It all happened so fast I couldn't even shout a warning. What was meant for a blow from the flat of the sword became a fatal stroke. The light was gone from Gareth's eyes even before he fell.

By then I was screaming. Lancelot reined in his horse, trying to puzzle out what had happened, but in an instant his men were surrounding him. "Go!" shouted Bors. "You have her!" Lancelot cast one more bewildered look at where the boy lay, then spurred his horse away out the gate, his men following.

Catlin saw the rest. Arthur, Mordred, and Gawain raced into the courtyard, all looking jubilant. Arthur was immediately surrounded by his men. A captain asked, "Shall we pursue?"

"No!" Arthur replied joyously. "No! Let them—"

Mordred put a hand on his arm, then turned him to see Gawain stumbling away from the group, toward his brother lying bloodstained and crumpled on the ground. He fell to his knees beside the boy and cradled him in his arms. There was a silence, and then Gawain raised his face to Arthur. It was a mask of ferocity.

"Oh aye, we will go after them. And I will kill him myself. And by all the gods, I will kill any man who stands in my way. Any man, Arthur."

I thought our flight might be stopped by the troops at the northern hill fort, but we passed under the walls without incident. I suspect they had been told that less than perfect vigilance would be tolerated. We thundered through the dark for some time before pulling up in a secluded glen. I had finally stopped sobbing, and Lancelot had maintained a grim silence through the ride. I slid from the horse but howled and fell; I could not bear weight on my blistered feet. Lancelot picked me up gently, wrapped me in his cloak and carried me to where I could sit comfortably, then threw himself down beside me.

"Who was it?" His voice was rough with dread. I tried to embrace him, but he wouldn't have it. Again, he demanded, "Who?"

"Gareth. He refused to display his—"

Lancelot let forth a groan that would linger in my ears forever. "No... no." He crumpled forward, burying his face in his hands. Again, I reached for him, but he leapt up and crashed through the brush, away from the milling soldiers and horses. I couldn't follow.

Someone built a small fire, and soon Bors approached me with a cup of warmed wine. I accepted it with a nod, but we didn't speak. In fact, all of my rescuers kept a careful distance from me. I caught mutters and dark looks now and then. My wine was replenished, and despite the pain in my feet, I began to feel drowsy. I had nearly nodded off when we heard a horseman approaching.

The soldiers leapt to attention, closing ranks between me and whoever approached. But the rider hailed them quietly, and they relaxed. It was Grance, and my tears broke out anew when I saw Catlin astride behind him, clinging for her life, her eyes screwed tight shut. When the horse stopped, she opened them and began searching frantically. The soldiers moved away, and when she saw me, she tumbled from the horse, landing hard in a heap. Though she must have been badly jarred, she scrambled right up and ran to me. We clung together in silence, our tears mingling. But soon she took a deep breath, sat up and shook herself and wiped her eyes. "Let's see those feet," she said.

One look, and she had the men scurrying to carry out her orders. There was a brook nearby, and she demanded constant refills of helmets full of the cool water. She tore strips from her skirt to make wet compresses, including some herbs she managed to find. Eventually the pain began to ease somewhat. Men were sent to find a large, moss-covered log for me to rest my feet on, higher than my hips to keep the swelling down. She found willows growing by the brook and stripped bark for me to chew and plied me with more wine. Finally, she tore more strips, gently dried my feet, and bandaged them loosely.

As she stood, I began to laugh. It was the last thing I expected to do, but it was uncontrollable. With all the strips torn from her gown, it now hung raggedly above her knees, and she appeared for all the world like an acrobat or rope dancer. She gave me a look, then commented drily, "Well, at least *I'm* not in my shift." She made sure I was comfortable, then lay down beside me and we both collapsed into the deep sleep of exhaustion. Lancelot had not returned.

He was pacing among his men when I awoke. Occasionally he gave a direction or answered a question about our logistics, but mostly he was silent as a stone. He did not come to us until Catlin called out to him as he passed by.

"Sir Lancelot! Wherever we are going, our lady cannot ride. I don't think my bones can stand it again, either." He came to us rather reluctantly.

"I've sent men out to find a cart. It's far from perfect, but we should be at Joyous Garde by dark tomorrow. We'll wait there until we find out what is happening in Winchester. And until your wounds are healed, of course," he said to me, with formal courtesy.

"Lancelot..." I said, reaching out to him, and Catlin limped off to give us some privacy. She needn't have. Lancelot ignored my outstretched hand. "It wasn't your fault," I said, trying to control the pleading note in my voice. "It was purely an accident."

"No, Lady," Lancelot replied. "It was God's punishment for our adultery." He turned on his heel and started away.

"Come back here!" I demanded. "Don't make me try to hobble after you." He relented and turned back, his face and body stiff with what seemed to be rage. "Lancelot. Why would God punish Gareth for our misdeeds?"

"He's not the one who is destroyed," Lancelot responded. "Gareth died in his full innocence, and if anyone ever deserved to sit at the right hand of God, it is he. As for me..." He turned and walked away again, and this time could not be called back.

Catlin and I made the rest of the journey in a farmer's cart that smelled strongly of dung. We were both well relieved when we arrived at Joyous Garde to find all had been prepared. I still could not walk, but it was Bors, not Lancelot, who carried me to the chamber held in readiness for me. Someone had, indeed, gathered clothing from the ladies of the castle. With their help, Catlin soon had me bathed and dressed respectably and ensconced in a comfortable chair with my bandaged feet resting on a stool. No one had considered that her gown might be ruined, or even that she might be with us, but the women soon found something she could wear.

Our meals were brought to us until my feet healed, and in that time I did not see Lancelot. Grance brought us the news from Winchester, and we learned Gawain's vengeful oath was not a passing grief, but had become an immovable obsession. Lancelot sent word back that he would in no way take arms against Gawain or the King, but preparations for an attack continued unabated. The people of Lancelot's holdings treated me with respect, but very little warmth.

At last I was able to walk for short distances, with some support, and so sent word I would be present in the hall for the evening meal. I think I half expected Lancelot to absent himself, but he was there. He seated me at the center of the dais, with himself on my right hand, thereby announcing that he still considered me High Queen of all Britain, and therefore superior even over him in his own holdings.

There was little conversation, and that was grindingly polite. He told me of his plan to remove himself to Benoic, his birthplace in Less Britain, across the Narrow Sea. There he was a king in his own right, and he hoped his sovereign standing, combined with the difficulty of bringing men across the sea, would discourage Arthur and Gawain from following.

"And what is your desire, my lady?" he asked coolly. I did not take his meaning, so he asked again: would I prefer to make the journey, or stay in Britain, perhaps protected at Joyous Garde or taking refuge in a convent if Arthur refused to accept me back.

I was so astonished at the question that at first I could not answer. To my mind, any decision had already been made. Arthur had condemned me, however reluctantly, to be burnt. Lancelot had rescued me. We had loved each other clandestinely for all these years, and now we were together in the eyes of all the world. It seemed to me the playing stones were cast, and our moira had made the difficult choice for us. And now he was asking me this? Rage and humiliation overwhelmed me, but I refused to surrender my dignity in front of the whole hall. "Let us discuss this tomorrow, Sir, and I will give you my answer then." He nodded, and we turned again to our repast.

I spent a sleepless night, which meant, of course, that poor Catlin did too. Lancelot's household was primarily Christian, and we heard the dragging steps of heavy-eyed servants heading to early morning mass before we finally drowsed off. We turned Lancelot's emotions and reasoning over and over, but the result of all our nighttime conversation was simply that I must tell him truthfully what I wanted and ask whether he was inclined to oblige.

I waited until the day was well underway before requesting his presence, partly so he could discharge some of his duties, and partly, I confess, in hopes I wouldn't look so hag-ridden by then. The face looking back at me from the bronze that morning had swollen eyes, sunken cheeks, and a sagging jawline.

Catlin made me some burdock tea with which to bathe my eyes. I put on a sapphire blue surplice over my gray gown and tucked my hair into a silver coif. When his approach was announced, I pinched some color into my cheeks and waited for this man I loved, who no longer seemed to love me in return.

He greeted me politely and enquired about the healing of my burns. But the joy that used to light his face when he saw me wasn't there. I bid him be seated, and let the silence between us lengthen, in hopes he might say something that would ease my mind. He said nothing, so I began, hoping no trembling in my voice or in my fingertips would betray my emotions.

"Last night... last night you asked me whether I wished to continue with you to Brittany. I have no wish to remain here. My return to court is impossible and hiding in a convent suits me not." He was gazing at the floor, and made no reply, so I continued. "But neither do I wish to go where I am not wanted. And so I must ask you plain, Sir Lancelot, what is your desire? Do you want me with you, or has your love for me died? If it has—" Still, he stared at the floor. "You must speak, sir, and tell me your wish."

I hated the sound of my own voice. The stiff, formal phrasing was not how I wished to speak with him, but I dared not let myself speak more personally, for fear I might break down altogether. Still, he stared at the floor, as if lost in the swirls of the mosaic, but I noticed his hands were clasped so tight it looked like the skin across his knuckles might split. His silence lengthened until I thought I must scream.

"Well," I said finally, "it seems I have my answer. May the gods go with you and keep you safe." I was bringing all my will to bear but could not prevent my voice from breaking. I rose to flee into my private chamber, since he showed no sign of leaving. But before I reached the door, he spoke.

At first it was barely a whisper: *"Jesu Christi!"* I stopped and turned to him, and finally he raised his ravaged face to me. "How can you think I don't love you? By all that's holy, woman, you have been my life since my eyes first fell on you. For all these years!" He was almost shouting now. "I betrayed my King and my dearest friend. I gave up my knightly honor for you. And now it seems I must give my soul as well."

He had risen and was striding around the room in a passion. I groped my way to my chair and sat, overwhelmed by his emotion, unable to respond. He stood with his back to me for a long moment, grasping the ledge and staring out the window. Then he turned, and in a rush, came across the room to me and threw himself to his knees, wrapping his arms around me. "So be it. I've already suffered hell in this life, loving you and never having you. If I'm condemned in the afterlife as well, at least I'll have my paradise now."

And that was the end of language. Inarticulate sounds became fraught with meaning, and the heaviest words lacked all sense. When Catlin scratched at the door, Lancelot was trying to lace back on one of my sleeves which had come undone. "They are looking for you in the hall, sir," she said, with no expression whatsoever.

"Do this for me, will you? I don't seem to be very good at it."

She did the sleeve as he bowed to me and left, then stood back to look at me. I had lost a shoe, my hair was sprung loose from its coif, and my face was abraded by his beard. I started to laugh. "I know," I said. "All your hard work undone."

"Actually," she replied dryly, "it seems to have done just what it was supposed to do."

Lancelot and I were in rapture. For the first time, we were without fear of discovery, and we spent every moment we could together. I'm sure we disgusted many in the company, acting like lovers in the springtime of their ardor. We could not stop touching, nor wrest our eyes from the other's. We had almost a fortnight of such delight amid the hubbub of preparation. Then he came to me and told me all was in readiness, and we would sail for Brittany on the morrow.

I can tell you nothing about the journey. Catlin and I spent it in our cabin, taking turns holding a bowl for the other to spew in. October was not the best time for a sea crossing, and neither of us had been on the water before. We both prayed heartily we never would again.

Chapter 30

Worsening weather closed the sea soon after, so Gawain and Arthur were unable to follow. I suspected that Arthur moved slowly, hoping the delay would serve to calm Gawain's fury somewhat. It did not. From time to time we heard messages about his continuing dire threats. Arthur would be suffering, torn between the two men he loved more than any other. Truth be told, Lancelot was closer to his heart, despite all. But Gawain was his kinsman, and if Arthur failed to support his own clan, the entire north, from the Orkneys down, would likely rebel against him.

Bors, Lionel, Ector de Maris and others of Lancelot's clan were deeply pleased to return to their homeland, but Lancelot had been sent to Avalon at such a young age that he held few memories. After the official greetings, at which we were both welcomed warmly, life at the keep was quiet. Nearly everyone here was Christian, but there was little of the hostility between sects that was rampant in Britain.

The Christians still brought in greenery by the armful to deck the castle in December. For them, it signified the eternal life promised by their savior. For us, it was the eternal life of the greenwood, the unending cycle of the year. Images of the Great Mother remained but were venerated as representing the mother of Christ. Wreaths were fashioned to bring back the sun, and the Yule log was burned. There was, of course, no battle of the Oak and the Holly, for who could take Gawain's place? But overall, the season was one of celebration and good fellowship. Arthur would have been pleased to see Christians and pagans living together without rancor.

Arthur. It may seem strange, but I missed him mightily, as did Lancelot. Lancelot was my soul mate, and our passion for each other never faltered, but Arthur had been our closest, dearest friend; we both grieved his loss. And Lancelot was often beset with guilt and sorrow over the death of Gareth. At such times, he would take himself away to the forest of Broceliande, where he stayed for a time in a hermit's hut, doing penance. There were those who said he suffered bouts of madness, but he wasn't crazed, just grief-stricken. After spending time in prayer for a few days, he would return and take up his duties. I learned to let him go without protest or worry, and he always returned with a full measure of devotion to me.

As Imbolc passed and Ostara approached, the Breton household began to buzz with new activity. Arthur had not been able to persuade Gawain to renounce his blood oath, and Lancelot continued to assert he would not raise a weapon against him or the King. So we prepared for a siege. A new well was dug within the keep. We expanded the gardens and made enclosures so we could bring the livestock in when needed. Lancelot's advisors wanted to blaze the land surrounding the castle, so an invading army could find no sustenance or shelter, but he refused. "If they attack the castle," he told them, "we will defend ourselves. But I will take no action against them unless forced." They grumbled and argued, but finally acceded. Bors took longest to convince.

On a soft, mild evening in early April, the signal fires kindled, and a shout went up from the watchmen. Arthur's ships were approaching. Catlin and I were exhausted; we'd spent all day carding wool from the newly shorn sheep and our arms ached. We had both retired early, but when the shouting began, we rushed from our rooms and ran to clutch each other. Then I pried myself away, wrapped a shawl over my sleeping robe and hurried out to the battlements.

Lancelot was already there. He and his men were staring out toward the sea, though we were too far inland to see anything. Bors, Lionel and the others were talking excitedly, but Lancelot stood silent and apart. I went to him, and he wrapped me in his arms. "It begins," he murmured into my hair.

On the second day after the alarm, we saw them. They were still far off, cresting a hill, and all we could make out was a confusion of horses and men and banners and spears. I was reminded of the day my father went out to join

245

forces with Arthur against Ryance, how the High King's army had been silhouetted as they were now, looking like a huge spiky beast crawling over the landscape. Who could have dreamt then that we would see Arthur leading his forces against us? But I had not yet met Lancelot, and that changed all.

He was quiet and withdrawn, trying to temper the excitement of his men. All winter they had waited, and now the moment was at hand. Despite the blood and pain and death, warriors welcome war. They are always restless and cantankerous in winter, but this one had been especially bad, since everyone expected Arthur would come in the spring. There was an air of ferocious joy among Lancelot's men, though he kept telling them they would not ride out to meet the opposing army.

When we awoke the next day, we were surrounded. Tents and pavilions had been set up overnight, with an empty space between them and the keep. Arthur's armies always moved with utmost precision and efficiency. Latrines had been dug, cooking tents set up and provisioned, the horses tethered in their line, and soldiers were moving purposefully about the camp. They were too far away to make out faces clearly, but it was evident which tent was Arthur's. I stood on the outer wall, alone, gazing at the pavilion over which the Pendragon fluttered in the brisk April breeze. As I watched, a man came out, and even at that distance, I could see it was Arthur: his straight yet easy carriage, his bright hair, undimmed by the gray, his air of authority that held no hint of cruelty. I tried to turn away, but could not.

This was my husband, to whom I had been wedded for many years, and whom I loved deeply. And I knew that even now, my love was returned. How could it be that there was such distance between us, that we each had armies at our backs, and that we were each other's foe? He turned, and his gaze scanned the wall of the keep. It stopped when it came to me. I held no doubt he recognized who stood vigil there. His vision was always better than mine, but even had I not known that, it was clear from the way his body tensed, and he stood stock still.

I don't know how long we stood like that, our gazes locked. At length, a man approached him—Gawain?—and the spell was broken. As I turned away, I nearly collided with Lancelot, who was standing close behind me. How long had he been there, watching?

All day messengers rode back and forth between the keep and the encampment. Despite protests and shouting from our men, and no doubt from Arthur's as well, the two were in agreement: neither one would take aggressive action against the other. Lancelot would remain within his walls, and Arthur would not attack. But neither could he withdraw. That was made clear to us when, late that afternoon, one man came riding out from the encampment.

It was Gawain, and he didn't come as a messenger. He came decked in full armor, with his double-headed eagle banner flying. He galloped right up to the main gate and wrenched his charger to a stop, dust flying. Then he took off his helm and tucked it under his arm. He raised his face to where we were gathered on the battlements, and cried out in a loud, terrible voice that I would never have recognized as his.

"Sir Lancelot! I charge you by your honor as a knight and Companion, come out and do battle! Ken ye well that I will never leave until we have met, and I have been avenged for my brother's death."

There was a lot of angry muttering among our men, but Lancelot stepped forth and leaned over the wall to address his former friend. His voice rang out calm and clear. "By my honor as a knight and a Companion, Sir Gawain, I swear I will never raise a sword against my Lord King."

"Then let the King stay behind. You shall close with me, Sir, for there will be nae other course. I must be avenged."

"I could no more raise my sword against you, Gawain, than I could stab myself in the heart. I share your grief. It was never by my will—"

"Liar! Mordred saw it all. Gareth showed himself to you and you killed him in cold blood." Our men stirred even more angrily at the accusation. Lancelot spoke vehemently, but still without rancor.

"I did not. How could you take the word of—"

"You will face me, Sir, if I maun beleaguer ye a year and a day." He replaced his helm, drew his sword and raised his shield, which had been hanging by his side. Catlin was pressed up close against me, and I could feel her gasp as she saw it. Gawain's coat of arms was gone. Instead, his shield was covered with white linen, as Gareth's had been, and the pure white field was splashed with crimson. It looked like it was soaked in blood. A silence fell over us. Gawain turned his horse and spurred back toward the encampment, brandishing his sword. As he galloped away, we heard his voice floating back to us, rough with choked emotion. "For Gareth!"

Despite the stifling heat of August, all the leathern curtains were drawn tight. And still we heard the muffled voice, unremitting, ragged and hoarse, as we had heard it every day without surcease for nearly half a year. "Sir Lancelot! Come out and face me. You maun pay with your life's blood for that of my brother. Come out, Sir Coward! Even a stinking weasel can't hide in its hole forever."

We were all frayed to tatters. There had even been a few minor rebellions among Lancelot's men. Though they were contained without incident, the soldiers were sullen and fractious. Rations were short, since we needed to stockpile as much as we could against the winter—no one doubted Gawain would stay forever if he had to. Now and then a hunting party slipped out the postern gate, but they were ordered to stay far away from the encampment and were strictly forbidden to engage should they meet Arthur's men. Even the horses were restless, having no chance to run, and my blood roiled with them.

Catlin and I were snappish with each other, and as the weeks passed, Lancelot withdrew further and further into himself. Unable to repair to Broceliande, he had carved out a chapel for himself in a remote corner of the keep and spent much of his time there. I kept to my rooms as much as my duties allowed, for everywhere I went, I was met with scowls and sneers.

Once, I was passing near two soldiers who sat on the battlements dicing, though with little interest. Gawain's voice, now ragged and thin, floated up to them, as it had day after day after day. "Send him out. Make the coward face his fate. Are you men? Are you knights? Send Sir Runaway out!"

"I'd like to go down there and cut his throat myself. Damned if I'll be called a coward's man." one soldier growled.

"Who ever thought we'd come to this? And all for a bit of sweeting..."

I turned to flee before they saw me, but just then Bors approached, and I was forced to stay in the shadows. He had heard the last remark. "That 'bit of sweeting' is a Queen and a lady. What would you have him do, let her be burnt when the fault was half his?"

"No, sir. But as it lies, at least he could let us fight."

248

"No honorable knight does battle against his King. And you can wager Arthur doesn't want to ride against Lancelot either."

"His honor is our shame! Why doesn't he at least ride out to Gawain and meet him man to man?"

"*Sir* Gawain. They were brothers in arms, the two best knights of all the Companions. Your lord would count it disgraceful to offer combat to his friend, when he is clearly deranged with grief. And if you are your lord's true men, you'll follow his command." Bors stomped off, and I slipped away, leaving the two men grumbling.

I found Lancelot sitting alone, a plate of food and a flask of wine untouched beside him. I poured the wine and offered it to him. He took it without speaking, or looking at me. I watched him for a moment, as he sat with the cup unregarded in his hand, then dropped to my knees beside him and looked up into his face.

"Lancelot. Only three things ever mattered to us: love for Arthur, service to Britain and our love for each other. We've lost Arthur and our honor, and those losses will haunt us all our lives. Let us not lose each other too." He looked at me then and drew me into an embrace. But somehow, he was still far from me.

By late November, the land was dressed in the drabbest of duns and grays, and despite the approaching Yuletide, there was as little cheer within the keep as there was outside. Nothing had changed, except the rations were getting shorter and people were ever more sullen and frustrated. Catlin and I sat spinning, a chore I detest. Lancelot was in the room—at least his body was. He didn't even look up when Bors came in.

But when Bors said, "I'm going to take one more sortie out tomorrow, try to get some game before the snow closes us in," Lancelot leapt to his feet.

"I'll go with you. I haven't been out of soft clothes or ridden a horse in months."

"But they may be doing the same thing. What if we..."

"I'll take that chance. I've got to see something other than stone walls!"

For the rest of that day, Bors, Lionel and the rest tried to convince him it was folly. Leaving the keep was risky indeed, and I was not at ease with it, but

I made no effort to persuade him not to go. It was obvious he needed some sort of release from the tedium of his days and the grating voice outside our walls.

He came back injured, but calmer, more tranquil than he had been for a long time. He told me little as I dressed his wound, only that he had clashed with a boar, and the beast was dead. Lionel, Ector and the others were also close mouthed. Lancelot wasn't the only one wounded—several of the party were battered and bruised, and there were even a couple of broken bones and knife cuts. It seemed clear that all that damage resulted from something more than a boar, but no one was answering any questions.

It was Catlin who finally pried the tale from Warrick, a young squire who had been present. Lancelot, Bors, Lionel and a few other knights and squires were entering a clearing when they heard a snorting, snuffling sound. Lancelot held up his hand for silence. The sound came again, and a wild boar, a huge beast, the lad said, came trotting out from the brush. Lancelot gestured the others back and set his spear. But then, instead of riding at the vicious creature, he dismounted and drew his short sword.

"Are you mad?" Bors shouted. "Spear him and be done! At least call the hounds if you're—"

But Lancelot was itching for combat, even if only with a savage brute. He approached slowly as the boar set its feet and lowered its head. Lancelot feinted, the boar swung its menacing tusks, and Lancelot thrust at him, trying to get behind his head. But the animal was too quick and turned, ripping Lancelot's forearm with a tusk.

Ector sounded the horn for the hounds, who came crashing through the forest and attacked, darting and retreating, several getting ripped or gored. Lancelot waded into the melee, weaving, and shifting for an opening, while his men shouted to him to get away. Finally, he saw his chance, stepped forward and thrust his sword into the neck of the beast. He stood there panting and bloodied, but with a smile on his face, Warrick said, that no one had seen since Arthur's troops had landed.

Bors was muttering in disgust at his bravado, but before they could get into a quarrel, they heard horses crashing through the forest behind them, then shouts and the clash of steel. Lancelot leapt onto his horse, and they galloped in the direction of the tumult.

When they reached the clearing where some of their men had been cleaning game, they saw those six were beset by eight or ten of Arthur's men and were fighting furiously for their lives. It seems an arrow from the king's party had landed among them, and they took it for an attack, though it may have simply missed its target in the woods. Some on both sides were shouting, trying to stop the confrontation, but it was too late.

Our men swept into the skirmish, and several more of the king's men joined from the other direction. Both parties were armed for hunting rather than battle. The men on the ground fought with skinning knives and cudgels, unable to use their bows. The mounted knights fought with short swords and small leather hunting shields, nearly face to face. No one was wearing armor, except for leather helmets, nor were there any banners or badges.

The boy reached the clearing in time to see Lancelot gallop into the crush and immediately dispatch a knight by grabbing his arm and twisting it, sending the man flying off his horse. He whacked another in the back with his shield, unseating him as well. Clearly, Warrick said, he was trying not to kill anyone, though his sword was drawn.

Another mounted warrior entered the fray and charged toward Lancelot, who turned just in time to meet the attack. His entire attention was focused on the opponent's blade as they thrust and parried, chopped, and blocked. Then came a moment when they crossed swords and strained toward each other. It was only then that they actually registered each other: it was Arthur Lancelot was fighting. Both men froze.

In that moment, Lionel struck a blow from behind that sent Arthur tumbling over the pommel of his saddle. But his foot caught in a stirrup, leaving him helpless in the chaos of the battling men afoot and unable to control his stallion. He strained upward but couldn't quite pull himself up into his saddle.

Without a moment's hesitation, Lancelot leapt from his horse and lifted Arthur back up. The squire told Catlin there was a moment when the two men simply looked at each other, Arthur in Lancelot's arms like an embrace. Then Arthur regained his seat, Lancelot leapt back into his saddle, and they both turned and spurred away, calling to their men to follow. They had not exchanged a word.

The first snowfall came on Yule, the day of the sun's rebirth. But there was little celebration, even among the few pagans at the court. A small boy lifted a curtain and leaned out to look at the snow. The child was roughly pulled away, and the leather fell back, but still we could hear it. Gawain's voice held a flat, hoarse tone by now, but the message was unchanging.

"Come out, coward. You killed my brother. I'll bide till one of us is dead."

The men in the room looked sullenly at Lancelot, who refused to meet anyone's eyes. Suddenly a soldier entered from outside, breathless, brushing off snow. "A party coming, Sir! They bear the Pope's banner." We all looked up, startled. Lancelot's eyes met mine for the briefest moment, then turned back to the messenger.

Gawain's rant fell silent, and we all rushed to the battlements. Gawain was arguing fiercely with the advance men of the party. Then their leader approached him, riding daintily on a palfrey and dressed in all the splendor of an archbishop. Gawain continued to argue for a few moments, but finally turned and rode back toward Arthur's camp. The archbishop looked up at us on the battlements, and the last vestige of my peace was annihilated: it was Edalwurf, and whatever the message he might have brought, I knew it would be to my bane.

Chapter 31

Lancelot and I stood side by side as the Archbishop and his party paced ceremoniously into the hall. Resplendent in his gold-embroidered robes, Edalwurf did not deign to look at me. He stopped before approaching us closely, and held out his hand, scarred by his burns. Lancelot abhorred the man as much as I did but was ruled by respect for the Archbishop. He stepped forward, crossed himself and kneeled to kiss Edalwurf's ring.

"I bear an edict from the Pope himself, Sir Lancelot. This division of Christian against Christian must end. Before the sun sets on Christmas Eve, three days hence, you are to return the woman Guinevere to her rightful husband."

The court gasped. I flinched as if this hateful man's words had slapped me across my face. I quickly drew my emotions under control but could not help a flicker of my eyes toward Lancelot. He carefully kept his gaze on Edalwurf.

"I will not return her to be burnt."

"His Holiness has commanded the King to accept her without vengeance, and he will obey."

"Have I no voice in this?" I demanded.

Edalwurf smirked at me. "As you are not Christian, madam, His Holiness addresses himself to Sir Lancelot and the King." He turned back to Lancelot.

"And I'm to be handed around at their will?"

Edalwurf made a show of stifling his irritation. "We can offer you an alternative. The King is only bound to accept your return, not to live with you as husband. Therefore, the holy sisters of Amesbury are prepared to take you in."

"A convent! I—"

"Arthur has agreed to this?" I resented Lancelot's interruption, but I too wanted to know the answer.

"He has indeed, to keep his realm from interdiction. And you, Sir, will agree as well. Elsewise you, your family, your household, and your entire clan will face excommunication."

Again, those in attendance gasped in dismay, and Lancelot paled. "I will parley on Christmas Eve, and make my decision known then."

"And I," I said, stepping forward to glare at Edalwurf, "will ask the Goddess to forgive you and your arrogant Pope for treating a priestess and a Celtic Queen as if she were chattel." I turned my back on him and walked out, leaving Lancelot to deal with the formalities.

It wasn't until evening that we came together. Lancelot sat on one side of the brazier, I on the other, and we both kept our gazes focused on the flame. I was doing my utmost to keep my tone level and conversational.

"I didn't realize your Christianity ran that deep."

"At first it was just a concession to Elaine. But as the years went by... And then when you were imprisoned..."

I waited, and after a moment he continued. "I prayed constantly. And I vowed if I could save you from the flames, I would never again doubt His power, and would ever after serve God with my entire heart." He raised his eyes to meet mine. "You are safe."

In truth, my decision had already been made. How could I continue putting all these good men in danger, both Lancelot's and Arthur's? If there was any hope that my return to Britain might allow them to make peace, I had no choice. The woman in me grieved, but the Queen knew where her duty lay. Still—my foolish pride—I wished Lancelot would beg me to stay with him. He did not.

"It's not just me," he continued. "Galahad! He has a true vocation in the Church. All my men, all my clan, those good men Bors and Lionel and Ector, consigned to hell because of me?"

"What kind of God is that? Do you truly believe innocent people would be punished—eternally—for something in which they took no part?"

He stopped pacing for a long, long moment. Then he met my eyes, and I could see the pain in his. "How can I take that chance?"

"I'm a priestess of the Great Mother. How can I go to a convent?"

"Arthur will take you back."

"Is that what you want?"

"I want to be the man I used to be. I want to stand beside Arthur again, not against him. I want to honor my knightly vow. And I don't want the blood of any more good men on my head." His voice was so weary, so desolate, that again I found tears welling. I lowered my head and nodded, almost imperceptibly. Then I got up and walked out before I lost all dignity.

There was snow on the ground as we rode from Joyous Garde under a hard blue sky. Arthur, Gawain, and Bedwyr, in ceremonial armor, rode into the clearing. Lancelot and Bors accompanied me. I was wrapped in a fine fur robe, and held my head high, but I could barely focus on anything.

Lancelot and Arthur trotted out to meet between the two factions. Their eyes were locked on each other, an intense searching look. Lancelot slipped gracefully from his saddle and knelt in the snow before Arthur, who was clearly moved by his humility. "My lord," Lancelot said, "I return your Queen to your keeping. And I ask—"

"Your job is done here, traitor!" shouted Gawain. "And the Pope's safe conduct ends with your errand. Run ye back to your burrow so I can follow."

Arthur gestured to him commandingly, and he retreated to a simmering silence. When Arthur turned back to Lancelot, he tried to maintain his majesty, but couldn't help the raw emotion coloring his voice. "I accept the return of my lady, with thanks for your care of her." For the first time, his gaze traveled past Lancelot to me. I sat frozen for a moment, then nudged my palfrey forward. Lancelot, with a last longing look at me, took my reins and handed them to Arthur. He in turn handed me off to Bedwyr, who led me back to join Arthur's party, his expression not at all sympathetic. As much as I wanted to yank my reins from all their righteous hands and ride away, I controlled myself.

I had refused to look left or right, but when I heard a snicker from Arthur's men, I glanced back. There was Catlin, on a broken-down mule, jouncing hard, her elbows and knees sticking out, riding out from Lancelot's party to join me. Even Arthur could barely hide a smile. Then he turned back to Lancelot.

"You're sorely missed among the Companions, Lancelot. If you and Gawain could—"

"NO!"

Bedwyr attempted to hold him back, but Gawain shook him off and galloped between Lancelot and Arthur, reining up in a fury.

"This caitiff killed my brother! Gareth was your kinsman, too, Arthur. How can ye—"

"Gawain, it was all confusion, and he wasn't bearing his arms. I didn't know him!"

"Mordred saw it. He told me."

"You'd take the word of Mordred over what your own heart must surely know? I knighted Gareth! He was as dear to me—"

Gawain turned his back to Lancelot and addressed Arthur. "Bring this man back, and you'll lose my allegiance and that of all Orkney and Lothian. Either ye war against Lancelot, or ye war against me."

Arthur wiped a hand across his face.

Lancelot looked at him, pleading. "Arthur... please..."

"Let us have a truce for Christmas at least. The day following, we'll meet again and a decision will be made. Agreed?"

"Agreed," Lancelot said, and Gawain nodded reluctantly. Arthur turned to Bedwyr. "In the meantime, Bedwyr, escort the Queen back to Winchester. She will rule with Mordred as co-regent until my return." I shuddered with hatred at the mention of that name. I was to hold converse with him, hear plaints with him, eat with him by my side? Was there no end to what was asked of me? I set my jaw and said nothing.

Bedwyr saluted and we moved off. Lancelot and Arthur returned to their parties. Neither had spoken a word to me. I too was silent as I rode away.

Crossing the Narrow Sea to Britain in winter was even worse than the voyage out had been. When finally we were on land again, the trails were slick with snow and ice on some days, and hock-deep with mud on others, so it took us the best part of a month to traverse from the coast to Winchester. We managed to find a small, gentle pony for Catlin to ride, but her lack of skill had also slowed our journey. As plodding as we'd been, however, the messenger I sent to learn what happened after the Christmas truce hadn't returned by the time we were approaching Winchester.

As we broke from a forest trail into a clearing, Catlin reined up and called to Bedwyr, "Tell them to set up the pavilion. And get the cooks to—"

"It's less than half a day's ride. Why stop now?" I asked, and I'm afraid my tone was sharp and irritable. Truth be told, I had been unpleasant company during the whole journey. Bedwyr and I no longer had the easy comradeship we used to enjoy, and Catlin's attempts to cheer me only made me cross.

"You need to rest and eat and make yourself presentable. You can't enter into Winchester looking like a beggary hag."

"Always the flattering tongue, Catlin. But what does it matter what I look like in a dungeon cell?"

"There won't be any cell," snapped Bedwyr. "Arthur has said you're to take your place as Queen and regent."

"Arthur's in Brittany. Mordred is here. He's the one who set the trap that started this whole disaster. Why should I think Mordred would welcome me?"

"I have little love for you, madam, after watching my brother suffer as he has. But if Mordred tries to harm you, he'll deal with me, and then, the gods help him, with Arthur."

Catlin nodded briskly and unceremoniously hauled me down from the saddle. "Let's get that pavilion up!" she commanded the men.

It was evening when we arrived at court. I drew a deep breath as the great doors opened. Catlin had done wonders, as usual. Somehow she had managed to procure for me a simple but beautiful silvery grey gown, and even more startling, a spectacular ruby necklace. I gaped as she drew them forth from her saddlebag, but she would say nothing about how she came to them. For once I didn't complain as she fussed with my hair, taming the wild, neglected curls into a dignified coif.

So I looked like a Queen as I rode into the Great Hall, but I felt like a frightened girl. Bedwyr, afoot, led me in to where Mordred sat on Arthur's throne. He was splendidly arrayed, though in a deep forest green rather than Pendragon scarlet. The court was assembled, all wearing Mordred's colors. As

I looked them over, I saw few faces I recognized. Most of them bore pagan tattoos, and a Druid priest stood in Edalwurf's usual place.

Mordred rose with a smile, and came to help me dismount. He positively beamed at me as he led me to the dais, then turned with me and presented me to the crowd. "Your Queen!"

To my amazement, they cheered me wildly! This was hardly what I expected. Most of those who had been my partisans were with Lancelot in Brittany. I was at a loss, and tried to hide my confusion as I returned their greeting. I turned to Mordred, who was basking in their cheers. "I beg your pardon, Prince Mordred, but I am entirely wearied by my journey. May we put off the court business until morning?"

"Of course," he said heartily. "You must be longing for the comforts of home. Come, I'll escort you to your quarters." He maintained his pleasant, courteous manner as we began walking down the stone corridor, and I began to relax somewhat. "I'm surprised Edalwurf wasn't on hand to report my arrival to the Pope," I said.

"Well, that would have been awkward, my lady," Mordred said jovially. "Edalwurf's dead."

"Dead! He seemed hale enough in Brittany. What did he die of?"

"Cold steel." His reply was cheery, almost playful. My smile froze on my face as I turned to him.

"Did you...?"

"I did indeed. May the White Christ welcome him! I'd like to send his scrofulous Pope to join him, but that will have to wait."

"But...why?"

"He'd done his duty. Thanks to him and his Pope, we got you back. Once that was done, there was no need for any more Christians around here."

"But half the court is Christian!"

"Not now, it isn't."

"The King is Christian!"

"The King is not at court. Nor will he be again. You're free of him, my dear."

I checked my astonishment. It was becoming clear to me that his cheerful demeanor was, in fact, madness. I smoothed my face and chose my words carefully. "What do you mean, Mordred?"

258

"I'm your consort now. I rule Britain in Arthur's absence. And no one at this court wants his return. Least of all us," he said with a chuckle.

"By 'us' you mean... the pagans? I noticed there were many –"

"Well, yes, but mainly I meant you and me." We had reached the sleeping quarters. Mordred stopped, kissed my hand, and gestured over his shoulder to his chamber, which was across from mine. "The waiting will be hard, but not long. Morgan will do our handfasting at the new moon."

My heart was pounding so hard I was sure he could hear it, and my mouth filled with sand when I tried to speak. "I... I'm not sure I take your meaning. You intend to marry me?"

"Of course. We'll let no one say our rule is improper."

"But I am already married!"

"Morgan has declared that marriage invalid, in view of the great good we will do. Together we will bring Britain back to its pagan legacy. And I love you, Guinevere. I'd marry you whether we had a kingdom or no."

"Mordred, you were my enemy. You came with those men, and... They would have burned me!"

"If Lancelot hadn't saved you, I'd have stopped it somehow. But you see, we needed to set him and Arthur against each other. There's no way we could have broken them elsewise. And even so, it nearly didn't work. I honestly believe he might have pardoned you both and let him stay. But fortunately for us, there was Gareth."

"Ah. So as for your father, you intend...?"

"My father? You mean the man who wanted to murder me at birth?"

"Arthur, then. How will you..."

"With luck, Gawain will bring Arthur to war and Lancelot will cut them both down. Once I spread the word of Arthur's death, we'll send our outraged Britons after du Lac, and be rid of all."

"And if Arthur wins?"

"Well, when he returns to find his court pagan, his Queen and his country mine, then it'll be between him and me, won't it."

"I see," I said, though in truth a black mist was spreading across my vision, and I fought to keep from swaying on my feet.

"Ah, I knew you would," Mordred said happily. "Some people said... but I remember how you used to look at me and stroke my hair—"

"When you were a boy! As your stepmother, of course I—"

"I know what mother love is. And clearly your love was something very different from Morgan's." He bent to kiss my hand again, and for a moment I was certain I must snatch it away, or cry out, or otherwise betray my panic. But I was still maintaining some control when he straightened. I gestured to my door.

"Well. We had best..."

"The new moon is too far off," he said, with bizarre gallantry. "But after all these years, a few more days will pass soon enough, I suppose."

"Yes, well... Goodnight, Mordred."

His eyes were glowing as he watched me slip into my chamber. I smiled at him, then closed the door and leaned my back against it. Catlin was bustling around, laying out my sleeping robe. "Catlin," I said. "Pack a small saddlebag and send the back way for Bedwyr." She glanced up, surprised, but when she saw my face, she set about packing with no questions.

We waited until the castle folk were settled for the night. Mordred had assigned no guard at my door, apparently believing I was in full accord with his plans. There was only a dim sliver of the old moon hanging in the sky, shedding barely enough light for Catlin and me to glide across the courtyard, clinging to the shadows. A guard stood near the gate, yawning, and chafing his cold hands. An arm reached out from the shadows, covered his mouth and dragged him out of sight. We heard a grunt, then silence. After a moment, Bedwyr stepped out and looked around. Stealthily, he opened the gate and gestured.

We lurked in the shadow of the castle wall until the battlement guard passed, then scuttled across the open space into the forest, where half a dozen mounted men waited with three riderless horses.

When it was almost full day, we left the road and went into the brush where we could walk down the horses unseen. When I had caught my breath from the long, hard gallop, I approached Bedwyr. Though still not as warm toward me as he used to be, when he heard about Mordred's plan, he had not hesitated a moment.

"How quickly can you get word to Arthur?" I asked.

"Not quickly enough. And crossing the sea... he'll be lucky to get here by Ostara. We have to find you someplace safe until then. Where will you go for refuge, lady?"

I had given it no thought until Bedwyr asked the question, and then it seemed inevitable. "With most of the country hereabouts supporting Mordred, it appears there's only one place I can go. The nuns at Amesbury will give me sanctuary."

Bedwyr nodded gravely. Catlin stared at me, open-mouthed.

Chapter 32

A drenching rain accompanied the last leg of our journey from Winchester to Amesbury, the kind that makes oiled hoods and capes of no use. We were a shivering, bedraggled group that presented ourselves at the convent doors, with no way to know how we might be received.

Edalwurf had said the sisters were prepared to take me in, but then, Edalwurf was gone. What might have happened in the meantime? Had Mordred left the convent in peace, or included them in his anti-Christian campaign? From what I knew of their beliefs, they must offer sanctuary to anyone in danger or grave need. But would they take in a pagan priestess if Mordred had harried them?

I stood back as one of our escorts knocked loudly on the door. The wooden slat covering the viewing hole slid back, and wary eyes looked out. "No men are allowed here," said the guardian of the door.

"I understand. We are escorting Queen Guinevere of Britain, who requests sanctuary with the holy sisters."

There was a gasp from behind the door. "Wait," she said, and slammed shut the viewing hole. The next thing we heard was a shriek, and then the sound of many scampering feet. When the door was yanked open, it seemed the whole community were clustered in the hall, agape with excitement. Then one of the gray-clad nuns pushed her way to the front, even elbowing aside the Mother Superior. I was surprised by the lack of decorum, but then I saw who she was: Wynyth, the girl who had been disgraced by Father Thomas years ago.

She threw herself at me and hugged me hard, then seemed to remember herself and backed off into a courtesy. "Your Highness! You are safe!"

The Mother Superior glared around her at the excited nuns, and some order was restored. She came out to me and looked searchingly into my face. Hers was grave and deeply wrinkled, a face to inspire obedience, but as she examined me, her faded blue eyes softened. She dipped a shallow courtesy, and I bowed my head respectfully to her. Then she reached out and took my hand. "Come, Your Highness. You'll be wanting a hot drink."

The sisters at Amesbury, unlike Christians I had known at court, did not lump all pagans together as savages. I held many long conversations with Mother Alyce, during which we discovered our beliefs had much in common. As for little Wynyth, the young nun treated me as if she were my elder sister and showed utmost care and concern. She and Catlin rubbed against each other at first but came to a kind of comradeship. Often, they made common cause bullying me out of melancholy, insisting I eat or rest or do something to which I was not inclined.

All in all, I was treated with respect, but not fawned over. No one tried to persuade me to take the veil. The days passed in preparing good but simple meals, keeping the convent spotless, and tending the garden and animals. While they were at their devotions, I was free to do as I wished. I must confess much of that time was spent worrying about whether Arthur would arrive in time to prevent Mordred's usurpation.

Mordred discovered where I was, of course, and presented himself at the convent door not long after I had arrived. Though he was accompanied by armed men, he made no immediate threat against the convent. I refused to see him, so he sent me a message: "I am to be crowned at Winchester come Ostara. I can wait."

We had little outside news. Occasionally a workman or farmer came to the back gate with an offering for the sisters, or travelers would request a stay at the guest house they maintained. I was planting peas when one such group appeared. If their meager possessions hadn't told me they were traveling out of need, not pleasure, the haunted look they carried, even the children, made it clear.

Mother Alyce went to the guest house to greet them and returned to her quarters walking hastily, barely keeping herself from running. I was summoned to her presence, and quickly rinsed the soil from my hands and brushed my apron. When I went in to her, I was startled by her expression of deep sorrow. Usually, she and the other sisters carried an aura of utter serenity. She came out from behind her desk and embraced me, which was totally unexpected. Then she drew me to two chairs and sat down facing me. "Your Highness..." She reached for my hand and held it in both of hers. "My dear, word has come that your husband has been killed in battle in Brittany."

"No," I said calmly. "No, that is not possible. Who—" My throat closed, and I began to choke. Mother Alyce poured me some blackberry cordial, but I simply sat with it in my hand, staring at her, unable to speak.

"Prince Mordred—" her lips twisted with the name, "announced it in court. The group that arrived today are fleeing before he is crowned King at Ostara. I'm so sorry."

It was like living underwater. Time floated silently past me, punctuated by the worried faces of Catlin, Wynyth and Mother Alyse. I saw they were speaking to me, but I did not hear. I was turned completely inward, struggling with the question of what to believe.

"It was Lancelot, milady," one of the travelers told me. "He and Sir Gawain met in single combat, and after long striving, du Lac struck the sword from Sir Gawain's hand. The prince yielded, but du Lac delivered the murderous blow regardless. The king was enraged and charged him, but he was no match for that one. He was killed quickly, Your Highness, and did not linger with a wound, if it is any comfort."

This was the official version according to Mordred. I refused to believe it. Lancelot, that most chivalrous of men, striking a dishonorable blow? Yet in a distant corner of my mind, there was a whisper: hadn't he confessed to Catlin that he killed Maelgwyn despite the villain's surrender? I tried to still that whisper but could not.

From all reports, Mordred's coronation was tumultuous. Morgan le Fey invested him with a silver crown, fashioned to look like woven branches and centered with an enormous emerald. He addressed the crowd, demanding that troops go to Brittany and avenge his "beloved father" by slaying Lancelot. But voices called out, saying Arthur was alive and on his way from Brittany. Mordred's partisans shouted them down, acclaiming that the old gods ruled in Britain once again. I took hope from this report, but could not be certain it was truth.

The stream of those fleeing from Winchester swelled to a flood, and Mother Alyse was hard pressed to provide refuge for them all. Most were Christians, of course, but there were also many pagans who refused to recognize Mordred or approve his forced return to the old gods. "No pagan religion, Druid or any other, has ever been forced on anyone. Mordred condemns the Christians, but he's doing the same thing," said one old traveler, his beard quivering with anger. Mother Alyse welcomed pagan and Christian alike, and we gave them what aid we could.

It seemed each new group of travelers bore a different version of events. Though most believed Arthur had indeed been struck down in Brittany, others swore he was alive and on his way to confront the rebels.

"Take what comfort you can from not knowing," Mother Alyse advised. I recognized the wisdom of her words, but as the days passed, I began to think it would be better to know the truth, however bleak that might be.

And so, for the first time, I sought out a vision using only my own powers. Both Catlin and Wynyth had been deviling me about my lack of appetite, so I expressed a craving for some sorrel soup. I knew that would send them to a distant meadow to gather the herb. When I was sure they were gone, I went to the kitchen and found a bowl suitable for scrying. I filled it with water, took it back to my chamber, sent fervent prayers to the Goddess, and bent over the shimmering surface. At first, I saw only my own face, and was becoming convinced that the only way I could channel the Sight was by touching someone who held the memory. But then...

The water darkened, then glowed with light. I could see blue sky, and the field near Lancelot's keep in Brittany. Though it was early summer now, this vision showed snow on the ground, and I understood I was about to witness the confrontation between Lancelot and Gawain, shortly after Yule. I steeled myself for what I was about to see. Would Lancelot kill Gawain after he had yielded? And then then kill Arthur, as Mordred put it about? Or was I about to watch the death of Lancelot? Whatever it might be, I could no longer bear the unknowing. I gathered myself and bent again to the bowl.

Arthur and Gawain rode up to the castle. Their men followed on foot and unarmed. The gates of the castle opened and Lancelot and Bors rode out to meet them. Their men arrayed themselves facing the other army. The four riders met in the middle. Lancelot dismounted and knelt for the blessing of a priest. Then Gawain, too, dismounted and came to stand face to face with his opponent. "No arms on either side save for the champions," said Bors. "And both sides agree to abide the winner. Swear it." Both men swore on the pommels of their swords.

Lancelot made one last desperate effort. "Gawain..."

"Ye are a murtherer, a coward and a traitor to your king. Defend it with your life."

Lancelot looked past him to Arthur, whose face was drawn and anguished. "My king, I have borne all I could, to keep from harming you or your kin. But unless your nephew accept my peace, I must defend against him, by my will or no."

"You are the two best knights and finest men who ever lived." Arthur said. "I think the world has lost all wisdom when it falls out that one of you must die."

"Can you not—" Lancelot began.

Though Gawain had delivered his challenge evenly, without emotion, he began to break now from the strain of keeping up this obsessive pursuit of a man he respected so highly. "Lancelot! By all the gods, man, leave off your blithering and let me ease my heart."

There was nothing to be done. Arthur and Bors returned to their armies. Lancelot and Gawain remounted and rode off from each other. They settled their lances, closed their vizards, and waited for the signal to charge.

When it came, they rode at each other like thunder. They met squarely, and both were so powerfully seated that their horses stumbled and fell. The combatants leapt to their feet, drew swords, and took up their shields. Lancelot was prepared before Gawain but waited before closing with him.

Gawain struck first, a stunning blow that landed across Lancelot's back as he twisted to avoid it. He staggered but kept his feet and backed off as Gawain pressed him. Gawain lashed out again, and Lancelot deflected the blow but didn't follow up on the opportunity he was presented. They continued in this way, Gawain stalking, Lancelot tracking and traversing, keeping himself covered with his shield but not striking back except to deflect. Gawain roared in frustration, and the men on both sides were shouting fiercely.

The chill sun was low in the sky, and still the battle continued. Both men were bloody and exhausted. Lancelot was still only defending; Gawain was weakening, but fought on in weary rage. He made a wild lunge, and Lancelot was too worn down to completely avoid it. The sword struck across his left shoulder, breaking the collarbone, and his arm fell limp. With his shield dangling useless at his side, Lancelot was defenseless. His people roared in dismay. Gawain gathered himself for the fatal blow.

Lancelot saw there was no way to simply defend. He used that second's delay to strike. The blow landed on Gawain's temple, and he fell like a tree. He lay there stunned and bleeding.

Lancelot leaned on his sword a moment in utter exhaustion, then turned to walk back to his people. Gawain tried to stand but couldn't. His men started toward him, but he gestured them back.

"Dinna turn away now, Lancelot!" His eyes were terrible.

"Gawain, it's done."

"Leave me like this, and as soon as I'm whole I'll come after ye again. For the love of all that's holy, kill me!"

"Come if you will, Gawain. I will not strike." He turned and dragged himself back toward his keep. Arthur and his men came for Gawain and carried him off.

I slumped back and buried my face in my hands in relief. Nothing had been resolved, but I had seen for myself that the vicious story spread by Mordred wasn't true. How could I have thought, even for a moment, that it was? I still didn't know where Arthur was, but I willed myself to believe he was on his way to take what was his back from Mordred.

A young woman arrived at Amesbury asking for me. It was Greta, the granddaughter of Davek, that grizzled knight who had doted on me when I was a child. The girl I'd known was now a comely young woman. A tiny boy, still wearing a padded bonnet, stood by her side. As Greta made her obeisance, the child saw one of the cloister cats strolling by and made a lunge for it despite his leading strings, almost toppling his mother. Laughing, Wynyth gathered up the boy and carried him off for some sweets in the kitchen.

I hadn't seen much of Greta at court, and now she seemed somewhat overawed in my presence. I sat on a bench and patted it beside me, inviting her to sit down. It took a few moments for her to get her message out.

She had come to tell me that Owen, her husband, had been snatched up to serve in Mordred's army. "Among his men, Mordred makes no attempt to keep up the pretense of King Arthur's death. It is common knowledge the king is on his way to confront Mordred. He will land at Dover, but the coward Mordred will not be there to meet him. Instead, he has made a pact with a band of bloodthirsty Saxons to do his fighting for him." I shuddered.

"Mordred was gathering an army to make a stand should the king survive the Saxons. But many, like my Owen, were taken up by force, and are still loyal to the king. Owen escaped and got a message to me. He's heading to Dover to help the king when he lands. He asked me to get a message to you if I could find you. And I did," she said proudly.

"Mordred plans to leave Winchester. He intends to set up camp on the Salisbury Plain, not far from here. Owen will take this information to the king. He and his army should be here by midsummer."

I was delighted with her news. Arthur was alive and had learned at last of Mordred's treachery! He was coming to take back Britain.

But first he had to get through the Saxons.

As soon as Greta and her child had been cared for, I rushed to my scrying bowl. But I could see nothing that day, nor for several more days. It seemed battle had not yet been joined, and I was not vouchsafed to see the future. Then there came a day when the air was so heavy with foreboding that I knew Arthur's ships must be nearing land. That night, I sat before my scrying bowl...

The battle was fierce. The Saxons, their hair bleached with lime, wearing rough furs and much heavy jewelry, were waiting on the sand when Arthur's boats appeared. Fire arrows flew, setting some boats ablaze, but Arthur's men were well trained and efficient. The flames were contained, the boats beached, and Britons poured out to join battle.

Soon the strip of sand under the chalk cliffs was drenched with red, and the iron scent of blood overcame the salt breeze. Arthur, Gawain, and Bedwyr were in the thick of it, laying about them with broadswords. All three were hard pressed, and no one noticed the Saxon behind them who wasn't as dead as they thought. Slowly, he got to his knees, then to his feet, and picked up his battle axe.

He braced himself and swung, just as Gawain caught sight of him and began to turn. The blow caught Gawain on the side of the head, where Lancelot had struck him.

He fell. Bedwyr finished off the Saxon while Arthur dropped to his knees beside Gawain, who was gravely wounded but still alive. The howl of agony came not from the broken prince, but from his king.

Their men protected them while they lifted Gawain and carried him back to their boat. Arthur shouted for bandages. "Nae," said Gawain. "Leave be. Send me a scribe."

"What? You mean a priest?"

"A scribe, mon. I want a scribe!"

"I can write," said Bedwyr.

"Find a stylus. As for you," he said, turning to Arthur, "what kind of king skulks in his cabin when there are Saxons to be slain? Go back to your men."

Arthur was reluctant to leave him, but Gawain refused to acknowledge any kind of farewell. He pointedly waited for Arthur to go. Then, with a groan, he hitched himself up to await Bedwyr.

When Bedwyr returned, Gawain began to dictate a letter, between gasps of pain. "Sir Lancelot: I am dying of the dunt you dealt me at Benoic. Though a muckit Saxon dealt the last blow, I claim my death at your noble hands. In the name of the love that was once between us, I beseek ye to cross from Brittany with all speed and all your strength. Arthur is foul beset, and it is my fault he lacks the best knight in the world at his side. Come..."

He had used up all that remained of his strength, but he managed to reach out and put his mark on the missive. Then he lay back and turned his head away.

The vision faded, leaving me perplexed. It was for Arthur's safety I feared, but instead I saw Gawain. His noble letter put me in tears, and I was glad to know that at the end, he had forgiven his old friend. But why was this knowledge sent to me?

Chapter 33

Mordred's army arrived and set up camp against the limestone ridge, a good position to defend. They had harrowed the countryside along their way, forcing men into their ranks, burning the crops, and fouling the water. After the long siege in Brittany, the sea voyage and the ferocious battle with the Saxons, Arthur's army now confronted a hard march westward, with little succor.

At Amesbury, we waited in a state of terror. The army was so close that we feared Mordred would be at our gates at any moment. Surprisingly, though, he left us unmolested. Perhaps a group of women weren't worth worrying about. Or mayhap he was biding his time until after the battle. I held no hope that he had forgotten I was there.

We spent our days preparing bandages and herbs, ready to aid the wounded once battle was joined. At last, we heard that Arthur's army was only four day's march away.

Sleep evaded me that night. The convent walls were thick, which helped keep it warm in winter and cool in summer, but that August was particularly stifling. The walls soaked up the heat all day and exuded it at night. My sleeping robe clung to me, my hair was damp and my scalp prickly. I wished Catlin and I shared a bed again, but the cells in the convent were small, with narrow pallets. I wandered into her room, hoping we might talk until I could sleep, but she was already trumpeting away.

At last I fell into a fitful doze, and soon found myself sitting at a campaign desk in a tent, maps spread out before me. I was wearing a robe lined with fur and a cup of seethed wine stood nearby, but still I was chilled to the bone.

The tent flap opened, there was a swirl of snow and Gawain strode in, snowflakes clinging to his face and hair. "God's hammer, lass, give me some wine! I'm half frozen."

"Your manners haven't improved any since I saw you last." I poured him a cup of warm wine. Gawain gulped it, then leaned on the map table, brushing unmelted snow from his eyes.

"Arthur canna go into battle yet. He maun find a way to delay it. Offer talks, something."

"Gawain the hothead counselling delay? Now I know that Saxon broke your brain."

"Hark! I came all this way to warn him, but he wouldna listen: if he meets with the bastard as planned, he canna win the day."

This was dire news indeed. "Gawain, why are you telling me this? What can I do?"

"Go to him. Make him hear. Lancelot is but five days behind him, with all his troops."

"Lancelot!"

"Aye. If Arthur can delay the battle until he gets here, he shall live and conquer. Tell him." He faded away in a swirl of snow.

I woke with absolute surety that this was a true dream, and that I had to find a way to get to Arthur immediately. But between us stood Mordred's army.

I knew I could not tell Catlin of this, nor Mother Alyce nor any other here. But I also knew I needed help...and help of a more than ordinary kind.

I sent a message to Avalon, in the fervent hope that Nimue was there. I bid her come to me privily, and as soon as ever she might. She was there much more quickly than I had expected, and with a second pony for me. "I prefer to ride Etain."

"We must go at all speed," she replied. "These ponies are of Avalon. You haven't seen their like. What is it?" she asked, seeing my face crease with anxiety.

271

"Catlin. I can't bring her, but she will raise an unholy howl when she finds me missing, with no knowledge of where I have gone."

"Tell her you are going and that she cannot come," Nimue said, as if that solved all.

"You have met Catlin, have you not? She would just follow."

"Then we must be well away before she finds out."

It seemed cruel to leave that way, but I could think of no better plan. *I will pay for this when I return. If I return.*

Nimue was right about the ponies. They ran with such grace and speed that the countryside flew by. In truth, there were times when it seemed I was indeed flying. We reached the limestone ridge sooner than I would have thought possible. Mordred's army was arrayed below us, an enormous host. I shuddered at the size of it. How many men did Arthur have left?

Nimue seemed to intuit my fears. "Arthur's army is smaller, but loyal. Many of these will turn their coats and fight on his side when it comes to it."

But how were we to get past them? It seemed they filled the entire valley below. I found myself wishing Nimue's ponies could, in fact, fly. I was quickly disabused of that notion.

"We'll have to go the rest of the way on foot," Nimue said, dismounting. "For tonight we'll stay up here."

"How are we going to get through?"

"What we must do tomorrow will take much of our vital force. If we use it all, we die. We need to rest tonight. And you need to learn."

Before I could ask, "Learn what?" Nimue was unpacking the ponies and handing things for me to carry to a sheltered spot she picked out.

We talked little until the ponies were attended to and we'd had a repast of oat cakes and cheese. We gathered kindling for a small fire. Nimue bid me light it, and I reached for tinder and spark. "Guinevere," she said, and gave me a scornful look. I was instantly abashed. Of course I could make fire. It was one of the earliest powers any priestess learns. But I had lived my life outside that realm for so long that I had almost forgotten even the simplest of earth magic.

The fire blazed up. "Small," she said. "We don't want to garner anyone's attention." I calmed the flames. We settled ourselves, facing each other.

"You have far more power than you know," Nimue said. "Most people do, but you are a priestess, under the eye of the Mother. That gives you special gifts, and now you must take them in hand. Respect these talents; they can be dangerous. But never fear them. They are given you by the Goddess."

I started to tell her I had been using the Sight, but it wasn't Sight she spoke of. She held out her hand. "Watch." I had seen shapeshifting before, when she or Merlin were taken by some strong emotion and suddenly looked different, more commanding, even younger. But as I watched, Nimue clenched her pale freckled hand. When she opened it again, it was not her hand. It was huge, rough-skinned and scarred: the hand of a warrior. I gaped. "Now you." I looked at her helplessly.

It was an awe-inspiring evening. Nimue taught me how to bring my will to bear upon my own body. At first, when she told me to grow tall, all I could do was stand very straight and try to stretch my spine. But she taught me how to lock and unlock my bones, how to bulk my body out or gather it in, how to crease my skin, how to make my blood run vigorously or laggard. "There is nothing to be done about the eyes," she said. "You can set wrinkles and pouches about them, but your eyes are your eyes and won't change."

I could see what she meant about shapeshifting taking a lot of life force. By the time we gave over, I was more exhausted than I had ever been, even though she had been lending me some of her power to help my learning. We spread our cloaks and lay down. Weary as I was, I could not banish from mind the menacing throng we were going to have to walk through on the morrow. But then a thought hit me and I began to laugh.

"What?" Nimue asked.

"Do you mean to say," I choked out, gasping with laughter, tears running down my face, "that all this time I could have been taller?"

I think I was asleep before we finally stopped snorting and snickering.

The next morning, two soldiers stood atop the ridge. Nimue had brought with her everything needful—we would have looked ridiculous in our gowns. I was taller than myself, not by much, maybe two hands. But I reveled in it. I was less pleased with my distended belly and the deep lines carved into my sallow face. Nimue was a pock-faced youth with a ruddy complexion and a limp.

"Remember this is illusion," she said. "If you ease your attention, even for a moment, your true self will flash out." She looked me over carefully and nodded. "The ponies will conceal themselves here. If you should return without me, just call for them and they will appear."

Return without her? The suggestion was so dismaying that I banished it from my mind, lest it make my disguise fail. We started traversing down the ridge.

Seldom have I been so frightened as when we reached the edge of the disorderly horde and plunged in. I gripped my new identity so hard I was in danger of using myself up. "Be easy," Nimue said quietly. "Apportion your power."

It took hours to weave our way through the milling soldiers, who paid little attention to us. As time passed and we were not challenged, I began to calm somewhat. Around us men were preparing for imminent battle, sharpening axes and knives, oiling leather breastplates.

At last we reached the forefront of the assembly. We were more conspicuous here, a pair of ragtag soldiers among resplendent knights, and we collected some curious looks. We were very close to the front now, and I began to think we might actually succeed.

But then I heard a familiar silky voice say, "What are those knaves doing up here? Get them back where they belong." Mordred.

I froze as two beefy hands grabbed me, and my guise flickered for an instant. Then there was a surge and I regained control: Nimue was aiding me again. The knight grabbed us and spun us around. I kept my eyes on the ground and shuffled my feet in the dirt, hoping to appear dull-witted. Of course, Mordred also knew Nimue, but I trusted in her superior skill.

My heart was leaping like a hare, and for all Nimue had taught me, I was unable to still it. Mordred's gaze flicked over us without much interest, then turned to a messenger who was spurring toward him. The knight gave us a shove and we lumbered off as the messenger, breathless, leapt from his mount and approached Mordred.

As soon as we were out of sight, Nimue clamped a hand on my arm and whispered urgently. "That messenger!" She steered us to where there were fewer bodies jostling. "Arthur is come sooner than expected," she said softly, pretending to help me with a gauntlet. "He intends to join battle tomorrow."

"He must not!" I gasped. "We have to reach him, warn him!"

"We will never find him in time." She turned from me a moment, thinking. When she turned back, there was a resolute set to her jaw. "I can get you to him. But I can't go with you."

"How? What will you—"

"I'll work my way back to the ridge and await you. When you are ready to return, call out to me and I'll fetch you there." She paused, and grasped my hands tightly in hers. "Don't tarry overlong."

I never had a chance to ask her how she did it. I sensed an odd tingling, as if my skin were all abuzz, and looked down to see my body traced with a bright white light. It shimmered so intensely everyone must see. But a soldier looking directly at me seemed to notice nothing. The aura grew brighter and brighter...

I stood at the edge of a clearing in the soft summer night, away from the flickering of the campfires, and called out to Arthur in my mind. It seemed an age before I saw him falter out of his tent and look around, perplexed, but it was probably only moments. I called to him again, and watched him stagger through the encampment, as if in a daze, to where I waited in the shadows. He passed near Bedwyr, but did not seem to see him. Puzzled, Bedwyr followed at a distance.

I was hooded, wearing the coarse gray habit of a nun. At first he didn't know me. He stumbled up to me, almost reeling, his eyes blank, uncomprehending, like a stunned beast. I could barely manage a shallow breath as I reached out to him, afraid to touch him, unable not to. His eyes began to clear, and he took both my hands in his, then pulled me close and wrapped his arms around me fiercely.

"Am I dreaming?" he murmured into my hair, his breath warm, his voice rough with longing. "Where did you come from?"

"I'm at Amesbury. I needed to see you."

"Amesbury?" He held me at arm's length, and his face grew even more astonished as he took in my raiment. "You're... a nun?" In his bewilderment, the years fell away, and he looked as vulnerable as a child. At last I was able to breathe and summon up a small smile.

"No. They're sheltering me until... You plan to go into battle tomorrow?"

"Yes."

I was back in my own small person, but I made myself look as commanding as possible. "Arthur, you must heed me. You cannot attack tomorrow, or you will die. You must delay!"

To my relief, Arthur didn't laugh, or brush away my importuning like some irksome gnat. Instead, he asked, "Why?"

"Gawain came to me."

"Gawain is—"

"I know. But he came to me in dream and told me Lancelot is coming to your aid."

"Lancelot!"

"You must delay until he arrives."

Bedwyr had been standing a little away, his eyes constantly scanning around us, his body tense and alert. When he heard this, he came forward, astonished and more than a little fearful. "This was a true dream, Arthur. Gawain sent for him."

"It couldn't be!"

"I wrote the letter. He bid me tell no one."

Arthur's face twisted in pain, and his voice was bitter. "Gawain may have sent, but why should Lancelot come?"

I stepped close to him again, reached up and turned his face toward me. I cradled that dear face in my hands as I waited for his eyes to meet mine. "He'll come," I said firmly. "He never stopped loving you, Arthur." My voice caught as I said what must be said. "Nor did I."

"Truly? You loved me as well, Guinevere?"

There was such an ache in his voice, and his face was so naked, so full of need, that I hesitated. To lie to this man now, to mislead him in any way, would be a greater transgression than any I had committed. I closed my eyes a moment, asking myself whether, after all the anger and betrayal, I was absolutely certain. I opened my eyes and looked into his again.

"Always." My voice was choked with tears.

Arthur's face softened. There was even the ghost of a gentle smile, though his eyes were misted. "What a magnificent heart you have, to hold two such loves."

We clung to each other one last time. I was not ready, I would never be ready, but I felt an urgency to return to Nimue. I tore myself slowly from Arthur's arms and took a few steps backward, unable to wrench my eyes from his face. The white light began to glow...

Dawn was glazing the plain with gold and the sky was full of birdsong when I found myself standing on the ridge above Mordred's army. Nimue's ponies were cropping peacefully nearby, but I did not see Nimue. Then I noticed a place where the tall grass was bent down. I thought at first it was a fawn nestled there.

She was still wearing the guise of a soldier, but that plump youth was wizened and shriveled almost to bone, her garments pooled around her. When she stirred and gazed up at me, I was shocked to see Nimue's green eyes still shining and vivid, though her face was raddled with pain. "We have done what we might," she whispered, "each in our own way. Even the Goddess could ask for nothing more. Whatever happens, remember that."

"Nimue!" I cried. But slowly her eyes closed, and the breath left her.

I lay there in the grass a long time, cradling her small remains. When my grief had wrung itself dry, I rose and considered what I must do. A priestess, any priestess, must be sent to the Mother with proper rites. And this was Nimue, chosen successor to the Lady of the Lake, and my dear friend, who had sacrificed herself for me and for Britain. I began to pace. Should I risk staying here and being discovered? Should I take her back to Avalon and deliver her to Morgan? With no decision made, I turned back to her, only to find she had come to my aid one last time. She was gone.

The Avalon ponies swiftly returned me to Amesbury, then trotted away to their home. Catlin intercepted me, embracing and berating, before I had taken three steps. Mother Alyse was not far behind. Though I was weary to collapsing, I sat them down and tried to explain my mission. I hesitated at speaking of the magic, the shapeshifting and transmutation, before the Mother Superior, but she listened raptly, and only absent-mindedly crossed herself.

Catlin burst into a wail when she heard of Nimue's sacrifice. Mother Alyse, crossing herself with full emotion this time, said, "May God bless her. And the Great Mother, and whatever benign spirits may be. With her help, you have saved Britain."

After much cosseting from Catlin, I was at last allowed to go to my rest. I slept through the rest of the day, and most of the night, feeling secure in the knowledge that Arthur had taken my warning to heart. Battle would not be broached for several days.

I was torn from my peaceful sleep by a sense of foreboding so dire, so overwhelming, that I could not stop screaming, even when Catlin and Wynyth and others burst in. "What, lamb, what is it?" Catlin folded an arm around me and smoothed back my tangled hair. "Shh, shh. What, my dove?"

"I don't know I don't know!" I babbled. "A snake. A sword. We are lost!"

She pressed my head to her shoulder and rocked me like a babe. "Only a dream it was. That's all, only a dream…"

At last I calmed. The sky was greying quickly, so I was about to start the day, but Catlin insisted I take a while to gather myself. She went off to bring me a cup of wine. I was lying on my pallet, drained, when I heard her returning. Her footsteps stopped. She gasped. And the cup hit the stone floor.

She stood like a statue in the passageway, staring out the casement. Far to the east, we could see a great cloud forming, but from the ground, not the sky. Faintly, a whisper, a murmur, a rumbling was carried to us on the morning breeze. It was the sound of men and horses screaming, of clash of arms, of pain and fury and destruction, all gentled by distance. Then the sun sent a finger of light over the horizon, and the great cloud turned red.

Chapter 34

Hour after hour passed as we waited for news, watching the dust of battle rise across the plain. I tried to hold a picture in my mind of Arthur galloping up to our gates, triumphant and whole, but I could not make my heart believe it. When the late summer sun hung low in the sky, I could bear to wait no longer.

Like Glastonbury, Amesbury has a sacred spring. Glastonbury's Chalice Well is claimed by both Christians and pagans, but at Amesbury it is sacred to the Goddess alone. I took a wide bronze bowl from the scullery, dipped it in the spring and made my way to a secluded copse of oaks, bidding Catlin to stay behind and prevent anyone from seeking me. I sang a praise song for the Mother, purified myself, then knelt to gaze into the water.

The sun was casting long shadows over a plain littered with dead and dying as far as the eye could see. With my breath rasping painfully in my throat, I searched for Arthur. At last I found him, accompanied by Bedwyr, wandering among his fallen men, bent nearly double with grief. He shut the eyes of a staring corpse. He offered a word of comfort to a man in his last agonies, then gestured to Bedwyr to ease the man's passage. He glared across the battlefield to where a few scavengers already crept to strip the armor and weapons from fallen warriors, but there was nothing he could do.

They came to a small rise. They climbed it and stood, both of them exhausted, bleeding, barely able to keep their feet, but alive. Was it possible Arthur might return to me, however maimed, however defeated? A spear was stuck in the ground in front of him. He let Excalibur drop and leaned heavily on the spear as he looked in all directions, searching.

He found what he was looking for. Barely visible in the haze and shadows, Mordred picked his way among the corpses. He was alone, turning this way and that. His vizard was up, and he looked lost, and very young. A hoarse shout rang out across the wasteland, all of Arthur's grief and rage behind it. "Mordred!" My hope died. I tried to call to him. *No, Arthur! Leave it. Let it end here.* But I could not reach him.

Mordred looked up wearily, then closed his vizard. Arthur wrenched the spear from the earth. They looked at each other across the carnage for a moment, then charged. Each man was so exhausted that it was a slow, lumbering run, each thudding step echoed by my heartbeat.

They picked up speed as they approached each other and issued a tremendous scream as they came together. I watched in terror as Arthur drove the spear up under Mordred's shield. The thrust was aided by the force of their charge, and the point pierced through the leather jerkin, into his chest, and then, enrobed in gore, out through his back. I tried to wrench my eyes away but could not.

For a moment, Mordred and Arthur stared at each other with something like sorrow. Then Mordred reached out with his left hand and grasped the shaft of the spear. Dragging his sword in his right hand, he pulled himself, inch by agonizing inch, up the shaft of the spear, leaving a glistening trail. Arthur stood as if transfixed, watching him come slowly nearer, while my mind screamed *No! No! No!*

The look on Arthur's face was one of anguish, and utter hopelessness. His eyes flickered from side to side, taking in the loss of his devoted men, the loss of his ideals, the loss of his realm and all it stood for. Then he looked back at Mordred and held his eyes. When Mordred had dragged himself to within a sword's reach, with his last strength, he struck. Arthur did not draw back from the blow. They fell together. Tears streamed down my face, but I was unable to move, even to sob.

Arthur untangled himself from the corpse of his son and crawled away, then collapsed. Bedwyr reached him and fell to the ground beside him. He lifted Arthur's head and cradled it in his arm, and the king opened his eyes. "Tell Guinevere. Make certain she's safe." He closed his eyes, and I began to keen, rocking back and forth. But then he spoke again. "Excalibur must go back to the Lake. It belongs to the Mother. I should never have turned it from the old gods. Take it there, Bedwyr."

A voice spoke from behind them. "We'll take it together, Arthur."

As the pale, ageless face came into view, I toppled forward, inches from the scene displayed in the sacred water. It was Morgan le Fey.

Seeing the dark-haired woman, at first Arthur whispered, "Guinevere?" But then his vision cleared—"oh"—and he turned his head away.

"My brother, why have you tarried so long?" She dropped to her knees in the churned dirt and blood of the battlefield and reached out for him. Bedwyr scuttled back from her, as if she were some loathsome beast, but Arthur turned his head again and met her eyes, dark and deep as an ancient well.

"You take me to my death," he said, unafraid. "I saw the barge with the black sails. The veiled women." Now I was wailing, silently. Not Morgan. Not her.

"That's as may be. It is for the Mother to decide. But I am the Mother's daughter in healing." *You, heal him? You, who first pierced his heart?*

"Do you think your story ends here? Shall the greatest king Britain has ever known die in the dirt and be buried in darkness?" She gathered him into her lap, wiped the blood and grime of battle from his face with her veil. I reached to brush away her hand but stopped before I touched the water and broke the vision.

"All men die," he said.

"You are not just any man. Come with me to Avalon."

Arthur, no! Stay where you are. I will find you.

"Let me use my arts, and with the Mother's help, it may be I can heal you. You can rest then, for as long as you need. Forever, if you wish. Your work is done, but your name will never die. As long as this island remains above the sea, the name of Arthur Pendragon will be revered."

"Morgan? Is this true?" His voice had faded to a whisper.

Don't listen to her! She is corruption—she knows nothing of honor.

She smoothed back the once-golden hair. "The day you were born, Arthur, I held you in my arms. A child myself, and yet I knew a great destiny awaited us both."

This vision was not in the scrying bowl, but in my own mind: a girl-child, an infant nestled in her lap. She was smiling as the infant grasped her finger and tried to gum it, staring up at her with Arthur's gray eyes. I, who had never held a child of my own, remembered the rush of love for Catlin's bonny boy when I first took him in my arms, he who was none of my own blood.

In the scrying bowl, Morgan continued. "Igraine was besotted with Uther, so I took care of you. And I was besotted with you."

More glimpses came unbidden: the girl walking with a crying baby and whispering comfort, scooping up a toddler to keep him away from the hearth, tussling with a tiny half-naked boy, trying to get him dressed. The little boy suddenly embraced her, and I swear I could feel her heart swell as she fiercely hugged him back. I was scrying not just the scene taking place on the battlefield, nor my own imagining, but into Morgan's mind.

"I thought we would grow together. I thought we... Then you were taken. And I was cast out." In my mind I saw her screaming, restrained by Uther Pendragon as Merlin walked away carrying the child with the golden curls, who was straining to reach her.

"Let me take you home, brother. You lost your way. I foresaw it and tried to prevent it, but I lost my way too. We can find the path again. Come to Avalon, where our Mother waits to welcome you."

The full moon had risen, and its silvery light touched them. Arthur shuddered in pain, grimaced, and tensed. "But...Guinevere?" he whispered.

Morgan's face had been bent to his, but now she raised it. As she had once so many years ago, she looked straight through the scrying and met my eyes. We gazed long at each other. "She would want you to be at peace," Morgan said.

I took a deep, shuddering breath. Then once again, I sent my spirit out to Arthur. *Go, my love. Be healed if you can. Rest, if you can. And if you can, come into our world again.*

I don't know whether my voice reached him, but he closed his eyes, acquiescing. Nine priestesses, veiled in black and silently weeping, paced into view and surrounded him. It seemed their small white hands barely touched him, as he was wafted gently from the ground and laid on a litter.

Bedwyr started to protest, but as Arthur opened his eyes again and looked at Morgan, he seemed transformed, almost beatific, the years, wars, and sorrow falling away. She too seemed to glow with an unearthly light.

The women lifted the litter and carried Arthur away. He raised one hand in a gesture of farewell, and Bedwyr did the same, tears flowing down his cragged face. Morgan followed, carrying Excalibur, stepping over Mordred's crumpled body without a glance. Bedwyr watched until the king and the women had disappeared, swallowed up into the night.

I tipped the bowl and let the sacred water flow into the earth, then lay for a long time and wept.

Chapter 35

Woefully few survivors found their way to our gate during the next few days, but Grance, by the grace of the Goddess, was one of the first. Catlin had been uncharacteristically silent in the aftermath of the battle, but when she saw him, she screamed at the sight of his wounds, began seven treatments at once, and asked more questions than any mortal could answer.

There was one question foremost in my mind: why? Gawain had returned from the otherworld and Nimue had given her life to help me get the message to Arthur, yet the battle started without the needed delay. Grance was too far back in the ranks to have seen what was happening, but it was known that the King had intended to parley with Mordred.

It wasn't until Bedwyr arrived that we learned how the calamity came about. After we had tended his wounds and grieved together, he gathered himself to tell the tale, surrounded by avid listeners.

"We took position just before dawn, the two great armies arrayed against each other. There was such total stillness that the clop of my horse's hooves rang clear in the air as I paced into the space between them, bearing a white banner. Mordred gestured for his lieutenant Mattias to come out to meet me.

"I delivered my message, that King Arthur wished to avert shedding the blood of his countrymen on either side, and bid Mordred meet him between the hosts to discuss terms of peace. Mattias nodded and rode back to Mordred.

"The two leaders, with me and Mattias beside them, paced to the center of the field and saluted each other. The troops on both sides had been told to keep their weapons sheathed until a command was given. But there was little—nay, no—trust on either side, and the soldiers shifted restlessly, eyeing each other across the narrow gap.

"The bastard was so haughty I wondered that Arthur could hold patience. 'Here are my demands,' he said, without waiting for the King to offer terms. First, he wanted rule of the north: Orkney, Lothian, all of Gawain's lands. Since all the Orcadian princes were dead now, Arthur agreed easily. But Mordred didn't stop there. He also demanded rule of Britain after Arthur's death. Actually, what he said was that he would allow Arthur to remain as King until..."

We who listened were shocked, but not surprised. That arrogance sounded like Mordred, at least the Mordred I had seen at Winchester. I remembered the quiet, polite boy he had been. Had that boy ever actually existed, or was he only the reflection of my own longing?

"I acted as though I was alarmed," Bedwyr continued, "and started to protest. Arthur turned and barked at me—'He is my son!'—and I pretended to be subdued. Arthur agreed that if he ruled the northlands well, he would be named as heir. I thought Mordred might protest the condition, but he had yet a greater demand to make.

"'Return Britain to the old gods, under the Lady of the Lake,' Mordred says. At that, despite the plan, Arthur quailed. He led his horse off a few paces and beckoned to me. I could sense the troops on either side becoming even more strained and alert at this hint of dissent. Arthur was shaking his head. The idea of giving Morgan power over Britain..."

"But he wasn't, really," I said. "He was only feigning agreement."

Bedwyr was silent a moment. "We talked long that night after you left, my lady. My brother was a man of unbending honor." Catlin grew rigid at my side. "Giving a false oath did not lie well with him. I tried to convince him that the likes of Mordred must be dealt with by any means necessary."

"I should think!" Catlin muttered. I poked her to be quiet as Bedwyr continued.

"Arthur finally decided to tender the oaths in good faith, keeping in mind that Lancelot was only days away, and that many in Mordred's army were there by force and might turn. At the slightest hint of Mordred's abuse of power, we could take it from him. Even so, the idea of allowing Morgan... well.

"As we talked, the men on either side became ever more disquieted. My horse shied at something in the grass, and I saw a snake, an adder, slide past. I gave it no thought.

"Finally, Arthur steeled himself to return to Mordred. I turned to our troops, intending to calm them. That's how I happed to see it." He choked, then took a sip of wine and continued. We all leaned hungrily to his words.

"The snake slithered over the foot of a soldier in the front line. An adder's sting isn't fatal, but it would put a man out of combat. The soldier started to draw his sword to kill it. I shouted to prevent it, and he checked. But Mattias had seen the man draw and heard me shout. He thought... he thought we were attacking. Just as Arthur reached his hand to seal the compact, Mattias pulled Mordred away and shouted to their men.

"A huge roar went up, and both armies charged. In an instant the carnage had begun."

I sat there a moment, stunned.

A snake? That was it? A vile mischance, a gesture wrongly parsed? This is what brought Britain down and cost the life of our finest king? I got up and walked away, motioning to the others not to follow.

When I sent Lancelot away, when I returned from Brittany, even when I stood on the pyre, at least I had made the choices that brought me there. But this... this seemed like some fell joke played by a malevolent spirit, though in truth I did not blame the Goddess. We pagans don't believe our gods are all-powerful. We believe they love us and wish us well, but our actions are our own.

Many, of course, would see it as punishment, the price we paid for an illicit love, and for the arrogance of pagans trying to prevent Christianity's ascendency. I didn't want to believe this, but what other answer was there? Random chaos? I sat in a dark corner of my room, brooding.

Catlin came in and dropped down heavily beside me. After a moment she began talking, as if to herself. "Was it the snake's fault? Na, he was just on his way to break his fast or find a rock to bask on when the sun rose. The man who drew his sword? But if Mordred hadn't raised an army against his king, they wouldn't have been there. If Morgan hadn't seduced Arthur, Mordred wouldn't have been there. Gawain! If he hadn't insisted on following us to Brittany...."

"What are you babbling about?" I asked irritably.

"I'm just trying to think who's to blame," she said. "It must be the ones who held evil intent. But Morgan and Mordred saw themselves as defenders of their faith. Was that evil? If you hadn't fallen in love, if Arthur hadn't turned Christian, if Lancelot hadn't been Lancelot...."

She turned to me and took my hands in hers. "I have no learning," she said. "But it seems to me if everyone is to blame, no one is. One thing built upon another, and this was the outcome. You can blame yourself, you can blame the poor wee snake, in the middle of a battlefield without his armor..." She looked for a smile from me, but I couldn't manage one. "Or," she said briskly, getting up and pulling me to my feet, "you can start thinking about what you might do next, and how you can help this country heal. In the meantime, there are wounded men to be cared for."

Once again I thanked the Goddess for Catlin, and followed her out.

The Saxons overran the entire southeast of Britain that summer and early fall. Other tribes—Angles, Jutes, Vandals—were preparing to follow. We could put up little resistance with most of our warriors gone, but there were surprisingly few atrocities. The sisters of Amesbury had been left in peace, and their companionship helped me through the worst of my grief.

I planned to leave after Mabon, when the heat of the summer had broken, but before winter made travel difficult. My intent was to return to the western marches where I had been a girl. I longed to see Cameliard again, though with the country in such utter disarray, there was no official role for me there: where there was no longer a throne, there was no need of a queen.

Early one September morning, I was standing at the casement in my smock, savoring the freshness of the air. The sky was vivid blue, but there were still rags and drifts of mist along the ground, swirling in eddies here and there as red squirrels scampered off to hide conkers for the coming winter. The road that led to the front gate was lined with oaks, sycamores and chestnuts, their leaves just beginning to take on color.

Idly, I watched an unfamiliar grey gelding pace slowly toward the convent, disappearing and appearing again in the mist. Then, even before I could see the rider's face, I let out a stifled cry and bolted from the window, crashing into Catlin, who was setting the room to rights. I raced to the front gate, Catlin close behind. "Open. Quickly!" I bid the novice tending it, then ran out into the road, the brisk air cutting through my sleeping robe, pebbles bruising my bare feet.

There I stopped for a moment, feeling suddenly small, and old, and despondent. A wave of grief washed over me for all that had happened since we were last together. I gathered myself, straightened my back, and raised my head to greet him with a faltering smile. Catlin, panting, caught up to me. She looked into my face, then to where I gazed. She grasped my hand tightly, then returned to close the gate and shoo away the sisters who stood peeping.

Lancelot slid from his horse and leaned wearily against its withers. He wore a plain brown robe. His face was craggy and battered, his grizzled hair pulled back roughly and bound in a leather thong. He lifted his head and looked at me, tears coursing down his face. Before I could take a step toward him, he threw himself to his knees. His voice hoarse as a raven, he cried out, "Forgive me!" and collapsed insensate in the road.

I sat beside him for hours in the little cottage the convent provided for guests. When at last he opened his eyes, he lurched up and frantically enfolded me in his arms. "I tried," he rasped into my hair. "I tried with all I had."

I made gentle noises to lull him and eased him back onto his pallet. He would not release me, so I lay beside him, stroking back his wild hair.

"I left Bors to bring the rest of my company, and I went ahead. I rode Rudigh so hard I foundered the poor beast. But by the time I got there..." He choked into silence. I wiped the tears from his face with my veil and waited. I had no desire to hear the carnage described to me. I had, after all, seen it for myself. But he needed to speak of it, lest it fester and rankle for the rest of his life and drive him mad.

As in truth it had. After he had raged through the charnel field, easing the passage of those who still suffered, he came upon Bedwyr, alone and in despair, sitting on a log in the midst of the mayhem.

"Arthur's blood was still wet on the ground. I plunged into the forest to follow, but again, I arrived too late to say a word of farewell to my liege. I broke through onto the bank only to see the barge with its black sails far out in the water. I could not see the king." He fell silent for the space of a few ragged breaths.

"I don't know how long I lingered there, watching until the black barge disappeared, then staring at the empty expanse of water. After that, *rien...* nothing."

The telling had exhausted him. I slipped from his side, though he made feeble efforts to keep me, and prepared him a posset of wine and valerian. I had checked for wounds when we brought him to the cottage, and he bore none, save scrapes and bruises from his sojourn in the wilderness.

His body healed quickly, but his soul... Lancelot was ever a scrupulous man, blaming himself far more than others did for any lapse. His wits were disordered for some time. One moment he would be talking with perfect sense, and the next he would be lost in the forest again and did not know me.

Mabon passed, and I found I could not leave him. Samhain passed, and Yule. With rest and nourishing food, and the peace offered at the sanctuary, he began to have longer periods being rational, until by Imbolc he was almost himself again.

He had built a hut on the convent grounds, to free the cottage for the many who needed shelter after the devastation of the war. He repaid the sisters' hospitality by providing game and doing the heavier chores. I continued to live in the convent, my healing skills much in demand.

We spent all our free time together, but without bodily passion. We seldom touched, except when, if talking about Arthur, or Gareth, or Gawain, we were overcome. Then we would cling together, and weep.

At last there came a morning, nearing Ostara, when the wind lost its bite and the air began to smell of earth and water. We were sitting on a bench outside his hut, soaking up the new warmth. His face was tilted to the sun and his eyes closed when he said, "Joyous Garde is overrun, so we should go to my holdings in Brittany." I closed my eyes in turn. The time had come.

"I'm not going with you, Lancelot." He turned to me, puzzled. "Our old world is dead, but we live. We have to find our new purpose. My purpose is here in Britain."

"Here? You can't mean to stay in a convent. You're a priestess, a Queen!"

"Yes. And I have obligations. Britain is full of widows now, women without protection. Christian women come here, ladies and peasants alike, and live out their lives with some safety and tranquility. I'm going to gather the pagan women, and any others who want to come, to start a convent of our own."

He stared at me, bereft of words. "These women who've sheltered me, despite our differences, they do good, and they're very wise, many of them. I haven't been wise, Lancelot. That's all that's left to me now. I can offer my people healing—not just their bodies, but their souls. Christian and pagan can no longer be at odds, not with the Sea Wolves ravening. If our people are to remain safe, and find some peace—"

"I can keep you safe! We can find our peace together."

"Oh, my dear. We have too many memories to ever find peace. And we cannot think only of ourselves. You have a purpose, too."

"My purpose has always been to love you. We can be together now, at last, with no one to say us nay. Don't you…?" He trailed off, looking miserable. I put a comforting hand on his arm.

"Of course I do. But Lancelot, we have played our part in this devastation. If Britain is to survive, we must do what we are given. It's my moira now to keep the Goddess alive for as long as I can."

"And mine?" he asked bitterly. "What is my fate, my moira? To live without you? I could wish I hadn't survived my madness."

"But you did. And Bedwyr lives, and Grance. There will be others of the Companions, scattered and grieving. Find them and bring them together again."

"You think they would follow me? I, who caused Arthur's death? They must hate me!"

"You didn't kill Arthur. Mordred did. And what did Bedwyr do when he saw you?"

"He embraced me," Lancelot answered reluctantly.

"The memory of what Arthur did, what Britain was, must not die. Think of this as your greatest quest: to keep the memory of Britain's glory alive."

He bowed his head in sorrowful acceptance. We sat quietly a moment together. Then he rose and turned to me. He said nothing; there was nothing to be said. He reached his hand to raise me and I took it.

With few possessions, he was ready to leave shortly after midday. But then the sisters loaded him down with so many gifts and so much provision that he was obliged to accept the gift of a pack mule, too. I walked him out to the road, bidding Catlin close the gate behind us.

We stood in an embrace for a moment, then slowly stepped back. Lancelot took both my hands in his. "Will we never be together?" His voice was rough, and his eyes shone with tears. Mine welled in response.

"Who can say? It may be, when our duties are done..."

"We have loved for thirty years, Guinevere."

"And if I'm given thirty more, you'll still be in my heart. Despite all, I count myself the most fortunate of women, to have been loved by two such men as you and Arthur."

I touched his face. And though it took all the will of a Celtic Queen, I turned back to the convent gate, where Catlin waited, to begin a new life in service to my land, my people, and my goddess.

The Wheel has turned, and turned, and once again we prepare for winter, perhaps our last. My eyes are dim, but I can see the glorious colors of the trees and the last of the season's wildflowers: betony, bellflowers, aster. Winter is mild in the western marches, where we are sheltered by the mountains from both harsh weather and the depredations of barbarians.

Though much has changed, much has remained the same. I praise the Goddess as I ever did. Catlin still orders me about, though these days, from her chair by the fire. There are always people who need succor, and we take them in, whether pagan or Christian, man or woman.

There are few pagans left in Britain now, and little magic. Avalon has retreated into the mist, dwindled almost to a rumor, and the Christians plan to build a church atop the Tor. The rule of law Arthur established has fallen, and dark times have come again.

The days of Britain's glory are gone now, but not forever. The soul of the Old Religion is our certainty that what dies will come again. The sun goes, and returns. Trees and flowers and grasses die and are reborn. The Wheel turns.

Bedwyr is out in the world, and Grance. I charged them, as I had charged Lancelot, with the duty of keeping our story alive for those who will come after. And I have told mine, in all its love, hope, and sorrow.

I have no knowledge of where Lancelot may be, but I feel sure I would know if he had left this world. And I would know if Arthur had returned.

He has not. But the darkness will not last forever. I won't see it, nor may any for a long, long time. But the light will come to Britain once again.

Author's Note

This is a work of imagination, not history. The era in which these events are set is called the Dark Ages for good reason: we know very little about Britain between the end of the Roman occupation and the Anglo-Saxon conquest. I have adopted certain conventions in telling my tale.

As much as possible, I have avoided using words that either did not exist at the time, such as *noon*, or that had a very different meaning, such as *fun*, which at the time meant trickery. When necessary, I allowed words that had Latin roots, since the Roman occupation had been very recent. Of course, these conventions are simply expedient, since many languages were spoken at the time, and none of them were English.

Place names and the names of characters have also varied widely. In most cases, I have used modern place names such as Winchester, to make it easier for modern readers. For the names of characters, I have preferred the older Celtic versions rather than the French: Bedwyr as opposed to Bedivere. Some characters, such as Maelgwyn, had so many names (Melwas, Meliagrance, etc) that I simply took my pick.

There is more about the characters that shift besides their names. For example, Mordred has been ascribed many motives, and in some tellings, he is the hero. Nimue has not only been called Niniane, Vivienne, and more, but in some tellings she is an absolute villain. Some versions say that Morgause is Mordred's mother rather than Morgan le Fay. In early versions, before the French gave us Lancelot, Bedwyr took his role. Gawain might be the noblest, most honor-bound knight of the realm, or a hot-headed troublemaker. And of course some characters, such as Catlin and Edalwurf, are my own invention.

Any story that has survived for nearly two thousand years and still captures our imagination must be considered a living thing. Everyone who comes to the Matter of Britain leaves fingerprints on it. The story we know today is vastly different from the earliest sources, yet certain themes persist:

honor, loyalty, religious beliefs, envy, revenge…all the values and emotions that humans evince.

Over the course of the many years that I have been working on *Guinevere: Bright Shadow,* I have read anything I could get my hands on that related to this story, far too many to include here. My most useful sources include, but are not limited to: Geoffrey of Monmouth, Sir Thomas Malory, Mary Stewart, Persia Wooley, and Marion Zimmer Bradley. I am grateful to every author who has added their bit to this living legend.

Pronunciation Guide

Cymru - *Come-ree*

Taliesin - *ta·lee·eh·sn*

Tintagel - *tin·ta·jl*

Samhain - *Sow-wen*

Lughnasa - *LOO-nah-sah*

Nimue - *Nim-oo-ay*

Pryderi - *pruh-dair-ee*

Gorlois – *Gor-lois*

Palomides - *pal-o-MEE-deez*

Cei - Kay

Ygraine – U-grain

Acknowledgements

I am eternally grateful for the help and encouragement of many people on this book's long journey.

The patience and discerning eyes of the Wednesday Writers' Group has been essential. Special thanks to the Old Guard who were there from the beginning: Donna Dakota, Susan Comenzo, Ginny Folger, Tom Willemain and Phyllis Kulmatiski.

Friends and family have also been important along the way. Edwina Trentham has been my stalwart for more decades than I care to admit. Anne Logan is a more recent blessing in my life, but her belief in me is ferocious.

Mina Panetti, Melissa Miller, Karen Hartwig and Dianne Alois have been especially supportive among my friends. Thanks also to Frances Driscoll for allowing me to use a line of her poetry. The Provost family, especially Mal and Ajay Provost, have provided much encouragement.

At Willow River Press, thanks are due to my editor, Penny Dowden, art director, Morgan Bliadd, Cherie Fox for the beautiful cover, and marketing coordinator, Jace Martell.

A residency at the Virginia Center for the Creative Arts provided indispensable time and space for me to work on this project. It is also where I met Lily Hamrick, who has been my faithful and incredibly helpful writing partner for several years, even though we live on opposite coasts.

Sarah Provost is a poet, playwright, screenwriter, and novelist, currently living and working in upstate New York. A collection of poems, *Inland, Thinking of Waves*, was published by the Cleveland State University Press. Her stage plays have been produced off-Broadway, in London, Los Angeles, and a couple of states beginning with K. No screenplays have been produced, but she made a decent living writing for Paramount, Disney, HBO, and others until Hollywood broke her heart. After a period of recuperation and relocation to a place with much worse weather, she began writing *Guinevere: Bright Shadow*, her first novel. A second novel, *The Real Girl*, is in progress.

9 781958 901199